Down in the Hollow

Timothy Hobbs

WICKED HOUSE PUBLISHING

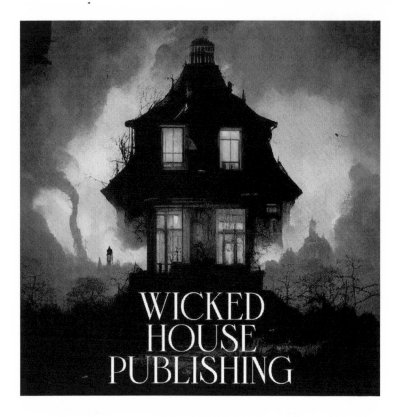

Down in the Hollow
By Timothy Hobbs

Wicked House Publishing

Cover design by Christian Bentulan
Interior Formatting by Joshua Marsella
All rights reserved. Copyright © 2022 Timothy Hobbs

A Special
Thanks From
Wicked House Publishing

Cynthia Collins
Taffy Homyak
Mary Kiefel
Kimberly Cabler
Kathleen Kuipers
JJ Murphy
Rita Auletto
Tara McAleese

PROLOGUE

Eli Snow dreamed of the battlefield.

In this dream, The Spanish American War approached its final days.

Looking for any sign of conflict, Eli rose, went outside, and gazed at a ruddy sunset burdened with lamentations from ravaged soldiers below. He then glanced down and discovered the devastated body of a man crawling toward him, the man's mouth agape, his lungs void of air for a scream.

Eli woke then from the dream, suddenly realizing he was in his cabin in Deer Hollow, Texas, the war long over, the pain and mutilations only ghosts now rattling in his head. He then heard piercing squeals nearby, glanced over, and saw a wild hog he'd captured the day before, thrashing inside its cage.

Eli sighed and went to the cabin door, opened it, and discovered twilight had arrived. He frowned and picked up the cage with its feral occupant. "They should be risin' about now. Best get them fed and see the ring of fire ain't gone out."

By the time he trudged across a portion of cleared land that ended in heavy forest growth, Eli thought how much he wanted this to stop. What his son had become was no fault of Eli, and the thing his son created damned sure wasn't.

Eli's wife committed the blasphemous act when he was at war. The witch seduced their only son, Arlis, and then gave birth to the incestuous result a month before Eli came home. He'd been furious with her, but she only laughed at him. He beat her and Arlis but never made them leave. He decided the baby had no responsibility in it and chose to raise the child, bastard or not. There was no way he'd accept his wife's and her family's background of black magic, and no way he could have known what the bastard child would become. But his wife did, and it was enough to make her abandon them. One morning, she was gone. Eli never heard from her again.

And now, as he moved to the remains of a storm cellar where the forest started to clear, Eli decided to do this no more.

The ring of fire around the cellar's door was down to just a few flames and intermittent sparks. Normally, Eli came here throughout the night and added fuel to keep it burning. But tonight, with the caged hog's weight feeling nearly unbearable as he held it, Eli decided to let the fire go out. When the things in the cellar realized the flame no longer burned, they would come to the cabin soon enough, hungry and thirsty for any warm-blooded creature.

Once back in his cabin, Eli put the cage down. The hog, now exhausted from its struggles to be free, thrashed occasionally before rasping feeble, pitiful squeals.

Eli sat motionless in front of the cabin's front door.

"Ain't but one way to do it," he said to the tired and frightened hog. "Have to take their heads off."

———

FEELING A MEASURE OF CAUTION, it rose from the cellar and turned its head quickly from side to side.

"Not like the old man to forget about the fire," it said out loud and then looked down into the cellar's gloom. "Come on up."

A hiss rose from the darkness below.

A gruesome smile spread over its feral face revealing terrible teeth. "Don't be shy now. The old man's probably dead. Heart gave out, maybe. Or his giant gut finally burst."

"*No. You go.*" The words drifted up in a childish, ghoulish whisper.

"Don't worry," it replied as it pushed itself out of the storm cellar's open door. "I'll bring back the body."

———

IT WAS ALMOST midnight when the scratching began.

Gripping an ax by its handle above his head, Eli walked on trembling legs to the side of the cabin's front door. The wild hog's exhaustion vanished under the sudden movements of Eli. Sensing danger, the animal squealed and thrashed in the confinement of its cage.

A voice from outside the door came low and menacing. "I think I hear supper. Pork? Again?"

The front door opened slowly, its hinges creaking like rusted notes from ancient orchestra instruments. When the top part of a head emerged, Eli pushed himself back as close as he could against the wall.

"You in here, old man?" Then, it discovered the caged hog.

Its raging hunger paramount over anything else, it rushed in and ripped open the cage door, never hearing the whoosh of the descending blade.

The first cut did not decapitate. It took repeated, erratic, battering blows to finally detach its head.

Finally, Eli stood above the twitching form and collapsed to his knees, shaking so hard he felt certain his body would fragment. The wild hog rushed by him with a terrible shriek as it escaped through the open door. Eli screamed in surprise at the animal's escape and screamed again when the headless body, arterial blood spurting from its ravaged neck, rose and started swinging its arms in a desperate attempt to flee.

The staggering, headless body then somehow managed to discover the cabin's open door. It turned briefly as if still possessing sight, and then swirled around and stumbled into the night.

His flesh cold and clammy, Eli fell to the dirt floor of the cabin, his eyes locked on a spiteful stare from the severed head still opening and closing its jaws in a frenzy to taste blood.

PART ONE

ONE

Northern Hamilton County
Deer Hollow, Texas
October 31, 1926

It all started with the head

Hung over from moonshine, Donny and Adam Cross were reluctantly up early for the first day of quail season, the brothers bedraggled from chasing a different sort of quail the night before.

Donny stopped to catch his breath, hacked and spit a phlegm wad. His aim flawed, the clump landed wetly on the toe of his hunting boot. "Goddamn!" he hissed, wiping the boot on a cluster of weeds. "Should we even be out this early? My head's poundin' like a judgment."

Eighteen and the oldest of the brothers by two years, Adam Cross leaned against a barbed wire fence separating their family's land from that of Eli Snow.

"Quit your yappin'," Adam said, shivering against a cold October morning. "If your head hurt as much as my pecker, I might find some sympathy for you." He ran a hand across a runny nose. "That Ida Perkins done rubbed mine raw with that mess of wiry twat hair she's sprouted."

Before Donny could respond, their hunting dog, an aged pointer named Turk, sent a chorus of yowls from somewhere beyond the fence. The brothers couldn't see Turk, but the dog's howls seemed to come from a thicket of mesquite trees further down on the Snow property.

Donny walked to the fence and stood by his brother. "Wonder what stirred Turk up?"

Adam bent down and carefully spread open the barbed wire. "It ain't quail, that's for sure. That dog may be old, but he still can point with judicious silence." He motioned for his brother to crawl through. "Hand me your shotgun and slide between the wires. You can hold it open for me when you're on the other side."

Donny handed Adam his twelve gauge and said, "Snow told Pa he don't want us huntin' on his land no more. Remember? Pa was pretty specific about it."

The dog's racket turned into eerie, extended howls sending goose bumps over Adam. "Just crawl through, Donny. We ain't huntin'. We're just gonna see what's got Turk all riled up."

By the time the boys passed through the barbed wire and headed toward whatever the old bird dog was focused on, a light drizzle started to fall from an overcast sky.

"Damnation," Adam said, raising the collar of his heavy fleece coat. "It would start to rain. Let's get down to them trees."

Adam took off in a jog, Donny following close behind. When the boys reached a thicket of mesquite trees, they found Turk standing on the rim of an old well, the dog's tail tucked between its hind legs, its body trembling. When the dog saw Donny and Adam, it threw back its head and let another long, low, morose, spooky howl materialize from deep in its throat.

"Damn," Adam said. "Ain't that the God-awfullest thing you ever heard?"

Donny approached the dog, grabbed the animal by the nape of its neck, and gently pulled Turk away from the well. "Come on, old boy," he said tenderly. "What's the matter?"

The dog gave Donny a forlorn expression and then surprised him by licking his face, where Adam knew Turk's tongue would be a warm and wet and somehow disgusting offering from his own experiences with such.

Donny swiped a hand across his face and released his grip on the dog. "Ugh, Turk. I didn't need that."

"Better than what you got last night," Adam said with a low chuckle. "Bet Sissy Perkins' tongue ain't half as good as old Turk's."

"No, but it's a damned heap more versatile. And she sure knows how…"

The dog stood up on the rim of the well and howled again. Shivers ran up Adam's spine.

"Okay, okay, boy." Adam walked to the rim of the well and stared down into darkness. Unable to see anything in the gloom, he picked up a loose stone and dropped it in the well, a dull thud wafting up shortly after. Turk stopped howling and stared at Adam as if encouraging him to keep looking.

"Sounds dry to me," said Donny. "Bet it ain't been used in a long while."

"Yeah, Pa said one of the freshwater springs over his and Snow's land dried up years ago. But they got plenty of others around. I reckon the one this well was built for sure played out though."

Light snowflakes started to fall as the dog renewed a chorus of melancholy wails.

"We should've stayed in bed today, brother," Donny said, watching the white flakes flutter around them. "Don't know why you were so intent on quail huntin' no how. No meat on them birds' bones. Not like a good steak, anyhow."

Adam started gathering what twigs and dry grass he could find. "Hush your bellyachin' and help me get somethin' together we can burn."

"Burn? You plan on makin' a campfire?"

Adam stared at his brother in exasperation. "No, you idgit. I'm gonna get a clump burnin' and drop it down in the well. Maybe we can see what Turk's so shook up about. You still got them matches you carry for smokes, don't you?"

Donny nodded and helped his brother pick up anything that might make for decent kindling. Between trying to coerce their dog to stop the horrible baying and gathering matter for a fire, the boys finally collected enough separate bundles of material to illuminate the bottom of the well. It took a few tries, but they finally got the first makeshift torch lit and dropped it down. Turk, who usually would've run from any flame, stood his ground on the edge of the well.

The fireball had fallen and left a trail of sparks as it did, landing with a whoosh. But all the brothers saw were scattered debris of old papers, broken pieces of wood, glass bottles, and what grass and weeds had laid claim to the dirt. What flammable material there was in the bottom of the well started to burn, making a large enough fire so the boys had no need to prepare another fiery bundle.

Donny and Adam peered into the well. The heat from the fire below rose and touched their faces like a warm breath. Then the stink came. The stink of burning flesh.

The boys covered their mouths and noses, and Turk began howling all over again.

"Ain't that a hell of a stench?" Adam asked.

Donny gazed down and pointed at something. "There," he said with excitement. "There, over on the far side."

Adam came closer and looked in the direction his brother pointed. "What the hell? That looks like..."

"A head. A goddamned head."

The fire started to abate as snow and sleet fell harder, dousing some of the flames. The brothers turned to each other, Adam saying, "Better go get Pa."

Two

L ucas Cross was the third born of five children, a brother and sister coming before him, and a sister and brother coming after. When Lucas was eight, his father had hatched an idea to gather the family and relocate from Georgia to Texas.

"You jest gonna leave our farm behind?' Mrs. Cross had asked with anger and disbelief. "We ain't got much, but it's somethin'. No need actin' a fool because of some misguided notion."

But Mr. Cross could not be swayed. He stated he was "Right tired of workin' like a mule and getting' nothin' back for it." He was certain by all he'd heard of the great state of Texas that the Crosses were sure to find a better life there. So, he sold his one hundred and sixty acres of farm land for a ridiculously low price, at least as far as Mrs. Cross was concerned. Then he purchased train tickets for his family, and booked passage to the thriving cattle town of Fort Worth, Texas where he intended to invest in and raise the lumbering beast of the plains.

It was a monotonous trip for the Cross children, the oldest boy being ten, the youngest five, the rest chronological as Mrs. Cross was impregnated regularly after each birth until her last, when she had complications too advanced for a mid-wife to deal with. So no more Crosses could be created in her womb, but not for lack of trying by Mr. Cross, who still got randy and chased his wife around the house to the innocent delight of their children.

But such feisty activity from Mr. Cross was cooled by the train ride and the cold, dreary November weather. Mrs. Cross, still brooding about leaving Georgia, turned an even frostier shoulder to her husband. The children, sensing their parents' chagrined behavior, stayed clear of Mom and Dad and inflicted as much teasing and punishment on each other as possible.

By the time the Cross family arrived in Fort Worth, they were a disheveled group with even Mr. Cross doubting his rash decision to leave Georgia. And the rank, heavy manure and animal smell hanging in the Fort Worth air only added to their misery.

Mr. Cross had no trouble finding work in the stockyards. But he only had experience with dairy cows and none with the bad-tempered and uncooperative cattle raised for food, so he soon lost whatever dreams of ranching he'd hoped for. Luckily not all hope was lost, and as it so happened the boarding house where the Cross family stayed was for sale. By putting down most of the money obtained from the sale of his land in Georgia, Mr. Cross purchased the home. There was more than enough business because of the comings and goings of cattle workers and buyers to allow Mr. Cross enough profit for his family's needs.

Eventually, the Cross children were placed in school, and by the time he was seventeen, Lucas decided he wanted to go out on his own. He never cared for the business of housing people, and, unlike his father, had a knack he'd developed from an afternoon job at the stockyard for working with cattle.

Lucas soon courted a girl from his school named Lisa

McDonald, her father a major cattle buyer who got along well with Lucas. The Crosses and McDonalds were quite favorable of the pairing, and by the time an engagement was announced, Lucas had saved up a tidy sum for the purchase of two hundred acres of land in Deer Hollow, Texas, about sixty miles south of Fort Worth. This distance gave the young couple independence but situated them close enough for family visits.

As a wedding dowry, Lisa's father gave the newlyweds one hundred head of prime cattle, allowing Lucas to start up his ranch while his brothers and sisters stayed with the family boarding house endeavor in Fort Worth. Lucas' two brothers eventually opened boarding houses of their own in the city. One sister married a cattle man and moved to Montana, his other sister later acquiring an old maid status as a local schoolmarm.

Lucas and Lisa prospered in the ranching business and soon had their first child, a girl they named Bonnie, after Lisa's grandmother. The next child, a boy named Adam, came along three years later. Two years after that, the last child, due to the fact Lisa died after the birth, was received with mixed emotions. Because Lucas was so stricken by his wife's passing, he tended to ignore the newborn. Lucas' mother stayed around long enough to see the baby received proper care and named the boy Donny after a favorite uncle back home in Georgia.

Tragedy struck the Cross family again when Bonnie disappeared. She was ten years old at the time. Despite extensive searches by authorities, the Cross and McDonald families, and friends and neighbors, Bonnie was never found. There were many drifters passing through Texas at that time, mostly migrant workers from Mexico. Lucas always believed one of the more desperate ones snatched Bonnie for reasons Lucas could only imagine and torture himself with.

It could be said that Lucas, with an ongoing melancholy for the loss of his wife and daughter, kept a simmering grudge against his youngest son even though he knew it was in no way Donny's fault Lisa had died or that Bonnie had been abducted. It was just that Lisa's death after childbirth was always in the back of Lucas' mind every time he set eyes on Donny. And that troublesome reproach still existed when his youngest came rushing into the cattle shed with news of what had been found in an old well that last day of October 1926 with his older brother Adam not far behind.

THREE

"The thought probably crossed your mind, Lucas," Bertram Stone, sheriff of Hamilton County, said as he held the reins of his horse and stared at a rope ladder descending into Eli Snow's well.

Lucas nodded. "I know it's been over ten years, but I still think Bonnie's remains will show up more likely than she will."

Adam and Donny stood nearby with Turk sitting between them. The old dog had ceased its howling as soon as Lucas arrived at the well with the boys. Lucas motioned for Adam to take the reins from Bertram. The sheriff handed them over and approached the well.

"I was still a Ranger when your girl went missin'," Bertram said, leaning over the rim of the well. "I seem to remember we scoured the land adjoinin' yours first thing includin' this well." He tugged on the rope ladder, that motion sending little clouds of dirt from the weathered stone rim. "This don't seem too steady, Lucas. You have any trouble getting' down."

"Naw, it's still pretty solid. Just a might crumbly on the surface."

"And damned sure dry," the sheriff added as he peered down in the well.

"Yeah, it was full of water back when Bonnie disappeared. That's why I thought... Well, you know, we couldn't rightly do no more than drag for her body then."

The sheriff stuck his hands in the pocket of a wool-lined jacket. He wore khaki pants, a long-sleeved white pearl-snap shirt, a bolo tie with a silver horseshoe slide, light tan leather boots, and a gray Stetson. At six foot two without the Stetson, Bertram was a good head taller than Lucas, but the sheriff of Hamilton County was considerably heftier, his expanding paunch stretching hard against his shirt's material.

"You done seen it, I suppose?" he asked Lucas.

"Yep. As soon as my boys told me about it, I had Adam ring you up. But I had to go down first myself just in case it was Bonnie's remains down there."

"And?"

"Well, course they weren't. I should have knowed better. Hers would be nothin' but bone by now. I just wasn't thinkin' straight."

"You say them boys of yours found it?"

"Actually," Donny broke in, "it was old Turk here found it. He was standin' on the ledge and howlin' like a devil. We just come..."

A sharp look from his father shut Donny up. The reprimanded boy lowered his head and started stroking the old dog.

"Sorry to cut him off, Sheriff," Lucas said with a grin. "But it'd be nightfall before he'd get it all out."

Adam giggled and received a similar glare from his father, so he clammed up and huddled in his coat, pretending to shiver.

"Thanks for not draggin' the head out. Never good to move evidence." The sheriff took a set of fur-lined gloves from his coat pocket and put them on. He then walked to the rope ladder and swung his legs over the rim of the well. "Would you do me a favor and hold this ladder, Lucas. Even though you had no trouble with it, I get a might skittish lumberin' down old, loose stone like this."

The rancher grabbed the end of the ladder hanging over the outer rim. "After you get started down, I'll sit on it. It won't go nowhere then."

"Much obliged." Bertram gripped the rope ladder and positioned his body downward to the first, wooden rung. When the sheriff started down, Lucas sat on the rope ladder facing the inside of the well so he could watch Bertram's progress.

After a short time, Bertram's voice came up. "Looks like somebody started a fire down here."

The rancher frowned and glared at his boys, who quickly looked back down at their feet. "Yeah, rather than come get me these two potato heads decided to put together a grass torch so they could see what was down there."

A laugh echoed up from the bottom of the well, and Lucas couldn't seem to help but chuckle himself in response.

But the sheriff's humor stopped suddenly, and he called up. "Lucas, have that boy of yours holdin' my horse take the rawhide bag I slung over the saddle horn and pitch it down to me."

Adam heard the request where he stood and retrieved the bag and walked to the well. "Here it comes, Sheriff," he said as he held the bag over the edge and let it fall.

Lucas rolled his eyes from Adam to Bertram's horse, a roan mare named Lucy that had been with the sheriff as far back as his Texas Ranger days, and the only female keeping Bertram company through most of those years.

Adam smiled weakly at his father before he headed back over to pick up the reins
and hold the mare.

A few minutes passed before the sheriff could be heard

knocking against the interior of the well as he climbed back up the rope ladder. The rawhide bag, stretched and bulging with its grisly contents, appeared over the rim before he did.

"Go ahead and get off the rope and take this, Lucas," the sheriff said. "I want to get my carcass out of this creepy hole."

The rancher did as he was asked, and Bertram soon pulled himself up and over the edge of the well with a sick look on his face.

"Damn, I hate the smell of burnt flesh," he said, casting a wary look at Donny and Adam. "Don't appear to be too damaged though. The hair's all singed, but the face is still intact except for one cooked ear and what the insects and weather have been workin' on." He swallowed audibly and held out his hand. Lucas offered him the rawhide bag and the sheriff took it and then looked up at the overcast sky. "Looks like we'll be in for more ice or snow later. No need lookin' for anything else down there just yet. Weather's supposed to clear up tomorrow. I'll have my deputies Gus and Howard come out and have another look around then."

"Thanks for comin' out," Lucas said. "I hope you weren't involved with nothin' important."

"Naw. I was just about to sit down to a mess of eggs, steak, and coffee at the Koffee Kup Kafé, but they can always fry up a fresh batch when I get back." Bertram looked over at Donny and Adam. "Thank you, boys, for alerting your pa. You did okay, even if you did barbeque the evidence a bit." Lucas and Bertram chuckled as the sheriff walked over to his horse, tied the rawhide bag on the saddle horn, took the reins from Adam, and swung up in the saddle. "And thanks for lookin' after Lucy, young Adam."

"Yes, sir," Adam said.

"By the way," the sheriff said, directing his attention back to Lucas. "Do you recognize who this noggin belongs to?"

The rancher shook his head no.

"How about you boys? You know who it is?"

"We didn't get a good enough look at it, Sheriff," Adam said. "We could just tell it was a head down there, is all."

"Well, I ain't gonna open that bag right now. Probably spook Lucy if I did. But ya'll come on into town tomorrow with your pa. You can have a look-see while your pa and me fill out an official report."

Both boys answered, "Yes, sir."

Bertram motioned Lucas over. "I'm gonna have to parley with that cantankerous Eli Snow tomorrow. This well is on his property. Just barely, but it's his land." He sighed and a breath of warm vapor escaped his lungs, frosting the air. "I believe I'd rather eat horse dung than talk to that old coot. Think I could impose on you to come along, you being his neighbor and all?"

"Well, Eli don't get along with nobody, especially his neighbors. But if it'll help you out, I wouldn't mind. Be interestin' to see how that old bastard reacts to a head being found in his well."

"Thanks, Lucas. We'll head out to Snow's cabin after I take an official report from you tomorrow." The sheriff pulled the reins back gently and clicked his tongue. "Come on, Lucy." Then he added, "This is one hell of a way to start Halloween."

Four

The city of Hamilton, Texas was also the county seat. It was a small berg with a central courthouse built in the usual Doric style with a statue of Lady Justice perched high on the top spire.

Sheriff Bertram Stone's office was in the courthouse basement. This removed any windows to view Hamilton's Main Street, which was quite all right by Bertram. As far as he was concerned, if you'd seen one small Texas town, you'd seen them all. They had an eclectic assortment of mercantile establishments: a barbershop, a post office, numerous churches in eternal competition for wayward souls, and even a movie theater—The Lone Star Bijou being the one in Hamilton.

Around these central establishments other businesses sprouted: a stable with a blacksmith, an apothecary, and a doctor's office. All along with the last stop for all the inhabitants and customers of the shops on Main Street—the undertaker and his funeral parlor.

The Hamilton Public School system, where Donny and Adam Cross spent useless time whenever they attended, had been constructed toward the edge of town for tax purposes.

And presently, in this sleepy little settlement the day after Halloween, Bertram Stone waited patiently in the courthouse basement for Lucas Cross and his boys to arrive.

It was almost eleven o'clock that morning when the Cross family's collection of boot heels could be heard clacking down the courthouse stairs.

"Mornin', Lucas," the sheriff said as Lucas Cross and his sons walked through the office doors. "Have any spooks out your way last night?"

The rancher surveyed the sheriff's office. It was a rectangular area around thirty feet wide and fifty feet long. The walls were stone just like the outside of the court house. The floor was hard wood, polished but scarred from the many boots and errant spur tracks inflicted on it over the years. A large mahogany desk with neat stacks of papers arranged in a two-tiered holder—one labeled **IN** and the other labeled **OUT**—occupied the rear of the room. An Underwood typewriter sat on the left-hand corner of the desk, just above its descending line of the drawers. It was evident to any casual observer that Bertram Stone had a penchant for neatness.

A dark, leather chair sat just in front of the sheriff's desk, and it was there that Bertram motioned for Lucas to sit. A matching sofa was located by the far wall beside the office door. A row of filing cabinets occupied the other side of the doorway.

"You boys don't have to stand," the sheriff said to Donny and Adam. "Take a load off on that sofa."

The boys glanced at their father, who nodded his approval. They sat down on the sofa, removed their cowboy hats, placed them in their laps, and waited for the adults to carry out their business.

Bertram opened the middle drawer of his desk and took out some papers. "Let's get the borin' stuff out of the way before we go and have a better look at that head." He then asked Lucas and his sons the details concerning their discovery the day before.

The interview didn't take long. The sheriff liked to keep things short and to the point. Lucas' vision would stray between Bertram's questions and the black and white snapshots hung on the wall behind the sheriff's desk. Many of the photos were of men on horseback. The figures sometimes looked to be joking with each other. But in other poses, they were deadly serious, holding cigarettes with their hands draped over their saddle horns. Or sometimes they had their heads bowed, looking at bodies lying on the ground in front of their horses.

As Lucas stood staring at the photos he heard Bertram offer, "All them is from my Ranger days."

The sheriff held the report papers together and tapped them on the desk so they lined up with all corners flush before he placed them in the **IN** box now that the interview was concluded. He leaned back and turned around toward the wall and rose out of his chair.

"Come on over," he said to Donny and Adam. "You too, Lucas."

The group gathered in front of the photos on the wall.

"This here's my favorite," the sheriff said, and tapped the glass covering of one picture. It showed three men on horseback with two bodies draped in lariats on the ground in front of them. "That handsome devil is me."

The sheriff brushed a finger over one of the horsemen. "The Ranger next to me is Billy Williams. He was killed in a shootout about a month after this. We were in the middle of the Las Norias Bandit Wars when this picture was taken in 1915. Those two Mexican desperados on the ground had killed about ten people before we caught up with them. One of them scoundrels was a half-breed. Ten scalps were still hangin' off his saddle when we gunned him down."

He shook his head. "Them was lawless times, not like today with all the legislators in Washington and Austin makin' the rules." A strange smile passed over the sheriff's face. He pointed to the horseman standing apart from him and Billy Williams. "That is none other than Captain Monroe Fox. Monroe was seventy years old then and could still outride and outshoot any of us. He never was wounded. I mean, none of us got off clean like that. I still got two chunks of lead in me."

The sheriff ran a hand across his ribs and over his left shoulder. "Hell," he continued and turned his head so Lucas and the boys could see the partial remains of his right ear. "I nearly had my head split open by a machete wieldin' crazy-ass wetback. Just happened to duck in time. I was lucky the tip of the blade sliced my ear and not my skull." The sheriff squared his jaw before he added, "Blew that fella's face plum away with my Colt though."

The room went silent. It was Donny who broke the spell. "Whatever happened to that Captain Monroe?"

Bertram looked at Donny as if the boy was from another planet. "What?"

"You said Captain Monroe was never wounded. He still alive?"

Lucas and Adam glanced at Donny before turning their attention back to the sheriff with apologetic looks on their faces.

The present bout of nostalgia deserted Bertram. He let out a sigh and said, "That old sumbitch retired and bought a ranch down near Pedernales. He died durin' an influenza epidemic. Imagine that. After all them years in peril as a Ranger, some fool thing like influenza gets him."

There was only one photo with an automobile in it instead of horses. It pictured Bertram much as he looked now and one other Ranger holding a short, stocky man. The prisoner had his hands cuffed behind his back. His face was dark and broad. He had a thick head of hair and indeed seemed hairy overall. The man's naked arms and the part of his broad chest exposed above the top button of his shirt were covered with twisted masses of curls.

"That's a Model T." Lucas pointed at the photo. "You boys give up on horses by then, Sheriff?"

"Mostly," Bertram said. "If we had to go out in rough terrain, we still went on horseback. But that's all different now." He tapped on the photo's frame. "That was my last arrest as a Ranger. I decided to retire after we caught this fella."

"What'd he do?" Adam asked.

"That there is—or was, rather, 'cause we strung him up not long after this picture was took—Alfredo Vincenza." The sheriff looked directly at Donny and Adam before saying, "Nice Italian boy who liked little Neegra girls; the younger the better. Liked to rape them and slit their throats with a straight razor after he got what he wanted." He stared at the picture a moment and then added, "Vincenza had a novel way of gettin' rid of the bodies too. He ate them."

The room grew deadly silent.

After a long pause without a word being uttered, Bertram said, "Well, Lucas, why don't we head across the street and take a closer look at that piece of evidence your boys came across in the bottom of Eli Snow's well."

———

THAT FIRST DAY of November was clear and cold, and a north wind howled down Main Street as Bertram, Lucas, Donny, and Adam exited the courthouse.

"Left that head over at Doc Peterson's," the sheriff said loudly over gusting wind. He held his hat in a firm grip on his head as did the rest of the company. "Doc did some forensic work for the state before he settled down in Hamilton."

The group made their way across the street where they walked down wooden floorboards past The Hamilton Inn, the town's only hotel, which was next to the funeral parlor. Shortly after, they came to a halt in front of the medical office.

"Strategically located," Bertram commented with a grin while pointing to the hanging shingles **James Peterson, M.D.** and **Newell Scruggs, Undertaker** facing each other from their perspective locations. Lucas and his boys forced a strained chuckle as the sheriff pushed open the door to the medical office without knocking.

If Sheriff Bertram Stone's office was a model of tidiness, Dr. James Peterson's was the antithesis of it. Loose papers were strewn haphazardly over a dilapidated, collapsing wooden desk made of anything from pecan to oak to hackberry as any recognizable wood tone or polish had been stained away by errant spills of whiskey and lab reagents.

The rest of the office fared no better. An odd collection of mismatched chairs were spread around the room. Several coatracks stood helter-skelter, holding discolored, once-white laboratory smocks, an assortment of tainted suit and winter coats, various Stetsons, and out of place berets, as far as Texas haberdashery was concerned.

The room was damp and reeked of chemicals and stale tobacco, the perpetrating butts of partially smoked or chewed cigars filling various standing and desk ashtrays around the room. An examining table covered with more disordered items and loose papers rested against a wall near the front door.

Sitting amongst the clutter behind the chaotic state of the desk, James Peterson, M.D. held the remains of a cigar clamped between his teeth. He turned to look at those entering the medical office as if annoyed by their intrusion. In a moment, he pulled the cigar butt from his mouth, picked up a dented spittoon from the floor, spat a wad of dark juice in, and wiped a long, brown string of mucous from between the spittoon and his lips before reinserting the cigar butt.

"Afternoon, Bertram," he said with a frown.

The doctor stared at Lucas as if in ignorance of who the rancher was before recognition arrived.

"Lucas Cross," the sheriff said. "You and your boys find a chair and sit." He pointed at the various covered objects around the room. "Just knock whatever's on them to the floor."

The doctor then grinned and winked. "I'll have the maid straighten up later."

All those present laughed, breaking what rigidity was present.

Peterson rose from his chair behind the desk. He was shorter than anyone in the room, even the youngest Cross boy, Donny. The doctor seemed frail and stooped under his filthy lab coat. He had a hawkish nose on which rested heavy spectacles with thick lenses, giving the doctor an impression of a crow-like creature with eyes too large for its skull, and a scraggly black beard and sideburns which added to the aspect of his gauntness.

The doctor watched as Donny and Adam removed their hats and searched for a place to sit, each finally picking up rather than wiping clear whatever clutter stood in the way of sitting in the chairs they'd chosen. The boys placed the clutter in the bowls of their cowboy hats and then sat the hats in their laps.

"You," Peterson said, snapped his fingers, and pointed at Adam. "You're Adam, the oldest." The doctor glanced briefly at Lucas and then back to Adam. "Let's see. I haven't had to deal with you much over the years. I seem to remember a rather persistent boil on your backside."

Adam squirmed and forced a smile.

"But we eventually bested it with sulfur powder." The doctor tapped a finger on his head of thinning, black hair.

"Then there was a broken wrist during branding one season. Bother you any over the years?"

"Not much," Adam said. "Pains me when the weather's damp or cold. But not enough to cause concern."

"Good." Peterson put his hands in his pockets and leaned back on his heels. "Healthy young man. Good." He nodded at Adam who was fidgeting a bit and walked over and whispered in the boy's ear. "No need to mention the other. A dose of the clap gives us all a little character."

Adam turned toward his father, who was about to ask just what the doctor had confided to his son when Peterson stopped any such parental question with a loud, "And you." He pointed this time at Donny. "I recall you weren't so lucky as your brother. Two bouts with pneumonia, wasn't it? Came on after the flu, I believe. We caught the first infection in time, but, by God, we almost lost you that second time."

He turned to Lucas, who still wanted to know what was whispered to Adam. "Had to move him down to Beaumont for treatment, didn't we, Lucas?"

"Yeah, we did. But, hey, Doc. What's up with my oldest? Did he—"

"Close call, that one." The doctor patted Donny on the shoulder. "Good man, though. Came through just fine."

Lucas held up a finger, but before he could continue his inquiry about Adam, Peterson surprised them all by racing across the office. He bent behind the desk and fetched the rawhide bag containing the head from Eli Snow's well.

The doctor unfastened the ties and held the bag upside down, letting the macabre object roll onto the desktop, the head coming to a halt next to one of the cluttered ashtrays. At an angle, the casual observer would have mistakenly believed the head's shriveled lips to be puckering up for one of the half-smoked cigar butts.

Peterson studied the head momentarily before picking it up, grasping it as one would when guessing the weight of a melon. "And this..." The doctor turned the head's face toward his own in an odd façade of a Hamlet to Yorick pose. "This is quite a prize you brought me, Bertram. Quite a prize."

The sheriff swallowed hard, and asked, "Doc, did you...?"

Peterson held one hand away from the head to silence the sheriff. "Did you know," he said with an odd distraction, continuing to gaze at the mangled face held in his hands, "there are certain pagan tribes in the mountain regions of India who will take the severed head of an enemy and play a game of polo with it?" He turned away from the head and looked intently at the occupants in the room. "Amazing when you think about it—all those Ivy League chaps at Yale and Harvard. I mean, if they had any idea where the uncivilized roots of one of their favorite and select sporting activities originated..."

The doctor sighed and placed the head back on the desk. "Oh, well, enough of my observations on mankind's civility." He then took an unsharpened pencil from his lab coat pocket and traced the severed area of the head's neck. "Whoever did this was most uncivil indeed."

Donny and Adam stood up from their chairs and walked with Bertram and Lucas closer in front of the desk and bent over slightly to get a better view as Peterson shared his conclusions. "What we have here is the head of a young male. I'm guessing by the wear on the teeth—except the four that were removed, which I will address momentarily—that this young man was in his mid to late twenties. The fleshy part of the face has been victimized by insects and scavengers, but not to the extreme. What I'm getting at is, if someone is familiar with this person, they might be able to offer identification." He looked at the group gathered around the desk. "Any ideas who this might be? Gentlemen, boys?"

Bertram and Lucas shook their heads no, Bertram then asking, "Adam, Donny... You two said you didn't get a good look yesterday. Have any notion who this head belongs to?"

The boys moved closer. "Maybe if we saw the eyes," Adam said.

Donny nodded in agreement.

The doctor smiled and pulled opened the eyelids.

"Ugh," the boys said in unison as a black-green fluid ran out of the orbits, spilling down the side of the face like grotesque tears.

After letting the eyelids snap shut, Peterson said, "First things a scavenger goes for are the eyes. Kind of like a sweet jelly or jam treat, I would imagine."

Adam shook his head and turned away, and Donny felt a rush of nausea.

"Looking a little green around the gills there, Donny," Peterson said with a grin. "Still don't recognize this unfortunate soul?"

Donny put his hand over his mouth and answered with a muffled, "Nope."

"Me neither," Adam added.

"Oh, well," Peterson said. "Course the hair and one ear have been burned away by," he shot a glance at the two boys, who had backed up a considerable distance from the desk, "our budding detectives. But I still think someone might know who this is. It's a small community, Bertram. Maybe we could put it on public display to see if someone can give this head a name."

"We could do that," Bertram said. "You might have to put some kind of powder on it to kill the smell. People aren't apt to get close enough to a thing like that anyways, especially in its state of decomposition."

"That will be easy enough. A little formaldehyde should do the trick." The doctor laid the head on its side and lifted a portion of the ragged neck tissue. "I can inject it here," he said while pointing to an area with his unsharpened pencil. "Right into the carotid artery."

"What could have tore up a neck like that, Doc?" Lucas asked. "Some kind of animal?"

"Actually, I've asked myself that question. I mean, it's not a clean decapitation. I've seen heads chopped off skillfully with swords, hatchets, and machetes." The doctor glanced at the sheriff's scarred ear. "No offense, Bertram."

"None taken."

"Anyway," Peterson continued, "I've seen about every way a head can be removed except by guillotine, which, I assume, is probably the quickest and neatest way to decapitate due to the speed of the falling blade and its keen edge. The guillotine's blade was so efficient that it's been documented the heads sometimes actually lived on for a while—the victim rolling its eyes around and moving its lips as if to speak. Imagine looking back and seeing your own headless body."

There was a dry cough from one of the group and then a short, tense silence.

"But this fellow." Peterson tapped the end of his pencil on the top of the head. "Had no such luck." He pulled a hemostat from his lab coat pocket and clamped its ends on the neck tissue and pulled it back. "See these marks?" He motioned for Bertram and Lucas to come closer. "There are definitely erratic slice marks in the muscle and tissue. Evidence of a botched or nervous hacking."

"You mean somebody chopped this head away like a Thanksgivin' turkey? And did a bad job of it?" Bertram asked.

"Exactly." The doctor pointed out some severed cervical vertebra. "You can really see the patterns in the bone here. Probably caused by nicks in the blade." He paused a moment before saying, "I certainly hope the fellow was already dead when this occurred." A visible shudder ran over him. "How gruesome if he wasn't."

"Good Lord," Lucas whispered.

Donny and Adam had retaken their seats by now. Chemical odors, musty tobacco, and an ascending reek off the head made both boys appear sick and claustrophobic.

Their father glanced at them briefly and frowned, then turned back to Peterson and asked, "Why would somebody cut a head off like that?"

"Must have been mad as hell," Bertram said.

"Or scared," Peterson added.

"Scared?" Bertram asked. "Looks like the hacker had the upper hand over the hackee, so to speak. What in the world would he be scared of? I'd presume the one getting' his noggin cut away would be the one in fear."

"Remember those teeth I told you had been removed?" the doctor asked. "Well, bend down here and take a look at this." Peterson unclamped the neck tissue and attached the hemostat to the upper left lip of the head, then took a second hemostat from his pocket, clamped the lower left lip and pulled both lips away from the teeth. There were two gaping holes—one on the upper jaw and one directly below on the lower jaw. "It's the same on the opposite side of the mouth. Someone pulled the maxillary and mandibular canines out."

"The maxil what?" Lucas asked.

The doctor smiled widely, running a finger over his own teeth. "These two. The upper and lower canines. The sharp ones."

"Yeah," said Bertram. "I been bit enough over the years by prisoners. Those teeth make a hell of a puncture."

"Especially these four canines," Peterson said. "See how wide these holes are? And look..." He inserted the end of his pencil in the tooth's socket. "These teeth were much bigger and deeper rooted than normal human canines. Exaggerated in size." He unclamped the hemostats and pointed out scarred erosion areas above the upper and lower mouth. "In fact, from this scarring, it appears our victim's lower canines protruded above the upper lip and the upper canines hung over the lower one."

"Like an animal?" Lucas asked.

"Yes," the doctor said. "Like a wild animal. So maybe whoever killed this man was frightened by his appearance. Or actions. Maybe we have a killer's head right here in front of us. Maybe somebody was just protecting themselves."

"But why cut off the head?" Bertram asked.

"I have a theory on that," said Peterson. "Whoever did this may have been superstitious enough to believe..."

The front door of the medical office creaked open, putting a halt to the doctor's theories. The group in the room, under the effect of the bizarre events concerning the doctor's discoveries and the eerie mood, turned quickly toward the sound, Donny so jumpy he appeared to forcefully bite his lower lip to stifle a response.

A tall, shadowy figure loomed in the medical office doorway. "Afternoon, gentlemen...boys," announced a low voice in the heavy tone of a church organ's bass pedal.

Peterson asked, "What brings you over, Newell?"

The city of Hamilton's undertaker, Newell Scruggs, was so tall he had to stoop to avoid the top of the doorframe, even after removing his stovepipe hat. He hesitated a moment before entering the medical office.

THE UNDERTAKER certainly dressed the part: a ubiquitous funeral-black suit and a glaring white starched shirt pulled together at the neck by an ebony tie with a centered ruby stick pin. A flower, today's looking suspiciously like a yellow cactus flower that was still perky in the November cold, donned the left lapel of his suit coat.

Newell was extremely thin, his facial bones sunken and austere enough to make him resemble a client rather than a proprietor.

"Dr. Peterson, Sheriff Stone, Lucas." Newell snapped his fingers, and added, "and Donny and Adam, I believe." Nodding his head at the boys, he cast a sly eye on Donny and said with dark humor, "Seems I missed my date with you the second time you had pneumonia, young man."

The boy visibly shivered.

"You've got to be the damnedest, most morbid person I know, Newell," Bertram said with a strained laugh.

"Please forgive my joviality in regard to such a solemn subject." Newell walked to Donny and placed his bony fingers on the boy's shoulder. "I meant no disrespect, lad. I'm afraid the occupation of undertaker sometimes moves my demeanor in a rather bleakly humorous aspect. But, of course, I am happy to see you and your brother and father in what appears to be the best of health."

"What can I do for you, Newell?" asked Peterson.

With his fingertips, the undertaker rolled the brim of his stovepipe hat. "I couldn't help but overhear your voices through the wall of our respective establishments." He stared then at the head on the desk. "Business being rather slow, I thought I'd stop in and join your company." He pointed at the head. "I assume this object being the topic of discussion, I might be able to offer some help in the matter."

Peterson glanced at Bertram.

The sheriff shrugged his shoulders to indicate he didn't mind the undertaker's intrusion.

"Sure," Peterson said. "Six..." he said before correcting

himself by tapping the head on the desk. "I mean, seven heads are better than one."

Everyone but the boys laughed, Donny still seemingly unnerved by the cold fingers on his shoulder long after Newell had lifted them.

"I was just explaining why someone might cut off a head in this manner," Peterson said to the undertaker, who had craned his long neck down to have a closer look at the head. "I told Bertram and Lucas that many people are still superstitious enough, even in these enlightened, scientific times, to believe in supernatural creatures. Ghosts, ghoulies, vampires and such."

"Oh, indeed." Newell arched his eyebrows as he pulled the head's upper and lower lips apart using his own fingers without revulsion or hesitation. "I see the canines have been extracted. By the look of the socket width and, I am assuming, depth, this fellow had quite a quartet of fangs in his mouth."

"Looks that way," said Peterson. "Enough to make a gullible person believe he's dealing with a terror rather than a biologically deformed human."

"Exactly." Newell ran fingers across the flesh of the head's face and neck as if appraising it. "Believe me, in my business I've witnessed many curious acts by people over the years. I've seen coffins filled with salt to keep an evil departed family member or friend from rising. On other occasions, families have removed the head of the deceased, albeit a bit more ceremoniously and neater than this one." He made a circle with his hands to measure the circumference of the head. "The mourners sometimes stuffed the head with garlic, silver, and, on one occasion, the bereaved beheaded being of Russian heritage, blessed Icons."

The undertaker glanced at the boys, who sat silent and fidgety in their chairs. "Once, I wouldn't agree to what one family asked me to do," he said, a gruesome look forming along the shadowy lines of his cadaverous face. "But the family dug up the coffin long after the ceremony was over and did what they wanted, anyway."

"What did they do?" Adam asked, taking the bait thrown out by the undertaker.

Newell walked over to the boys, bent over, and said in a low whisper, "They drove a wooden stake into the corpse's heart."

The boys' faces went ashen.

Newell straightened up and faced the men around the desk. "Damndest thing, that coffin was filled with fresh blood like the corpse's heart had never ceased beating, although I knew that was quite impossible."

Bertram elbowed Lucas. They both looked at Donny and Adam and couldn't help but snicker.

Peterson didn't join their laughter. His face was set and serious. "We don't know everything. Even us men of science. Inexplicable events occur daily. And superstitions have roots in some truth, natural truth, though it well may be."

The undertaker coughed dryly and, to break the sudden seriousness, asked, "Is there a body to go along with the head? I could offer my services either way, but it would seem more complete with a body."

Peterson looked at the undertaker as if he wasn't aware Newell was there. "What? The body?"

"Yes," Newell said. "Is there one?"

"Actually, the head was all we found," Bertram explained. "It was in a well on Eli Snow's land close to the fence borderin' Lucas' ranch. I sent my deputies, Gus and Howard, out early this morning to do a little diggin' in that well and search the general area for any evidence or clues."

"I see," Newell said. "Eli Snow, you say? Now there's a character. I'd hate to be the one to approach him regarding this matter."

Lucas frowned. "I told Sheriff Stone I'd go out to Snow's

place with him today, which probably ain't all that wise now that I've had time to think on it."

"I was out to Eli's cabin long ago," the undertaker said. "Let's see... Must have been over fifteen years now. Eli's older boy, Arlis, came into to town to fetch me. Said his younger brother, Jacob, had been sick and passed away, and they needed my services. Damnedest thing was, Eli wouldn't let me come in and get the body. Just stood there with a double barrel shotgun in the doorway of that dilapidated cabin the Snows called home. He cursed me for all I was worth and ordered me off his property. Arlis did everything but get down on his knees and beg his father to let me come in and take Jacob's body away. I never will forget the look on Eli's face when he growled at Arlis and said 'You know damned well Jacob ain't dead yet. You crazy or somethin', boy? Bringin' this corpse peddler here.' He then looked at me with the coldest eyes I'd ever seen and told me to git before he made me a customer of my own services.

"Well, I've never been foolish. And that demented old man didn't have to try any harder to persuade me. So, I left. I figured Eli would see to the burying if the boy was dead or dying. Arlis tried to convince me the body needed to be embalmed, that Jacob had suffered from some contagious disease. But there hadn't been any cases of anything like typhoid that I knew of, and if it was influenza, it wouldn't have mattered. You can't stop that from spreading.

"I climbed into the hearse and headed back toward town. Looking over my shoulder, I saw Eli whipping Arlis, but I couldn't help that. You men know as well as I do you can't get in the middle of a family matter without catching the brunt of it, so I returned to Hamilton and let the matter drop. Always felt bad about Arlis, though." The undertaker raised his eyebrows and placed a hand on the side of his face as if trying to recall something. "Arlis was killed in France. Wasn't he?"

"Believe he was," said Lucas. "Buried somewhere over there like so many were durin' the war."

"Eli Snow has got to be around ninety years old now. I heard he fought in the Spanish American War," Newell said. "He may still be cantankerous, Sheriff Stone, but I doubt he can get around all that well anymore. He shouldn't be able to cause you or Lucas much grief at this stage of his life."

"You'd think that was true," Lucas said. "But last year Eli came over to my place madder'n hell. Had that shotgun with him you mentioned, Newell, waving it around like a crazy man, ordering me to keep my boys off his land because Donny and Adam had been huntin' quail there. Hell, I didn't see no harm in them bein' on Snow's property. He didn't have up any **NO HUNTING** signs, or least ways nothin' down around where our properties meet. Eli must have heard my boys' guns. Anyway, I told him to get off my porch and to put that shotgun where the sun don't shine, and damned if he didn't cock the hammers back and level that thing at me.

"I don't think anybody in town can give an accurate description of that old fool, Eli being more a hermit than sociable. But I got an eyeful of him that day on my porch. He may well be close to ninety and bent over some, but he's still as burly as they come. Near as tall as you are Sheriff and stocky as a bear. It was about as cold that day as it is now, but that old bastard only had on a set of shabby overalls with no shirt underneath. His arms and chest were covered with thick hair, so I guess he didn't need no coat. And he was barefoot to boot. I thought he had gone Grade A crazy and held up my hands and told him to settle down, and that I'd see my boys stayed off his land.

"I kept a close eye on the finger he had on that shotgun's trigger in case I needed to move quick, but he eventually took it off and clicked them hammers back down real slow. Then he smiled at me in a threatenin' kind of way. I'll never forget his face. He didn't keep a beard, but his cheeks was dark with stubble. His nose looked like it had been broken on more than one occasion, and his lips were all dried and cracked. He was damned near completely bald—just had a ring of gray fuzz circlin' his head. His eyes were deep black like a bird's. All in all, he was one ugly sumbitch. And when he bent them lips back in that malicious smile, he revealed the nastiest set of teeth I'd seen. They was green with crud and crooked. Right there in that cold air I could smell the foulness when he breathed over them.

"Guess he didn't want to turn his back to me 'cause he backed off my porch facin' me. He then turned and went the way he'd come, I reckon, since he'd crept up on me to begin with. Don't guess he had no horse or car as he was hoofin' it."

Bertram said, "Hell, you men keep talkin' about that old scoundrel and I just might send Howard and Gus to talk with him. Don't know as I want to deal with any double barreled shotgun."

There was a pause, followed by a brief round of nervous coughing among the men. Donny and Adam sat glued to their chairs and did not utter a sound.

"Well, gentlemen," Newell said after a moment. "If you need my expertise on making that head look as presentable as possible, you know where to find me. And if no other body parts are discovered, I can prepare a small box for its burial." He glanced at Bertram. "That would be the Christian thing to do. I'm certain all here would agree on that point."

"I suppose the city could spare a little tax money to pay you, Newell," Bertram said. "But let's see if we can find out what happened to the owner of that head first."

"By all means, Sheriff Stone. As I said, business is quite slow these days, anyway." The undertaker smiled mischievously at Peterson. "What with the cunning scientific advancement in medicines to combat microbes that once brought me customers and the very prescriptions our good Dr. Peterson employs, my yearly numbers have drastically declined. Of course, there is no cure for old age, so I still do have clientele from that venue from time to time."

Peterson shuddered momentarily. "Newell, you're just not much for pleasant conversation, are you?"

The undertaker bowed slightly. "As I said earlier, it's a peril of my profession."

"Anyway, putting all this gruesome talk aside," said Bertram. "Newell, could you clean up our piece of evidence a bit after the Doc pickles it? We're going to put it on public display eventually in the courthouse square and see if any good citizens recognize the unfortunate victim."

"Well, now that's an excellent idea. I would be more than happy to help the city with its investigation as best I can." The undertaker then addressed Peterson. "Just let me know when you've finished your preparations, Doctor. Unless you'd care to have me embalm the object myself."

"No, I'll take care of the formaldehyde. I want to conduct a few more examinations first."

"Then I will await your instructions." Newell then turned to walk out of the office. As he passed Donny, the undertaker ran a bony hand over the boy's head and tousled Donny's thick mop of brown hair. Donny looked up with what seemed a forced smile. "Good day, gentlemen." Newell then glanced at Donny and Adam. "Boys." The undertaker made a slight bow just before walking out the medical office.

Peterson, Lucas, and Bertram stared at each other and let out a shared sigh of relief.

"On second thought," Bertram said. "Maybe a visit to Eli Snow won't be so bad after all. Might even lighten the mood after listening to Newell."

"Imagine having that black scarecrow, Newell, come by for

trick-or-treat last night," Peterson said. "That would raise a person's hackles."

"Well," Bertram said, "we've put this off long enough. Lucas, I'll follow you and the boys back to your ranch and check on Gus and Howard before we go out to Snow's."

"All right, Sheriff." Lucas motioned to Donny and Adam. "Come on, boys."

Before leaving, Bertram told Peterson, "I'll check with you when we get back, Doc."

"Afternoon, Doc," Lucas said, buttoning his coat and arranging his cowboy hat.

"Lucas. Boys," the doctor replied.

Positioning their own coats and hats, Donny and Adam offered a feeble wave goodbye.

Once the group had left the medical office, Bertram closed the door behind them. Stepping into the street, the sheriff scrutinized the sky. "Cloudin' up again. This new norther's gonna bring us more precipitation for sure. You bring your Model T Runabout, Lucas?"

"Sure did. We're in the habit of not ridin' horses much anymore."

"Sign of the times, I suppose. Think I'll give Lucy a break, too. Let her stay in the warm stable and munch on oats in her feedbag. I'll follow you boys in the city wagon."

"That old Ford is the city paddy wagon, ambulance, and hearse, ain't it?"

"That it is. And not necessarily in that order."

FIVE

While fighting agony from broken legs, Eli Snow dragged himself more than a quarter mile in the early morning hours after Halloween, passing out several times in the process. Dizzy from blood loss and pain, he woke up in a small cave without recollection of when or exactly how he'd made it there, his breath now ragged, blood steadily seeping from a neck wound.

Many years ago, native Indians used the cave as a hideaway. Eli had found it by accident while searching for a missing steer. It was not a large cave but spacey enough for an average adult to stand in, the interior roughly twenty-five feet in diameter, ending in a wall of earth permeated by plant roots probing from the ridge above. Eli had converted the cave to a storage area for moonshine brewed from a hidden still.

But the days of selling hooch were long gone, the still dry and barren since Eli's youngest, Jacob, had taken ill.

Now, as he lay hurt and confused in the cave, Eli tried to clear his head, concentrating on how to save himself from the terrors that had visited him just after the witching hour.

The previous night, he'd prepared the cabin as best he could from the danger he'd been expecting for many days. He'd covered the windows with heavy boards and fortified the only door to the cabin with wooden planks and large stones, precautions he'd practiced every night since decapitating his son.

He'd then situated himself in front of the door and waited with his shotgun ready.

———

HE HADN'T HAD any way of knowing the hour but guessed it had been around midnight when the sound of something dragging its feet moved methodically on the dirt path outside the cabin.

Beads of sweat running down his flesh in the cold autumn night, the hairs on Eli's body bristled when he heard a child's soft laughter, the steady dragging noise nearer and louder.

The dragging sound eventually stopped outside the cabin's front door, a whispering childish voice saying, "In there. For both of us."

Eli added his bulk to the fortifications against the front door. "Go away," he screamed. "I done killed you once! Get and take that hellish thing with you!"

After an extended silence, he heard the wind pick up and moan through cracks along the doorframe, and he soon relaxed, believing the unwelcome visitors had left. As his eyes welled with tears, he let out a strained breath, saying, "God Almighty, thank you for delivering me."

A sudden blow to the door was so powerful that Eli catapulted across the room, the shotgun flying out of his hands. He scrabbled toward the weapon quickly, cocked the hammers, and leveled the barrels at the door just as the wood and stone defenses flew straight at him like shrapnel when the door burst open. The debris caught him in the face and he fired wildly, missing the headless body gesticulating its arms in a flurry of disorientation hunting for Eli.

The thing stumbled through the broken wood. It tripped and then righted itself, its body naked and putrefying, white bone gleaming through damaged muscles, areas of decomposing tissue outlining the deep wounds inflicted on its once hale form. Scavengers had away eaten its genitals, leaving only dark globs nesting in matted, black pubic hair.

The thing's arms and legs were in constant spasmodic motion, the remaining neck muscles rotating left and right, moving an absent head to hunt with missing eyes.

Then something drifted into the cabin and hovered over the decapitated body of Jacob Snow.

A small girl, her thin dress so tattered that nothing remained but strips of frayed material barely hanging on her body. The child's flesh was the color of white marble, her near sexless body easily seen through the sheer garment: pale; twin dark, flat nipples; and the only thing distinguishing her from a boy—a vertical fissure of skin below her navel severely constricted inward by time and death.

The girl's hair was the complete opposite of her flesh—dark brown and lustrous, seeming to possess a life of its own undulating in thick swirls around and over her shoulders. The girl's face, however, was a horror, her eyes bottomless pools of burning blue nesting under eyebrows as dark as her hair, the lips on that face drawn back in a cruel snarl, revealing slender canines hanging over and beyond her pouting lower lip.

"There," the girl hissed, and somehow, even without eyes to see, the headless thing knew where to go.

By now Eli had managed to get up. He looked around and

searched for anything to use as a weapon. He stumbled toward the wood stove at the back of the cabin and heard the girl laugh as he pulled a carving knife from the stove's top. The arms of the headless corpse suddenly encircled Eli as he gripped the knife's handle, Eli shrieking when the thing lifted him high over the stump of its neck, throwing him against the cabin's back wall.

Eli slid to the dirt floor and immediately tried to crawl away. He then felt an enormous weight on the back of his right leg just before the femur cracked in two. The pain was unbelievable, heightening his senses enough to experience more anguish as his left femur was then broken as well.

Eli howled and rolled. The carving knife still gripped in his hand, he swung the blade forward and felt it slice through soft, decaying flesh like a rotten tomato. He had no idea he'd cut the headless body's abdomen open. The strong smell of rotten bowels filled the cabin, and Eli choked on the odor. Overcome by it and the agony of his broken legs, he felt consciousness slip away. The last things he was aware of before fainting was a sensation of something sharp tearing at his neck and slurping sounds.

———

Now in the cave, Eli wondered why he wasn't dead. There was no part of his body that hadn't suffered mortal agony. He tried to move his legs and was rewarded by such pain that he lost his breath and cried out in a soundless wail. Outside, the sun was high in an overcast sky. He stared at passive light mixing with swirling dots of his tortured vision and lay as still as possible until the ache in his legs reduced to a steady throb. He felt a warm, wet sensation on the side of his throat and carefully moved fingers over it, bringing back sticky blood.

"Oh no," he said.

He ran his fingers over the wound again and found the two punctures he feared would be there. Tears spilled down his grimy cheeks. He knew the sun had a long way to fall and that evening had just as long a wait to reach the midnight hour.

And he knew it didn't really matter. He was already dead, even if his heart was still beating.

Six

"Howard ain't too bad, but that Gus can be one lazy fella." Sheriff Bertram Stone cracked the Ford's driver window, pulled a Bugle Boy tobacco tin from his coat pocket and took out one rolled cigarette. "Smoke?" He held the tin toward his passenger, Lucas Cross.

"Don't mind if I do." The rancher took one of the cigarettes from the tin. He then cracked his window slightly, reached in his jean pocket, and pulled out a box of matches. He struck the match head across the side of the box and held the flame out to the sheriff.

"Much obliged," Bertram said, lighting his cigarette.

Lucas then lit his own smoke and shook out the match. The men sat in silence as they inhaled the luxurious tobacco and slowly blew out gray smoke.

The sheriff felt a twinge of irritation as he thought of Howard Sparks and Gus Greenwood. Bertram had arrived at the Cross ranch just after Lucas and his sons and found the two deputies sitting on the porch huddled in their coats against the wind and drifting off to sleep.

———

Bertram passed by a grinning Lucas Cross, who had sent Donny and Adam back down to the well to see if the deputies had left any kind of evidence laying around.

Taking off his Stetson, the sheriff slapped both of the dozing deputies on the head with it.

"Hell's bells," Howard yelled. His eyes were still cloudy with sleep and it took a moment for him to realize who it was thumping his head. He jerked up with uncoordinated motions and nearly fell down as he got up from the porch chair.

Gus, on the other hand, slipped deeper into the false security of his coat and uttered a muffled, "Oh shit."

"Damnation, Howard. Gus." Bertram returned the Stetson to his head. "You two are supposed to be diggin' in the bottom of that well for any clues that might be there, not lazin' away like it's Sunday afternoon and you're being entertained by Lucas and his boys."

Howard lowered his head. "Hell, Sheriff, we done dug about all we can. Ain't nothin' down in that old dried up well but bits of wood, glass, and other useless trash. Sure ain't no more human parts there." He couldn't hold back his celebrated country humor and added, "Lessen they crawled out before we arrived."

A muffled snicker came from the confines of Gus' coat.

The sheriff's face turned beet red. "And I suppose you two just decided there was no more to do after diggin'. Didn't occur to you to spread out and have a look-see around Snow's land?" Howard lowered his head again, and Gus went silent inside his coat.

"Gus," Bertram said. "You ain't no terrapin. Stick your head out that coat and pay attention to me."

Gus' head slowly emerged. "Yes, sir, Bertram. I mean, Sheriff."

"We were going to go back to the well and look around after we warmed up here out of the wind," Howard said. "Guess we got a little too comfortable."

Bertram shook his head and glanced at Lucas, who had been watching and listening with amusement while leaning against the porch railing. "Well," the sheriff said, "while Lucas and me drive out to Snow's cabin, you two look around the land close to that well."

"Donny and Adam will help," Lucas said. "I sent them out there to do some snoopin' already. The four of you could catch all directions from the well that way."

Howard nodded as did Gus, who by now had risen from his chair.

"And I don't want to come back here and find you two in the house roastin' weenies and shootin' the shit with Donny and Adam neither," said Bertram.

Gus grinned and said, "No, sir."

"Come on then," Howard said to Gus. The two ambled off the porch and walked in the direction of the well. Neither one looked back, avoiding the cold stare Bertram placed on their backsides.

——————

BERTRAM ROLLED down the driver's window and flicked out his cigarette butt and rolled the window up again. Lucas tapped the fire off the end of his smoke and let it fall to the floorboard where he ground it with the tip of his boot. He took what was left of the unfinished cigarette, placed it in his shirt pocket and then rolled up the passenger window. Glancing through the glass, he spotted Eli Snow's cabin materializing in the distance.

The cabin had been built in a natural hollow, smaller than the sunken valley from where Deer Hollow, Texas got its name, but low and deep enough to keep a north wind at bay.

It was evident by weather-worn logs and gaping holes between them that Eli had neglected the cabin for many years. The roof was sagging in the middle with numerous, crude patches to keep out precipitation. On one side of the cabin, the remains of a chimney climbed in disjointed, brittle pieces. Any smoke traveling up its wounded bricks would be dispensed as if flowing through a sieve.

Bertram parked the Ford about twenty yards away, and he and Lucas got out and walked slowly toward the cabin. Bertram unfastened the trigger strap on his side holster, his hand at the ready on top of the butt of a Colt .45.

Lucas had no weapon, so he walked slightly behind the sheriff letting him take point. In the event that Eli Snow emerged with that double barrel shotgun Lucas had already experienced firsthand, Bertram could understand his potential reasoning.

The late afternoon sky was now so overcast that very little light filtered through the clouds. The wind had died down, but the air was still damp and chilly, penetrating down to the bones. Approaching the cabin, a visibly shattered front door came into the men's view. Bertram motioned for Lucas to stop and stay where he was. The sheriff then inched forward, cautiously pulling out the Colt.

Bertram moved to the side and away from the ragged opening of what was left of the cabin's front door. He held the Colt up and inched around the busted frame. Surveying the mess inside, he said under his breath, "God Almighty." The sheriff then motioned for Lucas to join him.

Inside, the cabin was saturated with the smell of old grease and smoke permeating the interior walls from years of cooking bacon and other meat. It was savory, but at the same time rancid.

The place was a mess. A cluster of unwashed plates and glasses and frying pans were gathered chaotically on top of a wood burning stove. There were empty and half eaten cans of beans and peaches strewn haphazardly along with intermittent mounds of soiled clothes amassed in the corners of the cabin.

Besides the general and obvious routine bedlam populating the cabin, there was the recent destruction. Splintered wood from the shattered front door and the many, large stones Eli had fortified the entrance with were spread inconsistently about as if shot by a cannon, not to mention the shotgun blast that had blown a ragged hole in the ceiling when Eli had fired wildly, that shotgun now resting sideways with a broken stock against the wall.

Bertram holstered his Colt. "Ain't no revelation at the state of this place. I never figured Eli Snow to be of any housekeepin' persuasion." He bent down and picked up a carving knife he spied on the floor, its blade cloyed with dark gore. A reek of putrescence clung to it making him turn his head away and frown.

"Shooee," Lucas said when the odor wafted his way.

Bertram placed the carving knife back down where he'd picked it up and then lifted his hand and sniffed it. He frowned again and started to wipe the offending fingers on his coat, then decided against the notion of touching anything with those soiled fingers.

"There's a lamp back on a little table near the stove." Lucas pointed in that direction. "Reckon you might try that to kill the stink on your hand with that kerosene."

Lucas strained a smile as he watched the sheriff take the chimney off the lamp, tilt the base, and flood his reeking hand. Bertram took another sniff of his hand and made a funny face.

"God, what is on that blade?" He doused his hand again, found a soiled dishrag by a wash basin, and wiped his hand with it. "Smells like old, sour shit. Don't it, Lucas?"

But the rancher had turned his attention to the earthen floor where fragments of clotted blood mixed with dark stains resembling those on the knife. "Look here, Sheriff." He directed Bertram's attention to more of the streaks heading toward the door. Amongst the clutter of the cabin, both men had failed to see the blood trails when they first entered.

"Well, that tears it." Bertram pulled a watch from his khaki's watch pocket and opened it. "Goin' on four. Won't have light much longer." Before replacing the timepiece, he ran his fingertips over the silver chain until they rested on an old cartridge shell he'd made into a fob. "Mind followin' that blood trail with me, Lucas? I know you ain't no official deputy, but we're goin' to be hampered by twilight before I can drive back to your place and get Howard and Gus."

"Don't mind at all, Sheriff. Got a lantern in that Ford? Might come in handy."

But there was no lantern in the Ford, only the lamp from the cabin. So the sheriff replaced its chimney and brought it along as he and Lucas followed the spotted trail of blood leading away from the cabin.

The trail went on for a good quarter mile and then disappeared. But there were other tracks—jumbled markings in the dead grass and dirt like someone had danced a dervish.

"Think Eli got up and started walkin'?" Lucas asked.

Bertram bent down and touched the marks, studying the area ahead of them. "If he did, he wasn't bleedin' no more." The sheriff inhaled through his nose, wrinkled it, and pointed down. "Damn if the same stink on that cutting knife ain't out here, and damned if there ain't some more of them darker stains."

"Maybe somebody carried Eli away."

"Well, let's trail these new signs and see where they lead until it starts getting' too dark."

They followed the dark stains, which soon disappeared. When daylight was failing, they saw the beginning of a cliff rising into the wooded area of Eli's land. Approaching with caution, Bertram and Lucas discovered the entrance to the cave where Eli once stored his illicit liquor.

"I'll be," Bertram said. "Didn't know this cave was here. You ever seen it?"

Lucas shook his head no. "Never came out this way. Rumor was Eli used to have a still and run moonshine from his woods. I figured it was safer to keep clear of this section of his land."

"You still got them matches on you, Lucas?" Bertram took the chimney off the kerosene lamp.

"Yep, sure do."

The rancher reached into his jean pocket and brought out the matchbook, then struck a match and held it to the lamp's wick. The familiar and comforting smell of burning kerosene soon filled the damp air as Bertram moved into the cave's opening with Lucas close behind, the lamplight bouncing off the walls, producing long, undulating shadows. And it wasn't long until Bertram and Lucas discovered Eli Snow lying prostrate on the ground.

Eli's legs were badly swollen and stretched the material of his torn overalls, dark spots spreading out on the front around his thighs where broken bone had ripped through the flesh.

The sheriff held the lamp close to the wounded man's face. It was then he and Lucas saw the wide puncture wounds on Eli's throat.

"Good Lord," Bertram said. "What in the world got a hold of you, Snow?"

On hearing his name, Eli opened his eyes and moaned.

"Well, at least he's still with us," Lucas said.

Bertram squatted down to get a better look at the neck wounds. "Wonder what kind of animal could've done this?"

Lucas grimaced at the ragged flesh around the puncture wounds. "Maybe a mountain lion. Ain't seen one in a while, but if they get hungry enough, they'll come down outta them cliffs around Erath and Hamilton counties lookin' for livestock. I heard it ain't been above their nature to occasionally attack a human."

Bertram glanced back at Lucas whose face seemed gigantic and hovering in the lantern light. He then shivered and returned his attention to Eli. "Snow?" The sheriff gently touching Eli's shoulder. "Snow, can you hear me?"

Eli opened his eyes wide and attempted to speak, but only a dry rasp that sounded like *them* came out. He groaned and moved his trembling hands down to his legs and then looked back at Bertram. In the light cast on Eli's face, the sheriff saw that even in the cold air Eli's head and cheeks were covered with perspiration.

"Your legs?" Bertram asked. "Something wrong with your legs?"

Eli moved his lips, trying to speak again, then scowled and closed his eyes in evident pain. The sheriff directed the lamplight down Eli's body and the swollen legs. He saw the stains then and set the lamp down and told Lucas, "Help me turn Snow on his side. Something must've happened to his legs we can't see from the front."

Lucas bent and helped Bertram roll Eli, whose groan turned into a scream once they had him on his side. Moving the lamp closer, Bertram and Lucas saw the broken femurs poking through the overalls, the fabric torn around the jagged bones, bits of flesh and muscle clinging to their shattered ends.

"Mercy," Bertram said as he and Lucas rolled Eli back over.

Eli's screams declined, and he started to breathe spasmodically. His eyes widened as he reached up for Bertram. "Them," he gasped.

"Them who?" Bertram asked.

Eli rolled his bugging eyes toward Lucas and seemed to have a sudden recognition. His mouth twitched as he raised a trembling hand and extended an index finger, pointing at the rancher. "Her," Eli said in a shaky voice that rose in volume. Eli moved his hands down and tried to get up, but he stopped quickly as intense pain smashed him back down. "Aiiieee!" he wailed. He took a long, ragged breath, and then passed out.

"What in the world did he call me *Her* for?" Lucas asked

"I imagine the poor devil's seeing things. Suppose I would be too if my legs was as busted up as his are and my neck tore open like that."

"I guess it weren't no mountain lion after all. Wouldn't have broke Eli's legs like that. Unless he fell fightin' it and broke them hisself."

Bertram placed his hand on Eli's forehead. "He's burnin' up. Don't reckon no mountain lion did this to his neck though. If one of them gets a hold of your throat, there'd be two punctures on the other side as well." The sheriff opened his mouth, tapping the upper and lower canines. He then closed his mouth and grinned. "Lessen that cat done lost two teeth along the way."

Lucas snapped his fingers. "Say, Doc Peterson said that head from Eli's well had upper and lower teeth plucked out. You don't think..."

Bertram stood up and dusted dirt and dust from his pants. "No. That head had been ripenin' for a while. I'm bettin' Snow's injuries happened last night or early this mornin'." A thought then crossed the sheriff's mind. "Unless that head's got a twin around here somewhere."

Lucas shuddered and looked back over his shoulder outside the cave. "We better get Eli into town. Light's about gone."

"Okay, you want to stick around here or go get the Ford?"

Bertram could see from the look on his face that neither idea appealed to Lucas, but apparently being cooped up in that cave with Eli Snow proved to be less alluring than the alternative when he said, "If it's all the same to you, I'll hightail it back and get that Ford."

Bertram reached in his pocket, took out the keys to the Ford, and handed them to Lucas. He then pulled the Colt .45 from its holster and gave the gun to the rancher. "You better take this along just in case."

Lucas hesitated. "But what if...you know, somethin'—whatever it is—comes back after Eli?"

"Well, I got my old pocket knife. That and the fire in this here lantern might make it think twice. So, I'll be okay. Besides, Snow may come to and tell me what happened."

"I'll be back directly then." As he slipped the revolver between his belt buckle and jeans, Lucas put a finger to his hat brim and left the cave.

Bertram stared at Eli Snow, whose breathing was now faint and shallow. Outside in the distance something howled balefully. A chill creeping down his spine, Bertram pulled the collar of his coat up higher. He noticed then that Eli had a soiled shirt on under the overalls. "Well," the sheriff said. "At least I don't have to look at your curly body hair like Lucas did on his porch that day you came a callin'."

The howl came again but seemed further away this time. Bertram pulled his collar tighter and put a hand in his pocket, searching for security from the long-handled pocket knife there.

SEVEN

E li Snow remained unconscious on the rough ride over dirt and gravel roads Sheriff Bertram Stone navigated toward the town of Hamilton.

Earlier, the sheriff had dropped Lucas Cross off at his ranch and picked up deputies Gus Greenwood and Howard Sparks, who had been in the middle of eating supper with Donny and Adam Cross at the time. Neither the deputies nor the boys had uncovered any new evidence at the well where the head had been discovered or anywhere around it, so the objective now was to get Eli to Dr. Peterson in Hamilton as soon as possible.

The men in the Ford said little to each other on the trip. The temperature outside had dropped significantly and a few random flakes of snow drifted across the headlight beams.

Amid intervals of Eli's moaning in the back seat, Gus could no longer stand the quiet and asked, "Why does it smell like kerosene in here, Sheriff?"

Bertram turned around and briefly glanced at Gus, who sat in the back seat next to Eli. He then looked at Howard in the passenger seat before turning his attention back to the road. Glancing down at his fingers, Bertram said, "Just never you mind, Gus. You keep an eye on Eli back there and don't worry about what smells or don't."

Howard looked over his shoulder and winked at Gus.

"Yes, sir, Sheriff," Gus said, making a face behind Bertram's back.

———

SILENCE TOOK over again and snowflakes began to fall in earnest, twisting over the headlight beams in a swirling ballet of white.

At this same moment as he rode unaware toward Hamilton, Eli Snow's subconscious was occupied by another cold evening. One from years ago. One in which he and his eldest son, Arlis, had trudged through an unusually heavy snowfall in search of Eli's youngest son, Jacob.

Both Eli and Arlis were dressed in heavy coats, Eli holding a kerosene lantern in front of him as he walked through the drifts. "Jacob!" he cried over a fierce north wind. "Give it up and come back home, boy!"

Holding on to his cowboy hat with a gloved hand, Arlis walked close behind, keeping his head buried in the folds of his coat.

Eli stopped to catch his breath, then swung around and held the lantern near Arlis.

"Dammit!" he said between gasps for air. "How many times I got to tell you, boy? Your brother cannot be let out of his chains."

The boy's head was so bundled up against the cold, Eli only saw a slight glitter from the light reflected in Arlis' eyes. "Sorry, Pa," came through muffled.

"What's that?" Eli held the lantern even closer to Arlis' face.

"I said I'm sorry, Pa." Arlis' face was now somewhat visible in the lantern light. "Just don't seem right to tie him up that way. Besides, it was still daylight. I didn't think he could go out durin' the day."

From the meager areas of Arlis' exposed face, Eli observed the boy's fair complexion standing out starkly against the contrast of his dark, black hair. Even in the subdued light, the boy's aquiline facial structure from Spanish ancestry was evident, which he felt a sudden twinge, thinking Arlis so closely resembled Eli's missing wife, Carletta.

The frosted fog of Eli's breathing slowed. "Ain't your fault, I suppose. You didn't bring this on us." He turned then and trudged forward. "But in this overcast weather, even the Lord's sun don't affect your brother. Best find Jacob soon before he does somethin' he shouldn't."

A sudden jolt from a hole in the road broke through Eli's subconscious and brought him into painful reality. He howled with excruciating grief as the fractured bones of his legs further penetrated his tortured flesh.

———

GUS LEANED over just in time to see the injured man grimace and pass out again. "Damn, Eli don't look so good," he said, watching Eli's face grow even pastier than it had been.

Bertram responded by flooring the gas pedal, the Ford fishtailing briefly, then dashing through the snowy night toward Hamilton.

———

DR. JAMES PETERSON lived in the room above his office and had been sound asleep in the quilted cocoon of his bed when the disturbance below rudely awakened him.

Peterson stumbled from bed. Recalling then he was dressed only in grubby long johns, the doctor grabbed a robe from a chair next to the bed, cinched its belt securely about his waist, and coughed out what night had settled in his lungs. He then shook his head and rubbed his eyes, turning immediate attention to the annoying rap-rap-rap coming from below.

Pulling on a drop chain, he turned on one of the ceiling pendant lights nearest the stairway snaking down to the medical office. Still half asleep, the doctor staggered a few times before reaching the bottom of the stairs, and upon entering his office, twisted the wall turn key switching on a larger, incandescent ceiling light before approaching the front door.

He looked through the glass pane on the door and asked in a loud voice, "What the hell is going on out there?"

Bertram pressed his face flat against the pane and startled Peterson. "Let us in, Doc! We got a dying man out here."

The doctor opened the door, and Bertram and his deputies hauled an unconscious Eli Snow into the office.

The men waited as Peterson cleared his examining table of a chaotic collection of items settled there, a few loose papers flying through the air like dying birds as the doctor hastily swung his arms across the table. "Sorry, Bertram," he apologized once the table was clean and the men had placed Eli on it, leaving him on a tarpaulin Lucas had placed the injured man on in the cave. "Don't get too many cases that need a body exam these days."

The sheriff backed away from the examining table, saying." Don't know as you can do Snow much good. He's been severely mistreated."

Peterson pulled a set of eyeglasses with thick lenses off his desk, slipped them on, and approached the body on the table. He then placed a hand on Eli's wrist, frowned, and shook his head, asking the sheriff, "Where'd you find him?"

"Me and Lucas found him in a cave," Bertram said as the

doctor turned Eli's head to one side, revealing the neck wounds. Peterson sighed and gave a brief look to Bertram, who continued with facts about Eli's cabin and the mess inside, the blood trails, and the discovery of the injured man in the small cave. "Somethin' broke both his legs too. The bones cut right through the skin on the back of his thighs."

Gus and Howard were transfixed by the scene and said nothing until the doctor turned Eli over on his side, exposing the broken femurs with tangled tissue and clotted blood hanging from their ends.

Gus groaned and turned away while appearing to hold back rising vomit.

"Holy shit!" Howard said with a sort of morbid fascination. "I ain't never seen nothin' like that. Not on a human, no ways."

Bertram shot Howard a stern look and shook his head with disgust as Gus staggered out of the medical office door, grabbed the support pole on the porch, and retched what supper he'd eaten with the Cross brothers onto the snowy street.

Being in a serious examination mode and interested only in the man on the table, the doctor paid none of the men any attention. And after studying the compound fractures, he turned the burly form of Eli Snow back over.

"Ain't you gonna do somethin' to them legs?" Bertram asked. "I ain't no doctor, but I imagine it might not be in Snow's best interest to keep his weight on them fractures."

His vision fixed on Eli's open, glassy, bulging eyes, Peterson said, "The state of his legs no longer matters. Eli Snow is dead and in no more mortal pain."

DEPUTY HOWARD SPARKS was sent home to his wife and Deputy Gus Greenwood to his parents. "That boy ain't never gonna get away from his mama," Sheriff Bertram Stone said as he craned his neck to watch Gus amble down the street huddled in a coat against the wind.

Bertram let out a long breath and went back into the medical office. After closing the door behind him, Bertram discovered Dr. Peterson had obtained a soiled sheet from somewhere and covered Eli Snow's body with it. Under the clinging fabric, the corpse's contours struck Bertram as somehow disturbing. He shivered as he wearily pulled up a chair and sat in front of Peterson's desk, the doctor seated on the other side.

Peterson rummaged through the desk's middle drawer and eventually found a partially smoked cigar, which he clamped between his teeth but did not light. He then glanced up at the sheriff.

"Sorry, Bertram." Peterson searched through the drawer again. "I'm certain I have more cigars." He looked at the sheriff briefly and grinned. "Might even be a whole one hiding in here somewhere."

Bertram felt his fatigue fade a little and smiled. "No thanks, Doc. My stomach's a bit off right now, anyway."

"You sure?" Peterson asked, still fumbling in the drawer.

"I'm sure," Bertram said, feeling exhaustion embrace him once again.

The doctor closed the drawer and chewed on the cigar butt for a while before spitting into a mauled spittoon at his feet. He then removed his glasses, set them on the desk, and closed his eyes. He placed his hands behind his head and leaned further back into the chair. "Something sure messed Eli up."

Bertram felt his eyelids getting heavier. He rubbed them for a moment before saying, "Had to be an animal, didn't it? Those bite marks couldn't have come from no human."

"Normally, I would say no human could do that much damage." The north wind picked up and rattled the medical office's glass windows. Peterson cut his eyes to the noise momentarily and then closed them again. "But you have to admit these last two days haven't been typical for such a tranquil town as Hamilton, Texas."

"You tellin' me human teeth made those marks?"

The doctor leaned forward and opened his eyes and gazed at Bertram. "None that I ever studied in anatomy classes. But the teeth that were pulled from the head you brought in here aren't like anything I've ever seen or heard of either." He paused a moment, then said, "Maybe that head has a twin somewhere, because what size I imagine those canines to be certainly could make wounds like those." He pointed toward the covered body. A slight chill then grabbed the doctor. "Could almost make one believe in the Boogeyman."

The sheriff let out a nervous laugh. "Funny thing, you sayin' that about a twin, 'cause Lucas and me voiced the same speculation. And if I wasn't so tired, I could almost agree with you. But there ain't no such thing as ghosties and ghoulies. You and I both know that. We seen enough of what a vicious thing the human animal can be." He sighed and stood up. "I must be tired. I never took off my hat or coat."

The wind yowled against the side of the building again. "You probably were still chilled, Bertram. It's damned cold out there."

"A little early for it too. Usually late November before we get a winter storm like this."

Peterson got out of his chair and felt late hour coldness creep under the front door and into the office where it spread across the floor, wrapping icy fingers around his feet. "Well, I'll go next door, wake up Newell and get him to help me move Eli over to the funeral parlor."

"Maybe you ought to let Newell sleep and tell him about Snow in the morning."

"No, my industrious neighbor will be more than happy at being disturbed due to the prospect of a job, even if it comes from meager funds the city provides. I hardly imagine Eli had much money to leave anyone. By the look of what wasn't damaged on his body, I'd say he didn't live high on the hog, albeit much like one. Besides, I don't relish the idea of sleeping with Eli's body down the stairs from my bedroom."

The sheriff cleared his throat. "Well, I might feel the same if I were in your shoes. All this talk of wild animals and monsters could spook anybody, especially in this gray weather and late hour." He then asked, "You need me to help transport Snow next door?"

"No, I'll see to it." Peterson felt an unexpected sense of being childish come over him. "I must be a bit fatigued myself. I feel ashamed of what I said about sleeping with the body here in the office. Guess all this grisliness had more of an effect on me than I realized."

"Then you gonna wait 'til mornin' to tell Newell?"

The doctor glanced over at the covered corpse again and felt that same shudder crawl over his flesh. "No, I'll go with my original plan." He forced a grin. "And if you really don't mind sticking around until I rouse Newell and get him over here, I'd be grateful for your help lifting the body. Eli Snow doesn't appear to have been a stranger to the dinner table, so three men should be better able to transport his body's dead weight."

"Sure. Be glad to help. Probably won't get much shut eye, anyway. Not after this day's events. Sometimes I'm so tired I feel like I can't take another step, but damned if I can fall asleep. Kind of ironic, ain't it?"

Peterson hastily pulled one of the many coats around the office from a rack and lifted a wayward hat from a cluttered chair. He put both on and moved toward the door. "Fatigue can do a lot of strange things." He opened the office door, the wind immediately sweeping snowflakes in. "I'll only be a moment, Bertram." The doctor closed the door behind him.

With a brief gust of biting wind as the door closed, Bertram turned to stare at the corpse on the table. The brief gust of air resulting from the door being closed had been strong enough to lift a corner of the sheet from Eli's face, revealing one glassy, sightless eye seeming to gaze directly at the sheriff.

"God Almighty," Bertram said under his breath, the gloom of a different kind embracing him.

Eight

Lucas Cross had arrived home agitated after discovering Eli Snow's wrecked body in the cave. When he'd gone back to get the Ford, leaving Sheriff Stone in the cave with Eli, Lucas could have sworn he'd heard something tracking him. Even above the increasing wind, he'd heard faint, chaotic shambling movements parallel with his in a pace matching his own. At the time, Lucas had convinced himself he was being childish, that the macabre nature of Eli's condition affected his nerves. Still, when he came to the vehicle and opened the driver's door, he was certain he'd glimpsed a shadowy mass slinking behind Eli's cabin.

But Lucas never mentioned the incident to the sheriff and again dismissed it to his own imagination.

———

EARLIER, once he had gotten back at the cave, Lucas and the sheriff were faced with the dilemma of how to move Eli without causing more trauma to the broken legs.

"Normally, there's a stretcher in the back of the Ford, but I think it's over at Doc Peterson's," the sheriff had said. "Never had much use for it since after picking up Sam Weathers when he fell off his barn last summer. You remember that, don't you?"

"Yep. Didn't kill Sam, but put him a wheelchair for good. Lucky he has those three sons and his wife to keep the farm going. We still get our pork and eggs from there."

The sheriff had snapped his fingers in sudden recollection. "But there is a tarpaulin under the back seat. Newell Scruggs stores it there to keep loved ones dry at a gravesite if the weather's gone bad."

So the two had positioned Eli on the worn canvas as best they could and lifted the ends of the tarpaulin, giving the injured man a painful trip to the Ford. Eli had thrashed about in agony and eventually fainted once they had him settled in the back seat.

———

THE ORDEAL HAD BEEN ENOUGH to make any man edgy and disagreeable—just the conditions Lucas found himself in when returning home. And after the sheriff and his deputies left to transport Eli Snow to Hamilton, Lucas lit into his sons first thing. "You two clean up this mess you made! Why'd you have to fix supper for those two lazy deputies anyhow?"

Donny and Adam knew it was best to tidy up and get to bed as soon as possible to avoid their father's wrath, a wrath they knew would escalate after their father pulled down a bottle of Rye whiskey and sat at the kitchen table with a glass promptly filled.

Lucas glared at his sons just waiting for some excuse to further berate them and found it when Donny dropped a plate that shattered on the hardwood floor. "Damnit, boy!" He shouted. "Good thing your momma ain't here to see one of her prized china dishes broke. She..." The consumed whiskey backing up his gut and burning his throat, Lucas abruptly stopped talking and looked at Donny, who had turned away and lowered his head. Lucas heard passive sniffles and knew the boy was crying, and he chided himself for reminding Donny about the tragic circumstances of his birth. "Don't think nothin' about what I said, Donny. Ain't nobody's fault what happened to your momma."

Adam pulled Donny over and helped him finish drying the dishes. Silence weighed heavy in the cold air then until Lucas said, "You two get on to bed now. Need you up early to spread some hay. Them cattle'll be hungry with this cold weather settlin' in."

The boys said "Yes, Pa," and then hurried off to their rooms.

Lucas sat at the table and started drinking again, trying to shake off the effects of the day's morbid circumstances. Eventually, he fell asleep, waking hours later with his arms stiff from their unnatural position on the tabletop. He rubbed his eyes and shook his head. He saw the whiskey bottle was almost empty.

"What the hell," he said, shrugged his shoulders, poured what whiskey remained into his glass and drank it down in one swallow.

After a short while, Lucas got up rigidly from his chair and walked to the south side of the house where the boys' room was located. He found them covered up completely in the goose feather quilts Lucas' mother gave him several seasons ago.

The old bird dog, Turk, was under Adam's bed, where he'd taken up residence earlier before the boys retired for the night. The dog was curled up in a wad of old blankets Adam put down for him previously. Because of the dog's advancing age and arthritis over the last few years, Lucas allowed the animal to stay in the boys' bedroom during cold weather, a tradition he never regretted as Turk's presence added a sort of security to the boy's bedroom.

Lucas watched until he saw a brief rise and fall of chests under the quilts as Donny and Adam breathed in their sleep. As he was about to leave, Lucas caught Turk opening a wary eye. After recognizing the intruder, the old dog closed that eye, letting out a relieved hush from its aged lungs.

The rancher smiled and turned away, then went back to the kitchen. He extinguished the wall mounted kerosene lamps and, as was his nightly habit, silently cursed the Gulf States Utilities Company.

"Sumbitches don't think ranchers or farmers need wires strung out here," he whispered through gritted teeth. "Not worth it to them money wise, I guess."

Instead of extinguishing the last lamp, he lowered the flame just enough to leave a little light in the front room. He then walked to the east side of the house to his bedroom, built there so he and his wife could watch the sun rise each morning, that reason never occurring to him much anymore, it only being a place to lay his weary bones and try to rest these days.

Lucas took off his boots and stripped away his shirt and jeans, keeping his long johns on since the air had turned frigid. He glanced briefly in the shaving mirror and found his skin red and chafed from exposure to the north wind earlier that day. It was hard now for Lucas to imagine himself being young once. The flesh of his cheeks had developed a leathery appearance from years of work in the blistering Texas heat. Crow's feet trailed a little more each year from the corners of his eyes. And his once thick, coal black hair was now thinning and peppered with gray.

There was still enough alcohol in his blood to bring on sudden melancholy. Tears filled the lower lids of his eyes as he bent closer to the mirror and whispered as if to a ghost beneath the reflected image, "Where'd you go to, boy?" One line of wetness then followed the length of his cheek, settling in a single drop on the middle of his chin. He rubbed a finger across the day's bristle of beard to brush the tear away and said, "None of that now."

Lucas extinguished the two lamps in his bedroom and checked to be sure the window was tightly shut beneath its heavy curtains. He then crawled into bed and pulled the quilt snuggly around him. Fatigue and the liquor took him down quickly, and he was soon dead to the world. It wasn't long until a dream glided into his subconscious like smoke—thin at first, then building into a thick fog.

Soon after his daughter, Bonnie, disappeared ten years ago, Lucas often dreamed of her. In some dreams, he found her alive and experienced amazing joy, that pleasure soon deteriorating to deep sorrow upon awakening. Other dreams were nightmares in which Bonnie was discovered murdered and mutilated. Waking from these was a great relief, for he clung to a hope she was still alive and unharmed. But as days turned to months and months to years without Bonnie being found, his dreams declined until he dreamt of his daughter no more. Until now, ten years later, when Bonnie arrived uninvited into his sleep.

In the present dream, Lucas walked across the front yard of his ranch in the direction of a barbed wire fence separating his property from that of Eli Snow's. He felt it should be cold but never sensed anything other than a neutral dampness around him.

The air was dense with fog, impairing his vision, but he could still distinguish objects like the barbed wire fence.

As if floating above it to the opposite side, Lucas moved over the barbed wire with no resistance. And when he found himself standing on solid ground, he heard soft laughter. Under the fog's influence, it was difficult to pinpoint where the sound had originated. If he moved toward it, the laughter shifted away to a different location.

Under the impression he was lost and wandering in a circle, Lucas stopped and stood still until he heard the subtle laughter again. This time the sound seemed much closer, and he walked slowly toward it, glimpsing Eli Snow's dilapidated well through intermittent breaks in the fog. As he came closer, Lucas noticed a figure materializing on the well's rim. The fog began to thin then, and the form sitting on the rim of the well emerged as Bonnie, who was humming, stopping occasionally to laugh.

"Bonnie!" Lucas cried, trying to run forward. But his legs were weighted, their muscles straining in a slow, plodding advance.

Bonnie looked up and saw her father and squealed and yelled, "Daddy! Daddy, over here. Hurry!"

She was dressed in a lacy, white chiffon garment with a frilly knee-length petticoat skirt resembling something worn for Easter, a dress much too thin for this damp dream atmosphere. A white bonnet cinched in a bow under her chin completed her ensemble.

Before voicing disapproval of her thin clothing, a revelation came to Lucas, remembering it was the exact dress Bonnie had worn the day she disappeared on a Sunday in mid-April ten years ago. The weather had remained cool then, but Bonnie wanted to wear her special dress to church the week before Easter Sunday despite the cold. And Lucas had refused her wish. 'You just want to flirt with the Simmons boy,' he'd said right before she threw a tantrum and ran out of the house. He had not followed immediately, certain his daughter would calm down soon enough and come back home. But she didn't return and was never seen again.

Now, in this dream, a wave of guilt and sadness consumed Lucas, and, without realizing it, his body drifted rapidly toward the well as if catapulted by an unseen force. Once there and standing next to Bonnie, a sudden revulsion seized him, and he found himself wanting, but physically unable to, back away.

Lucas instinctively avoided gazing directly at his daughter's eyes. The deep cobalt blue he so fondly recalled now seemed like a snare, a bottomless ocean into which he longed to but dared not dive.

Bonnie smiled and a rush of dread seized Lucas. She slipped from the edge of the well in a strange serpentine movement, her limbs appearing to bend unnaturally around the stony contours of the well. Then Lucas found he could no longer fight the urge to gaze at her face and turned his head to stare into those unnatural eyes.

Of Lucas' three children, Bonnie most resembled his deceased wife, Lisa. Like her mother, Bonnie's hair was a dark, chestnut color, falling beyond her shoulders in a natural mass of curls. And Bonnie now seemed no different than she had the day she disappeared—short and slender with a wispiness still about her, a fairy-like trait Lucas had held an endearing quality throughout her childhood.

But as she glided toward him now, Lucas slowly distinguished certain, subtle discrepancies, especially the tone of her skin. Bonnie had always been a little pale. But then so had her mother, this paleness never associated with illness. In fact, Bonnie had been a robust child and hardly ever sick with even so much as a common cold.

Now, as she drifted nearer, Lucas noticed the flesh of his daughter's arms, shoulders, face, and exposed area of her chest along the line of the dress' bodice had an exaggerated, pallid quality appearing slightly bruised and mottled.

As she continued to approach her father, Bonnie smiled, Lucas then suddenly assaulted by reminiscent smells: the soft, feathery scent of her baby powder along with the lilac toilet water he'd given her for her sixth birthday.

Bonnie then wrapped her arms around his neck and any prior trepidation or revulsion Lucas had experienced faded away. He immersed his face in her chest, sobs rising deep in his chest as her body meshed with his, entrapping him like gossamer webs.

"Oh, my sweet, little girl." He wept, his shoulders shaking. "You've been gone so long."

"Don't cry, Daddy." She pressed her mouth against his neck. "I'm home now." Her tongue flicked out, licking the flesh just above his pulsing artery, and the previous repulsion returned.

"Bonnie, what are you doing?" Lucas asked. A feline-like tongue gliding over his skin, Lucas tried to push her away, but her grip was unnaturally strong.

Lucas struggled, lost his balance and fell and landed on his back. A scream lodged in his throat as Bonnie lifted her head away from his neck momentarily during the fall, her face now transformed into a snarling horror, her blue eyes mixed with burning scarlet, her lips full and red, the upper canines protruding thick, pointed. With the expression of a wild beast, her nostrils flared. Lowering her head, she growled and bit deeply into the flesh of his neck.

Lucas tried to cry out, but what breath remained in his lungs had left under the jagged pain ripping into his neck. He struggled in vain to pull his daughter away, her teeth digging and tearing as she moved her head erratically from side to side like an animal in a state of frenzied feeding. Eventually Lucas' strength faded, and he surrendered. An unexpected sense of pleasure followed, and he hugged Bonnie tighter, wanting her to drink more.

The fog began to disperse, and Lucas realized his daughter had stopped feeding. A low snarl vibrating her throat, Bonnie lifted her head, her mouth sticky with blood trailing in streams from the corners of her terrible lips, mixing with her hair, clotting in its tangles. Lucas saw her dress was no longer the pretty gift he'd given her for Easter but decayed and ragged, flecked with moldy earth trapped in shredded fabric.

Glancing over her shoulder, Bonnie's eyes widened. She turned around, grimacing at her father, her tongue sliding out, licking clinging blood away from her lips. She then hissed and evaporated into an amorphous mist before his astonished eyes.

Lucas pulled himself up from the ground, vertigo assaulting him as he stumbled to the crumbling edge of the well for support. Sensing a hasty intrusion of light, he glanced up and saw the sun was rising. A repetitive howling sound grew suddenly near before he fainted and fell forward, the dream dissolving around him.

————

"*Pa*?" Adam shouted from the other side of his father's bedroom door, a long, baleful howl joining his cry. "Hush, Turk," Adam said, but the dog kept on howling until Adam along with Donny managed to push the door open enough to see that their father had fallen against it—the reason they couldn't open it in the first place.

"Pa!" Adam said, struggling to get through the door.

The brothers finally managed to force the bedroom door open. Lucas, still dressed in nothing but his long johns, collapsed to one side as they entered, a cold rush of air then accosting the boys.

"The window's open!" Donny said.

Adam glanced at the billowing curtains just before Turk rushed by him and jumped through the open window, barking wildly.

"Turk!" Donny yelled and went to the window. "Turk, get back here."

The blanket of snow that had fallen during the night

glared under clearing skies and a rising sun. Donny had to shield his eyes and adjust to the white brilliance before scouting out where Turk had run off to. Donny heaved a frustrated sigh having finally glimpsed the animal, still yowling, running up the hill toward the fence. "Hell, that crazy old dog is probably goin' back to the well." He then noticed an accumulation of snow covering the window ledge trailing down the wall where it gathered in little patches of white on the floor.

"Don't worry about Turk," Adam said. "Close that damn window and get your ass over here. We need to lift Pa off the floor and get him in bed."

Donny positioned his hands under Lucas' knees while Adam grabbed his father under the shoulders, and together they lifted Lucas and carried him to the bed.

Adam knelt beside the bed and shook his father's shoulder. "Pa, you all right?" He shook his father a little harder.

Lucas moaned and opened his eyes in thin slits.

Adam then let out a sigh that sounded full of relief. "Well, at least you're alive."

"Expect Pa had too much to drink last night. I saw that whiskey bottle was bone dry on the table," Donny said with a little laugh. He went to the other side of the bed and, with his brother's help, pulled the feather quilt from its rumpled mass at the foot of the bed, tugging it over Lucas.

As he arranged the quilt under his father's chin, Adam stopped abruptly. "Whew! Donny, get over here and look at Pa's neck!"

"What the hell?"

Adam gently turned his father's head to the right. Two jagged holes stared at them from Lucas' throat, the wounds raw, filled with torn tissue and dark blood clots, lines of dried blood trailing in rivulets down their father's left shoulder.

Donny then gazed in horror at the window he had recently closed. "Somethin' crawled through that window last night!"

"What?" Adam asked, still absorbed with the gashes in his father's neck.

"Look," Donny said. "I didn't spot those when I was by the window. I just now seen them from across the room."

Adam glanced up and immediately seemed to notice what his brother referred to: there in the light drifts of snow settled in patches on the floor were human footprints, small and delicate, resembling those of a child.

NINE

A tangle of stiff limbs, Sheriff Bertram Stone woke inside his sleeping bag. He'd been fighting in his troubled sleep with a renegade Comanche from his Texas Ranger days, the cold edge of the Comanche's knife at his throat fetching the sheriff back from the territory of dreams.

"Damn," he said.

He coughed phlegm and swallowed it back with disgust before getting bearings on where he was. He sighed then at the nagging ache in his bones and joints as he pulled himself out of the sleeping bag and sat upright on the office floor.

———

BERTRAM NEVER GREW accustomed to sleeping in a bed, not after all those years as a Texas Ranger where he spent most nights under the heavens in a sleeping bag or on a roll of blankets with a saddle for his pillow. Not that he hadn't tried, mind you, when he'd left the Rangers and decided to settle down with the job as sheriff of Hamilton County.

Because of a law enforcement profession, he'd never considered marriage. He'd seen enough of its failures or complications with his fellow Rangers, figuring his lifestyle was best spent alone.

When Bertram accepted the position, he bought a small house outside of Hamilton. He kept the furnishings simple and purchased a brass bed with a mattress. After a few restless nights, Bertram told a friend the mattress was too soft and made it seem like he was sinking in mud. So he started spreading a blanket roll on the floor of the house and found the old habitual sleeping arrangement with the ground best suited to his nature.

After living in the house for only a year, Bertram felt out of place. That's when he started spending nights in his basement office. The cold presence of those stone walls underground seemed to bring a comfort and security to him he couldn't acquire in a home of his own. Eventually, selling the house and the furniture in it, he stored what clothes he needed in his office and decided to make the basement his dwelling for as long as he kept the post of sheriff. He never thought about women all that much and didn't develop the yearning for any attachment other than an occasional trip to one of the brothels camouflaged as boarding houses in Fort Worth or Dallas.

———

THIS MORNING in the courthouse's basement office and in spite of complaints from his fifty-year-old bones, Bertram was at ease. The pictures from his Ranger days hung on the wall. The deep, earthy smell of the wooden desk, and the solid stone walls surrounding him brought a firm reassurance to his being. Some people might see his office as nothing more than a self-made prison, but he considered it home.

He'd slept in nothing but his undershirt and skivvies, which were warm enough inside a snug bedroll but a bit thin against the November morning once standing.

The sheriff shivered and went to a small closet and took out a pair of clean pants, a shirt, and a new set of socks and underwear. After slipping them on, he promised himself he'd take a bath next Saturday, seven days between washings being acceptable in his present job. As a Ranger he'd gone much longer stretches without a good scrubbing.

After getting dressed and ready for the day, he checked his pocket watch and found it to be a little past seven in the morning. He'd left Newell's establishment with Dr. Peterson after they transferred Eli Snow's body from the medical office to the funeral parlor at a little around three that same morning. So he'd only managed about four hours of sleep. But for Bertram that was plenty.

As he slipped on his boots and coat, Bertram couldn't help but chuckle having recalled Newell Scruggs' appearance when he and Dr. Peterson had toted the body of Eli Snow into the funeral parlor.

The skeletal undertaker had been dressed in a long, white nightshirt falling loosely to his ankles, the man's elongated feet resting snuggly in a pair of brown slippers. Matching the nightshirt, a nightcap, its end falling to one side, had donned Newell's skull. The sheriff had struggled through enough Charles Dickens novels in his day to be reminded of similar characters from those pages, a flickering candle the undertaker held by the curled stem of its brass holder only adding to any Dickens resemblance.

As Dr. Peterson had predicted, Newell was not upset at being awakened in the early hours of the morning. In fact, the undertaker seemed quite elated at having a new client.

———

"Gentlemen, please follow me," Newell had said, leading them down a short hall beside the viewing room.

After Peterson had awakened Newell earlier and made him aware of the situation and before the doctor returned to the medical office to move Eli Snow's body, the undertaker had lighted candles down the length of the hall in advance. He prepared and illuminated the embalming room located at the end of the hall as well with the more efficient kerosene lamps mounted on the walls. As Peterson and Bertram followed the undertaker down the hallway, the men's short shadows trailed just behind the longer outline extending from Newell.

Pointing out a flat, metal table in the center of the room, Newell said, "If you will kindly place Mr. Snow's remains there."

Bertram had been in the embalming room on other occasions, mostly when a death might warrant investigation, but it was an occurrence he never looked forward to, this visit being no exception. The room had a stark nature with the metal cabinets mounted on the walls, the various bottles of chemicals plus instruments of Newell's profession in those cabinets, and the array of tubing and suction devices situated by the center table for draining blood. Not to mention the ever-present stringent odor of formaldehyde along with a cloying scent of blood and body fluids beneath it. Add the antiquated kerosene lighting and the room's atmosphere was more akin to that found on a horror movie set.

With as much respect for the dead as they could muster in the cold room and the early hour, the sheriff and the doctor had placed Eli's body on the table, Dr. Peterson rolling the corpse to one side while Bertram pulled away the tarpaulin they'd transported the body on.

The sheriff folded the canvas as best he could and said to Newell, "I believe this tarp belongs to you. It sure came in handy for all of us involved today, though."

"Hmmm," the thin undertaker said with low articulation. "Yes, the rain tarp." He sat the candle down, blew it out, and then extended his hand, taking the canvas tarpaulin from Bertram. "I am pleased it came to your aid."

With a sort of strange ceremony, the undertaker placed the tarp into the bottom storage area of one of the wall cabinets, then approached Eli Snow's body and peered down on it. "My, my," he said, examining the corpse. "Those neck wounds. Quite hideous." He glanced up at the sheriff and the doctor. "Some animal bite perhaps?"

"That's what we're going to find out," Peterson said. "And that's why I need you to delay embalming for a little while. We need to get a better look at Eli in the morning when there's better light and clearer heads."

"I quite understand, Doctor. As cold as it's been lately, I think Mr. Snow will keep nicely for a while." The undertaker grinned. "But not for too long. Corruption progresses even in the cold. Slower, mind you, but persistently nonetheless."

"I'm going back to Snow's cabin early in the mornin'," the sheriff said. "Doc plans to come over here to get a better feel for what killed Snow while I'm gone. So the body shouldn't be here too long. If we need to drag things out, we can always ice it down for a bit."

The undertaker nodded in agreement. "Is there anything else I can do for you gentlemen then?"

"Don't believe so, Newell," Bertram answered, experiencing a shudder as he gazed on the undertaker's macabre face. "I'm sure Doc can use your assistance in the mornin', though."

"Very well." The undertaker snapped his fingers. The loud

popping sound his bony phalanges generated seemingly intensified in the small space making both Bertram and Peterson jump. "I almost forgot. I have finished restoring the head Doctor Peterson placed in my care. Would you care to view it before I bid you both good morning? It is a fine job of repair. One of my best."

Bertram and Peterson shook their heads no.

"I'll have a look later today when I come over and examine Snow further," the doctor said. "I think Sheriff Stone would rather wait as well." He looked at the sheriff, who vigorously nodded yes.

A bit disappointed, Newell replied, "As you wish, gentlemen. I'll see both of you out then."

Peterson turned to leave with Bertram but then stopped suddenly and asked, "Newell, are you ever going to convert over to electricity? It's readily available, you know? Gulf States could put wires behind your walls just like they did everybody else on this street. All you need to do is have them hook you up."

The undertaker clucked his tongue. "Too expensive for me, Doctor. In a bustling city like Dallas or Fort Worth maybe, but not in this sleepy berg. Just not enough business to justify the cost."

With Newell trailing methodically behind them, the doctor shrugged and walked with the sheriff toward the front of the funeral parlor.

———

AFTER ESCORTING the two men out, Newell closed and locked the front door. He then conscientiously snuffed each lighted candle in the hallway as he returned to the embalming room. There, he walked to the table where Eli Snow's body lay and bent closer to further examined the corpse. He lifted each arm and checked the joints of the shoulders, the elbows, and wrists, then scrutinized the fingers of both hands finding grime and dirt, but no apparent injuries. He palpated Eli's protruding abdomen and again felt nothing out of the ordinary.

Newell continued his examination on the lower trunk, pausing when his fingers went behind Eli's left thigh. "Oh, my," Newell said with surprise.

He rolled the body to one side and saw the broken right and left femurs jutting through torn flesh. "Dear me. This must have been an animal attack. Some wild and powerful beast." He then returned the body to its previous position. "Too bad the bones didn't penetrate from the front."

He began to carefully undress the corpse. "It would have brought a little extra money for cosmetic repair. The bones, you see, would jut through your pants. But your injuries being where they are will not be visible in the coffin." He paused and smiled, noting, "But I do still possess a magnificent pecan wood casket. I don't think the city would mind paying a little extra for one of its citizens."

The undertaker stared directly at Eli's dead face. "Do you, Mr. Snow?"

———

BERTRAM WALKED down the courthouse steps with his memory of the early morning occurrence at Newell Scruggs' funeral parlor fading under the smell of bacon and coffee wafting across the crisp dawn air. He glanced up at a clear sky and maneuvered cautiously over areas of packed snow in the street as he headed for breakfast at the Koffee Kup Kafé located just across the street from the medical office and the funeral parlor. The café had been in Hamilton since the town's inception and was still operated by descendants of its family founders.

"Mornin', Sheriff," Molly Cooper, a short, stout, jolly woman, hailed as Bertram entered the café.

The daughter of Pat and Vera Aycock, the original café owners, Molly had married her second cousin, Hunter Cooper. After the death of her parents, she and Hunter took over the café, an easy adjustment since both had been working there since they were children.

"Mornin', Molly." The sheriff sat in his favorite booth across from Dr. James Peterson, who had arrived about ten minutes earlier.

"Bertram," Peterson said as Hunter brought over the doctor's plate of sunny side up eggs with sliced tomatoes on top along with a cup of steaming water, a bag of Earl Grey tea, and a slice of lemon.

"Still eatin' healthy, Doc?" Hunter sat down the items and grinned. Then to Molly, "Doc here ain't never had your bacon, ham, steak, or biscuits and meat gravy, hon. Don't seem right to have a veg...vega... Just what the hell are you, Doc?"

"Vegetarian," Molly piped from behind the row of counter seats where she stood in front of a crackling grill already at work on the sheriff's customary order. "Doc don't eat nuthin' that has a face."

"Yeah, that," Hunter chuckled. "Don't seem right to have a vegwhatian in North Central Texas. Not with all the livestock around, not to mention the biggest stockyard in Texas up in Fort Worth."

There were other early morning patrons in the diner, mostly those who worked the general shops like the mercantile and grocery stores, and two employees who manned the post office. These patrons joined in Hunter's friendly bantering of the doctor. The café's business generally picked up around nine in the morning, when farmers and ranchers nearest Hamilton traveled to town for various necessities or business matters. And that's when Molly and Hunter's eldest of three daughters, the other two still in school, would come in and help them. But for now, the group in the diner was small and familiar with one another, so Peterson was quite used to being ribbed regarding culinary preferences.

The doctor smiled and patted Hunter's portly belly. "Well, at least I don't have one of these weighing me down."

The crowd guffawed even more.

Hunter then cocked his thumb at Molly and said, "You ain't got a wife at home neither, Doc. And my Molly can sure whip up a mess of delightful things to eat." He tapped himself on the stomach. "And this here's proof of it."

Molly yelled across the café, "You come on over and bring this plate to the sheriff, hon. No need in his breakfast getting' cold." When Hunter took the plate from her, she said, "And get started on the next batch of biscuits. Gonna get crowded in here pretty soon now."

Unlike the light morning fare the doctor preferred, Bertram's plate consisted of steak, eggs over easy, biscuits, and fried potatoes covered with cream gravy. And next to that crowded plate, Hunter set down a pot of coffee and a large mug for the sheriff.

Peterson eyed Bertram's breakfast, shook his head and removed the steeping tea bag from its cup, gingerly sipping a little of the hot liquid. "Keep eating like that and you'll be in to see me after all, Bertram." This was a general joke between the two men, as the sheriff had yet to seek medical attention from the doctor.

Bertram took his steak knife and sliced a hefty piece of beef. "Not if I can help it, Doc." He broke one egg's yolk with the meat he had forked and swirled the beef around in the viscous, yellow fluid. "I done all my own patchin' in the Rangers, or had one of my compadres do it. Reckon the only time you'll be seein' me is when I don't have anythin' left to say or air to say it with."

Peterson laughed and took another sip of his tea. He then glanced out the café window and saw Newell Scruggs emerge from the funeral parlor dressed in his usual black attire. The undertaker stepped into the street and walked toward the café.

"Well, I'll be damned," Hunter said from where he was concocting biscuit batter and gazing out the window as well. "Newell Scruggs ain't never ate in here. Not as far as I can remember. Has he, Molly?"

Molly stopped her cooking and glanced through the window at the thin man ambling toward the diner. "Not that I recall." As if a goose had walked over her grave, Molly trembled slightly as she watched Newell approach. She turned her attention back to her husband and stage whispered, "And I was hopin' it'd stay that way," before she returned to the grill.

Newell entered the diner and removed his stovepipe hat and grasped its rim in his hands. "Good morning, ladies and gentlemen."

Walking from behind the counter, Hunter said, "Mornin', Newell. What can I do you for? Some eggs and bacon maybe?"

A wily smile appeared on the undertaker's face. "No, thank you." He nodded at a man sitting on one of the counter stools. "Although I'm quite certain the cuisine is exceptional and hearty in this home-style eatery, I believe I will maintain my meager diet from the supplies purchased at the general store belonging to Mr. Tanner there."

"Coffee then?" Hunter asked, clearly having no idea what the word 'cuisine' meant and not certain if he and Molly should be offended or not, judging by his facial expression.

"Again, I must decline." The undertaker turned to the booth where Bertram and Peterson sat. "My business is with the good sheriff and the doctor." He nodded to Hunter and walked to the booth. "Gentlemen, if I may, I will only take a brief moment of your time."

Peterson glanced up at the elongated figure and smiled. "Certainly, Newell."

"By all means," the sheriff said as he wiped his mouth with a napkin and scooted over to allow room for the undertaker. "Sit down and take a load off."

Newell shook his head. "I wouldn't think of intruding on your meal. I just wanted to know about what hour I'm to expect Dr. Peterson for further inspection..." He paused and glanced around the diner before lowering his voice. "Of the unfortunate Mr. Snow."

"Just as soon I finish up here and make sure no patients are waiting at the medical office," Peterson said. "I'll probably take a quick cigar break before coming over to your place. I know you don't allow smoking."

"Because of the chemicals. They are flammable, you see."

"Of course. Anyway, I should be there around nine or nine thirty."

"Perfect. That will give me all the time I require to run a couple of errands."

The undertaker nodded to both men and walked to the diner's front door. Before leaving, he raised his hat, tipped it, and said, "Good day to all." He then placed the hat on his head and walked out.

"Take care, Newell," Hunter said with a weak smile.

As she took the pan of raw biscuit dough from her husband and shoved it in the wall oven, Molly shook her head. "Lord but that Newell's a creepy man," she said to no one in particular.

From his seat by the café window, Peterson scrutinized the undertaker as he walked out of sight down the wooden planks in front of the café. The doctor then drank the last of his tea and asked Bertram, "You still headed out to Eli's cabin this morning?"

"Soon as Gus and Howard wander in here for their mornin' feed." The sheriff sopped up the last gravy puddle with what was left of a biscuit. He chewed the gravy-soaked, buttermilk dough and swallowed it down with a drink of coffee, wiped his hands on a napkin, and then took out his pocket watch. "Which should be about fifteen minutes from now, if I know those two. I'll tell them to hold down the fort while I go out to Snow's and have a look see. What with it gettin' dark and Snow being in the state we found him in, me and Lucas didn't get to perform a proper search yesterday."

Peterson slid out of the booth and walked to a coat rack where he retrieved a rumpled, gray coat. He pulled a hound's tooth beret he was strangely attached to from one of the rack's upper pegs and positioned it comfortably on his head, then removed a multicolored ascot from one of the coat's pockets and draped it around his neck. He was perhaps unaware of the other patrons watching him, or their low chuckles in response to his odd wardrobe.

He went back to the booth, scratched at his beard, and pulled heavy spectacles from his shirt pocket and put them on. "Come over to my office when you get back from Eli's place. I'll enlighten you as to what, if anything, I discover after my thorough examination the body."

"Will do, Doc."

"And, Bertram," the doctor added with a mischievous grin. "You might want to stop by St. Jude's on the way out of town."

The sheriff smiled back, saying, "But I'm a Baptist, Doc. At least at election time, I am."

"Well, I don't imagine the priest at St. Jude's—Dobbins, I think is his name—will begrudge even a Baptist a blessed crucifix and holy water, do you?"

Still grinning, Bertram said, "I don't reckon I'll be dealing with anything a bullet can't stop." He appeared to glance out the window then and take note of his deputies with coat collars raised high and hats pulled down sidling over patches of snow and ice in the street. He drank the rest of his coffee a little too fast, the hot liquid looking to give him a measure of consternation, coughed slightly and moved out of the booth. "Looks like Howard and Gus are a little early. Let me get my coat and hat and I'll go out with you, Doc. I'll update those two on what's been goin' on when we're outside." He looked back at the café patrons and whispered to Peterson, "No use stirin' up any unneeded questions."

Peterson waited until Bertram put on his hat and coat before he walked with the sheriff toward the café's front door.

"Ya'll have a good one," Hunter said as he handed Molly another pan of raw biscuit batter.

"And keep warm," she added. "It's cleared up out there but still cold as a witches' heart."

The sheriff tipped his hat, and Peterson nodded as they exited.

Once outside, Bertram waited for his deputies.

Before walking across the street to the medical office, Peterson asked, "You taking the Ford out to Snow's place, Bertram?"

The sheriff cast a look up at the blue sky. "Naw. Think I'll go over to the stable and get Lucy saddled up. She's had a few days off, and I imagine she done ate herself into a stupor and could use the exercise."

"She's getting up in years. You might go easy on her."

"Old Lucy's still got some rides left in her. She'll advise me when it's time to let her graze out her days."

Peterson raised his hand in goodbye and headed across the street to his office. "See you later, Bertram. Deputies," he added just as Howard and Gus were stepping on the porch planks in front of the café.

"See ya, Doc," Gus said.

"Mornin', Sheriff," Howard said.

"Mornin', men. Before you have breakfast, let me inform you of my plans for the day."

TEN

The headless thing knew instinctively the child had come back to the storm cellar. It could not hear the rusty hinges complain as the cellar door was lifted nor see the bloated child stagger toward a mound of earth in the far corner where she would dig in and bury herself. And it could not smell the blood clinging to the child's lips or look into the deep blue of her lifeless eyes.

But it sensed all these things just the same.

Without a head, without a brain or eyes, the body had become nothing more than an uncoordinated mannequin controlled by the child. If the body had been whole, it would have found great irony in the fact its creation held dominion over the now headless thing, and was now its master.

In the dark storm cellar, as the sun rose steadily in the early morning sky, the headless thing could only wait now until the girl needed it again, until it felt her commands. The knife wound in the thing's abdomen would never heal, the protruding intestines already shriveled, no blood left in the dead husk of its body for any immune system's process to heal decomposed flesh. One day it would become a mass of putrefied tissue, unable to walk about. But until that day, the thing would obey the child, even if it had to crawl.

Now, as it lay motionless against the storm cellar's earthen wall, an occasional, isolated muscle twitch occurred along its arms or legs much like the hide of a horse when a fly touched down on it. And when the weather turned warmer, there would be flies and maggots, and the headless thing would become a squirming corruption unable to recall the night it had found the child wandering not far from the cabin. The night the thing's destiny was forever changed. The night the cabin was filled with smoke from a wood stove as Eli Snow dropped slices of pork meat into a pan of grease, several kerosene lamps burning in various locations, filling the interior with an oily light.

That night, so long ago.

———

"Arlis!" Eli shouted to his oldest son, who sat at a table, staring vacantly ahead. "Wake up from your dream world, boy."

Arlis continued to stare blankly and appeared not to hear his father's command.

Eli sat the pan down on the fire and threw a wet, stale kitchen towel at his son. It landed on the boy's face, and he shrieked, pulled the towel away, and stared wide-eyed at his father.

"What the hell you doing, Pa?" Arlis wiped at the residue left on his face from the filthy towel.

Eli frowned and went back to the pan of cooking meat. "I been tryin' to get your attention, you idgit. What's wrong with you lately? You act like you sleepwalkin' most of the time."

"It's just..." The boy lowered his head. "You know, Pa. Jacob's gettin' out of hand, and..."

Eli glanced over his shoulder at Arlis and appeared to register his son was shaking. "And what?"

Arlis swallowed hard. "I'm scared of him now."

Eli snorted. He set the pan down and picked up a decrepit spatula and flipped the pork over and then placed the pan back on the fire. "Scared? And you're the one who used to feel sorry for Jacob. Always wantin' to untie him like you did that winter night we hunted him down long after midnight. That night he killed them sheep over at the Cross Ranch. Lucky thing Lucas never found out what really killed them." He glanced back over his shoulder again and sarcastically said, "Scared? You're scared now, are you?"

"Jacob weren't but a child then." Arlis turned toward the front door. He stood and walked to the door and pulled the bolt in place to lock it. "He's full growd now. And he might not be satisfied with just livestock and wild animals no more."

Eli took the pan from the fire and drained the grease into a dented, metal bowl. "Arlis, stop actin' a fool and unlock that door right now. Then go outside and fetch your brother for supper, you hear." He watched the last of the bubbling grease slide into the container and mix with pig's blood he'd poured in it earlier. A look of revulsion crossed his face before he sighed and watched Arlis sit back down at the table. "Goddamnit!" Eli set the pan of meat on the side of the stove where there was no flame. Holding the spatula above his head, he marched toward Arlis. "You get out there and do what I say! I'll smack some sense into you if you don't."

Arlis jumped up and raced to the door. He slid the bolt free and opened it just as Eli was about to swing at him

Eli grabbed the top of the door before Arlis could shut it.

"You forget that lamp, boy?"

He went to the wall behind the wood stove and took down a kerosene lamp from its place on a peg. Then he set the spatula down on the kitchen table, retrieved a box of matches from the back of the stove, lifted the lamp's pane, and lit the wick. He then walked back to door and handed the lamp to Arlis.

When Arlis took it, Eli noticed the boy's hand was shaking. Arlis held up the light, making his father's face appear elongated and menacing.

"Boy," Eli said. "Don't get so worked up. Jacob ain't gonna hurt you. You're his kin. Besides, he's probably full of whatever he caught out there. If he don't want to come home with you, tell him I got a bowl of pig blood mixed with grease for him. He ain't partial to cooked food, but he does like blood mixed with a little pan grease, so that should get him back here." His eyebrows knitted as he frowned. "We need to sit down and eat supper together like a proper family. Even that hell bitch mother of yours wanted us to act like a family every once and awhile."

"Yes, Pa."

Eli closed the door, leaving his eldest son standing alone in the night.

ARLIS SHUDDERED and then slowly made his way down the side of the cabin until he was behind it. It was late April, the evenings and nights still chilly under the tenacious ghosts of winter, so he tugged the collar of his light coat high around his neck. He guessed Jacob was somewhere deeper into the hollow where a wild growth of trees and shrubs began. Arlis had gone looking for his younger brother there on more than one occasion, usually when their father had the notion they were still a normal family, not one with the horror infecting Jacob.

When Jacob was a child, Eli tied him up at night, not allowing the boy outside the cabin. Arlis felt sorry for his brother then and every so often took Jacob outside where he walked him with a rope tied around his neck like a dog. Eli didn't like it, but he let Arlis do this with strict orders that "If he gets loose, it'll be on your head to catch him."

And everything went well for a time. Besides the disgusting habit of eating fresh, raw, bloody animal flesh, Jacob really caused little trouble. In the daytime, he was docile, staying in a dark closet because of a burning effect sunlight had on his skin. At night when he was tied to a chain on the cabin wall, Jacob couldn't cause much mischief. It was true after sundown a restlessness disturbed him, a state usually eased with increased feedings of raw meat.

But as Jacob grew, so did his strength and cunning. After that one winter night when he escaped from Arlis and killed some sheep at the neighboring Cross ranch, things worsened, and he was no longer easy to control at night.

Eli finally laid down the law, forcing Jacob to live in an old storm cellar located on the east side of the hollow. There, the remains of a ranch house destroyed by fire years before Eli bought the land persisted amongst the overgrowth and the storm cellar itself sat nearly hidden nearby. Eli had only discovered it when looking for a place to hide a still for brewing corn liquor.

The cellar was dark and dank and filled with roots penetrating the earthen walls from above. Spiderwebs covered shelves placed there by the ranch house's former owner to store canned goods and preserves.

It was perfect for Jacob, who welcomed its darkness during the daylight hours. But it proved a hellish prison at night, the boy howling ungodly sounds when he couldn't get out of the door above locked by his father. Eli and Arlis brought Jacob nightly feedings, but it was apparent he needed something more for his cursed spirit. He threatened and pleaded until Eli finally agreed he'd be permitted to hunt at night as long as he didn't stray from the boundaries of Eli's property and occasionally joined his father and brother for a sit down supper in the cabin.

And tonight, as Arlis walked into the trees and brush where the woods began, he wondered what he would discover—a ravaged deer, wild hog, or stray lamb from one of the neighboring ranches? Or maybe he'd come across his brother lying in wait or stalking something that walked about on two legs, the flesh of wild or domesticated animals no longer satisfying his soul.

A light breeze drifted through the treetops. Somewhere in the forest, Arlis heard the faint hoot of an owl. Twigs crunched loudly under his slow pace, the breeze pushing sporadic cloud cover from a quarter moon whose pale light sifted through the trees, bathing the forest in ashen hues.

After walking for a long while and not being able to find any trace of his brother, Arlis decided to go to the storm cellar. It wasn't unusual for Jacob to take his prey there and eat the poor creature while it still lived. Arlis likened that inclination of his brother to a cat playing with a mouse, an image that never failed to make him shiver.

It wasn't long until Arlis saw the burned-out shell of the ranch through gaps in trees and bushes. The original builders had cleared a large area of the forest away, but over time wild growth moved back stealthily to reclaim the space. Eli had removed a mass of vines from the cellar door when he decided to keep his youngest son there, but even those crawlers had rebounded, crisscrossing the heavy door with tendrils resembling networks of veins.

Arlis held the lamp ahead of him as he reached the cellar, finding its door open. He stood in front and lowered his lamp into the gaping space, then gazed down and saw his brother, Jacob, sitting at the bottom of the cellar's rickety steps.

Jacob looked up and smiled.

Looking on the gore clinging to the prominent upper and lower canines protruding from Jacob's mouth, Arlis' stomach knotted. He had a sudden urge to turn and run.

Jacob then greeted him. "Well, brother. What brings you out on this cool night?" As was typical for his nighttime appearance, Jacob's face possessed a harsh feral countenance, his eyes reflecting a strange animal glow, the black hair on his head thicker than normal like the dark stubble of his beard.

Arlis started to say what their father wanted when he heard panting. He guessed whatever his brother had captured was still down in the storm cellar and alive. "It ain't right to torture what you're gonna kill."

Jacob chuckled and stood. Arlis saw his brother's ragged denim shirt and jeans were slick with dark stains.

"Anyways," Arlis said, even more afraid since his brother had assumed a standing position. "Pa wants you to come and have supper with us."

"Naw. I got plenty here." Jacob looked sideways into a dark corner of the cellar. His face lost its teasing nature, and he ground his teeth. "This here will hold me for a while."

There was a faint moan followed by a weak cry of "Help" from the darkness.

Jacob looked quickly at Arlis, who'd lowered the lamp deeper into the cellar's doorway.

"What was that?" Arlis asked. He watched his brother's face tighten, the muscles around Jacob's lips ticking nervously.

"Just my dinner." Then, with menace, he added, "And never you mind about it. Hear me?"

The cry came again.

"You got a human down there, ain't you?" Arlis bent as far as he could without actually going down the wooden steps. "Gawd Almighty!" He exclaimed when he saw a small shoe-covered foot appear in the diminished light at the bottom of the cellar. "That a child?" He then turned the light back toward Jacob. "What have you done?"

Jacob held a finger to his lips. "Hush now. I found her wandering around when I came out of this hole tonight."

He removed the finger from his lips and looked up into the lamplight. Arlis obscured his face with the bulk of the lamp, but his body was trembling.

"She must of got lost, I suppose," Jacob said. "Poor little lamb."

"But you have to let that child go. We need to find out who she belongs to."

Jacob frowned and, in doing so, made his teeth appear even more prominent and dreadful. "Too late."

He moved into the shadows and bent over. There was a slight gasp as he straightened and moved back into the light with a young girl in his arms. She wore a white dress with frilly petticoats, the material drenched with sweat, urine, and blood. Her thick hair flashed hints of dark brown in the subdued light as it fell in tangled curls behind her shoulders and above a white bonnet dangling free from her head. She breathed in rapid pants, her eyes wild and pleading, their dark blue color evident even in the dim light.

When the girl turned her head, Arlis saw gashes on her throat. "Jacob! That's Lucas Cross' little girl. That's Bonnie!"

"Hmmm," Jacob said. "I believe she is. However, she belongs to me now, and I plan to keep her."

"But you cain't kill her! Lord, all Hell'll break loose if you kill her."

With a sly grin, Jacob glanced at Arlis. "No, this one I won't kill. I'll make her my companion instead." He turned his attention back to the trembling girl in his arms. "I get so lonely down here, Little Lamb."

The girl's eyes rolled back in her head, and she fainted.

Arlis watched as her rapid breathing slowed down to frightening, sporadic movements.

"Jacob, you have to bring her out. I'll take her to the cabin. Pa'll know what to do with her."

Jacob moved back into the storm cellar's shadowy corner and gently lay the girl down. He walked into the glow of the lamplight and looked directly up at his brother and said, "No."

Arlis tried to swallow, but his saliva had dried up from fear. "They'll come lookin' for her. You know they will."

"You'll just have to help them then. And do remember to keep them away from this part of the forest."

"How on earth you 'spect me do that? They'll comb every inch of this area."

"Tell them to split up to make the search better and faster, only you come here and then go back and tell them you found nothin'. They'll be confused and tired. They'll believe you."

Arlis' brow wrinkled. "I don't think that's a good idea. What happens if they won't listen to me? What...?"

Jacob began to climb up the cellar's steps. Arlis gasped and lifted the lamp out and backed away from the cellar door. When Jacob's upper body came out of the opening, Arlis was seized by panic and he froze, his legs weighted by fright.

Once out of the cellar, Jacob, with his face set and horrid, moved close to his brother. The dried blood on Jacob's mouth and beard appeared black in the lamp and moonlight. "You do as I say, Arlis. Tell Pa you couldn't find me and act as surprised as a rat in a trap when Cross and whoever's helpin' him comes lookin' for this little girl."

Jacob moved even closer then. "If you don't..." He snarled and snapped his teeth together like a wild dog. "I'll tear you apart and eat you while you're still breathin'."

Arlis gasped when his brother grabbed him by the shoulders. As Jacob moved to within an inch of his face, the lamp fell from

Arlis' grip and landed upright on the ground. The smell of blood and sweat came off Jacob in ghastly waves.

"Do you understand?" Jacob asked.

As a warm stream of urine slid down his leg, Arlis shook his head yes.

Jacob relaxed his grip and lightly tapped Arlis on the cheek in a mock slap. "Good." He wrinkled his nose. "Best not let Pa know you pissed yourself. He won't cotton to it. He won't cotton to it at all."

ELEVEN

Sheriff Bertram Stone kept his horse Lucy at a slow, steady pace on his way to the hollow where Eli Snow's cabin stood. As it was earlier that morning, the sky remained clear and the north wind brisk but sluggish, as if resting until gathering enough strength for a future onslaught. The road had patches of snow here and there, but most of the freezing precipitation had been pushed to the side gullies by passing vehicles and the previous night's wind.

A few ranchers and farmers passed the sheriff in their automobiles or horse drawn wagons headed to Hamilton. All tipped their hats to Bertram, who returned their cordial greetings with one of his own.

"This part of the county's too low key for the sort of trouble we've had lately. Don't you agree, Lucy?" Bertram asked his plodding horse.

Lucy's ears picked up at the mention of her name, and she snorted briefly while maintaining a methodical, steady stride.

As he passed the Cross ranch, the sheriff started to veer off the road to pay Lucas and his boys a visit. He reconsidered when he checked his pocket watch and found it was near ten in the morning, telling himself he'd stop by on the return trip.

By the time ten thirty rolled around, Eli's cabin came into view and Bertram directed Lucy up the muddy, ice-crusted road winding toward the hollow and the cabin built into its recess. Once there, he took a good look in all directions before dismounting and leading Lucy to a dilapidated fence row where he tied her up. Sparse patches of winter weeds dotted the ground where Lucy began to graze.

"Not much to eat around here, old girl," the sheriff said.

He went to his saddle bags and took out a few apples and a small bag of oats he'd brought along from the stable. He set the apples down in front of the horse and spread the bag of oats open beside them, grinning when Lucy snorted, shook her head, and immediately abandoned winter weeds for tasty apples.

"I agree, old girl. Them weeds might give you the runs, anyway." He patted the horse on her hindquarters and then walked toward the cabin.

Approaching the cabin's shattered front door, Bertram, as he had the day before, slipped the trigger strap off his Colt .45. He moved forward with caution and then pulled out his gun. Turning into the open doorway, the cabin looked as it had the day before: sprinkled litter of food cans and cooking utensils, broken pieces of wood from the door, a scattering of stones that had been used to fortify that door, and a gaping hole in the cabin's ceiling from Eli's wild shotgun blast.

The sheriff stepped into the cabin and looked around for a while. He searched under the litter and combed the area around the wood stove and inside its bottom doors, finding only charred logs and more trash.

On one wall there was a photograph that went unnoticed the previous day. The frame of the photograph was cracked as was the glass covering its black and white picture, an image of a young soldier, a dough boy from WWI, the soldier's expression grim. The eyes gazing from under a helmet at Bertram did so with articulated fatigue, a look belonging to a very old man instead of the youth in a ridgid stance gripping his bayonet.

"Must be that oldest boy of Eli's," the sheriff said, tracing the image with his fingertip. "Heard he got killed over in France toward the end of the war."

He sighed and then redirected his focus on the clutter inside the cabin.

Soon, satisfied there were no clues other than those he'd seen the day before, Bertram decided to have a closer look outside the cabin. When he had one foot out the devastated front door, the sound of frantic scrambling made him swing around and cock his gun. He laughed nervously as a black cat yowled and ran past him. The animal had been hiding under some soiled blankets near the kitchen table.

"Whew," Bertram said, not the least bit superstitious about the animal crossing his path. "Guess that's one suspect I can eliminate."

The sheriff lowered the gun's hammer, holstered it, exited the cabin, and started his exploration out front. Circling the decrepit structure, he discovered nothing but some discarded and rusted farm implements and the partial remains of a surrey in the back. Other than those items and fallen bricks scattered in a chaotic pattern below the chimney, he found no useful clues. Not even any tracks, the ground encircling the cabin revealing nothing more than the home's bleak, failing structure, cowering like a skeletal shell.

As Bertram headed back to his horse to ride around the property and then into the wooded area, the cat that had fled from the cabin came up from behind him. Fairly sure this human meant it no harm and might have some food, the animal rubbed against Bertram's leg and purred.

"What's this?" he asked and bent down and stroked the cat's back.

The animal rolled over on its side and then righted itself and started rubbing against the sheriff again with its motor humming through Bertram's pants leg just above the rim of his boot.

"There's a good fellow," he said, scratching the cat behind the ears.

The cat looked up, its giant yellow eyes filled with pleasure.

Lucy whinnied and stomped her hooves, seeming jealous of the attention Bertram bestowed on the cat. Startled by the sudden noise, the feline hissed, and ran toward the tree line behind the cabin.

The sheriff giggled and said, "Scaredy cat." He then walked to Lucy and chided her. "Old girl, you ran off my only witness before I could question him."

He picked up the empty oat bag, stuffed it inside his saddle bag, untied and mounted his horse. Riding slowly over the surrounding property and again finding nothing of any interest, he then directed Lucy toward the beginning of the forest behind the cabin.

In the late, Texas autumn, most trees were leafless, but live oaks still held their foliage, giving enough cover to darken the area underneath them. And other than oak trees, the woods on Eli Snow's property consisted of an abundant variety of mesquite and scrub brush, making the region tough to navigate a horse through.

Along his trek, Bertram found traces of worn paths here and there with none leading to and ending at anything other than a bulk of brush. It wasn't long until the vegetation became too thick for him to continue on horseback.

He dismounted and tied Lucy's reins around the trunk of an oak young and small enough in width to allow it. "Don't have any more grub for you." He stroked the horse's neck. "But you've had plenty so far. I'll see you get a fresh feed bag once we get back to Hamilton."

Lucy snorted and lowered her head and searched then for any vegetation worth nibbling on.

Walking through thick brush, Bertram looked closely for any clues he might find in connection with Eli's death, his mind obsessing over Eli's broken legs and gruesome neck wounds. Even with the day as clear as it was, the woods still managed to convey a gloomy atmosphere, and he couldn't help but shudder, more from the recollection of Eli's ravaged neck than the chilly air.

Considering the wildness of the forest, Bertram thought it quite possible a mountain lion could actually be in the area, maybe a rogue cat come down from the steep hills and cliffs around Hico or Johnsville, Texas. Those bergs were close to thirty miles north of Hamilton, but it wouldn't be the first time a big cat traveled that far hunting for farm livestock or game, especially if human intervention made its local habitat dangerous.

But as he'd discussed yesterday with Lucas and Dr. Peterson, mountain lions have upper and lower canines. If such a cat had attacked Eli, there should have been punctures on both sides of the neck.

"Most likely it was a two-legged animal," Bertram told himself as he pushed deeper into the thick mass of bushes. "Some crazy sumbitch that thinks he's a wild animal." He then stopped when the woods began to thin out a bit. "Like the Wild Man in a carnival down San Antonio way I saw back when the Rangers was trackin' a renegade."

He shook his head and laughed. "That Wild Man had a bone through his nose and ate live chickens." He stopped laughing when he realized he'd been talking out loud to himself.

"Bertram," he said under his breath. "Maybe it is time to consider putting yourself and Lucy out to pasture."

An icy breeze whisked by the sheriff as he found himself in an area once cleared of trees and brush. It was evident the forest was inching back in for reclamation, but the vicinity was, for the most part, uncluttered by the thick foliage he'd recently been fighting.

At the borderline where the woods started up again there stood the burned out remnants of a ranch house Bertram vaguely recalled from ten years ago. When he was close to ending his days with the Rangers, Bertram had been called in from Fort Worth to help search for a missing child named Bonnie Cross in Hamilton County. He had hardly done any real investigations at that time but consented on this missing child case as a favor to an old friend.

He remembered scouring most of the land around Cross' ranch. If his memory didn't fail him, it was Eli's oldest son, whose name he couldn't recall but was more than likely the same young man in the photograph hanging on the wall in Eli's cabin, who'd volunteered to search this area. And because of his familiarity with the landscape, no one thought the young man was being anything other than helpful. In fact, he recollected Lucas Cross had asked the Snow boy if he had checked out the old ruins of the burned-out ranch house when the search party gathered at the end of the day. The young man stated that he had indeed, and much of the surrounding forest as well. He also said he'd seen no evidence of Bonnie.

Bertram had asked Lucas about the ranch house then. That's why he now remembered the place. Lucas had told the sheriff he knew little other than it was there. The rancher said he used to hunt deer around that spot before Eli bought the land. That's when he'd first come upon the burned remnants of the home.

Now, in the clear afternoon, Bertram viewed the charred bits and pieces with a touch of unexpected dread. Somehow, with elongated, irregular shadows cast by remaining walls and partial beams, the ruins resembled a wounded, dangerous beast hunched and prepared to lash out in defense of its sorry hide.

But he shook off the feeling and scolded himself for being silly and then approached the scorched relic with a renewed interest in looking for clues. But, as with his previous explorations that day, he found nothing other than scattered bits of burnt furniture surviving over the years and a few other items that were unrecognizable from being melted long ago in the fire.

The sheriff took off his hat and scratched an itch that predictably materialized on top of his head when he'd found no clues. He stopped scratching and sighed at the lack of hair once crowning his head, then put his hat back on and walked toward what was left of a chimney on the north side of the burned ranch house. And it was there to the side of the chimney, not far from the house's foundation, Bertram discovered the bulge of a storm cellar door.

He moved to that spot and found the cellar door covered in a mass of vines connecting it to the edge of the encroaching woods. Upon closer inspection, he noticed some vines had been ripped away from one edge of the door. He bent down and pulled up that side and carefully lifted the door, its old hinges creaking, until he finally set the door on the ground beside the cellar's entrance.

"What have we here?" he asked, staring into the dark recesses below.

Daylight only penetrated so far, allowing him a dim view of a set of descending steps, but how far down they went he couldn't judge because of the darkness.

He poked his head into the opening and an odor of earth

and mildew coupled with something else—a smell he recognized but could not distinguish— touched his nostrils.

Bertram removed his Colt .45 from its holster and then prepared to climb down the steps. As he lifted his head out of the cellar's opening, he detected a movement below, just enough of a divergence in the thick gloom covering the cellar's belly to alert him something had definitely shifted.

"Hello?" he asked. "Somebody down there?"

Again, he thought he glimpsed a subtle movement, this time accompanied by a scratching sound as if something dragged itself across the dirt floor.

"Look here," the sheriff said as he decided it would be better to inch down the stairs feet facing out just in case there was something down there, something that could easily jump on him if he backed down in the conventional way. "I'm coming down. If you're a critter, there's no need to worry. But if you stand upright on this earth, be prepared 'cause I got my gun drawn and ready."

He took one more glance into the cellar but saw no further movement. He sat down and let his legs fall into the opening and then inched forward. Tapping the wooden slats of the steps with his boot heels until he was far enough inside to pull himself down, he held his gun with one hand and gripped the side rail with the other.

"Probably ain't nuthin' but a raccoon or possum," he murmured under his breath. "Hell, best not be a polecat." He recalled how he had been sprayed on two occasions in the past and how long it took the pungent odor to wear off.

Sensing the wooden stairs' age and fragility as they bent under his weight, Bertram descended with slow determination one boot heel after the other, until his head was almost entirely inside the cellar. He halted abruptly when he heard the distant, frantic neighing of his horse.

"Good lord!" He backed up and out of the cellar.

Once on solid ground, the sheriff ran toward the panicked noises he knew came from Lucy and admonished himself for leaving the horse alone. If in fact there was a mountain lion roaming the area, that could well be the cause of his horse's alarm.

When he entered the thick border of brush and trees, the sheriff saw foliage parting in front of him. He froze and held his Colt ready. Whatever had spooked Lucy was coming straight at him now, and it was moving quickly.

Bertram lowered himself to one knee, cocked the gun's hammer, and took aim as the movement in the scrub brush rushed forward. When a scratched and wild-eyed Donny Cross appeared, the sheriff let out a sigh of relief.

"What in the world's goin' on, Donny?" He re-holstered his gun and stood up when the boy halted, bent over, and panted for air.

Donny was a mess, his denim coat, shirt, and jeans bedraggled. Because the cowboy hat he usually wore was uncharacteristically absent, his head was bare, disclosing a mass of brown hair matted with burs and broken twigs.

"Sheriff," he said, still gasping. "It's my pa. Adam sent me... He... It..."

Bertram walked over to Donny and put a hand on the boy's shoulder. "Settle down, son. Get your breath back and take it slow."

The disheveled boy looked up. Bertram noticed nicks and cuts on Donny's face. "Yes, sir, Sheriff," Donny said and nodded.

The sheriff waited until the boy calmed before asking, "Now, what's that you wanted to tell me 'bout your pa?"

Donny breathed slower now but was still bent over with his hands placed right above his knees. "Me and Adam found him this mornin', Sheriff. Somethin' crawled through Pa's window last night and…" He glanced up with a pitiful expression. "And bit him."

"What?"

"Bit his throat." The boy put a hand on his own neck. "Right here. Bit him right here."

Bertram knelt down by Donny. "Bit? You sure?"

Donny nodded yes, then swallowed hard and said, "He ain't dead, though. Just weak. Me and Adam wanted to load him in the Runabout and go to Doc Peterson, but Pa wouldn't hear of it. Told us to leave him be."

Bertram stood and a sinking feeling hit his stomach at the thought of yet another attack in this normally quiet community. He then turned his attention back to Donny. "How'd you get here, anyway? And how'd you know I was here?"

"Adam called your office. Deputy Howard told him you rode out to old man Snow's place." He glanced over his shoulder. "I drove the Runabout out here, but the scrub brush was too thick to navigate through, so I left it a ways back and came lookin' for you on foot." He smiled weakly. "Didn't mean to scare your horse."

"Well, we best get back to your pa and see what the matter is," the sheriff said, turning to glance in the direction of the storm cellar. And there, standing on its open door, was the cat the sheriff had encountered earlier at the cabin. It was in the distance, but he could make out it was the same animal. The cat, oblivious to Bertram and Donny, nonchalantly groomed itself.

"Must have slipped in while I was opening the cellar door. Didn't notice it until it made some noise being a busy body," the sheriff said.

"Sir?" Donny asked.

"Hmm?" Bertram turned to the boy. "Nothin'. I'll come back after I get a good look at your pa."

"What about your horse, Sheriff? You cain't leave her out here."

Bertram's brow wrinkled. He didn't much warm to the idea of someone else riding Lucy. However, he realized in this case he'd have to make a concession. "Tell you what. Let me take the Model T so I can get to your pa as quick as possible. You ride old Lucy back to your ranch for me. How'd that be?"

"Okay, but you think she'll let me?"

The sheriff placed a firm grip Donny's arm and directed the boy toward the forested area. "She'll be obliged at the lighter weight," he said as they walked forward. "The Koffee Kup Kafé has put some extra poundage on her regular rider."

———

When Bertram turned the vehicle off the main road, he found the gate to the Cross Ranch open. Adam stood by it and waved as the sheriff slowed the Model T Runabout to a stop.

"Hop on in, Adam," Bertram said.

Adam pulled the passenger door open and crawled in beside the sheriff. The young man's face was pale and strained. "Where's Donny?"

"He's riding my horse back here for me. Now, what's this about your pa?"

Bertram asked, driving down the dirt and gravel path leading to the ranch house.

Adam proceeded with the same tale Donny had offered but adding the information about footprints left in the snow in front of the open bedroom window.

"You sure they was human?" Bertram asked.

"Weren't no wild animal tracks. Unless there's something like that with ten toes."

The sheriff winced as the ranch house came into view. "You say they were small, like a child's?"

"Yes, sir."

Adam placed his hands on the dashboard. Bertram saw weariness, fear, and worry lining the boy's face. Adam turned that face toward the sheriff and asked, "But they couldn't be, could they? No child could have done...that kind of bite, could they?"

"'Spect not. Suppose those tracks have melted by now?"

"Yes, sir. Didn't take long for them to turn to mush."

Bertram wheeled the Model T toward the house, but Adam stopped him. "No, Sheriff. Pa ain't in the house no more. He wandered outside. I tried to stop him, but he damn near throttled me even as weak as he is."

"Well, he cain't have gone too far."

"It's okay. I know where he went. I weren't about to let him meander around alone." The boy pointed to the east. "He's down at Ma and Bonnie's graves. Just over that rise."

The sheriff drove in the direction Adam designated but already knew where the small cemetery was. Once over a slight incline, Bertram stopped the vehicle when he saw the gravesite and Lucas, who was on his knees in front of the gravestones.

When he saw his father, Adam's breathing increased, and he made to bolt from the Model T, but Bertram grabbed the boy's arm, saying, "Steady now. Let's take it nice and easy." Adam struggled to free his arm from the sheriff's grip. "Hold on now, Adam. There ain't no need to rush down there and spook your pa. We need to go there as calmly as we can. Understand?"

The boy struggled briefly and then stopped. Under the brim of Adam's hat, the sheriff could see rivulets of sweat. "You okay?"

Adam's respiration slowed. He swallowed and nodded yes.

"Good. Let's go see to your pa."

The graves Lucas Cross had made for his wife and missing child were encircled by a wrought iron fence with posts about three feet high. Time and the elements had blemished the metal with areas of rust and pits, but the spot still held a sense of reverence about it.

As the sheriff and Adam got out of the vehicle and walked slowly toward Lucas, Bertram recalled the day he had attended the mock funeral of Bonnie Cross, the day Lucas decided his daughter would never be found and was, more than likely, dead. The rancher buried an empty pine box next to his wife's grave. A formal ceremony, presided over by a local Baptist minister, was performed as if the grave contained the earthly remains of Bonnie. As far as the sheriff knew, Lucas had not set foot in a church after that day.

Now, as Bertram approached the small graveyard, the first thing he noticed was that Lucas wore only the insulated underwear he had bedded down in the night before.

Bertram walked cautiously around the rancher and motioned for Adam to stay slightly behind, even though it was evident the boy wanted to go to his father immediately.

"Hey, old hoss," Bertram said with caution as he placed a hand on Lucas' shoulder. "A bit cold out here for just long johns, ain't it?"

Once it rested on Lucas, the sheriff had an impulse to pull his hand away. Despite the insulated material on the rancher's shoulder, an icy cold penetrated through the fabric embracing Bertram's hand with an awful foreboding. Then, adding to the eerie atmosphere, from the opposite side of a small rise above the grave site, a terrible howl arose. It was the most unnatural sound the sheriff could recall and sent a tingle of dread over his flesh.

"Lordy," he whispered under his breath.

The yowl was repeated, and the sheriff then spied the lone

figure of the Cross' old bird dog, Turk, standing on the crest of the ridge above them.

"It was Turk's barkin' that got Donny and me out of bed this mornin'." Adam's voice made Bertram jump even though the sheriff was quite aware the boy was behind him. "That's how we knew something was wrong in Pa's bedroom."

As Bertram turned to face the boy, a voice rose in a hollow, soulless intonation emerging from deep in Lucas Cross' chest. "Hush, now, Turk."

Because of the dog's age and its distance from Lucas, there was no way the animal could have heard the rancher speak. Despite that impossibility, the dog abruptly ceased its howls, tucked a tail between its legs, and sauntered over the ridge and then out of sight.

Bertram lifted his hand from Lucas' shoulder, stepped back. "Let's get you into town and have Doc Peterson take a look at you." Bertram removed his coat, stepped forward, and draped it around Lucas, who gave no indication he noticed the sheriff's gesture at all.

"Those stones," Lucas said flatly.

Bertram glanced at the two headstones. They were gray granite and held nothing other than the inscriptions: **LISA CROSS 1886-1910** and **BONNIE CROSS 1905-MISSING 1916**. "I remember you said you had to go to Hico to get those made. Only stone mason around these parts at that time had his shop there."

"Bonnie's has to be removed." Lucas turned his head around and staring directly at Bertram. It was the first time he'd done so since the sheriff and Adam came down, and it was the first time the sheriff was able to clearly observe the two wounds on Lucas' throat. They didn't appear as vicious as those inflicted on Eli Snow, but they were ghastly enough with ripped tissue and ugly bruising.

Bertram sucked air across his teeth. "Whew, man. What happened to your throat?"

Lucas smiled and raised a hand to cover the injuries, then turned his head back toward the graves. "Bonnie's stone has to be removed," he repeated, ignoring Bertram's question.

"Why, Lucas?"

"Yeah. Why, Pa?" Adam asked.

When Lucas answered, he did not turn around, keeping his attention on the harsh stone in front of him. "Because she ain't dead." He rubbed the bites on his throat with a suggestive, curious affection. "Ain't missin' neither."

Bertram put his hands under the rancher's shoulders. "You're not well, Lucas." He made to lift him from his kneeling position, but it was like trying to lift dead weight. "Here," Bertram said to Adam. "Come help me get your pa up. I'll drive the Model T down when he's standin' and you've got a steady hold on him. We can get him into town then."

It took a while, but the sheriff and Adam finally got Lucas on his feet. Adam then held his father, who swayed as if he might collapse at any moment, with a firm grip.

"I'll be right back with the Model T," Bertram said, heading up the ridge.

———

"PA, YOU'RE GONNA BE OKAY," Adam said. "Once Doc Peterson takes care of you, you'll be all right."

Lucas' body stopped swaying and went rigid as he turned his attention to Adam. The rancher's hazel eyes were flat and void of human emotion. "She's come back to us, son."

Adam shook his head. "Cain't be, Pa." He felt like he would cry. "You're just imaginin' things. We get you into town and you'll think clear again."

Lucas' eyes went wide. "No! Take me back to bed where I can wait for Bonnie!"

"Pa! Be still!"

But Lucas' sudden outburst was coupled with an unexpected flood of strength. He pushed his son to the ground and started up the ridge on unsteady legs. The rancher had made it about halfway up before meeting the vehicle Bertram drove.

———

IT WAS HARD TO ACCOMPLISH, but eventually Bertram persuaded Adam to stay behind and wait for Donny.

"I'll get your pa situated in the Model T and covered up with blankets. As soon as I get to Hamilton and take your pa to Doc Peterson's, I'll head back here. You and Donny can come to town in this then, and I'll ride Lucy back to Eli Snow's place."

Bertram had convinced himself whatever was up to mischief around the county originated on the Snow property. The footprints Adam had mentioned were the biggest mystery, but, then again, the boy was distraught and probably didn't see exactly what he thought he had.

"Just be sure and see my horse gets put up safely in your stable. She ain't agreeable to too many changes in her livin' quarters, but I imagine she'll do okay until I can get back, 'specially if you give her a hefty feed bag. Think you can manage that?"

Adam, dividing his looks between Bertram, who was standing by the passenger side of the vehicle, and Lucas, in the passenger seat and slumped against the door, nodded. "Yes, sir, Sheriff. Just please hurry and get Pa to the doctor."

"You hop on back and we'll go to the ranch house and get those blankets." The sheriff walked around the front of the Model T to the driver's door. Once inside, he stuck his head out and called to Adam now on the back of the Runabout's extended back end. "After I head back to town, telephone my office and tell Howard or Gus I'm comin' in with your pa."

The sheriff put his head back in and turned the ignition. He glanced at Lucas and saw the rancher had passed out. He didn't care for Lucas' color at all. At the gravesite, the rancher had been pale, but now the man's flesh had an unhealthy gray tone.

"Guess I could call ahead myself. But I ain't got time to spare if that party line out this way is tying up the phone lines," Bertram said to himself.

After he gathered a good number of blankets from the ranch house and covered up the cold, clammy Lucas Cross, Bertram drove toward Hamilton at the top speed the vehicle could muster.

With his eyes alternating between the rancher and the road, Bertram kept a nervous vigil as he sped down the gravel and dirt. Lucas made no movement or sound until they were about five miles from town, when he let out a moan and gasped. The sound was sudden and unexpected and gave the sheriff enough of a scare that he jumped out his seat for an instant.

"What is it, Lucas?" Bertram tried to watch his passenger and keep an eye out for the sharp turn leading into Hamilton.

"The light!" Lucas groaned with his face creased in a scowl. "It's too bright!"

It was early afternoon, the sun high in the sky. And although the day had remained clear, the temperature was low enough to give anyone a chill, which made the sheriff even more concerned as to the critical nature of Lucas' health.

"Hang in there, Lucas," he urged, coming upon the turn into Hamilton. "We'll be in town shortly. I'll go right to Doc Peterson's office."

The rancher moaned again, clenched his eyes shut, and pulled the blankets up over his face and head.

When Main Street finally came into view, Lucas started

screaming and thrashed under the blankets. Bertram thought the rancher would surely cause the passenger door to open and he would fall out of the Model T before Bertram could get Lucas to the medical office.

Bertram pushed the accelerator to the floorboard and then, just as he arrived there, skidded to a halt in front of Peterson's office. He then scrambled out of the driver's side and started banging on the doctor's door.

"Doc!" The sheriff pounded on the door. "Hurry up and get out here. Lucas Cross has been attacked and is in bad shape. He's—"

A hand gripped Bertram's shoulder. He spun around and found Dr. James Peterson standing behind him.

"Bertram?" Peterson asked with a concerned look. "What's going on?"

"Thank the Lord," the sheriff said. He grabbed the doctor by the arm and directed him toward the waiting vehicle. "I got Lucas Cross in here." He pulled open the passenger door.

Lucas was still completely covered by blankets, but his screams had ceased, his struggling now an intermittent series of twitches.

Peterson guessed the seriousness of the situation and asked no more questions. He instantly helped Bertram remove the rancher from the Model T. Once they had Lucas out, the sheriff grabbed the rancher under the armpits and waited as Peterson opened the medical office door. The doctor then returned, bent down, and grasped Lucas by the ankles.

The two men lifted the rancher and carried him into the office where they placed him on the examining table Eli Snow had occupied in the early morning hours of that same day.

Bertram sighed and pulled back the blanket from Lucas' face. "We got another one, Doc." He looked at the bites on Lucas' throat and noticed the wounds had almost closed, the torn and bruised flesh appearing to have healed with unnatural quickness. "That cain't be," the sheriff said as Peterson examined the wounds. "Doc, them bites was wide open less than an hour ago."

The doctor glanced up, frowned at Bertram, and then went back to his examination. "Less than an hour? You sure about that?" He placed his fingertips on the rancher's wrist just above the radial artery. The doctor then bent down and positioned his ear next to Lucas's closed lips. "I barely get a pulse on him, Bertram. And a very faint, weak one at that." He removed the cover of blankets from Lucas. "His breathing is diminished as well." He then checked Lucas's abdomen by pressing lightly around the stomach area. "What happened to him?"

"Adam was supposed to call and have Howard or Gus come tell you before I got here."

"No one said anything to me." The doctor rolled Lucas over on his side and prodded the small of the back around the kidneys. "I've been on the courthouse square along with everyone else." He rolled the rancher back to a supine position and examined the rest of his body. "Matter of fact, Howard and Gus were on the square. If Adam called your office, there probably wasn't anyone there to answer."

The sheriff turned to look out the window. "What do you mean you were out there with everybody?" Down by the courthouse, Bertram noticed a crowd. "Hell's bells! Must be everybody in Hamilton down there, Doc." He turned back to Peterson, who was pulling the covers back on Lucas. "What's going on?"

"I tried to talk them into waiting until you came back." The doctor tucked the edge of the blanket under the rancher's chin. "It was Gus who couldn't stand it. Not after Newell came over to get instructions on what to do."

"Come on, Doc. Instructions for what?"

"The head. Newell finished his restoration and wanted to know what to do next. So Gus took the initiative." Peterson grinned slightly. "Seems your deputy might have aspirations to run against you next election and thought he could pull a little authoritative action of his own."

The sheriff grimaced. "He didn't."

"I'm afraid he did."

"And it's—"

"Yep. There in the middle of the courthouse lawn, sitting on a slab of hickory wood placed across those two five-foot stone columns normally standing in front of Tanner's General Store for idle leaning and the spreading of local gossip."

"Sumbitch!" Bertram shouted. "As if I didn't have enough to worry about right now."

"Thing is, Bertram, our prim elementary schoolmarm, Matron Vivien Hagler, says she knows whose neck that severed head belongs on."

TWELVE

Sheriff Bertram Stone had to admit, Newell Scruggs had performed an amazing reconstruction on the head. He'd filled in the eye sockets and placed wood inserts into the gaping holes where the teeth had been extracted, which gave the head a certain aspect of its original shape.

"I took the liberty of sewing the mouth shut to keep the jaw from sagging." Newell stood by his work on the town square, advising Bertram. "A little makeup here and there, a dollop of mortician's wax, and a light trim and combing of what hair wasn't singed away made a great difference. Don't you agree, Sheriff?"

Bertram glanced at a group of citizens gawking at the grisly object. "Does look more human, Newell."

The sheriff made a quick mental note as to who was present and studying the head—mostly people he recognized from Hamilton. There were a few farmers and ranchers the sheriff knew slightly, but the two onlookers who gave him pause were the Davenport brothers, Ezekiel and Noah, from south of Hamilton. Although never proven, the Davenports had a history of more than one run in with the law for supposed rustling.

They were also suspected of making and selling corn liquor, but that too had never been confirmed. The sheriff felt the hair on the nape of his neck rise when he saw those two hovering on the edge of the spectators.

Ezekiel noticed Bertram's attention and elbowed his brother in the ribs. The two men grinned with rotten teeth and chuckled. Noah spat a hefty wad of tobacco juice between juvenile snickers. The sheriff gave the Davenports one long stare with emphasis, but the brothers were not intimidated and made no move to leave the crowd gathered around the head.

"Sheriff!" Deputy Howard Spark's voice interrupted Bertram's scrutinizing. "Just got Adam Cross' phone call. The boy was frantic. Seems he's been callin' for hours, but me and Gus was out here, I guess, and didn't know Adam was tryin' to get a hold of us." He smiled sheepishly. "See you got here okay though, Sheriff. How's Lucas?"

"Not too good right now. I didn't figure on puttin' that evidence," Bertram said, pointing at the head, "on display 'til I had things settled down around here about Eli, and now Lucas."

The deputy lowered his head. "That's what I told Gus. When Newell came over to see what to do, I told Gus we should wait 'til we heard from you."

"Uh-huh. Where's Gus?"

"Down in your office with Missus, I mean, Miss Hagler," Howard remarked with a frown. "Don't go callin' her Missus, Sheriff, she'll lecture you hard enough to make you think you're back in school."

Bertram smiled. He knew the woman probably had both Howard and Gus in her class when they were boys—that is, on days when those two actually attended school.

"Doc Peterson told me she might know somethin' about our head." The sheriff glanced back at the assembly of bystanders and discovered the Davenport brothers no longer there.

"Yes, sir. That's what Gus is talkin' to her about."

"Guess I better go join in that conversation. Howard, them Davenport brothers were part of this crowd a minute ago. I'm not sure where they got off to, but I want you to nose around town and see if you can find them. You know those two, don't you?"

"Zeke and Noah?"

"Them's the ones."

"Yes, sir. I know them two skunks all right."

"Well, if you find them, keep a close eye on those boys. They's just mean enough to have somethin' to do with all the mysterious goings on around here what with the supposed competition Eli had with them distillin' and sellin' corn liquor."

"Yes, sir. I'll get right on it."

Bertram watched the deputy move through the crowd and head up the street. The sheriff then approached Newell Scruggs, who was sharing his expertise with a young married couple, the wife appearing greener by the second.

"You see," the undertaker said in his deep, pipe organ timbre. "By filling the eye sockets—"

"Pardon me for interrupting." The sheriff then addressed the couple. "You're the Crawfords, right?" The man answered they were. "Just married and moved down here from Benbrook last summer?" Again, the man nodded yes. "Well, I think your missus here is a bit overwhelmed by all this, young man. Maybe you both should walk over to the cafe and get a nice cup of tea to settle her stomach."

The man stuttered an apology to his wife, took her by the arm, and walked in the direction of the Koffee Kup Kafe.

"Newell, you would do me a great favor by taking our guest," the sheriff said, indicating the mounted head, "back to your establishment. I think we've had about everybody in and around Hamilton ogling it today. Don't you agree?"

"Most assuredly, Sheriff. I was entertaining the same idea myself."

Bertram patted Newell's bony shoulder. "Good man."

THE UNDERTAKER LIFTED the head from its resting site and then placed it inside the leather bag Bertram had originally used, a feeble moan of protest rising from what curious spectators remained. It was a short-lived objection however as the sheriff cast them a wary eye and they hastily ambled away.

Before Bertram went to his office to see what Vivien Hagler knew or thought she knew, he asked Newell, "Would you mind checking in with Doc Peterson after returning the head to your place?"

"Is the Doctor in some type of difficulty?" Newell cinched the bag closed.

"No. It's Lucas Cross. He's in Doc's office and in bad shape." The sheriff put two fingers on his own throat. "If you catch my drift."

The undertaker's eyes widened. "My goodness, Sheriff. Just what type of criminal has invaded our generally quiet town?"

"That's what I'm workin' on. And I'm goin' to find out somethin' damn soon. You can bet on it."

———

As HE MADE his way down the basement steps to his office, Bertram recognized the stuffy voice of Vivien Hagler echoing down the hallway.

"You never did take to math, did you, Deputy? Your partner Howard did, though. I had high hopes for that young man." Bertram watched Vivien Hagler turn toward the office door as he strode through it, her neck craned from her position where she sat in front of the sheriff's desk. "Well, it's about time you got here, Sheriff." She looked back at Gus, who was sitting in the sheriff's chair. "I told your deputy I wanted to wait and give my information to you, seeing as you are the first authority when it comes to law enforcement in Hamilton County."

"Sheriff," Gus said as he stood up from the chair and glanced down at Vivien with exasperation. "She may have been waitin' for you to get here so she could say whose head she thinks it is, but that ain't stopped her from conversin' none."

Bertram grinned and walked around his desk. "Miss Hagler, I heard you might recognize the evidence in question."

Vivien turned her attention to the sheriff. She was a lean, dry spinster approaching seventy years of age without trepidation, her lips perpetually puckered in a non-committal expression making it hard to guess her actual mood. She wore her grayish-brown hair in a tight bun on top of her head. A light dusting of makeup powder covered the prune-like consistency of her face along with a wisp of pink lipstick, which she'd prudently added to her thin lips. The only item absent from her starched figure with its drab tan blouse and matching skirt touching her ankles when she stood was a stereotypical set of spectacles. Vivien Hagler would announce to anyone in a heartbeat that her vision was still as razor sharp as when she was a girl.

"Well, yes, Sheriff Stone," Vivian said. "Despite my age, I still have the bright and focused eyes of a child." She glanced at Gus who had positioned himself behind and to the left of Bertram after the sheriff sat down. "Much like your deputy once had when he was in elementary school."

The sheriff glanced over his shoulder at Gus and grinned. The deputy frowned and fiddled with the brim of a cowboy hat he held in front of his chest. "Gus, you had Miss Hagler here for a teacher?" Bertram asked with mischief.

"Yes sir. And so did my pa."

"And your father was a better student," Vivien said with indignation at the deputy's reference to her age.

Gus glanced up and found the sheriff staring at him with a big smile plastered on his face. He lowered his eyes then and said, "Yes, ma'am, I reckon he was."

Bertram suppressed the giggle in his throat and turned back to Vivien. "So, please, Miss Hagler, tell me who you think the head belongs to."

"Why, that head belongs, or rather belonged, to Jacob Snow."

"Really? Eli Snow's boy?"

"No mistake, Sheriff Stone. That is Eli Snow's youngest son's head your deputy had the bad taste"—here she gave Gus an accusing glare—"to luridly display on the courthouse square."

"I see." The sheriff looked over his shoulder at Gus and whispered, "I'll need to have a chat with you later about your deciding to do that." The deputy swallowed and nodded, keeping his eyes focused downward. "Just what physical features make you so sure that it's Eli's boy?" Bertram turned back to Vivien.

"Why, the relation of his nose to its position between his upper lip and the heavy eyebrows. You could say, although in this instance I suppose it would be considered bad taste, that it's as plain as the nose on his face."

The sheriff couldn't swear to it, but he though he saw the teacher briefly smile. "To be honest, I didn't see much on that head that could be particularly unique even with Newell Scruggs workin' his mortician's magic on it. Besides, Newell tells me Eli's older son—Arlis, I believe his name was—came and got him some fifteen years back so Newell could bury Jacob Snow. And when Newell went out there old Eli run him off with a shotgun." Bertram raised his eyebrows and then asked, "So, are you still certain that head is Jacob Snow's, being that boy's been dead for a long while?"

Vivien seemed shocked by this news. "I don't recall anything ever mentioned about Jacob Snow dying. I do remember that Arlis was reportedly killed somewhere in France during the War. Was buried over there, I believe."

"I think you're right about Arlis. But as far as Jacob's passin', well, maybe Newell got his dates mixed up. I imagine he was just gettin' his business started back then, so he might not have said much about it, not knowin' folks around here all that well. But I doubt he was that far off in regard to it bein' quite a while ago."

Vivien visibly stiffened at her word being challenged. "I do know this. Whenever those Snow brothers had the notion to attend school, I thought Arlis was quite nice and very soft spoken. But Jacob—and that's why I know that's his head outside there on the square—had the look and disposition of a wild animal. I imagine he was born with it. The bones of his face and the way his eyebrows bridged together, well, I had a hard time looking at that child. He gave me the willies." She paled a little and then added, "And I've had more than occasional night-mares populated by that face."

The sheriff leaned back in his chair and let out a sigh. "Just how often did they come to school, Miss Hagler? You'll have to excuse my presumption, but Eli doesn't impress me as a great supporter of higher education."

"Indeed, he was not. In fact, I went out to his cabin once to find out why those boys weren't attending classes on a regular basis. Even if Jacob frightened me, I still had duties to perform as an educator, and I could not justify the way I felt about a child's looks to make me sway from those duties either."

"I'm supposin' Eli didn't cotton to your intrusion, did he?"

"Hmpf," she said with disgust. "That Eli Snow's a loathsome, filthy creature. It's no wonder one of his sons looked more feral than human."

Bertram considered telling Vivien that Eli Snow was dead and resting on a metal table in the back of Newell Scruggs' funeral home, but he decided not to let that cat out of the bag just yet nor to offer any information about the attack on Lucas Cross either.

Vivian continued. "He treated me in much the same manner you said he did Mr. Scruggs, without a shotgun, however. He told me—or rather, snarled at me—that his boys had work to do and didn't have time for such foolishness as... book learnin' I believe was his exact, ignorant statement."

"Do you remember when you went out there?"

"Let's see, that would have been either 1909 or 1910. Come to think of it, it was the spring of 1910. I remember because that's when they started building this very municipal structure we are presently occupying. There was only a jail here up to that time. There was no courthouse."

"And you never saw Jacob after that?"

"No, I can't remember seeing him after my visit. But I did see Arlis in town every so often. He even came back to school intermittently. I asked him about his brother once, but he just shook his head and wouldn't answer me."

"Well then, Newell's story could have been accurate as far as the time period. It would have been a year after your visit out to Eli's. But if Jacob was dead at that time, it cain't be his head we found at the bottom of the well. There wouldn't be anything left of it but bones at this late date."

Vivien huffed and jumped out of her chair. "If you must keep disputing me, I will take my leave." She walked to the coat rack and took down a full-length coat matching the same drab tan material as her dress.

"Hold on now, Miss Hagler," the sheriff said and stood up.

"It ain't that I don't believe you. Newell never saw a body when he went out to Eli's. For all we know Arlis, who we cain't very well question, may have only thought his brother dead."

The schoolteacher put on her coat, tied its fabric belt snuggly around her waist, and then turned back to Bertram. "I only know that head belongs to Jacob Snow. I don't care what you believe." She then turned to leave but stopped just before reaching the office door and whirled around to face Bertram. "One other thing, Sheriff Stone."

"Yes, Miss Hagler?"

"These photographs hanging on the wall."

"Yes?"

"I imagine some are quite nostalgic for you. I know of your history with the Texas Rangers, and I expect there were some hard and dangerous days in your former law enforcement activities with them."

"And?"

"Well, do you really think it appropriate to have photos of the bandits or renegades or whatever purveyors of lawlessness you had to contend with dead and lying on the ground in front of you as you and your various fellow Rangers sit on horseback relaxed and smoking and talking? I mean, keeping such displays in the privacy of your own home is one thing, but in your office? You must have women and children down here occasionally, and I certainly don't believe they should be subjected to those pictures in such a nonchalant manner, do you?"

Bertram felt a brief pang of anger as he eyed the woman standing rigid in his office doorway. He couldn't help but think just what those outlaws would have done to such a prim and proper matron as Vivien Hagler, no matter what her age. He imagined she'd welcome the photographs of the dead bodies of such outlaws had she survived their repeated rapes and debaucheries. And the schoolteacher would find nothing improper about her feelings of revenge either. Of that fact, he was certain.

"I'll definitely take your observation into consideration, Miss Hagler."

"Well then, I'll be on my way. Good afternoon, Sheriff Stone. You too, Deputy."

As Bertram and Gus watched her walk out the door, the deputy said, "My pa said she was a good looker back when he was a kid. Imagine that."

Bertram sighed and decided not to chastise Gus about putting the head on public display. The interview with Vivien Hagler had been enough punishment for them both.

"Well," Bertram said. "I used to be thin. Don't make no never mind now; pretty or thin, it's just the way of it all."

The phone on the desk rang. Bertram picked up the receiver and answered with, "Sheriff Stone's office. Sheriff Stone speakin'."

Adam Cross' excited voice came over.

"Right now, your pa's fine," Bertram told Adam, not really sure if that was the truth or not. "Doc Peterson's checkin' him over."

Gus tapped the sheriff's shoulder and gave him a questioning look.

"Somethin's come up here I have to deal with, Adam," Bertram said into the receiver. "You and Donny need to sit tight for now. I don't know if I'll be able to get back out there today with the Model T after all."

The sheriff nodded his head. "I'll try, Adam. But if I don't make it out your way, you and Donny be sure and keep my horse stabled and warm. If I don't get back to the ranch today, I'll be there first thing in the mornin'."

He nodded again at Adam's reply. "No, you don't have to comb down Lucy. She'll be fine until tomorrow." He glanced up at Gus while telling Adam, "I'll let you know how your pa is. In fact, me or one of my deputies will call you later if I don't get a chance to drive your pa's truck back tonight."

There was a pause and then Bertram said, "You boys keep an eye out. Whatever attacked your pa might still be roamin' around." He was then sorry he'd made that statement and realized too late it would probably frighten Adam and Donny, but he also believed he had to warn the boys in case something or someone did come back to the Cross ranch. "Uh-huh. I'll be sure and let you know."

He placed the receiver in its hook and saw Gus' concerned and questioning gaze. "Might as well fill you in on what transpired out at the Cross ranch early this mornin'. Let's head over to Doc Peterson's. I'll talk as we walk."

————

THE CROWD that had been drawn in by the macabre evidence put on display on the courthouse square had now taken their leave, continuing on with their own concerns. Meanwhile, Bertram communicated the specifics concerning the assault on Lucas Cross to Gus as he and the deputy walked briskly across the street to the medical office.

"What in the world is goin' on with these attacks, Sheriff?" Gus asked as they arrived at the medical office.

"I hope Doc can help answer that." The sheriff reached to try the knob on the office door. Finding it unlocked, he opened it and discovered Dr. James Peterson and Newell Scruggs standing by the examining table where Lucas Cross lay. The doctor stepped away and Bertram was relieved to see a sheet had not been pulled over the rancher's face.

"What did our schoolmistress have to say, Bertram?"

Peterson asked as he picked around the clutter on his desk until he found a pocket ruler.

"Miss Hagler thinks the head is that of Jacob Snow."

"But that would be impossible," Newell said. "That boy has been dead for over fifteen years now."

"I'll discuss what Miss Hagler had to allow later," the sheriff said and walked to the examining table. "I'm more interested in this man's condition right now."

With a grim tone, the doctor said, "His vital signs are not improving." He then placed the end of the pocket ruler next to one of the bites on Lucas' neck. "I should have done this when you first brought him in." He took a notepad and pencil from his lab coat pocket and made an entry.

Bertram glanced down at Lucas' throat. "It don't take a measurement for me to tell them bites is closing up faster than they should, Doc."

"That they are. But now I'll be able to gauge just how much they are closing and at what rate." The doctor glanced at the sheriff and Gus. "Any references I can gather will be needed because, honestly, I've never seen anything like this."

"What do you think it could be?" Gus asked.

Peterson put his fingers on Lucas's wrist to check the rancher's pulse. "It can't be bacterial. The wounds wouldn't be healing like this. Don't know much about how a virus introduced through the bites could affect the healing process. I suppose it's possible the immune system could be over stimulated but..." He rubbed his forehead in thought. "I've never come across any medical articles about the known existence of such an organism."

"Will he be all right?" Bertram asked.

"Honestly, I think we should keep him here this evening and through the night. I can log a record of his pulse and respiration and blood pressure every fifteen minutes. Right now, these seem to be consistent. Not good, mind you, but consistent. If he doesn't show any change for the better by morning, we should transfer him to Methodist Hospital in Fort Worth. He may need more thorough treatments to pull through, options I can't provide here."

"Have you given him anything?" Bertram asked.

"I considered giving him a thing or two, but that's all I've done. I don't think it would be appropriate to administer any of the usual pain relief or anti-inflammatory drugs because of his reduced blood pressure and heart rate. I think he needs fluids more than anything else, but he is unconscious and unable to drink, and, as I mentioned, I don't have set ups for the more complex tending he's apt to need. Over the years I've referred patients requiring that kind of care to Methodist Hospital in Fort Worth."

The sheriff shook his head. "This is the damnest thing, and it's now gone beyond the attack on Eli and finding that head. Looks like I'm goin' to have to call in some help from Dallas or Fort Worth. At least before somebody else gets assaulted."

Before anyone could respond, Deputy Howard Sparks entered the office. "Sheriff, those Davenport brothers must have hightailed it out of town. I couldn't find hide nor hair of them."

"You think them two's involved, Sheriff?" Gus asked.

"It's somethin' to consider. What with Eli havin' a competing business in the liquor trade and the history of those Davenport scoundrels." Bertram raised his eyebrows. "Wouldn't hurt to look into it. Matter of fact, Gus, why don't you and Howard see if can find out what the Davenports were doing in town today. Ask around and see what you come up with."

The deputies nodded but stayed where they were.

Bertram eyed them and said, "I meant like now."

They answered "Yes, Sheriff" and exited the medical office, giving a hasty goodbye to everyone else in the room.

The doctor grinned. "That should keep them occupied for a while, Bertram." He prepared to take Lucas' blood pressure.

"And out of my hair. Were you able to come up with anything else concernin' Eli's body? You said you were goin' to take a closer look at it this mornin'."

"Not much." Peterson pumped up the arm cuff. As he slowly turned the pressure release knob, he watched the mercury gauge descend. "Only that Eli died from shock and extreme blood loss."

"It is curious, don't you think, Doctor?" Newell chimed in. "That the wounds on Mr. Snow's neck did not take on the rapid healing effect that Mr. Cross' did."

"I would assume it's something to do with having enough circulating blood." The doctor removed the cuff from Lucas' arm and then logged the blood pressure numbers in his notepad. "That and still being alive."

Bertram sat down heavily in one of the medical office chairs. "Do you have any idea, Doc? Any idea at all what could be doing this?"

"Looks like the work of a vampire to me," Peterson said with an odd laugh.

"Come on now, Doc... We've been down this road before. There ain't no such things. And you well know that, and I well know you do."

"However, Sheriff," Newell said. "There could be a deranged person who thinks they are just that type of being. As I mentioned before, I've come across some strange superstitions in my years. Consider those deep tooth sockets found in the jaw of that head. And as Dr. Peterson has told me of his speculation about the exaggerated condition of the teeth that filled those sockets, wouldn't it be plausible there is some type of genetic malformation at work here."

"Well, Newell, I don't think that head was still on a body when Eli and Lucas were attacked," said Bertram.

"Yes, but perhaps some type of condition from inbreeding affected more than one person. Say a twin or another sibling."

Peterson retrieved a wrinkled blanket draped over a chair. He spread it out and covered Lucas and then pulled the end under the wounds on the rancher's throat. "Newell might have a point. I've seen some genetic evidence of such inbreeding like webbed fingers or additional digits." The doctor sighed and sat in the chair he had removed the wadded blanket from. "There was one family from those high cliffs around Chalk Mountain whose teenage girl gave birth to a pathetic, twisted thing with rudimentary gill slits developing on one side of its neck." The sheriff couldn't help but cringe. "Lucky for all involved that pitiable creature was stillborn."

The sheriff scowled. "More than likely one of the girl's brothers got to her. It ain't an unusual occurrence in regard to some of the isolated families around here, especially the dim-witted and poor ones."

"That's true enough." Peterson closed his eyes against a mounting fatigue. "That family I spoke of had eight kids running around their shack. They ranged from toddlers to hulking forms approaching adulthood—a potpourri of all shapes, sizes, and gender, so anything of a creepy sexual nature could well have been possible." Here Peterson opened his eyes and after a slight pause added, "Even the father could have been suspect. As I recall, he was a rather grim, hairy specimen with the dullest eyes I've ever encountered."

The sheriff coughed nervously and asked, "You ever hear of Eli havin' another child, Doc? A girl, maybe? Reason I ask is that what you and Newell are sayin' might have some real levity concernin' the events that unfolded over the last two days."

"Newell?" Peterson asked. "You've been here a bit longer

than me. Ever hear any evidence concerning more than two Snow children?"

The undertaker thought for moment. "No, I've only heard of the two boys. However, I do remember one of the Aycocks, Molly Hunter's mother Vera, talking about the Snow boys during visitation hours for her late husband Pat. I overheard her say how Arlis had been helping them out at the Koffee Kup a few nights a week. The boy had been bussing tables and dishwashing. I remember she said they really didn't need the help, but her husband felt sorry for Arlis and thought it the Christian thing to do so the boy could earn a little extra money. She said she'd told her husband '*I just hope he keeps it for himself and doesn't give anything to that no good father of his or...*' and here I remember Mrs. Aycock trembling, '*that frightening brother of his.*' So I imagine if there had been another child in the Snow household, Mrs. Aycock would have mentioned it."

"Well," said Bertram. "I'll swing by the Koffee Kup in the morning and ask Molly or Hunter if they have any information about the Snow family."

The undertaker cleared his throat, saying, "Gentlemen, as the afternoon is fading, would it be acceptable if I began the embalming process on Mr. Snow's body? Since the good doctor here made a thorough examination this morning, would there be any other reason to delay?"

"If Lucas hadn't been attacked," Bertram said, "I wouldn't have objection, Newell. But since whatever got to Eli has now done the same to Lucas, I'm thinkin' we might need to send Eli's corpse to Fort Worth and get the medical examiner to do a formal autopsy."

Peterson agreed. "With Lucas being injured, an autopsy on Snow would be the best course to take. The manner in which Lucas' neck wounds are healing might indicate a pathogen being transmitted by the bites. It wouldn't do to have some epidemic get started here. I've seen and read about things spreading more rapidly than Typhus, wiping out small towns in a matter of days. So it's better to be safe than sorry." He noted a look of disappointment on the undertaker's face. "Newell, I know the medical examiner in Fort Worth. Robert Callahan's a good man and very thorough. He's also very expedient. He'll have Eli put back together and returned to you in no time."

The undertaker forced a smile. "I see. Of course, I will comply with whatever you men think is best."

"If Lucas doesn't improve by mornin'," said Bertram, "we can transport Eli's body when we take Lucas to Methodist Hospital. I might need you to help Doc with that, Newell, since there's gonna be a lot of things for me to look into here and back at Eli's cabin tomorrow. Would you mind?"

The idea seemed to lift the undertaker's spirits. "Why, not in the least. It would be my pleasure." He went to the coat rack and took his long, black coat from it. "One gets out of Hamilton so rarely it would be a luxury, even though surrounded by the tragic circumstances prompting such a journey. If there is nothing else, gentlemen, I will excuse myself and organize supper and get to bed early so I can be up and ready on the morrow."

The doctor visibly shuddered at the suggestion, likely because he would be the one accompanying the undertaker if Lucas didn't improve. "I have nothing else, Newell," he said.

"Me neither," Bertram added. "Other than it may be you have to drive the Ford up to Fort Worth. Doc here is goin' to be up most of the night, so I don't imagine he'd be too keen on drivin'."

Newell glanced at the doctor. "That, too, would be quite acceptable. I have been told by mourners I've escorted to graveside services that I am an excellent driver." From a hat rack on the wall, he removed his stove-pipe hat and placed it on his head. "Doctor. Sheriff. I will bid you good afternoon then."

Bertram and Peterson offered their cordial farewells as the undertaker exited. The sheriff then chuckled. "Well, Doc, at least Newell won't be driving *you* to no graveside service."

Peterson grinned and glanced at his watch. "Not anytime soon, I hope." He then walked to the table where Lucas lay and prepared to check the rancher's vital signs. "Still unconscious," he remarked, placing a finger on the rancher's wrist. "It's going to be a long night for me. But it won't be the first time I've endured this type of vigil." He lay Lucas' arm down and wrote his finding in the notepad. "What are your plans, Bertram? Going back out to the Snow place?"

"No. It'd be dark by the time I got there or near dark anyways. And even if I did beat sundown, I wouldn't have long enough to get a good look see."

"Where's your horse? You brought Lucas here in his Model T, so you must have left your horse at the Cross ranch, right?"

"That I did. Donny and Adam will tend to Lucy." He watched Peterson adjust the blood pressure cuff on the rancher's arm. "Lucas raised them two boys right. They get a little rowdy sometimes I suppose, but boys that age always do."

The doctor was the one to chuckle this time. "Yes, boys that age discover heads without bodies in wells, don't they?"

"Oh, I expect that object would have come to light someday with or without the Cross boys' aid." The sheriff smoothed out wrinkles on the legs of his khakis. "You want me to relieve you later so you can grab a bite to eat?"

"No, I'd better stick to my timetable. Lucas' vitals are still low but constant. However, I know by experience they can plummet in the blink of an eye, so I'll stick around. You could, if you don't mind, bring me a plate back for supper if you are going to be around."

"Be glad to. I'll go get my supper over at the Koffee Kup around six and then bring you somethin' over after."

"That will be fine. I appreciate it."

"What can I bring you?"

"Let's see," Peterson said as he placed Lucas' arm back under the sheet. "I'll have whatever vegetables Molly's whipped up for the night, a good helping of their pinto beans—unless they put pork in them, which they sometimes do—and if that's the case, then bring a big helping of the potato soup Molly makes daily along with several slices of their homemade bread and a good size pad of butter."

"Still no meat?"

"I don't have a bone to pick with anything from the animal kingdom, so I'll stick to vegetables and grains."

The sheriff put on his hat and coat. "Mind if I keep you company over here tonight? You might need a nudge if you happen to doze off. Besides, I'd kinda like to keep an eye on Lucas myself. Gus and Howard can work a split shift. It won't hurt them none."

Peterson nodded and said, "I'd appreciate your company. We may even be able to come up with some answers as to what's going on around here." The doctor then adding, "Might I suggest you instruct your deputies not to mention the attacks on Eli or Lucas to any of our townspeople just yet. No need in causing a panic."

"I made that point to them yesterday after we brought Eli in, and I'll reinforce the issue now that Lucas was attacked. I just hope Adam and Donny don't call nobody besides me about their pa."

"Did the boys ever get through to your office?'

"Yep. Adam called after Miss Hagler left."

"I suppose someone on their party line might get wind of it, but we'll just have to deal with that situation if it presents itself."

"I reckon people are gonna find out soon enough, but, like you said, I'd rather have a little more time so I might be able to explain all this and keep the good people of Hamilton calm."

Peterson sat down in the chair behind his desk, saying, "Amen to that."

Bertram tipped his hat and left, closing the office door behind him.

———

As the doctor sorted through some half-smoked cigar butts until he found one that appealed to him, he struck a match, and lit the cigar's end. He leaned back and took a long drag and held the swirling smoke in his mouth to tickle his palate. Then he closed his eyes momentarily and jerked up when he heard a faint moan that seemed to come from the direction where Lucas lay.

Peterson shoved the cigar in the crowded ashtray on his desk and quickly made his way to the examining table. "Lucas?" he asked, watching for any response on the rancher's inert face. Continuing to study him, Peterson thought he glimpsed Lucas' left eye open and close for a split second. "Lucas?" But the rancher showed no hint of movement.

The doctor discarded what he thought he'd seen to fatigue. As far as he could determine, the rancher was still unconscious. He then took out the small ruler from his lab coat pocket and re-measured the wounds on Lucas' throat, looked at his initial data on the notepad, and raised his eyebrows. "Closed another two centimeters," he said under his breath, wondering what could cause such accelerated healing. He checked the rancher's pulse and then went back to his desk, sat down, retrieved the cigar butt, and relit it.

Taking another lengthy drag, Peterson glanced at the antique clock on the wall, a gift from his parents when he completed medical school, and saw it was close to five at night. He made a mental note to rewind the clock before midnight, glanced briefly at Lucas Cross' supine form and then closed his eyes to allow himself a few minutes of rest.

————

A LITTLE PAST seven that same evening, Peterson was stirred from another catnap by someone knocking on the door. He rubbed his eyes. "Enter. It's unlocked."

A muffled reply came then from the other side of the door. "I got my hands full, Doc. Cain't turn the knob with my teeth."

The doctor smiled and got up, stretched momentarily, and walked to the door. Opening it, he discovered Bertram on the other side holding two covered dishes of food.

"Supper has arrived," Peterson said, taking the dishes from the sheriff, the bottoms of the plates warm and comforting against the chilly temperature creeping through the open door. "Thanks so much, Bertram." He walked to his desk where he set the dishes amongst the clutter. "How much do I owe you?"

The sheriff closed the door behind him and rubbed his hands briskly together. "Molly said it's on the house. I told her a fib that you were catching up on patient records, and she said to tell you to go light on her family's bill."

Both men laughed quietly as the doctor uncovered the plates, steam rising from the warm food. "Ahhh," Peterson said and took in a deep breath of the vapor. "Beans. I love their beans." He looked up at the sheriff and asked, "No pork, eh?"

As he took off his coat and hat and hung them on the coat and hat rack, Bertram said, "Molly was just about to add some fatback when I went into the cafe. I told her to set aside a good portion of them pintos for you before she did." He then glanced at Lucas and asked, "How's he holdin' up?"

"The same, I'm afraid." The doctor unwrapped a large square of cornbread from a cloth napkin.

The sheriff sat down in one of the chairs free of litter. "Well, at least he's no worse. That's something."

Bertram leaned back and let the doctor eat in peace. Outside, a north wind escalated, rattling windows and rafters on the buildings of Main Street.

Thirteen

The headless thing sensed darkness was imminent, that no more light sifted through cracks in the cellar door above. Its decaying tendons flinched, its ligaments responding like rotten rubber bands.

From the cellar's corner, a mound of earth splotched with white crusts of mold and mildew rustled and heaved. A pale hand wiggled free from the dirt followed by a rising form clothed in a ragged Easter dress. Once Bonnie Cross' head appeared from its resting place and clumps of decrepit earth slid away from her face, her eyes snapped open like the shell of a marine predator. She rotated her head slowly to the right and then back to the left as if unaware of where she was. A groan then rose from her throat, a complaint of emptiness and aberrant hunger.

The headless thing stood stiffly, its abdominal wound now a corrosive, black outline. The stench of rotten intestines filled the storm cellar but fell on no complaining nostrils save a solitary rat backed far away and shivering in a corner.

Bonnie appeared glassy-eyed as the headless thing stumbled to her and held out one dead hand. She grasped it and was lifted upward. The thing clutched her in one arm and walked to the storm cellar stairs. Stumbling up the wooden rails with the coordination of a moth gamboling against an outside light fixture, it made its way out of the cellar and stood under a half-moon's pale light while awaiting Bonnie's instructions. The frightened rat then rushed up the stairs, scurrying quickly toward the beginning line of brush and trees.

———

"Sheriff told me we didn't have to curry her."

Adam Cross stood in the stable, watching his brother Donny run a curry comb over the gratified coat of Sheriff Stone's horse, Lucy.

"I don't mind none." Donny gazed with vacant eyes at the movement of the brush under his hand. "She's a good ol' gal. Didn't put up any fuss at all when I rode her here from Mr. Snow's place." He looked over at Adam. "Besides, I need somethin' to take my mind off Pa."

Adam glanced at the other three horses milling in their stalls. He walked to the tack area and pulled down four blankets. "Well, you probably need to quit combing her before you rub her raw." He handed Donny two blankets. "You cover the sheriff's and Pa's mount, then get their feed bags ready. I'll take care of our two nags."

"Gonna be a cold one again tonight," Donny said to Lucy as he covered her. "You'll appreciate this old blanket once it gets good and dark outside."

After preparing the horses for the night, Adam and Donny walked to the ranch house. The sun had almost completely set, twilight now filling the evening sky. Adam had put a pot of beans on the stove under a low flame before going out to get Donny, and the living room and kitchen were now filled with a warm, earthy smell from the pintos. Adam got bowls for the beans and glasses for milk from the cupboard while Donny stirred chunks of fatback into the beans and turned up the flame on the gas stove. While he continued to prepare for their dinner, Adam thought that Donny was simply watching bubbles form on the surface of the liquid covering the beans until he heard him say, "Wonder how Pa is."

Placing the bowls, eating utensils, and glasses on the table, Adam said, "I don't know. I wish Sheriff Stone had come back here with the Runabout. I'd feel better about Pa if I could go into town and see him."

Donny grabbed a hot pad, lifted the pot of beans off the stove, then went to the table and spooned out a large helping in each bowl. "Ain't nothin' we can do about it, I suppose." He placed the pot back on the stove and lowered the flame, which then embraced a glob of liquid that had run down the side of the pot when Donny spooned out the beans, sending the faint smell of burnt protein into the air. Donny wrinkled his nose before opening the stove's front panel where he removed a baking sheet holding a covered loaf of bread his brother had earlier placed inside to warm.

Adam walked to the ice box and brought out a bottle of milk and a tub of butter and set them on the table. The brothers then sat down on opposite sides. Donny bowed his head and Adam did the same, intoning, "Good food, good meat, good God, let's eat."

The boys chuckled, Donny saying, "Pa always liked that one."

"Yeah." Adam poured milk into both glasses. "Even if Pa did quit saying grace, he never minded that one."

Donny took the cloth off the bread and cut two large slices, handing one of them to his brother. "Reckon whatever it was, it got in that window last night?"

Adam was about to answer when he felt something bump against his leg. "Shit!" he screamed and jumped up, almost knocking over his glass of milk. The wet, droopy eyes of the old bird dog Turk stared up at him.

Donny laughed. "It's just old Turk's tail bumpin' around. He must have been under one of our beds and smelled supper and sneaked in here. He's old, but he still has a good sniffer on him."

Adam let out a long sigh. "Damnation, Turk." He rubbed the dog's head. "You scared the bejesus out of me." Adam sat back down, took a wad of fatback from his bowl of beans and held it under the dog's nose. Turk lapped it up with appreciation and anticipation for more.

"Whatever it was got to Pa last night," Donny said, "old Turk sure took out after it this mornin'."

Adam felt a chill grip him when he remembered those footprints in the snow. He unconsciously rubbed his neck as if in empathy for his father's wounds. "Hope he caught it, whatever it was."

"I still don't get them little footprints." Donny lay down his spoon. "Could it be a person that bit Pa?"

His hunger fading, Adam put his spoon down and set what was left in his bowl on the floor for Turk. With his tail wildly wagging, the old dog lapped at the beans voraciously. "How could it be a person?" Adam asked, watching the bird dog's gluttonous consumption, the animal's slurping taking on an unexpected, sinister tone.

Donny paled. "Are there such things as...? You know. Them things you hear about. Them things talked of in books. Them dead things that come back and drink blood."

Adam smiled grimly and said, "Probably not. But we better be ready if whatever it was comes back again tonight."

"You think it would?"

Adam quickly sobered as he placed a hand on Turk's back and rubbed the dog's grimy coat, the old dog looking up while licking brown residue from the beans off its muzzle. "'Spect it might," Adam said. "Everythin's got to eat."

BY THE TIME darkness fell over Deer Hollow, Texas, Adam and Donny had fired up every lantern in the house. The boys milled about nervously until Adam tried to call the sheriff's office to check on his father, but one of the champion gossipers of Hamilton County, Agnes Goad, was on the party line, and he couldn't get her attention because of interfering static.

"God damned party line!" Adam cried in frustration. He put the earpiece back in the phone's cradle and turned to his brother. "I don't know about you, but I ain't interested in going to bed any time soon."

Donny shook his head no. "Me neither. I'd just as soon stay awake in case... Well, you know."

Adam went to the screened-in back porch and brought back an armful of cut wood, placed it in a fireplace located on the side of the living room opposite the kitchen, and soon had a fire going. The brothers, with Turk following, took up residence on a leather couch sitting across from the fireplace.

Adam and Donny watched the flames in silence while Turk fell asleep at Donny's feet. Time passed at a snail's pace, Adam the one finally breaking the silence. "Pa's got a bottle of hooch hid in his cedar chest. If we're gonna be up all night, we might as well have a little nip to calm our nerves."

"I dunno. Pa wouldn't like it none if we drank up his whiskey."

"It's all right. We'll replace what we take out with a little water. He won't know the difference."

"Well, I suppose it wouldn't hurt none to have a nip."

Adam went to his father's bedroom and rummaged through a cedar chest until he found a bottle of rye whiskey. He then walked back to the living room and motioned for Donny to come over and join him at the kitchen table.

Donny got up from the couch, disturbing Turk, who had been comfortably asleep on his boots. The dog growled at being bothered, and walked stiffly around the couch and out of view. The dog would likely amble back to the boy's bedroom where, after the usual canine circling ritual, situate himself under Adam's bed in a wad of old blankets where it was more peaceful.

Adam saw the dog wandering down the hall and smiled. "Old Turk don't need nothin' for his nerves." He took two shot glasses from the cupboard, handing one to Donny, who sat opposite his brother just as he had at supper.

Adam pulled the cork out of the bottle and poured himself and Donny a shot. The boys clicked their glasses and then downed the dark, amber liquid.

The first whiskey shot was like fire going down, and both boys coughed and sputtered.

"Whew, don't it burn!" Donny's eyes watered, and tears spilled down his cheeks.

"Lordy," Adam said and coughed. He looked at his brother, giggled, then filled the shot glasses for another round.

The next drink was stiff, but went down easier, its route paved by the first one. And by the time the boys reached shot number five, the rye slid like silk down their throats, the intention of saving any of the bottle for their father a distant memory.

The strong north wind danced against the glass panes of the ranch house and attempted entry, but the boys didn't care much about it. They'd been reduced to a sniggering pair of inebriated teenagers whose boozy minds rapidly descended to the gutter.

"Know what?" Adam asked with a foolish grin plastered on his face. "Think I'll call up Ida Perkins."

Donny slapped at his knees and laughed. "Ain't you scared of that wiry twat of hers you was complainin' about the other day?"

"Hell no. I'm so numb, I wouldn't feel scratch one from that hairy booger."

Donny cackled, saying, "Ida got that sister of hers too. Maybe she could bring her along."

"Oh, yeah. She got a sister all right, but Turk's better lookin' than her!"

And so the bantering continued with as many insults toward neighboring farm girls the brothers could muster until the alcohol buried them in an anesthetized stupor. Both boy's heads now lay on the table, the bottle of rye standing empty between them. Simultaneous with their journey into drunkenness, the soft sound of a familiar voice traveled on the north wind, slipping into the brother's ears.

"Adam. Donny. Come out and play. We can go crawfishing down at the creek."

In their intoxicated state, the boys mumbled. Adam's hand dragged across the table, upsetting the empty whiskey bottle, which rolled off the end of the kitchen table and landed with a thud on the wooden floor.

FOURTEEN

Newell Scruggs had a secret habit.

For years now, due to the nature of his work and some of the grisly things he'd witnessed, Newell, before bedtime, mixed a teaspoon of laudanum into to his nightly cup of tea to help him sleep.

Tonight, with an unusual opportunity to accompany Dr. James Peterson to Fort Worth the following morning, the undertaker decided to add an extra teaspoon to his nightly tea in case he found himself overly excited about the trip and unable to fall asleep with his customary single dose of laudanum.

Like Dr. Peterson, Newell had an upstairs apartment as part of his place of business where he kept a small, portable gas stove for cooking his meager meals and boiling water for tea.

———

EARLIER, after he'd left the sheriff and doctor in their vigil over Lucas Cross, the undertaker went to his funeral parlor. He made his way to the embalming room and checked to be assured Eli Snow's body had not significantly advanced in mortification as well as verifying the bodiless head was safe and sound in its leather bag.

Satisfied all was well, Newell made his way upstairs for supper to be followed by plans of going to bed early to rise on time for the trip to Fort Worth.

Newell sliced two pieces of bread from the remaining half loaf he'd purchased two days earlier from Tanner's General Store. He then placed a thin slice of salami on the bread, added his favorite items—a long wedge of dilled pickle along with a slice of cheddar cheese—to the sandwich and then sat down for a negligible meal. Before eating, he'd placed a pot of water on the gas stove and lit the burner, which had started to boil as he munched his food. And by the time he'd consumed his sandwich, Newell had his cup, saucer, bag of Earl Grey tea, and a bottle of laudanum at the ready.

While the tea bag steeped, he took off his glossy ebony shoes, black suit, and white shirt, carefully hanging the clothes in an undersized, French closet. He then put on his night shirt and sat down by the bed in a small chair.

Newell removed the tea bag, placing it for reuse tomorrow night in one of his handkerchiefs. He then measured out the first teaspoon of laudanum, added the second, and leaned back in the chair where he sipped on the mixture of tea and narcotic opiate.

It didn't take long for the drug's increased dose to have an effect, and Newell found he was soon groggy with the need for sleep. He lit a candle on the nightstand, making certain there was enough waxy length of wick for it not to burn out before he awakened. He then extinguished the kerosene lamp on the wall and wound his Big Ben alarm clock, setting it for three in the morning, which would allow ample time to rise, eat a light breakfast, take a sponge bath, dress, and prepare Eli's corpse for the trip.

And by the time Newell placed the alarm clock next to the candle, his eyes were too heavy to keep open. He slid under the sheets and adjusted one of the few remaining possessions of his childhood, a feather pillow, under his knobby skull and fell fast asleep.

Normally, the laudanum instigated very few dreams, Newell usually awakening the next morning with a mind clean of any subconscious dallying. But tonight, for some reason, that extra spoonful of laudanum opened a gateway for his subconscious to flood with reminiscences.

———

In his dream, Newell was a young boy. His father, dressed in the same black funeral attire Newell now sported daily, exhibited a very different physical body than that of his son.

Isaiah Scruggs was a short, broad-shouldered man sporting a Quaker fashioned beard attached to stony jaws. His funeral parlor was located in Austin, Texas, and he had it in mind that Newell would follow him in that business. And since Newell's older brother had succumbed to a swift moving bacterial infection, Isaiah was even more obsessed with the idea his remaining child would carry out the family trade. So he drove Newell unmercifully in regard to duties at the funeral home.

Newell's mother, Naomi, had held the lean string bean physical characteristics Newell inherited. She was a dry, religious woman responsible for giving graveside services if the family of the departed had no minister of their own.

When Isaiah first exposed Newell to embalming procedures, the boy was horrified and ran screaming straight to his mother, who offered little comfort. "You will soon become accustomed to your responsibilities," she told him while reviewing the funeral home's monthly, economic tallies. "The corpse is after all, Newell, only the shell of what was once a person. The soul has fled and made its glorious journey to our Lord's heavenly home."

So, after countless nightmares, Newell eventually accepted the fate of being a mortician. His youthful smile vanished, replaced with a somber line of concession. And the day he felt no emotion while draining the blood from his father's corpse was the moment of Newell's complete cross over into the dreary role of undertaking. And it was that moment which now swirled in his laudanum-soaked brain.

"You will stay in Austin, of course," his mother, who stood behind Newell while he drained his father's fluids, said without emotion. "It is only proper you see to my needs now that Isaiah has gone to Glory, and that you keep our business abreast of its current status and accomplishments."

"Yes, Mother. I'll handle all just as Father did."

Naomi placed a skeletal hand on Newell's shoulder. "I know you will, Son." She then walked to the opposite side of the metal table where her husband's body lay. "We will place Isaiah in a plain box and dress him in a fake suit front instead of his good one." She glanced at her son, who preferred to finish his work and had not raised his head to look at her. "There is no need to buy a plot. Isaiah will be given back to the earth next to our first son, Zachariah, in the pauper's section. That land is donated by the city. No need in taking on extravagant expense for Isaiah's dead flesh. We will instead rejoice in his homecoming with our Lord and Savior, which no amount of money can be substituted for."

"Yes, Mother," Newell said, still not raising his eyes.

Naomi added, "I will be in the day room with customers waiting for information concerning the upcoming service of their grandmother, whose body is in route from the old folks' home. You will be sure this table is cleared and ready in the next hour, will you not?"

This time he did raise his eyes and look dryly at his mother, saying, "I will be certain all is ready." Then he went back to his work as Naomi turned and left.

From somewhere inside the embalming room came a low scratching sound like something being dragged over metal. Newell glanced down and saw his father's hands twitching, his dead fingernails grating across the table. But other than the fact dead hands should not twitch, and dead fingernails should not scratch, Newell found he was more concerned his father's fingernails, normally immaculate in their manicured length and cleanliness, were now long and sharp and grimy with what resembled caked earth.

Newell turned his attention to the corpse's face and found his father's head replaced with the decapitated one from Eli Snow's well.

The head's eyes suddenly flipped open, and Newell screamed, releasing the embalming tool still in his father's femoral artery. Newell backed away as the corpse rose and bent into to a sitting position, the long, metal, embalming probe sticking out like a spear.

Newell stared in horror as the head rotated in his direction with eyes now present in what were once empty sockets. There was something terrifying and haunting about those eyes holding the look of a newborn child shocked by entrance into a strange world, eyes with a profound black fathomless filling their stunned fury.

From deep in his subconscious, Newell willed himself to wake. But the heavy dose of laudanum he'd administered held his cognizant mind at bay as he pushed with futility to escape the dream, which was impervious to his efforts.

Then, as Newell increased his struggles to wake, the dream

became more vivid. A horrible putrefying odor filled the room when the corpse swung its legs sideways, pulled out the embalming tool, slid from the table, and landed in a heap on the floor. The corpse then tried to right itself, but found no support from its legs. It fell forward and kept its arms straight and crawled toward Newell, who was in such a state of fright he could only back away at an excruciatingly slow pace as if his feet were encased in lead weights.

The corpse craned its neck upwards and looked directly at Newell, the look in its eyes changing from confusion and surprise to feral hunger. Its mouth opened and closed rhythmically. Exaggerated upper and lower canines had re-grown and filled the empty tooth sockets, the gruesome teeth sliding over and above the lips in a snapping motion.

Newell screamed again when the corpse's hands wrapped around his ankles and dragged the undertaker to the floor. Newell scrabbled like a tick but slipped on the slick tiles of the embalming room floor, making no headway as the corpse began to climb on his back and claw its way toward his neck.

Newell flayed his arms backward in an attempt to knock the thing off, but his efforts failed, the vicious mouth of the corpse soon inches away from his neck and the blood flowing there.

And just as the undertaker felt the sharp tip of the canines penetrate his throat, he managed to pull himself out of the nightmare.

———

"OH, HOW HORRID! HOW WRETCHED!" Newell gasped, discovering his bed a ruined rumple of sheets, his blankets a mass of turmoil. He had drenched the bed and his nightshirt with sweat, and, much to his embarrassment, had urinated on himself and the bed covers.

"Oh, how dreadful," he said, getting out of bed.

His legs shook as he made his way across the room to a tiny wash station in the corner where he poured water from a porcelain jug into a wash basin. With unsteady hands, he pulled the nightshirt from his body, let the soiled, wet item fall to the floor and then lathered a bar of lye soap in the water basin.

As he began to wash himself, Newell's mind continued to clear, and he remembered fragments of the nightmare, trembling against those recollections in the early morning's chilly air.

Once satisfied he'd cleansed himself of sweat and urine, he moved his thin frame across the room to the closet where he grabbed a worn robe, covered himself, and then went about the business of stripping his bed of its damp sheets and blankets.

He glanced at the candle and found it had not burned more than a quarter down, then looked at the alarm clock, finding it was a little past two in the morning. He spotted the empty teacup and the bottle of laudanum, vowing a silent oath never to use more than his customary teaspoon ever again.

To his relief, Newell found the wetness on the bed had not soaked the mattress. He would only have to clean the blankets, sheets, and his nightshirt, a chore he planned to do before leaving for Fort Worth later that morning.

He bundled up the wet items and opened the door of his upstairs room, arranged the pile under his arm, then lifted the candle from the bedside table and walked toward the staircase. At the top of the stairs, before he descended, Newell heard a distant sound of something falling somewhere below. His nerves already on edge from the nightmare, he moved with vigilance down the stairs.

At the bottom of the staircase, he bent and placed the pile of wet items on the floor and then made his way to the first wall lamp, lighting its wick with the candle's flame. The strange sound returned about the time the lamp cast light down the hallway leading to the embalming room. Certain something had fallen in that room, Newell froze.

The dream came back to him then with the macabre vision of his father's corpse with the decapitated head attached crawling across the floor in search of blood. Newell shivered and a chill gripped him before he silently chided himself for being so ridiculous. "It was only a bottle or some metal container I left too close to the edge of the cabinet," he thought. "Some item unbalanced enough to fall of its own accord."

Even though he had convinced himself how free of sinister elements the situation was, Newell continued to have a moment of trepidation as he opened the door to the embalming room. The lamplight from the hallway sifted across the doorway, falling in a thin ray on the covered corpse of Eli Snow and the leather bag containing the head which, much to Newell's relief, still rested undisturbed on the metal cabinet.

He felt a rush of air flow from his lungs and shook his head, laughing softly as he walked through the door and lit the nearest wall lamp. As the flame jumped up and light filled the room, the sound came again, the disturbance now more in the direction of the rear entrance. Newell assumed it was only the wind, pushing itself or some object against the rear door.

He walked in that direction, stopping to light another wall lamp, then went to the back door and pressed his ear against it. The cold wood comforting against his head, he smiled as a tap came from the other side, then ceased and returned as the north wind filled his ear with a strange moan. While the intermittent tapping on the outside continued, he opened the door slowly and a piece of splintered wood from some unknown source rolled into the room.

With his head still outside the door, Newell made a quick scan of the area around the rear entrance and found nothing but gusts of wind. He then closed and locked the door, picked up the wood fragment and deposited it in a trash receptacle he kept in a corner of the room.

Content that the source of the mysterious noise had been solved, Newell walked away from the rear door with the intention of leaving the embalming room to retrieve the soiled laundry left at the foot of the stairs. He stopped short when he discovered the body of Eli Snow uncovered and sitting up on the metal table, staring with the same black, distant gaze cast by the corpse's eyes in Newell's recent nightmare.

FIFTEEN

Sheriff Bertram Stone was awakened by someone shaking his shoulder.

After a brief instant of sleep befuddlement, the sheriff found himself gazing into the face of Dr. James Peterson.

"Sorry to wake you, Bertram. It seems we both fell asleep."

The sheriff cleared his throat and then remembered Lucas Cross. "Is Lucas still okay? Did somethin' happen? God, how could I fall asleep like that?"

"Don't feel bad. I dozed off too. That heavy supper didn't help any." The doctor walked over to where Lucas lay unconscious and started his routine vital sign checks, commenting as he took the rancher's pulse, "But nothing happened while we were dozing. His condition is unchanged except that the wounds on his neck are now completely closed. I'll be quite interested in what the physicians in Fort Worth make of that fact."

Bertram got out of his chair and stretched to ease stiffness from sleeping in an awkward position. He glanced briefly at the antique clock hanging on the wall of the medical office and saw it was a little after midnight. "Well, at least we didn't sleep too long. Last time I checked that clock it was almost eleven."

"Actually, I forgot to wind that clock, or I guess I was asleep when it wound down. I have a pretty constant routine in regard to winding it, and the hands will freeze when they cross the number twelve if I don't follow that routine."

"What time is it then?"

"That's what I was going to ask you. You have your pocket watch on you?"

The sheriff pulled the chain out and retrieved his watch. He then flipped it open and found it was almost two fifteen in the morning.

"Guess we did saw a few logs. It's a quarter past two," the sheriff said, winding his watch.

Peterson slipped the blood pressure cuff off the rancher's arm, took out his notepad, and made the entry. "Almost the identical to the readings I took before we drifted off."

The doctor walked to the wall clock then and opened its glass face. After setting the hands at two fifteen, he took the turnkey from its slot beneath the number six, inserted it into the keyhole, and wound the mechanism.

"Guess you and Newell will be headin' up to Fort Worth soon," Bertram said, glancing at Lucas before positioning himself back in a chair.

Closing the door covering the clock's face, the doctor said, "Yes. I doubt there will be any drastic change in Lucas before sunrise, so we need to get him to the hospital there." He then sat at his desk, opened one of the side drawers, and took out a half-full bottle of whiskey. "Care to join me, Bertram?" he asked as he searched through the litter on the desk until he found a shot glass stained a ghostly brown from previous use.

"Little early for me, Doc."

Peterson nodded, poured a shot, and lifted the glass. "Then

here's to us night owls." He moved the glass to his lips when, simultaneously, a loud crash accompanied by a terrible scream came through the walls of the medical office.

The doctor sat the glass down abruptly, spilling some of the whiskey. He stared at Bertram. "Good Lord! That came from Newell's place."

But the sheriff was already on his feet and headed out the door of the medical office, so Peterson jumped up and followed.

Finding the funeral parlor's front door locked, the sheriff beat on it and shouted, "Newell! What in the hell's going on in there!?" He then beat harder on the door.

"Newell!" the doctor, standing behind Bertram, cried. "Let us in!" Another bloodcurdling scream filled the air.

"To hell with this," the sheriff said.

He pulled out his Colt .45 and smashed its butt through the door's windowpane, shattering the glass. Bertram then slid his right arm through the opening, a jagged piece of glass slicing his shirt sleeve and cutting his arm. But he paid no attention to the laceration as he was too busy feeling for the doorknob and its latch. When he finally found the latch and unlocked the door, Bertram rushed into the front of the funeral parlor with Peterson right behind. They were met with yet another shriek and a noisy crash of what sounded like falling metal.

"It's coming from the back. The embalming room, I think," Peterson said, the two men then rushing down the narrow, dimly lit hallway, the door to that room standing open with Newell Scruggs, dressed in a worn bathrobe, backing out of it.

"Newell!" Bertram cried. "What...?"

Before the sheriff could finish, the undertaker's head jerked around, a look of absolute terror in his eyes stopping Bertram and Peterson dead in their tracks. The face confronting them bore little resemblance to the normally sullen undertaker.

Newell's eyes stared wildly, his mouth agape as spittle flecked out from rapid breathing. "Help me!" he shrieked. "It's…"

Newell was suddenly thrust backward by some unseen force and slipped and fell hard to the floor, Bertram and Peterson watching in shock as the man scrambled for purchase to rise into a sitting position using a nearby metal stool, which he then held above him. Then they saw what had pushed the undertaker to the ground. It was all either could do not to shriek themselves, for standing in the embalming room's doorway, silhouetted by light behind it and slightly illuminated by the wall lamp in the hallway, stood the naked corpse of Eli Snow.

Peterson's initial thought was not how a corpse could be standing in the doorway of Newell Scruggs' embalming room, but rather how it could be standing on broken femurs, those bones somehow knitting back together at unnatural angles sufficiently enough to support the bulk of Eli's body.

The corpse focused its attention to the men standing behind the prostrate body of Newell Scruggs. Eli's face was a mass of muscular twitches, his eyes glassy, startled, and confused. He turned his head to the side like an inquisitive dog, nostrils flaring as if detecting a scent.

His head then abruptly straightened, his lips pulling back over upper canines emerging behind the old ones, pushing them up and out with thick, sharp replacements. A growl came from Eli's throat as he moved forward in a rickety gate. His naked body was covered by so much hair he resembled something part ape, part human. And for some reason his genitals were swollen, his huge, bloated testicles grotesquely swaying as he trudged forward.

The doctor glanced at Bertram and noticed the sheriff's bloody sleeve. "You must have cut yourself when you broke that front door window, Bertram." Then realization struck Peterson. He turned back and watched as Eli attempted to move forward.

"By God, he smells it," Peterson said, still bewildered by the scenario in front of him.

Bertram, mystified and trying to accept the reality of the situation as much as the doctor, asked, "What? Smells what?"

"Your blood. That thing smells your—" But before the doctor completed his statement, an enormous roar of gunfire erupted by his left ear, momentarily jarring him. He grabbed the left side of his head, now filled with a thunderous buzzing, and glanced up and found the corpse no longer stood in the doorway but was now lying partially back inside the embalming room.

Through the dizzying numbness in his head, Peterson heard a soft click. He turned to the sheriff, who had cocked his Colt .45 and was taking aim at the fallen corpse of Eli Snow. "Don't shoot that thing again!" the doctor cried over his ringing ears.

Bertram gave the doctor a puzzled look, then again took aim at the corpse.

Peterson grabbed the sheriff's arm. "Please, Bertram. I'm not going to hear a thing in my left ear for weeks now thanks to that canon of yours. Hell's bells, I may be permanently deaf in this ear because you fired that thing so close to my head."

The sheriff looked at Peterson with that same puzzled look before turning his attention back to the corpse, which now showed signs of movement.

A look of incomprehension spread over the sheriff's paling countenance. "Cain't be," Bertram said in low whisper. "Cain't be."

The doctor steadied himself and bent down to tend to Newell, who had shown no signs of life since being pushed to the floor, his arms still stiffly extended, grasping the metal stool.

When Peterson slid his hands under Newell's shoulders to lift him from the floor, the undertaker became swiftly animated and shrieked.

"Newell!" the doctor shouted. "It's me, James Peterson. For

goodness' sake, don't scream anymore. My having one eardrum shattered is quite enough for one night!"

Newell looked up at the doctor's looming face and attempted to get up, tossing the stool away as he did. Once Peterson had him on his feet, the undertaker grabbed the doctor in a death grip and buried his head in the doctor's chest where his frantic gibbering was both blessedly muffled and rendered incoherent. As he was trying to calm Newell, the doctor saw the sheriff's finger tighten on the revolver's trigger.

"I shot that man directly in the heart," Bertram said. "He cain't be itchin' to get up again." He glanced over at the doctor, whose body was still covered by the nerve-shattered Newell Scruggs. "You must have missed somethin', Doc. Snow couldn't have been dead, and, by Jesus, he cain't be tryin' to get up right now. Not after I just blowed a hole in his chest."

Peterson moved the undertaker toward Bertram. "Get him off me," he said, trying to push Newell away.

"I'm not taking my eyes off Snow," the sheriff answered and prepared to fire again. "You take care of Newell, and I'll make sure Snow don't get up again."

"Newell," the doctor said as calmly as he could. The undertaker raised his head from the moist chest it was buried in and stared at Peterson with the same terrified expression. "Look, Newell, you've got to get a grip on yourself. Bertram and I are here to help you. Understand?"

The undertaker's wide eyes seemed to take Peterson in and, while still sporting that look of horror, nodded slightly, and released his tenacious hug.

"Good," Peterson said, still fighting a buzzing head. "Bertram," he said as he directed Newell toward the sheriff. "Please don't shoot at Eli anymore." He watched the jaw muscles tighten on sheriff's face. "Bullets will not help. Trust me."

Newell stood behind the sheriff and let out a whine when he looked over Bertram's shoulder and saw the fallen corpse attempting to rise.

"Just take it easy, Newell," Peterson said. "Where do you store your formalin?"

The undertaker didn't quite understand. "Store my what?"

"Your formaldehyde and water solution. Where do you store it?"

"What?" Newell asked. "I don't understand. That will do you no—"

"Goddamnit, Newell!" Bertram blurted out. "Just tell Doc where that...that stuff—whatever he called it—is before Snow gets back up!"

The doctor stared coolly at Newell, who finally said, "There is a liter bottle in the bottom right shelf of the upper cabinet tier behind the embalming table. But I don't see—"

The doctor moved through the embalming room quickly, sidestepping the twisting corpse of Eli Snow on the way to the cabinet. On the bottom shelf of the right tier, he found a glass bottle with the printed label **FORMALIN**. He snatched it away, pulled out the glass stopper, approached the writhing thing on the floor with caution, and then poured the contents of the bottle on it.

The doctor noticed the candle Newell had brought down earlier was still burning on top of the embalming pump. He grabbed it and walked around the groping hands of Eli's corpse before rejoining Bertram and Newell.

"That stuff is flammable, I suppose?" Bertram asked, keeping an eye on Eli.

"Indeed, it is," Peterson said.

"So now what, Doc? We gonna burn that thing and Newell's place along with it?"

"Let Eli get up," Peterson said.

"You crazy, Doc? I think blowin' that thing's head off would do just as good as barbequin' it."

"Just listen to me, Bertram. Let Eli get up and we'll lure him outside."

Newell whined again, and Peterson said, "Just stay behind us, Newell. In case you didn't notice, Eli's not too agile right now. I think we can stay well out of his way."

Eli's corpse righted itself and stood up on twisted legs. It was in a rage now as it lumbered toward the men standing in the hallway. It clicked its teeth together. It snarled and grunted, its eyes wide and glassy and black.

"I hope you know what you're doin', Doc," Bertram said as the men started their retreat toward the front door, the sheriff keeping his Colt on the jerking form of Eli Snow while Peterson held the candle in a firm grip. Newell clearly fought the urge to flee, his knees shaking as he remained behind Bertram, keeping pace with the sheriff.

Once the three men made it out of the funeral parlor's front door, they moved quickly to the middle of the street. Evidently, the loud shot from the sheriff's gun had not disturbed any citizens living at their businesses as the street was empty and silent.

Eventually, the three men stopped and waited, and it wasn't long until the corpse stumbled out of the doorway. The night air seemed to stimulate Eli's corpse. It began to move at a faster pace toward the men, its legs bent at even more unnatural angles as it sped up its gate. Its swollen genitals swung in a grotesque rhythm and slapped against naked, hairy thighs, the smell of the formalin pungent in the air.

When the corpse entered the street, the doctor told Bertram, "You may shoot Eli now."

The sheriff seemed stunned. "But you said it didn't do no good, Doc. I thought you was goin' to burn that thing."

"Please, Bertram," Peterson said, moving away to protect his damaged eardrum. "It will knock him down."

The corpse had cut the distance between itself and the three men. In exasperation, Newell cried out, "For goodness' sake! Someone please do something!"

Bertram took aim at Eli's head and fired. The rear of the corpse's skull burst into fragments, a black stream jetting from it spraying the ground with gore.

Eli's body fell backward and landed with a dull thud. The doctor walked up and gazed in astonishment as the body once again struggled to get up.

"I'll be damned," Bertram said. "Should I shoot it again?"

Peterson held up his hand and then tossed the burning candle on the jerking form, which was immediately consumed in a whoosh of flames.

The doctor backed away. He, Bertram, and Newell stared as the body continued to twitch, even managing to utter a coarse moan as flames fed on it.

The doctor felt a chill from the cold night and shuddered. "I guess I shouldn't have readily dismissed all the superstitions I've come across over the years."

"There ain't no way Snow was dead," Bertram said. "These things just cain't be."

Newell gathered his robe snugly about him. "I'm afraid I have to agree with the good doctor, Sheriff," he said with an unsteady and fragile voice, glancing painfully at the burning corpse. "I too have seen some bizarre aspects of this world."

———

THIS TIME the shot from Bertram's .45 had disturbed a few residents. Molly and Hunter Cooper came down the back stairs of their apartment above the Koffee Kup Kafe, Hunter dressed in a nightshirt covering his long johns, his wife Molly bundled in a heavy cotton sleeper over which she'd placed a thick bathrobe. Hunter had instructed their daughters to stay put until he and Molly found out what was going on.

Once down the back stairs, they ventured cautiously into the street. When Hunter saw the three familiar men, he grabbed Molly's hand and hurried her along to where Bertram, Peterson, and Newell stood

The sheriff heard footsteps approaching and turned around, seeing other sporadic lights had come on down the street and catching a glimpse of Abraham Tanner's head poking out of the General Mercantile's entrance. "Appears we have disturbed our sleeping citizens," Bertram said. "Suppose they'll want to know what a burning body is doing in the street."

"Good Lord!" Hunter said as he and Molly stopped short and covered their mouths and noses. "What in heaven's name is going on, Sheriff?"

The fire had gone from an inferno to a smolder, the corpse motionless, the smell of burnt flesh and formalin filling the cold night air.

Peterson stepped up to offer his altered truth before the sheriff could say anything. "Eli Snow came after Newell," the doctor explained to the shocked couple. "Eli had a high a fever. I was treating him at my office. Bertram was there to help, and we both fell asleep. Eli wandered next door. The poor man was out of his mind and attacked Newell."

"Oh, dear," Molly said and tentatively patted the undertaker on the shoulder. A few sparks burst above the body in the street momentarily startling Molly and the others. She covered her nose again. "What a stink! Is that...Was that Eli?" She pointed at the glowing form in the street.

"I'm afraid so," Newell said, seemingly feeling better now that other people had arrived. He then decided to continue the doctor's fabrication. "I was in the embalming room. I couldn't sleep, you see, and decided to catch up my reagent inventory. I was measuring out some formalin when Eli burst in. It was careless of me not to have locked the front door."

"How terrible," Hunter said. "But how did he catch fire?"

"He accosted me, and we struggled," the undertaker said, now caught up in the invented drama. "He was much more powerful than myself and almost had me down. I threw the chemical on him. It injured his eyes and he backed into a candle I had there for light." He glanced at the tentative stares from the sheriff and Peterson. "Eli burst into flames," he continued. "He ran into the street and fell down there. It's just a lucky thing Dr. Peterson and the sheriff were awakened by the noise. He and Sheriff Stone were keeping the vigil on Eli, you see, and they both had dozed off."

"But the gunshot?" Hunter inquired.

"He was coming directly at us," Bertram stated. "I had no choice."

The sheriff turned back to take another look at the smoldering corpse when, incredibly, Eli's body rose and started ambling toward them. This sudden and surreal action shocked the sheriff so much he dropped his gun. Molly, Hunter, and Newell screamed simultaneously as the burnt figure hobbled forward. And by the time Peterson quickly retrieved the Colt and handed it to the sheriff, Eli Snow's corpse made one final motion, lifting its arms as if searching for something to grab before falling forward, twitching a few moments before it stilled.

The sheriff cocked the Colt's hammer and was intent on shooting the devilish, unexplainable thing at his feet when Peterson grabbed Bertram's hand and pushed it down to lower the weapon. "I think Eli's gone this time," the doctor said in a hushed voice.

Hunter moved close to the body. "Reflexes," Newell said to

Hunter. "It happens all the time. Sometimes even many hours after death."

"Poor man," Molly said.

From behind, Bertram heard the voice of deputy Howard Sparks. "Sheriff! Sheriff! What's goin' on?"

Bertram turned and found the deputy running toward the group gathered in the street. He holstered his gun and walked toward Howard. "Drawed the short straw, didn't you?" he asked.

Howard's face was red from where he had fallen asleep on his arm, his shirt half tucked in his trousers. "Yep." He slowed down his run to a fast walk. "Gus got the evening duty; I got the midnight run." His eyes widened at the burnt remains of Eli Snow. "What in the world?" he asked while tucking in the rest of his shirt.

"I'll tell you about it later," the sheriff said. "Go down to the livery stable and get some horse blankets so we can extinguish what's still smolderin' on that body."

"But?"

"Never mind. Just go on and do what I say. You can advise me what you and Gus found out about them Davenport brothers when we're finished here."

"Oh yeah, about them two. They took out this afternoon. Couldn't find hide nor hair of them. Only thing they bought was some coffee and jerky at Tanner's. Least that's what Mr. Tanner told Gus. You don't think they came back and had somethin' to do with this, do you?"

"I said I'd talk to you about it later. Now go get them blankets."

The deputy shrugged his shoulders and headed in the direction of the livery stable as Bertram walked back to where the others stood staring at the remains of Eli Snow.

"I was about to get up anyway before we heard the shot,"

Molly was saying to Peterson and Newell. "Me and Hunter will go on back to the café and get some breakfast started. Y'all come on over after you get finished here with poor Mr. Snow. You'll need some coffee and eggs after this night."

"Unless you need my help, Sheriff," Hunter said.

"We'll get this cleaned up, Hunter," Bertram said. "Much obliged for the offer of breakfast, Molly. We'll get over to the café as soon as we see to Snow here."

Hunter nodded and walked with Molly toward the café, their heads bobbing in active conversation.

The deputy arrived back from the stable with two bulky horse blankets in his arms. Bertram took them and covered the smoking corpse, then glanced at Peterson and saw a look of worry cross the doctor's face. "Don't worry, Doc. I doubt Eli will ever be getting up again."

"Hell, I thought Eli was already dead," Howard said. "Least ways that's what Doc told us last night."

"I said we'll talk about it later, Howard," said the sheriff.

"What I'm concerned with has nothing to do with Eli Snow," Peterson said, walking briskly in the direction of the medical office.

Bertram then realized what the doctor was talking about "My God. We forgot all about Lucas."

"Lucas?" Howard asked.

"Never you mind right now," Bertram said. "You stay by this body, Howard." The sheriff then cast a look at the rattled under-taker. "Come on, Newell. Let's go on over to the Doc's."

Newell nodded and walked with the sheriff toward the medical office.

"But, Sheriff," Howard said, glancing at the smoke rising from under the blankets. "Shoot." He shrugged and looked both confused and resigned to that fact. "Wish Gus had drawn that short straw."

When the sheriff and Newell arrived at the medical office, they found the front door wide open and went inside, discovering the doctor standing by an empty examining table, the sheets once covering Lucas Cross scattered on the floor.

Peterson sighed, looked at Bertram and Newell, and remarked, "Well, Lucas can't have gone too far. Not in his condition."

Sixteen

D r. James Peterson wore a weak grin. "Abraham didn't seem very enthused about us storing Eli's remains in his freezer at the mercantile. And I don't think Newell was all too cheerful about that decapitated head remaining at the funeral parlor."

Sheriff Bertram Stone, positioned behind the steering wheel of the multifunctional Ford, glanced over at the doctor. The sheriff's right arm now throbbed from the cut inflicted when he'd broken the funeral parlor's front door glass. Twitching his bicep, he felt a sting run the length of his arm. "No, I don't think Abraham cared for me throwin' my legal weight around, and Newell is plain spooked. Gus wasn't too pleased at bein' waked up so early, either."

Bertram kept the vehicle at a slow, steady speed, he and Peterson keeping a vigil for Lucas Cross on each side of the roadway leading to the Cross ranch. The sheriff had sent his deputies, Gus Greenwood and Howard Sparks, in the opposite direction to the north. Hunter Cooper and Abraham Tanner had been temporarily deputized by the sheriff, one sent west and the other east just in case Lucas Cross was confused and didn't take the path back to his ranch. Newell Scruggs asked to be allowed to join in the search party, but Bertram and Peterson agreed the undertaker had experienced enough excitement for one night and suggested he get some rest.

Peterson, having seen the sheriff's prior grimace, remarked, "I'd better have a look at that arm when we get back to town. It may need suturing."

"Might need some sewing all right. But I'm more concerned with locatin' Lucas right now."

"I doubt he came this way." The doctor watched the Ford's headlights spread out on the roadside. "We'd have come across him by now."

"You think so?"

"He was in such a feeble state I can't believe we didn't find him in town. I don't see how it's possible he could have wandered very far from my office."

The sheriff gritted his teeth, his eyes tired, their lids heavy, his injured arm aching. "Hell, I don't know what to believe anymore. If a supposed corpse can get up and walk, I guess anythin' is possible."

Peterson rubbed his head, holding his hand over his ear and grimacing. He knew the gun fired next to his ear and mounting fatigue conspired to bring a serious headache his way. "I am unable to explain what happened to Eli Snow. He had no pulse and no blood pressure. His pupils were fixed and dilated. There were no sounds of breathing at all. Clinically, he was dead."

The sheriff freed an irrational giggle and said, "There has to be some reason, Doc. Dead things don't get up and start walkin' around. Hell, I'm not sayin' you don't know what you're doin. It's just...Well, if Snow came back to life, I suppose we really should keep a close look see on the head in that bag. It might be grinnin' from ear to ear and us none the wiser!"

"I imagine there could be some rational explanation, Bertram. But damned if I can think of one."

"There has to be somethin'. Couldn't some weird disease maybe cause a body to do what Snow's done?"

The doctor removed his glasses, rubbed his eyes, put his glasses back on, and then took up his vigil through the passenger window again. After a few minutes, he said, "I've heard of cases of catalepsy making a person appear to be dead."

"Cata-what?"

"The victim's muscles go rigid. Their heart slows down to an imperceptible rate. From what I remember from my medical school days, and from journal articles, victims of the disease have been pronounced dead and then buried. There was one case where a coffin was dug up during a relocation process. Its lid was pulled to one side as if the corpse had tried to free itself. Scratches from fingernails were discovered on the inner side of the lid, further proof the occupant was buried alive."

"Lordy. Did Snow have that disease?"

"His condition certainly didn't present what one would expect to find in diagnosing catalepsy. And then there was the unusual postmortem fusion of Eli's fractured femurs. You certainly can't explain that away with catalepsy."

"But couldn't that be like those neck wounds on Lucas? Those marks were closin' up mighty fast. Couldn't Snow's leg bones have done the same thing?"

"The only possibility—and I mean it's a stretch for any rational mind..."—Peterson continued, "is that there is an undiscovered pathogen at work here. Some bacteria or virus that can make the host appear dead but is also capable of speeding up the immune system and instigating rapid healing." He paused, seeming to consider how absurd that theory actually sounded. "But that would defy anything known to science."

A large shadow fell over the headlight beams as something

dipped in front of the Ford and then disappeared. The sheriff glanced out the window and up into the night sky. "A night hawk, I reckon," he said. Pulling his head back in, he checked the dashboard clock and saw it was almost five in the morning. "Our lights must have fell on somethin' that hawk had a fancy for. Otherwise, it wouldn't have swooped in front of a moving vehicle."

He cleared his throat and glanced at Peterson. "Well, up yonder is the gate to Lucas' place. Guess you was right about him bein' too sick to head this way, unless he veered off the road and is lyin' out in the brush somewhere. Once we check on Donny and Adam, and I get Lucy out of the stable, you can take the Ford back into town and see if Gus and Howard, or Hunter and Abraham, had any luck." He looked out the driver side window again, saying, "'Bout an hour 'til sunup. Once I get Lucy, I'll take a look around on the ride back to Hamilton. I can get into the undergrowth better with my horse than I can this Ford, anyways."

They found the gate to the ranch open. As Bertram turned off and drove over the cattle guard, something ran in front of the Ford. The sheriff slammed on the brakes, sending dust and gravel spraying.

Bertram and the doctor jumped out, each hoping it was Lucas who'd crossed their path. Instead, the cowed and shivering form of Turk stared frantically at Peterson and the sheriff.

"That's Lucas' old dog," Bertram said as he slowly approached the trembling animal. He bent down and held out his hand. "Come on, old boy. We ain't gonna harm you none." He looked at the doctor. "Cain't seem to remember this old hound's name."

Turk's eyes were wide with obvious fear. He hunkered down and kept those eyes fixed on the sheriff.

"Looks like he's been scared by something," the doctor said.

"Looks that way all right."

The sheriff again extended his hand. Turk shuffled backward, looking unable to make up his mind whether to trust this human or not. "Come on, old man. Let's get you in the Ford. It's warm in there. We're headed to your master's place, anyway. We sure wouldn't begrudge you a ride down."

Turk eyed the advancing hand. When the sheriff's fingertips were inches away from the dog's nose, Turk's lips curled back in a snarl, and Bertram quickly pulled his hand back. The dog stood up and growled, barked one dry bark, and then turned and loped away into the darkness.

The sheriff stood up from his kneeling position. "Well, that's fine howdy-do for you," he said with a grin. He turned to Peterson who was also smiling. "Guess he's particular about the company he keeps." The sheriff walked back to the driver's side of the Ford. The doctor slid in the passenger seat as Bertram fired up the ignition and drove toward the ranch house.

———

From the crest of a slope, Turk watched the vehicle descend. The dog turned its head in the opposite direction and gazed at the headstones rising from the diminutive Cross cemetery at the base of the slope. Turk trotted down toward the graves. Once there, he huddled against Bonnie's vacant plot and headstone and closed his eyes. The north wind had now diminished to a sporadic, meandering breeze as a few pellets of sleet began to fall, peppering the old dog's thinning coat.

Turk then nuzzled into the pelt of his inner leg and shuddered.

———

Discovering the front door of the ranch house wide open, Bertram and Peterson entered with caution.

"Adam, Donny?" the sheriff called.

The living room showed no obvious disorder. The fireplace still held a few glowing embers and there was a pile of unwashed dishes and glasses on the sink behind the kitchen table.

"Boys must have gone to bed," Peterson said. "Probably forgot to lock the door. Must have been cracked just enough for the wind to push it open."

"You take a look down that hall." Bertram pointed toward Lucas' bedroom. "And I'll head down here." He walked toward the boys' room.

Near the end of the kitchen table, the sheriff tripped over an empty rye whiskey bottle. It rolled across the wood floor with a clank, prompting Bertram, along with the doctor, to stop and glance down.

Bertram bent and grabbed the bottle, held it up, and chuckled. "Looks like them two got into their pa's hooch." He extended the empty bottle toward the doctor. Peterson grinned and then turned around and walked back down the hall.

The sheriff sat the bottle upright on the kitchen table and continued toward the boys' room. When he got to the end of the hall, Bertram found the bedroom door closed. He then carefully turned the knob and opened it. The room was illuminated faintly by light filtering down the hallway from the wall mounted kerosene lamps. The two beds on opposite sides of the room were empty and neatly made, their covers in place and undisturbed, their pillows fluffed and unruffled by weary heads.

Bertram glanced around and saw nothing but items belonging to young men: a baseball glove on an end table, matching lamps with center supports cut in the shape of wagon wheels, a Winchester mounted on the wall, and a collection of boots poking out from under each bed.

Satisfied there was no one there, the sheriff exited the room and walked back toward the kitchen. Peterson arrived from his search at about that same time.

"Lucas' bedroom," the doctor said, "is unoccupied and looks quite normal."

"Same with Adam and Donny's bedroom." Bertram glanced down at the empty bottle on the table. "Probably got drunk and headed to town. Worried about their pa, I reckon."

"When boys that age get inebriated, there's no telling what they'll do. Their bravado swells. I know that from personal experience," the doctor chuckled.

Bertram nodded. "That's true. Them two might have gone out lookin' for some of the local female flesh around here. Could've forgot all about their pa."

"Adam has already suffered a case of the clap from one indiscretion that I know of. I hope he's learned to be careful," Peterson added, shooting the other man a toothsome grin.

The two men giggled as their own youthful encounters briefly haunted them.

After a while, the sheriff said, "Well, let's go check out the stable. For all we know, them boys may be passed out in the hay."

Peterson held up a small glass container. "Just let me borrow of few of Lucas' aspirins I found at a wash station in his bedroom."

The sheriff nodded and waited until the doctor thumped some of the white pills from the bottle, placed them in his mouth, and crunched them between his teeth.

"Like to take them that way myself, Doc," the sheriff said. "Kinda got a sharp flavor to 'em."

"Gets them into the bloodstream quicker as well," Peterson said, placing the aspirin bottle on the kitchen counter.

The men then walked out of the ranch house, the doctor

making certain the front door was securely closed behind them before they made their way to the livestock building.

Inside the stable, the horses milled nonchalantly around their stations searching the empty feed bags in hope of finding oat flakes. Lucy's head bobbed up as Bertram and Peterson entered, whinnying in recognition of her longtime companion.

The sheriff walked to where his horse was tied and petted the animal. "Good to see you, old girl." He placed a hand on the horse's long face. "Looks like them boys done you quite well for curryin' and a feed bag."

Lucy snorted and shook her head as if in agreement.

"Well," Peterson said. "Those brothers must have gone out on foot. It appears the rest of the Cross' horses are here."

"Maybe they went lookin' for them gals after all and didn't need their rides." Bertram walked away from his horse and gave the stable a good inspection. Finding nothing out of the ordinary, he shrugged his shoulders. "I guess we ought to get goin', Doc. I'll ride around the property just in case them boys are out there somewhere and then head back to Hamilton. You go ahead of me in the Ford and see what the others found in town."

Falling pellets of sleet began hammering the stable's tin roof. Bertram looked up and moaned. "I hope somebody found Lucas. Looks like we're in for more bad weather."

——————

As Dr. James Peterson suspected, Lucas Cross had not made it out of Hamilton. Abraham Tanner and Hunter Cooper, delegated by Deputy Gus Greenwood to search in Hamilton before looking outside of town, had explored the stores on Main Street, waking a few perturbed owners living above their businesses in the process.

It was Hunter who volunteered to search the old warehouse at the west end of Main Street.

The warehouse once served as a general delivery area, but over the years it became a shared storage space for Hamilton's merchants, Newell Scruggs being one of those merchants. Since his funeral parlor had limited space, Newell kept an inventory of surplus caskets there. But it never occurred to Hunter he should check inside those coffins. Why should he? If Lucas Cross was up and walking, he certainly wouldn't crawl in a casket. So after Hunter deemed the warehouse empty of any human life, he left the building and departed Hamilton to search for Lucas, unaware that Lucas, who'd instinctively realized he'd never make it back to his ranch before sunrise, was indeed in the warehouse curled up in a plain coffin with the lid tightly closed.

However, Lucas' sons Adam and Donny were in a different place entirely.

———

REGAINING slight degrees of consciousness while being carried through the thick underbrush of Eli Snow's property, Adam and Donny Cross were still too drunk to believe anything around them to be more than inebriated hallucinations. In fact, both grinned drunkenly as stiff stems of scrub brush scraped across the exposed skin of their arms and faces. And as quickly as they might start to recover, the boys once again passed out under the influence of rye whiskey.

When their minds finally cleared enough to feel part of the real world, the brothers found themselves lying on the dirt floor of a cellar.

Adam rose stiffly. His head throbbed and his stomach lurched. "Believe I'm gonna loose them pintos." He fell to his knees and bent over and heaved.

"Oooo wee," Donny said as he rolled facing away from his brother. "If I didn't feel like pukin' before, I sure will now after smellin' yours." He doubled up in the fetal position and repeated, "Oooo wee."

Adam heaved a second time, the taste left in his mouth a mixture of hot, half-digested beans, sour whiskey, and bile. He took a handkerchief from his pants pocket and blew his nose. Gagging, he said, "I hate it when that stuff goes up your nose. Just makes you want to upchuck some more."

Donny rolled up on his knees. "Damnit, Adam, now I'm gonna spew." But his retching halted when a smell worse than any human vomit filled the air and made him swallow back what threatened to come up seconds before. "God! What's that stink?" His head now clear, Donny became conscious he was kneeling on a dirt floor and glanced at Adam, whose eyes were wide with concern.

"And just where the hell are we?" Adam asked while trying to stand.

But before Adam could stand, a hand swung forward and knocked him down. Donny tried to get up and help his brother and received a similar blow to the head, sending him sprawling.

A figure moved around them in the shadows of the cellar, the horrible stench intensifying. The brothers groaned, their heads spinning.

"Adam. Donny."

The voice was frightening but also familiar to the boys.

Adam pushed himself into a bent position and saw something pale in the gloom. "Is someone there?"

The pale form moved forward. Faded light from a setting moon oozed through the open cellar door and down the steps, its insipid glow falling over the brothers. Donny struggled to get up. He glanced at Adam and caught the outline of the figure approaching. It was small and appeared to glide rather than walk.

"Adam. Donny. My brothers. My family."

Bonnie Cross emerged. The waning moonlight bathed her skin in an austerely white tone, the gruesome features of her face outlined against the harsh contrast of her dark hair.

Adam covered his mouth to suppress a rising shriek while Donny, suddenly thrilled, shouted, "It's her, Adam! It's Bonnie! She ain't dead. She's come back!"

Adam extended a hand and placed it on his brother's shoulder. Donny jerked his head around, a wide, exaggerated smile plastered on his face. "See, Adam. I don't remember her as well as you, but I know that's her. Ain't Pa..."

Donny's words caught in his throat when he saw the pained expression on Adam's face, shaking his head no and saying, "You know it cain't be her. Bonnie's been gone over ten years." He pointed then at the advancing shape. "Whatever that thing is, it ain't our sister."

"No, it is me, your loving sister."

Bonnie's lips parted. Her pointed teeth gleamed when her lips pulled back in a snarl.

"You ain't Bonnie," Adam yelled, gaping at the advancing horror dressed in a moldy, ragged dress. Her deep blue eyes swirled with scarlet waves, her tiny, mottled feet swaying above the dirt floor. He gasped and knew without a doubt what now hovered in front of him had left those footprints in the drifts of snow under the open window in their father's bedroom. "Let's get out of here, Donny." He looked at the rising cellar stairs. "Get up them steps quick!"

Donny struggled to get up and fell down in the process. Adam kept his eyes glued on the thing advancing toward him, certain it would lunge at any minute. But Bonnie's movements slowed instead. She had a mocking grin on her face as she watched Donny finally get to his feet and turn toward the stairs.

Adam backed up. "Go on, Donny. Speed it up, will ya?"

As Donny was about to put his foot on the first step, a large figure moved between him and the stairs, the overpowering stench from before flooding the area.

Donny stared at the decomposing, nude, headless body blocking his way. He backed into Adam and screamed. Adam turned away from Bonnie just in time to see the decapitated body move in jerky motions up the stairs.

"No!" Adam cried as the thing, now at the top of the stairs, reached to the side, grabbed the cellar door, and swung it shut.

The cellar was now almost completely dark, the only illumination being thin moonbeams penetrating cracks in the wood above.

Donny positioned himself close to his brother and they backed away from the floating presence again moving toward them. At the same moment, they found themselves trapped in a corner of hard earth.

Bonnie's grin went flat, her mouth opening wide with hunger.

SEVENTEEN

M olly Cooper hurriedly prepared food for café breakfast patrons who'd be arriving shortly. She was still upset that none of the men from earlier that morning, including her husband Hunter, had taken time to eat before going to hunt for Lucas Cross.

Since her husband had been temporarily deputized, Molly needed assistance in the café and had awakened her oldest daughter, Martha, to help prepare breakfast.

Martha was an attractive eighteen-year-old with thick auburn hair springy with curls. She had her mother's bone structure and would be prone to the same plumpness in later years. But at present her figure was slim and engaging.

"How come Mr. Snow and Mr. Cross got sick, Ma?" Martha asked as she stirred a bowl of biscuit batter.

"No one said nothin' about it yesterday," Molly said, pouring bacon grease on a hot grill. "Seems awful strange Sheriff Stone or Doc Peterson didn't mention it to nobody." She wiped her hands on an apron and went to the ice box, took out a large bowl of blueberries, and brought them to Martha. "I thawed these out overnight. Be a treat for the regular customers and those men out huntin' Lucas. Nice to have some berries around in late fall."

"Yessum." Martha dumped blueberries in the biscuit batter, thought a few minutes and then said, "Sure hope ain't nothin' like that flu bug goin' 'round again. Didn't kill many here in Hamilton, but I heard Dallas and Fort Worth had a lot of poor souls succumb to it."

"That was seven years back." Molly cracked some eggs and let the slick albumin and yolks slide into a metal bowl. "You had just turned eleven. I was scared to death you or your baby sisters would catch it." She then set the bowl of eggs down, grabbed a whisk and started beating the contents. "You're right, though. The sickness hit the big cities hardest. I only heard of a few cases nearby, and they was outside town."

Martha frowned and stopped stirring the batter. "Mr. Cross and Mr. Snow, they's both from out of town."

"That's true, but Lucas ain't been to no big city I hear tell of, and that Eli Snow was nothin' more than a hermit. He rarely come to town for supplies." She emptied the bowl on the hot grill and stirred the eggs as they sizzled and popped. "Anyways, I sure hope Lucas didn't have nothin' catchin'. He's got those two boys and they most likely would come down with it."

Martha grinned, poured out the batter mixed with blueberries on a long cookie sheet, and started molding the round balls she would place in the café's wall oven to bake. "Yeah, that Adam," she said with a chuckle. "He's kinda wild." She glanced up to be rewarded with her mother's glare. Martha cleared her throat and went back to shaping biscuit dough. "Course, that's what other girls around here say." She looked at her mother and added, "I wouldn't know myself."

Before Molly could chastise her daughter about impure thoughts or deeds, the bell above the café's front door sounded.

Hunter Cooper and Abraham Tanner entered, both men the persona of fatigue.

"You two have any luck, hon?" Molly asked Hunter while filling two plates with scrambled eggs, sausage links, thick slices of toast, and a small container of fresh butter.

"Nope." Hunter motioned for Abraham to sit down at the lunch counter.

"Wonder where Lucas could have wandered off to." Molly said. "Doc Peterson said he was real sick."

Hunter gave her a weary look. "God only knows. Maybe Sheriff Stone and the Doc found him."

He moved toward the wall where his apron hung, and Molly stopped him. "You just sit down and get somethin' in that stomach of yours, Hunter Cooper. Me and Martha got things under control here."

Knowing better than to argue with his plump wife, Hunter sighed and sat down next to Abraham who had already dug into his breakfast. Molly brought over two steaming mugs of black coffee and set them in front of the men. Hunter blew on his and slurped loudly with Abraham following suit.

"God, but that's good coffee, Molly," said Abraham. "Wish I could brew up something as devilishly fine as this."

Molly smiled, saying as she placed Hunter's plate down, "Secret's in the grindin', Abraham." She refilled his and Hunter's cups and then called to Martha. "Best get them biscuits in the oven. The regulars will be here soon, not to mention Gus, Howard, Sheriff Stone, and Doc Peterson."

"Gus and Howard are already back," Hunter told his wife, pointing to the scrambled eggs steaming on the grill. "I'll have another dose of those and some more sausage links." He then motioned for her to do the same for Abraham. "Them two deputies told us to meet at Sheriff Stone's office when we got back. They got there a little after Abraham and just ahead of me.

We told them two geniuses we didn't find nothing." Hunter and Abraham both giggled. "As if they couldn't see that for themselves."

Abraham smiled. "Well, they ain't the brightest bulbs in the bunch. That's for sure."

"Hush now, you two," Molly said, but she did so with a smile. "So I guess they'll be comin' over for breakfast?"

"Just as quick as they hash out a report to give to Sheriff Stone," Hunter said. "Course, they didn't find nothin' either."

"Speak of the Devil," Molly said, nodding at the front door.

The little bell above the door sounded again as Gus and Howard, both appearing wearier than Hunter or Abraham, walked into the café. The deputies took off their hats and jackets, hanging them on the coat rack.

"Mornin'," Gus said as he sidled toward the lunch counter, offering Martha a smile and a nod.

"Mornin'," Howard repeated from behind Gus.

"Guess you two are near starvin'," said Martha. She took the breakfast plates her mother had prepared and served the deputies herself.

Hunter and Abraham both looked at Martha, knowing she was sweet on Gus. Molly, on the other hand, frowned. She had bigger plans for her oldest than a dimwitted deputy.

The smell of sweet dough baking soon filled the café, and Molly went to the wall oven and took out the first batch of morning biscuits. Steam bathed her face as she looked with pleasure on the flaky biscuits studded with blueberries. Then she scraped the biscuits off the pan onto a large china plate and brought them over to the counter. She pushed Martha, who was busy chattering about the night's excitement with Gus, with one of her formidable hips and said with a mother's authority, "That's enough flirtin' for now, Martha Cooper. Just you get that second batch of biscuits goin'. More hungry folks are on their way."

Martha and Gus blushed, the ridiculed eldest of Hunter and Molly Cooper turning around briskly before marching behind the counter with a scowl.

Molly glared down at Gus. He gently eased his hand over and picked a blueberry biscuit from the china plate, the snickering of the men at the counter making his ears redder than they already were.

———

AN EXHAUSTED DR. JAMES PETERSON parked the Ford in front of the medical office. He got out of the vehicle, and headed straight for the Koffee Kup Kafe to self-medicate his throbbing head with large quantities of caffeine from Molly Hunter's renowned coffee, instead of his usual tea.

———

AFTER RIDING around the Cross ranch looking for any trace of Adam or Donny and coming across nothing but Turk huddled next to a gravestone in the Cross' small cemetery, the sheriff headed back toward Hamilton at a slow pace, guiding his horse in a zigzagging motion to facilitate searching off one side of the main road and then the other. But still he found no sign of Lucas Cross or the rancher's sons. By the time the eastern horizon revealed a broad band of a faint red and orange peeking under an overcast sky, fatigue from the last few days fell heavily on the aging lawman's shoulders.

Bertram now shivered despite being bundled in his winter coat. The cold morning air, damp with intermittent sleet, filmed his eyes and triggered his nose to run.

"Damned mess we have here, Lucy," Bertram said to his horse. "I'm bone tired, old girl, and I might as well get ready for wide eyed stares from the boys up in Fort Worth when I share the facts of what's goin' on in our normally quiet little county." He raised a gloved hand and wiped his nose. "Lucky I've got Doc Peterson and Newell as witnesses. Course them city fellas are still gonna have a hard time swallowing this situation."

A solitary crow landed on one of the fence posts paralleling the road and cawed raucously, its head bobbing as if in some ancient act of commentary. Bertram glanced at the black omen briefly before revisiting his thoughts. "Hell, them city boys would more than likely believe this danged crow could recite poetry rather than what I got to tell them, even if two other men support my report."

The sleet began to fall with more regularity, the sheriff pulling his coat's collar higher on his neck. Well off the road now, he spotted a thin line of smoke rising in the distance.

"I think that's the Walker place down there, Lucy. Bet they's all gathered 'round a nice warm stove havin' a hot breakfast." His stomach rumbled a loud protest. "As soon as we get back to town, I'm taking you to the stable and givin' you an extra bag of oats along with some shiny apples. Then, I'm dragging my weary bones over to the café and fillin' up with Molly's eggs, bacon, toast soaked with butter and gravy, and about as much coffee as I can drink." He reached down and patted his horse on the neck as they continued their steady pace off the side of the road. "Then, I'm gettin' some sleep before doin' one more thing. Gus and Howard can take over for a while. That's what the state of Texas pays them two for."

He noticed more lines of rising smoke scattered across the horizon, the world waking and preparing for another day whether Eli Snow was dead or Lucas Cross and his sons missing. The sheriff, realizing there was nothing he could presently do to change those facts, pulled back lightly on the reins, brought his horse to a halt, and continued gazing at divergent rising plumes of distant smoke.

Lucy shook her head and whinnied, her bridle clinking harshly in the chilly air.

"Smoke," Bertram said under his breath. "Smoke," he repeated and grinned, urging Lucy forward by gently tapping her ribs with his legs. "I wonder if that half-breed still lives on that steep hill between Jonesboro and Fairy." The sheriff chuckled at the strange name of Fairy, Texas and how out of place it seemed in the rough landscape surrounding it. He shook his head and said to Lucy, "Hell, if anybody can give some sense to all the weirdness that's been goin' on around Hamilton, old Smoke sure can."

PART TWO

Eighteen

Northern Hamilton County Texas
November 4, 1926

After Sheriff Bertram Stone arrived in Hamilton and stabled his horse, he went straight to the Koffee Kup and devoured breakfast. Afterward, he walked over to his office and gathered what information his deputies had in regard to the search for Lucas Cross. He then went across the street to check on Dr. James Peterson and Newell Scruggs and found them both fast asleep in the medical office and decided not to disturb them.

Since the missing persons now included Adam and Donny Cross, the sheriff felt it prudent to notify law officials in some surrounding towns.

After making phone calls to the nearby towns of Gatesville and Hico, Bertram's fatigue conquered him. He closed and locked his office door, unrolled a sleeping bag, and collapsed into a deep sleep, not waking until after noon. When he'd gathered his senses from dreamland, Bertram discovered Deputy Gus Greenwood waiting outside the office door.

"Damn, Sheriff. I thought you'd never wake up," Gus said.

Bertram, still a little sleep drunk, rubbed his eyes and asked, "What time is it gettin' to be, anyways?"

"Half past one in the afternoon. Day's already half shot."

"Anybody come down from Hico or Gatesville yet?"

"Officer Hoat came from Hico. He brought a couple of ranchers with him, but ain't nobody got here from Gatesville."

"Good. Ben Hoat's a wiry devil and a hell of a lawman. Them boys from Gatesville have more miles to travel. I reckon they'll be here directly."

"You want me and Howard to wait for the Gatesville crew, or you want us to start searching with Hoat and his team?"

"Where's Hoat now?"

"Him and the fellas he brought along are over at the Koffee Kup grabbin' some chow."

"Go ahead and get them together when they finish eatin'. I'll send you out with them later. Howard can wait 'til the group from Gatesville arrives."

"You comin' with us, or you gonna wait with Howard?"

"Neither. I'm fillin' up the Ford and headin' down to an area between Fairy and Jonesboro. There's an old boy I think still lives there I want to talk with."

"Think he has somethin' to do with all this?"

"No, but he might have some useful information."

"Uh-huh," Gus said and then giggled, adding, "best be careful around Fairy, Sheriff. Heard they got some bad ass leprechauns roamin' around."

Bertram shook his head. He wanted to scowl but felt more like joining Gus in his joke about a berg named Fairy.

"I'll keep my eyes open, Gus. You get on over to the café. I'm gonna touch base with Doc Peterson and check on Newell before I come back here and meet with you and the Hico group."

"I saw Doc earlier over at the Koffee Kup. Must have been before you got in. He was pretty tired. Newell actually came over and joined him for breakfast and confessed to sleeping in the medical office all night. I suppose even a mortician can get the willies given the right circumstances."

"I think me and Doc and Newell will have the jitters for a while after that event with Eli Snow."

"I thought Doc said Eli was dead that night we brought him to the medical office."

"We ain't quite sure what happened. Doc thinks it might have been some virus or parasite that just made him look dead."

"Howard said it might be somethin' else. 'Cause of them wounds on Eli's neck and all."

The sheriff raised his eyebrows. "Lord have mercy. You two don't get no rumors started about anythin' as crazy as vampires or monsters, okay?"

"I don't believe in them things neither. Howard was just puzzled when he found you all out there with Eli's body burnin', that's all."

"Well, that's what I'm goin' to discuss with that fella I know down Fairy way. Just you go on over to the café and get Ben Hoat and his crew. I'll meet y'all back here directly."

After Gus left, the sheriff headed to the medical office and found both Peterson and Newell sprawled out in chairs and still sleeping. He smiled and let them be, then took the Ford down to the mercantile and filled it at the gas pump, advising a weary Abraham Tanner to put the cost on the city's tab as usual.

About the time Bertram made it back to the courthouse to tell the search party what he wanted them to do, the group from Gatesville, one officer and one volunteer, were parking a newer Model T in front of the Municipal Building.

The sheriff escorted the men to his office where he found

Gus and Howard along with Ben Hoat and his group from Hico.

"Ben," Bertram said. "Good to see you could make it. This here is Officer Randy Sawyer and John Hobbs, who's a volunteer. They came from Gatesville to help out."

Officer Ben Hoat's demeanor was stony and all business. "Bertram. Randy. Mr. Hobbs. I brought along Lee and Ellis Carter from outside Hico. Their pa got about two hundred acres near Seldon. They've helped me out before, so I can vouch for them."

"Okay," said Bertram. "I sure appreciate all you boys comin' here. Let me tell you about the missin' man and his sons."

Bertram filled the group in about Lucas being ill and that the rancher's sons were missing now as well. He then laid out plans and the different areas he wanted the men to cover with Gus and Howard heading up the search parties. He left out any facts concerning the weird events connected to the situation, deciding it was best to treat this as a routine missing person's scenario for now.

After the parties left on their hunt, Bertram got in the Ford and headed out to see if his old comrade, Smoke, still lived on that cliff between Fairy and Jonesboro.

———

Fairy, Texas was founded in 1884 and named after Fairy Fort, the daughter of a Confederate Army captain whose given name was Battle Fort.

Fairy, the girl, never grew above the height of two feet, seven inches. She was married and divorced twice and lived to the age of seventy-three.

The road around Fairy, Texas hugged the side of a cliff. In the valley below was an expansive cemetery originally constructed to honor men who fought and died in the Civil War. The most recent occupants to keep the dead company there being those killed in World War I.

As Sheriff Bertram Stone drove the Ford carefully around the curving road, he glanced down at the odd collection of headstones. Some rose tall and stately while others were plain markers lying flat against the ground. In the older section, some wooden crosses still stood with names of the dead burned into their crossbeams.

As Bertram came out of the curve, he saw a rising cliff in the distance and made out the vague outline of a diminutive structure on top.

"Looks like somebody's livin' there," he said to himself. "If it's Smoke, I hope he remembers me."

The land between Fairy and Jonesboro, Texas was completely different than that of Deer Hollow and Hamilton. The cliffs around Hamilton and Deer Hollow ascended from valleys that rose and fell, some of them being natural hollows. The farmers there flattened their land for fields, but the ranchers left the terrain in its natural shape, allowing their animals to graze on the high slopes and in the low valleys.

Although the towns of Fairy and Jonesboro were in Hamilton County, the stretch of terrain between them was flat. What cliffs rose did so from level earth, the one Bertram approached being the highest in the area. A rough, rocky road wove up its side, and it was on this path the sheriff navigated the Ford.

The vehicle bounced and sputtered ascending the steep incline, Bertram feeling beaten by unseen hands as he was thrown from side to side in the driver's seat. A cloud of dust surrounded him, restricting his vision. He was thankful the windows were rolled up. That amount of dust would produce a coughing fit. But even with the windows closed, a fine powder of dirt infiltrated the Ford, and by the time he reached the top of the cliff, Bertram was in a sneezing frenzy.

The rocky road eventually gave way to a wide path covered with loose dirt and flattened, wild grass. Bertram put on the brakes and let the dust settle, his sneezing soon subsiding. "Damnation." He wiped his eyes and nose. "I hope I didn't go through this ordeal for nuthin'."

When the cloud of dust settled, the sheriff rolled down his windows and drove forward in order to clear out the haze of fine dirt inside the Ford, soon catching sight of the small house off to the east side of the cliff's apex that looked to be no more than a simple shack. Not far from the house stood an open shed.

Bertram pulled in front of that shed and saw a figure bending down beside a chestnut stallion, the right rear leg of the horse held between the figure's knees.

It was much colder this high up so Bertram pulled his coat tightly around him, saying, "Yep. Sure looks like Smoke in there shoein' that horse."

———

CORTEZ ORTIZ MENDOZA never answered to his given name anymore.

The only son of a Mexican bandit and a full-blooded Apache woman, Cortez was a natural tracker, and, after a checkered youth of gunrunning, murder, and drinking himself almost blind, his behavior radically changed when a Texas Ranger named Monroe Fox pulled Cortez's half drowned body from the Pedernales River.

Cortez changed his errant ways after that and joined Fox and Fox's fellow Rangers on searches for individuals fleeing the law. He used his tracking abilities to help bring many a criminal, renegade, or reprobate to imprisonment or a trip to the ever-lasting.

But he was never known or addressed as Cortez Mendoza. He was called Smoke because of his ability to be in and out of a campsite like a 'Wisp of Smoke.'

———

BERTRAM TOOK off his Stetson hat, dusted dirt from it, and then slipped it back on as he walked toward the open shed. The man shoeing the horse never looked up.

"Stone," Smoke said as the sheriff walked into the shed. "Long time no see."

"How in the hell did you know it was me?"

Smoke took the last shoeing nails from between his lips and pounded them into the horseshoe, then released the horse's hoof. He looked up at Bertram and said, "I never forget the sound of a man's walk. Especially if he still wears the same brand of boot."

The sheriff studied Smoke. The half-breed didn't look much different than the last time he'd seen him, years ago. Smoke was not tall but stocky and solid. His face was broad with high cheekbones, his nose completely flat against his face from being broken many times. Dark black hair fell thickly and trailed in braids over his broad shoulders. His eyes were clear and a deep brown—so deep, in fact, they appeared black.

Smoke was dressed in a flannel shirt, frayed denims, and scuffed, worn boots. Even though it was winter, the flesh of his face and hands was still a dark, reddish brown from years of working in the sun.

He laid down his hammer and gave the stallion a light tap on its flank. "Good mount," he remarked to the sheriff with a smile. "You still got old Lucy?"

———

THE COFFEE BERTRAM DRANK from a tin cup was very strong and brought back a flood of memories from his life as a Texas Ranger.

Inside Smoke's home, the sheriff sat at a small table. Smoke sat opposite him. There was no fireplace in the one room dwelling and no furniture other than the tiny wooden table and two chairs. A bedroll lay neatly situated in one corner. The floor consisted of natural earth the home was constructed on.

"Great coffee," Bertram said. "Kept a lot of us goin' when we was on the trail."

"You betcha. My mama raised me on chicory."

"See you still like to live simple."

"Yep. Got all I need up here. Plenty of game around. Natural spring just over yonder near Fairy. My horse and me do just fine."

"Only thing missin' is a Missus," Bertram said with a giggle.

"Tried one of those a few years back. She just never could get use to me or sleeping on the dirt."

"Still sleep on the floor myself. Course, it ain't dirt. Old hardwood."

"Dirt's softer, right?"

"Damn straight it is. I cain't see no stars through the ceilin' of the courthouse basement neither."

A smile spread over the half-breed's broad face. "Those were some hard days. But they were good, too."

The sheriff picked up the metal coffee pot and refilled his cup, blowing a stream of air across the liquid's surface before taking a sip. "Them days are over now. All these modern devices like cars and phones done cut the chase down. I still use old Lucy once and a while, but mostly she spends her time stabled. That's why I take her out every so often. She needs the exercise."

"I'm sticking to the old ways myself. Don't have no plans to change anytime soon. I suppose someone will want to build some fancy house up here one day. They'll probably run me off, but I'll just go find me another spot."

"Don't imagine either of us will live long enough to see too much more modernizin'. Don't think I'd like it much, anyhow."

"See you still wearing a badge. Looks like a sheriff's."

"Cain't seem to get it out of my blood. I thought this job would be a cakewalk compared to what we used to do for a livin'. And up to the last few days, it has been. That's why I come to see if you were still livin' up here. I got some questions for ya."

"Uh-huh." Smoke raised his eyebrows. "You think I been involved in something?"

"Oh, hell no. I remembered you used to talk about things that...well, things that weren't natural."

"You getting scared in your old age, Stone?" Smoke asked.

"I'm startin' to doubt what my eyes see. If the same things hadn't been witnessed by others, I'd think I was gettin' senile."

Smoke got up from his chair. He reached across the table, picked up the coffee pot, walked to the open front door, and poured what was left in the pot on the ground. He came back in and sat the pot near a bedroll in the corner, pulling a leather shoulder bag from behind that bedroll. He reached inside the leather bag, took out a Mason jar filled with a clear liquid, and then came back to the table and sat down, placing the jar in front of Bertram. "Looks like we need a different kind of *strong* if we're going to talk about spooks and such," he said, unscrewing the jar's lid.

The sheriff drank what coffee remained in his cup and then slid his cup over to Smoke. "Don't mind if I do," Bertram said as he watched a clear liquid slide from the jar.

———

By the time Bertram told Smoke the events of the last four days, twilight had painted the sky a deep purple, and a frosty mist surrounded the simple home on top of the cliff.

Smoke sat silent for a while. The sheriff, warmed by the corn liquor, knew the half-breed was considering all he'd heard about the head in the well, the attack on Eli Snow and Lucas Cross, and the strange, horrific resurrection of Eli Snow.

Smoke refilled both cups and then stood and took a kerosene lamp from its wall holder and set it on the table. He removed the chimney, struck a match, and lit the wick. A petroleum smell wafted up with a thin line of gray haze curling around Bertram.

Smoke then sat back down. The dying light outside coalesced with the lamp's glow and threw a soft shadow on the man's face. "I rarely leave this place. But once or twice a year, I ride over to Jonesboro. I don't go to buy supplies. I go to visit my cousins." Smoke leaned back slightly, the motion causing his braided hair to fall behind his shoulders. "Course, they ain't really my cousins. You know that. Cousin is just Injun for all of us havin' the same blood. Anyhow, there's a couple of breeds like me and one full blood from the Anadarko tribe. Most of his people got moved by the government to Oklahoma years ago."

"Indian reform," the sheriff remarked with disgust. "Officials in Washington got tired of the Army's bloodbaths, so they made up all them useless treaties."

"Yep." Smoke took another sip of liquor. "These old boys and me get together down at the local watering hole in Jonesboro. We visit, drink, talk about old times, stuff like that. Not many of us left around here anymore, half-breed or full blood. So we like to make contact to keep up blood bonds."

"This somehow connected to what I been talkin' about?"

"Might be. That Anadarko was acquainted with Eli Snow."

"No joke. How was that?"

"Bought corn liquor from Snow when the old man had a still. Said Snow got drunk with him one time and kept goin' on about how his wife done up and left him not long after he got back from the war."

"Spanish-American War?"

"Yep."

"One of my friends back in Hamilton said he thought Eli was in that war."

"That's what the Anadarko said. Said Eli went on and on about how that she-bitch had gotten knocked up when he was off fightin'. That's where the youngest son supposedly come from according to Eli."

"Well, that ain't an unusual occurrence. Women get lonely and spread 'em for strangers sometimes. Ain't nuthin' spooky about that."

"But it wasn't a stranger. It was Eli's oldest boy."

"*Arlis*?"

"Anadarko never gave no name; just said oldest boy."

"I'll be damned. No wonder Eli turned mean and uncooperative."

"That's not all. The Anadarko said Eli told him his wife come from a family across the border down near Reynosa, Mexico. Her mother was supposed to practice black magic. She was some kind of witch." Smoke started to take another drink but changed his mind and sat the cup back on the table.

Outside the sun had set, the air temperature quickly dropping due to the cliff's elevation. A lone cry from a night bird filtered through the window.

The sheriff shivered and asked, "A witch?"

"Not just a witch, a Tlahuelpuchi."

"Besides being a mouthful of a word, what's the difference?"

"Tlahuelpuchies possess a lot of power. They are said to give themselves body and soul to Satan for this power, participating in black rituals. They sacrifice babies and cannibalize the infant's flesh and drink its blood."

The bird cry came again, louder this time.

Bertram looked over his shoulder out the window. "Good Lord! What the hell's makin' that racket?" He turned back around, rubbing his arms. "Damned eerie noise. now we're talkin' about witchery."

The half-breed grinned. "Only a nighthawk, Stone." He picked up the Mason jar and refilled the sheriff's cup. "Probably after a rabbit or mouse."

Bertram took another drink, then lifted a hand and wiped his mouth. With the lamplight dancing in his eyes, he said, "You really believe in all that superstitious claptrap, don't you?"

"When I was boy down in Mexico, I saw things most Christian white folks would put blinders on for. Hell, Stone, it's all just natural, anyway."

"Natural?"

"Nature lets us walk around. But we are weak under the powers of this earth. Indians accept this, but you white folks don't. Anything unusual happens, you say it can be explained with logic. That's a failing of your race. You are blind to what's right in front of you sometimes."

"Hell, I just wanted to know if you could help me understand what's been goin' on in my once peaceful jurisdiction. I don't need no sermon about bein' white and close-minded."

Smoke chuckled. "Okay, back to your problem then. Those Tlahuelpuchies can get stronger. Move higher up the demonic food chain, so to speak."

"Huh?"

"When they eat human flesh and drink human blood, they can be possessed by a spirit my people call the wendigo."

"So?"

"It can be passed on to their children."

"But I ain't said there's been any evidence of flesh eatin'." The sheriff then remembered the bite marks on Eli and Lucas' throats and his brow creased. He frowned, glanced across the table, and added, "Course, now I ain't so sure about the blood drinkin' thing."

"Eli told that Anadarko he was certain his wife put a spell on the oldest son and then molested him. It wasn't for love or lust; it was to create a monster she could use for her own purpose since the oldest boy didn't seem to have inherited any of her tainted blood. Eli said he suspected his wife performed some kind of black magic ceremony when she got pregnant because that next child came into the world with something bad inside it."

"Bad? You mean like deformed or somethin'?"

"More deformed in its soul."

A slight grin lifted the corners of Bertram's mouth. "That cousin of yours ever say anythin' about vampires?"

"No, but he did say Eli told him they had to keep the youngest son chained up." Smoke paused, his face shadowed by intruding darkness. "Eli said that boy killed the wildlife around their cabin when he was just a small child, and that he ate it raw like a beast."

"So they kept him tied up after that?"

"Not then. The killing of wild animals didn't bother Eli. But the boy started roaming deeper and off Eli's land where he killed some neighbor's livestock, and Eli knew trouble would follow if he let the boy keep it up."

"That would have been Lucas Cross' animals, I imagine. He was Eli's closest neighbor."

"Well, the Anadarko never mentioned any names, but what you say makes sense. Anyhow, when the boy started to grow in earnest, so did his violent nature and Eli had to keep him locked up, especially after sunset."

"I hate to even ask." Bertram felt a little nauseous now from drinking on an empty stomach. "But why after sunset?"

"That's when the fiendish nature came over the boy—that thing the boy's mother produced by her unholy incest with the older son."

"Shoot," the sheriff said. "None of them that was attacked, Eli or Lucas, was eaten on." He placed two fingers on his neck. "They was bit right here. We thought it might be a mountain lion."

"You said that schoolmarm told you the head belonged to Eli's youngest son, didn't you?"

"That's what she said, but the condition of the evidence didn't cause me to feel all that optimistic about her identification." Bertram bent back. The warmth from the liquor was wearing off and he sensed cold air gathering around him, goose bumps covering his flesh. "Course, Doc Peterson down in Hamilton pointed out the empty jaw holes where teeth had been pulled from that head and speculated them teeth to be abnormally fierce. Only thing, if that head does belong to Jacob Snow, then that boy wouldn't have been alive the night Eli was attacked, nor the next one when Lucas was assaulted."

"Maybe that boy ain't the only thing prowling around your town."

"What do you mean? Surely there cain't be more than one of whatever is making mischief?"

"Don't forget, Stone, creatures of darkness like Eli's wife and son can make others, and what they make don't necessarily have to be like them."

"Then what kind?"

"Anything dark and hungry. Children of the Tlahuelpuchi and the wendigo. Creatures who crave human flesh and blood."

"Damnation." The sheriff looked down at his hands for a moment and examined the calluses and scars on them. "Let's say them things do exist," he said in a low tone while still gazing down at his hands and absentmindedly picking at the dry skin of a recent callus. "Just how would they be killed? Does it have to be magic or some other nonsense?"

"My people used to get a medicine man to make potions against evil spirits, but I imagine Christians like you got in Hamilton wouldn't cotton to those superstitions. But anything blessed by a priest or any other man of the cloth might help."

"Lord God. I can just imagine the look on the Catholic priest, Baptist minister, or the Church of Christ reverend in Hamilton if I asked for such a thing. They'd probably think I belong in a loony bin."

"You'd be surprised. Some men of the cloth would more than likely take you seriously."

"Hmpf. I doubt it."

"Well, if all else fails, there's always sunlight or fire. Seems what you told me about Eli coming back from the dead proves a good dose of blazing heat will stop anything."

Bertram felt the weariness of the past few days and nights tugging at him. "Well, guess I took up enough of your time, Smoke. Suppose I'll drift back to Hamilton and see if them search parties come up with somethin'."

"I got an extra bedroll if you want to rest up before morning," Smoke said as he rose from his chair. "Wouldn't mind the company."

Bertram smiled and stood up from his seat. "Naw. I done intruded on your hospitality enough." He extended his hand. "But it was damn good to see you, Smoke, and I thank you for the info."

Smoke firmly gripped the sheriff's hand. "Same here, Stone. Now that you know I'm still above ground, don't be a stranger."

"Maybe you could do the same. You're one hell of a tracker. Suppose you grab what you need and come back to Hamilton with me. We could sure use the help."

The half-breed grinned and shook his head no. "Don't know as I want to come down to anywhere except my rare trip to Jonesboro for those powwows." He hesitated and then added, "But I'll reflect on it."

Bertram nodded. "Take care, Smoke." Then, just as he was about to leave, he asked, "Did Eli ever say what became of his wife?"

"According to that Anadarko, the woman left not long after that second boy was born. Eli said even his wife was frightened by what she'd spawned."

Nineteen

L ight from a rising moon bathed the warehouse where Hamilton merchants stored their surplus items, where Newell Scruggs kept his empty coffins, pale moonbeams breaking through a partial cloud cover seeking cracks in the aged wood and tin.

The nocturnal creatures who resided in the warehouse's high rafters and shadowy corners now stirred, a raccoon peering cautiously from its nest behind some broken, wooden slats. An owl hooted in the dark recesses of the rafters where disturbed pigeons fluttered their weary wings.

And inside one of the coffins, Lucas Cross awakened.

Thoughts infusing Lucas' mind did not belong to him. That man—the rancher, the father—existed no more. In his place a new being dwelled, one consumed with deep emptiness and terrible hunger.

Lucas did remember his family and ranch, but those images seemed more like impersonal photographs. The strange force now flowing through his body burned with one desire: to drink in order to fill a shriveled stomach with hot blood.

Curled inside a coffin too small for his body, Lucas' movements to free himself were hampered and his progress slow. But eventually, he managed to push the coffin lid away.

Moonlight covered Lucas in erratic patches. He was still dressed in long johns, but the chill seeping through the warehouse walls brought him no discomfort, the coldness of his flesh proving a refuge against the elements.

Lucas rose from the coffin and inhaled deeply, the night air filling his nostrils with yearning. He slid over the body of the coffin in a motion more suited to a reptile than a man. His bare feet touched the earthen floor. He straightened his spine and then crouched like an animal preparing to hunt. His nostrils flared. The living creatures in the warehouse filled his nose and palate with luxurious scents. A line of drool hung from his lips in a sticky string as he moved his head from side to side in search of blood.

He ambled in the direction of the raccoon. The creature saw him and quickly retreated back into its nest behind the broken slats of wood, Lucas' snarling face hovering just outside that opening. The raccoon backed further into its den when a hand appeared through the wood slats. The fingers on that hand thumped across the dirt probing for the animal. When the raccoon found itself backed as far as it could go with no opening for escape, it lunged at the intruding hand and delivered a vicious bite. The wood around the broken slats then exploded as Lucas grabbed the animal with his other hand, pulled it to his mouth, and tore into its neck. His new canines were still not completely formed, but the upper points had pushed through far enough to be serious weapons.

The raccoon squeaked briefly as teeth ripped into its throat. The hot blood rushed into Lucas' mouth and pulsated against his palate. He swallowed and sucked for more, but there was not enough blood in the small creature's body to satisfy his thirst.

Lucas tore the raccoon apart and drew out as much blood as

he could from the raw tissue, heart, and other organs before tossing the carcass aside in frustration.

He loped around the warehouse. Aroused by the blood of a living creature, Lucas rummaged around the stored goods. He knocked over some empty coffins and then shredded bags of dry goods from Tanner's store in search of another living being to drink from. But by now even the lowest of creatures had fled the building. Only the unconcerned owl remained in the rafters, gazing down uncaringly at the strange form going berserk below.

The blood from the raccoon was rapidly absorbed by Lucas' body and a sudden jolt of emptiness filled him with a deep pain of hunger he knew must be satisfied quickly or more intense pain would follow.

He hopped easily from the dirt floor to the warehouse's loading platform and then jumped through an open door, landing on Hamilton's empty Main Street.

With his new, acute senses, Lucas sniffed the air. The town seemed dead and closed down for the night. He discovered just the slightest glow from an occasional lamp or candle burning above the stores of merchants residing there.

Lucas moved warily onto a long wooden porch running in front of the stores on that particular side of the street. He came to halt when he passed the Koffee Kup Kafe and inhaled air lingering around the café's front door. The aromas of grease and cooked meat were repugnant to Lucas now, but underneath those cloying scents a soft fragrance rose, one of copper and salt and sweat mixed with the clean smell of powder and soap.

Lucas crept to the corner of the café and looked eagerly up a flight of wooden steps built on the side of the building. He saw a door at the top of those steps along with a small window opening into the room of Hunter and Molly Cooper's three daughters, the window Molly closed against the cold night this time of year but never locked.

The muscles of Lucas' face stiffened, the corners of his mouth drawing back into a grimace of ravenous thirst as he placed one bare foot intently on the bottom step.

———

Sheriff Bertram Stone drove past the open gate leading down to Lucas' ranch house.

On the drive back to Hamilton, Bertram had tossed the conversation with Smoke back and forth restlessly in his brain.

Wendigos? Witches? Tlahue... Hell, he couldn't remember how Smoke had pronounced it, but he knew the word stood for something evil.

He then asked himself, "God, where can such madness end?"

Bertram understood why Smoke would adhere to such legends. It was in the man's blood and heritage. But to think that he, Bertram Stone, a retired Texas Ranger and an elected sheriff could even consider such childish notions came over both incredible and insufferable.

As he passed the open gate, Bertram glanced down at the Cross ranch house. He slowed and pulled the Ford over to the side of the road, then turned the vehicle around and went back toward the ranch.

"Better check and see if Adam and Donny ever came back home," the sheriff said out loud as he passed through the open gate. "Pretty sure one of those search parties has already been out this way today, but it won't hurt none to double check."

When he walked up the ranch house's porch steps, Bertram half expected to find Turk curled up by the front door. But there was no one there, not even the dog.

"Would've probably growled at me anyways," Bertram said,

pausing briefly to knock before entering through an unlocked front door.

It was dark inside. He searched for and found a kerosene lamp and then pulled a book of matches from his shirt pocket, struck one, and lit the wick. Everything looked the same as it had when he and Dr. Peterson had been there before. It was evident the Cross boys had not been back, but the sheriff checked both bedrooms anyway, finding not a soul.

Bertram extinguished the lamp and went outside, closing the front door behind him. He went to the stable and found the Cross' horses standing patiently in the dark. There was enough moonlight for him to find the stash of oats, so he filled the feed bags and untied the animals, certain they would stay put until they had emptied the bags.

Bertram then stepped outside the stable into an empty corral where he found the gate secured. He leaned against the wooden slat poles and pulled out a metal tin from his shirt pocket. He removed a rolled cigarette from the tin, then took a book of matches from his pocket and lit the cigarette. Bertram pulled a long drag and held the smoke deep in his lungs. It occurred then to the sheriff this was the first real moment of relaxation he'd had since he and Lucas found Eli Snow in that cave.

"How could so much go wrong in such little time?" Bertram asked himself.

He glanced up at the night sky. An erratic collection of clouds partially blocked the moon and stars, but he saw enough of the heavens to be touched with melancholy, the mood completed when one of the horses wandered out into the corral. He recognized the animal. It was Lucas' black mare.

Bertram walked to the mare and gently patted her flank. The horse snorted briefly but did not move away, eagerly accepting the admiration of the man by her side.

"Never got your name, gal," the sheriff said.

The smell of the animal, the dirt terrain of the corral, the cold night, the open land before him, and the sky above drove nostalgia deeper into Bertram's soul. He took the last puff of his cigarette and dropped it on the dirt, grinding it under his boot heel.

"Me and Lucy spent many a night under the stars," he said to the horse. The animal's ears flicked briefly, and it tossed its head as if in understanding. "Kinda wished I was doin' that again."

The other two horses strolled out, ambling to where Bertram and the mare stood. He patted them, saying, "Y'all need to stretch your legs awhile. I'll leave you out tonight. If it gets too cold, I know you three got sense enough get back inside. If them boys don't show up by mornin', I'll send Howard or Gus out to see y'all get tended to."

Bertram gave the horses one last pat each before walking back to the stable. There he emptied more oats into the feed bags and took a final, deep breath of the animal and earthy smells. He then went out of the stable and made his way back to the Ford parked in front of the ranch house.

———

HUNTER AND MOLLY COOPER, exhausted by the day's events and their own physical activities, slept deeply, their snores reverberating in the small bedroom. Across the hall, their middle and youngest daughters, Rose, a month shy of fourteen years, and Katy, twelve, slept fitfully. The Cooper's oldest child, Martha, had slipped out when she heard the first snores from her parent's room. She knew from experience they would be dead to the world until the early hours just before sunrise. Martha had arranged a clandestine meeting—not the first one of these events either—at the livery stable with Deputy Gus Greenwood. The stable was mostly unattended at night as Hamilton's deputy on duty periodically checked it and the other buildings on Main Street.

Tonight, the deputy on watch was conveniently Gus, and Martha planned to take up most of his shift in the livery stable's hayloft with her continuing sex education studies. They'd agreed on this meeting after the search parties from Hico and Gatesville found nothing, each having gone back to their respective towns following a substantial supper at the Koffee Kup Kafe.

So the three diminutive beds across from the oblivious, slumbering Hunter and Molly Cooper, held only two bodies, and those, unlike their parents, dozed restlessly.

———

Katy moaned and turned over as the window to their room slid up while Rose lifted herself up slightly in bed at the soft sound of the sliding wood. Rose rubbed her eyes and saw the window curtains part as a hunched figure passed through them. She gasped and tried to scream, but an icy hand gripped her throat. Her eyes widened as moonlight fell on the face of Lucas Cross. His breath flowed hotly across her face, reeking of old blood.

Lucas held Rose's throat in a steel grip. She beat at him with her fists and kicked at him with her feet. She could not breathe, her oxygen-starved lungs burning in her chest. Just as her vision faded into a mass of swirling, black dots, Lucas released his hold on her throat.

———

Rose then slumped down, fighting to pull air back into her lungs. Lucas glanced over briefly at Martha's empty bed and then looked at the one next to it where he was met by a frightened stare from Katy.

Lucas indulged in a feral grin when he saw Katy's mouth begin to open in what would most assuredly be a wail of terror. But his speed was alarming, and he had her mouth covered before she could utter a sound.

Lucas desired both the girls' blood and wanted it immediately. Just the thought of such gluttony made him groan, but he intuitively felt there was danger for him if he bled the sisters there.

Just as he'd done with her sister, Lucas grabbed Katy by the throat and strangled her until she passed out. At that same moment, Rose had recovered enough to stumble out of bed. She fell on the floor with a loud thud and made a raspy coughing noise. Lucas covered her mouth and pinched her nostrils together until she lost consciousness again.

Lucas then gathered Rose under one arm and Katy under the other. He paused momentarily to see if anyone else in the house had been disturbed. After hearing wet snores from across the hall, he smiled and slipped easily out the open bedroom window.

———

"DON'T STOP, GUS," Martha pleaded in a strained whisper.

They were in the upper loft of the livery stable. The only other creature in the place was the sheriff's horse, Lucy, who rested contently below with a full stomach.

Martha thrust herself against Gus and pulled him deeper inside her. Even though the air was chilly, the couple sweated.

"Almost there." She covered his mouth with her own to muffle a cry of passion. Their movements then halted, and Gus rolled off her and pulled up his jeans. With amusement, Martha watched his clumsy efforts at dressing. "You in a hurry or something?" she asked, restoring her cotton panties to their station between her legs.

Gus rolled the condom off his dwindling erection and shoved it under the mass of hay they'd been cavorting in. "Yeah, sorry," he said as he buckled his belt. "Sheriff Stone might be back anytime now. The way things been goin' on around here lately, I don't want to get caught with my drawers down." He winked at Martha and snickered at his own joke.

"Real funny, Gus."

Martha stood and straightened out her dress. Gus brushed errant patches of hay from her back, and she did the same for him. Before he put on his hat and holster, she pulled one long hay strand from his hair and giggled, running it over her tongue. "When can we meet up here again?"

"Depends on what Sheriff Stone wants to do next." Gus held on to her hand as she backed up to the hayloft's ladder and lowered her foot to the top rung. He followed her down, saying as he did, "We ain't found a trace of Lucas or his boys. Sheriff Stone's gonna be real disappointed."

After stepping off the ladder, the two embraced and kissed.

"Course, we could get married," Gus said with his lips still on Martha's. "Wouldn't have to sneak around none then." They broke the kiss. "Besides," he added with a laugh. "That dry hay's beginnin' to chafe me in some private areas."

Martha struck him playfully on his arm. "You devil."

Gus retrieved her coat from a hook on the stable's wall and held it as she slid her arms inside. He then put on his coat.

"And as for marriage," Martha said, sliding her arm inside his. "Why ruin all the fun we're havin'?"

———

"Now who's the devil?" Gus asked while peeking outside the livery door to make sure the coast was clear.

Still arm in arm, the couple entered an empty street and walked in the direction of the Koffee Kup Kafe. They conversed in general chit chat and giggled. When they passed by a narrow alley separating Tanner's General Mercantile from the post office, a movement caught Gus' eye.

He stopped abruptly and whispered, "Shush, Martha."

Martha poked him the ribs. "Don't you shush me, Gus Greenwood. I'll—" She stopped talking when something moaned, cutting off her threat.

Under the shadows of the two buildings surrounding it, the alleyway was almost totally dark. Gus stared hard into that darkness and could only make out a peculiar, hunched shape dressed in something a bit lighter in contrast to the gloomy atmosphere around it.

The sound of slurping then drifted down the alley along with an eerie groaning.

Gus pulled his revolver from its holster and motioned Martha to get behind him. He inched forward and asked, "Someone there?" There was no answer, so he moved closer. With the open palm of his free hand, Gus signaled Martha to stay put.

As Gus approached the hunched figure, the slurping noises got louder, reminding him of pigs grunting with pleasure while gorging on slop from a trough.

Gus cocked the gun's hammer and took aim at the shape while slowly moving toward it. "If you're a man, you best get up and show yourself. If you're a critter, you're about to be a dead one."

At the sound of the deputy's voice, the feeding noises ceased. Gus stopped walking then and held the gun steady on the form. Whatever crouched in the dimness now stood and the deputy saw it was a man. And for some crazy reason, Gus could have sworn that man was dressed in long johns.

"Who's there?" Gus asked and grinned at the silliness of finding someone out on this cold of a night dressed only in unions. "That you, Mr. Tanner? Been samplin' some of that hooch you keep hid in your office?"

By now Martha, her curiosity aroused, had crept up behind Gus. She covered her mouth to suppress a rising laugh when she too saw the figure standing in long johns.

Gus lowered his gun. "Come on out now, whoever you are. Let's get some hot coffee in you." He then added with a snort, "If you got the backdoor open on them thermals, you sure gonna need that coffee."

"Oh, Gus," Martha hooted, no longer able to contain her laughter.

Gus whirled around. "Martha, I thought I made it clear you was to stay put! This might only be a drunk, but you never know what—"

A snarl rose from the dark alley, escalating to a growl much like that of a cornered, mad dog. Chills shot up Gus' spine. He turned back toward the figure standing in the alley.

"Martha," Gus said with his back to her. "You get on back home and wake your pa. Tell him to fetch Howard and get down here." He then raised his gun and took aim again. "This ain't no drunk."

Before Gus could fire or Martha had time to turn and run, Lucas Cross' blood-stained body crashed through the couple, knocking them roughly to the ground.

Twenty

Bonnie Cross' signals were now so mixed and confusing, the headless thing no longer felt her influence. The thing had no way of knowing she had drank so much of Adam and Donny's blood she was as inebriated as the boys from the rye whiskey flowing in their veins. In fact, Bonnie barely made it back to her mound of loose dirt in the darkened corner of the storm cellar before sunrise, something she was usually very good about.

The headless thing instinctively, rather than by her design, moved from its position directly beneath the cellar's door where holes in the wooden beams allowed light to cast probing rays on the earthen floor below.

Adam and Donny Cross were sprawled in a corner near the cellar steps. They were barely alive, most of their blood taken by the predatory thing that was once their sister.

Donny regained consciousness late that afternoon and attempted to crawl to the ascending cellar steps, dizziness and nausea ultimately stopping his efforts. When he tried to get a view of his surroundings, the world spun around him. He then dry heaved, the fluid in his mouth tasting awful.

"Oh," he moaned. "Adam, I'm dreadful sick."

But Adam was still passed out. In his subconscious, the words *dreadful* and *sick* echoed faintly but meant nothing to his oxygen starved brain. Adam had been attacked first, Bonnie greedily draining almost all his blood. Donny had struggled to get away, but the headless thing had held him firmly until Bonnie was ready to drink more.

"Adam," Donny pleaded in a raspy voice. "You got to get up. We got to get out of here."

————

ADAM FELT HIMSELF RISE. He grabbed Donny and hoisted him on his back and began climbing the storm cellar steps. At the top, he pushed open the door and swung it to the side, emerging with his brother into bright sunlight.

"Thank God, Donny!" Adam said. "We made it. We made it."

He tried then to take a deep breath and the sky above him clouded. He could not fill his lungs with air. He strained harder and his vision faded. He opened his eyes and saw he had never left the dirt floor of the cellar, never having grabbed his brother and escaped.

Adam tried to speak, but there was no air left in his lungs to do so. The last thing he saw before his heart stopped beating was the heel of Donny's boot dug in the dirt.

————

WHEN SHERIFF BERTRAM STONE pulled the Ford onto Main Street, he saw lights burning in the medical office and funeral parlor. Deputy Gus Greenwood stood in the medical office's doorway while Deputy Howard Sparks stood in the doorway of the funeral parlor. Seeing this, the sheriff was optimistic Lucas, Adam, and Donny Cross had been found by the search parties and felt a surge of hope as he got out of the Ford and walked to the medical office. That hope quickly vanquished when he saw the look on Gus' face.

"It's bad, Sheriff," Gus said.

"What happened?" Bertram glanced over his deputy's shoulder and saw Martha Cooper lying on the examining table in the medical office with a cloth covering her forehead. Dr. James Peterson stood next to Martha, taking her pulse. Bertram and Peterson made eye contact, the doctor, who appeared exhausted and pale, shook his head and frowned.

"The bad news is about Lucas Cross, Sheriff," Gus said

"You found Lucas? What about Adam and Donny?"

Gus stared at Bertram with bloodshot eyes. "No sir, we ain't found them boys. We didn't find their pa, neither. He found us, in a manner of speakin'."

The sheriff saw the strain on his deputy. "Just go ahead and spit it out, Gus. I'm prepared for about anythin' these days."

"Well, me and Martha was out strollin'. I was on duty but didn't see no harm in visitin' with her while I made my rounds."

"That's fine. Go on."

"We heard somethin' in the alley between Tanner's store and the post office. It sounded like somethin' eating. It was a messy sound, like pigs in a ditch." Gus removed his hat, nervously rubbing the brim between his thumbs. "I told Martha to stay behind me, and I pulled my gun and went down the alley. I asked who was down there, and somethin' stood up that looked like a man. Funny thing, though; he only had long johns on, so I thought whoever it was they was just drunk. Thought it might be Mr. Tanner. He's been known to get sloppy drunk, ain't he, Sheriff?"

"Every so often. Was it Abraham?"

"No, sir. Whoever it was kinda growled."

"Growled?"

"Yes, sir. Like a wild animal. He charged me before I could get a round off. Knocked me and Martha down in the street."

"You see who it was?" Bertram asked, knowing this scenario was headed into something bad, and he wasn't certain just how much additional bad news he could stand.

"Yes, sir. It was Lucas Cross, and he was all covered in blood."

"You sure it was Lucas? Last time I saw him he could barely breathe."

"Yes, sir. It was him, but he was changed."

"Changed? How?"

Gus stopped fiddling with his hat brim and looked directly at Bertram. "His face, Sheriff. There was somethin'...ferocious about it. Not like when a person gets mad or anything. More like somethin' not human. More like a beast." He glanced back down at his hat. "'Spect you think me off my noodle sayin' somethin' crazy like that."

"Like I said, I cain't disregard anythin' after all that's happened. Hell, as far as I'm concerned, all of us that seen the craziness goin' on in Hamilton feel a little bit like we're off in the head ourselves."

"Yes, sir."

"Now, did you see where Lucas got off to?"

"Nope. By the time me and Martha calmed down, he was long gone." The deputy let out a long sigh. "Course then we found what else was in the alley." His voice then picked up a noticeable tremor. "And where all that blood on Lucas come from."

Bertram knew Gus was about to break down, so he called out for Howard, who had been standing in the doorway of the funeral parlor. But Howard was no longer there. Newell Scruggs now stood where Howard had been. The undertaker was dressed in his black suit, but the material seemed to be wrinkled and grubby. If he had looked cadaverous before any of the week's events, he appeared even worse now, more like a risen corpse than a living being.

"Sheriff Stone," Newell said in his deep voice. "Perhaps you should let Deputy Greenwood sit down in Dr. Peterson's office. If you come into my establishment, you will find out to what Deputy Greenwood is referring."

Bertram nodded okay. "You go on in and sit with Martha, Gus."

"Yes, sir, Sheriff."

"Where's Howard?" the sheriff asked Newell as he stepped into the funeral parlor.

"I asked him to keep an eye on Mr. and Mrs. Cooper. They are in the family room," the undertaker said as he directed Bertram toward the embalming area.

"Hunter and Molly Cooper?"

"Yes. They are in quite a state. And rightly so."

"What's goin' on?"

Newell opened the door to the embalming room. Necessity had dictated the undertaker bring a second metal table from its station by the rear door. Both tables gleamed dully under light from kerosene lamps, the bodies of Rose and Katy Cooper occupying the hard, metal tops. The girls were still in their cotton pajamas: Rose's a periwinkle blue, Katy's a pale yellow. Both sets of pajamas were stained a deep crimson in erratic patches, the girl's shoulders and necks draped with glossy, wet, lumpy clots of blood.

"Lord God," Bertram said under his breath. He felt his stomach flip and silently wished he had not drunk that corn liquor with Smoke earlier, now tasting the harshness of it along with stomach acid gathering in the back of his throat.

Fighting back his rising nausea, the sheriff stepped closer to the metal tables. Bertram had witnessed many terrible desecrations of the human body over his years with the Texas Rangers, worse than what he now witnessed on the embalming tables. But anytime children were the victims, the acts struck a deeper chord in his soul.

He had seen children skinned and had found others broken like dolls. One particular incident that always haunted him, he and his posse came upon a group of Comancheros. The bandits had overtaken a wagon of settlers earlier that day. They had killed the husband and wife and the eldest child, scalping all of them. But there had been an infant in that wagon as well. The Comancheros had impaled the baby through its rectum, the wooden stake exiting the child's mouth. The renegades then placed the ends of the stake in respective forked, wooden poles and cooked the baby over an open fire. Bertram and his men got to the Comancheros before they had eaten all the evidence, but he could never get the image of that half-consumed baby turning on a spit out of his head. Until now it had been one of his worst memories.

The Cooper girls' throats were savaged. The mutilations were not similar to the puncture wounds Bertram had seen on the necks of Eli Snow and Lucas Cross. Something had literally torn the flesh and muscle away and severed both of the girls' tracheas. It was as if the mangler's ultimate purpose had been to rip the girls' heads from their bodies.

"Were their eyes closed like this when Gus brought them in?" the sheriff asked, gazing on the grimaced rigor of the girl's faces.

"Oh, no, Sheriff Stone. I wish that had been the case. The horror I saw in those innocent eyes before I closed them is something I doubt I'll ever forget."

"Why would someone be so brutal? Looks like they tried to rip these children's heads off."

Newell seemed completely exhausted. His deep eyes had dark circles underneath and appeared sunken. "Remember last Monday when I joined you and Lucas Cross and Dr. Peterson in the medical office along with the Cross boys?"

"The day Doc Peterson summarized his theory on the head I took out of Eli Snow's well?"

"Yes. And, if you recall, I enlightened all present about the superstitions I've run across over the years in my business preparing the dead."

The sheriff glanced back at the devastated flesh on the girl's throats. A chill crept over him. "Are you tellin' me you seen somethin' like this before?"

"Not quite like this. Not as brutal. But there was one family convinced their grandfather was a creature that lived off human blood. They kept him locked up and fed him raw, bloody meat. This went on for several years until the grandfather died. As they did not want the body removed from their home, I was called out to prepare the corpse there. When I was shown the corpse, I found the head neatly severed from the rest of the body. The corpse lay stretched out on a bed, the head next to the vacant neck. I asked the family why they had committed this desecration. 'To keep him from a risin',' they told me, as if I were an idiot."

It hit Bertram then. The head found in the well. If it really was Jacob Snow's, had Eli cut it off to stop his son returning from the grave?

And now these two girls. Had this been done for similar reasons, or was there something else entirely that they could only guess at?

"Do you think?" Bertram asked. "Someone wanted to stop these children from...comin' back from the dead?"

"I only know from my examination so far there is virtually no blood left in their bodies."

"They must of bled out in the street then."

The undertaker shook his head no. "There was very little blood where they were found."

Hunter Cooper's voice shrieked down the hall. "Is that Sheriff Stone I hear down there with my *babies*?" The sound of struggling was followed by another outburst. "Damnation, Howard, let me go! Sheriff Stone will let me see my babies!"

"Hunter and his wife ain't seen the bodies yet?" Bertram asked Newell.

The undertaker pointed to the small corpses. "In this condition, no. I wanted to clean their wounds before the Coopers were allowed to see them. I just thought it important you witness the bodies appearances before any cosmetic alterations."

Bertram groaned. "I'll see what I can do to calm the Coopers down." He started to leave the room and then turned back around. "I never thought I'd see the day somethin' like this came out of my mouth, Newell. Would you be able..." He closed his eyes momentarily and swallowed harshly against a dry throat. "What I mean is, would you be able to cut off the heads?" The sheriff grimaced as a shudder clutched him. "I don't know why I'm suggesting such a terrible thing. I..."

Newell blinked his tired eyes. "I wholly agree with your request, Sheriff Stone. With the inexplicable activity as of late in Hamilton, I think such an action is a wise one. I can do what you wish and make certain the Coopers never suspect such an act was performed."

———

After Bertram and Howard were able to calm down a distraught Hunter Cooper, the sheriff assured both Hunter and

Molly it would be best to wait until Newell prepared their daughters before viewing them. Bertram then put Howard back in charge of the Coopers and went back to the medical office.

He found Dr. Peterson alone at his desk. The doctor looked in no better shape than Newell Scruggs. Peterson sat with half an unlit cigar dangling from his droopy lips, a shot glass with a hint of amber liquid in the bottom grasped in his hand.

Peterson glanced up when the sheriff entered. The doctor said nothing and wearily motioned for the sheriff to have a seat.

Bertram sat down in one of the chairs empty of clutter. "I suppose you seen them Cooper girls?"

Peterson grimaced and then nodded yes.

"Gus, take Martha home?" Bertram asked.

"I gave her a stout dose of phenobarbital." The doctor reached into his desk drawer and took out a bottle of bourbon. He brought out a second shot glass and filled it and his then slid one across the desk toward the sheriff. "I already told Gus to see Martha home and put her to bed. I also told him to stay with her until she wakes up." He glanced at the sheriff. "I hope that wasn't out of line, Bertram. It didn't occur to me at the time you might have other duties for Gus."

The sheriff eyed the bourbon, the ghost of Smoke's white lightning still fresh in his stomach's memory. But because of the state of the Cooper girl's bodies, he pushed the nausea aside and reached toward the desk and grabbed the shot glass. He downed it and surprisingly enjoyed the sting moving down his throat. Hair of the dog, he thought.

"I needed that, Doc," the sheriff said, placing the empty shot glass back on the desk, and Peterson refilled it. "Gus can stay with Martha for a while. I reckon Lucas cain't have gone too far."

"No?"

The sheriff downed the second shot of bourbon. "Nope.

Whatever Lucas Cross has become, more than likely it will be tryin' to get back to where it's been hidin' or make its way back to the ranch." He looked at Peterson and forced a strange grin. "The ranch is the only home Lucas knows, and God knows what he will do if them boys are there."

The doctor rubbed his eyes and tossed back another shot of bourbon. "Lucas will have to make it to the ranch before sunrise," he said, refilling both shot glasses. "Won't he?"

"Never would have occurred to me I'd be havin' such a conversation with an educated man," Bertram answered, accepting a third shot of whiskey.

The doctor took a match from a small box and slid the sulfurous head down the box's striker pad. "I suppose it's time to consider ghoulies, ghosties, and long-legged beasties," he said with a weird look as he lit the cigar. "Seems to be no other explanation for what's occurring in Hamilton."

The sheriff threw back the third drink and set the shot glass on the desk. "Guess I'll tell you what an old tracker companion of mine named Smoke had to say about the family of Eli Snow."

Peterson refilled the glasses and then leaned back and took a long drag on his partially-smoked cigar.

TWENTY-ONE

Lucas Cross moved through the brushy hillside outside Hamilton as if he were effortlessly flying, his recent, heavy blood meal not hampering him in any way.

Lucas had no urge to return to his ranch. He was being drawn through Deer Hollow toward Eli Snow's land.

It was his daughter Bonnie who beckoned.

Wary of any obstacle, animal, or human that might impede him, Lucas' eyes moved quickly from side to side. As he rushed through the night, Lucas licked his teeth in search of wayward clots remaining from the last feast.

———

"Sounds like some grim Shakespearean or Greek tragedy," Dr. James Peterson said after hearing Smoke's story from Sheriff Bertram Stone.

"Other than grim, I couldn't swear by what you say, Doc." The sheriff buttoned up his heavy jacket and arranged his Stetson. "Never was much on reading. Tried Dickens once in a while and was scratchin' my head most of the time. Expect I'll stick to them dime westerns. If nothin' else, I get a good laugh from some of the far-fetched scenarios in them."

The doctor grabbed a long coat from the rack by the front door of his medical office then put on a beret and tugged it tightly around his scalp. He took a holstered forty-five from a peg on the wall, slid the belt around his waist, and tied the leather strip at the holster's bottom around his thigh. "Hadn't seen much use for this firearm over the years. Don't know how much good it will be against Lucas, especially if your friend was accurate in his tale."

"If he's anything like Eli, standard bullets won't kill him, but they'll damn sure slow him down long enough for burnin'."

"Would silver bullets do the job?" Peterson asked.

"Don't imagine Abraham has any silver bullets down at his general store, and we ain't got time to make any." The sheriff patted his own side arm. "This will have to do for the present."

"I don't suppose we have time to stop by one of the churches before we go on our hunt, do we?"

"I ain't sayin' that's a bad idea. I just think blessin' things like water or bullets or us, for that matter, won't be the solution. A comfort maybe, but not a solution." Bertram opened the office door and motioned for Peterson to go ahead of him. "Fire's the answer. That or beheadin', and I don't imagine Lucas is goin' to lay his neck on a chopping block for us."

The doctor waited until Bertram joined him outside and then said, "Whatever attacked Eli and Lucas is still out there as well. Logically, it's going to be something just like the things it created."

"Yep. I got a gut feelin' Lucas will be searchin' for that thing to join it or kill it."

"I'll get the Ford while you collect Gus and Howard. I'd better see how much gas is left in the tank after your trip to Fairy."

"Yeah, I reckon you'll have to wake up Abraham to unlock the gas pump. Won't make him none too happy, neither." The sheriff paused before saying, "Think I'll just come along for now. I better leave Gus with the Cooper girl. I'll get Howard to keep an eye on the town. Lucas may still be here, but I doubt it. I'll tell Howard what to do just in case Lucas shows himself again."

"Just you and me then?"

"I believe Newell's got his hands full right now, so, yep, I think we can handle it."

"Maybe we should wait until sunrise. If we're putting sensibility aside, as we seem to be doing, and accept these night beings as truths, then wouldn't it make more sense to hunt them when they're most vulnerable?"

"More than likely. But I think now is the time. After sunrise, Lucas and whatever else is out there will be dug into some hidey hole like a tick."

"Well, I always wanted to be a cowboy like Wyatt Earp when I was a child. I guess my father was correct when he told me to be careful of what you wish for."

Bertram patted the doctor cordially on the shoulder. "Sure appreciate your coming with me, Doc," he said. "Sure do appreciate it."

Lucas Cross passed his ranch just after midnight. He glanced at it briefly and then headed toward the distant beacon drawing him.

Turk, still shivering by the tombstone he had not left all day, raised his head to the sky and uttered a long, miserable howl into the chilly night.

AFTER CHECKING in with Howard and Gus, Bertram joined Peterson, who was waiting in the front passenger seat of the Ford. Neither spoke much as they drove down the road. Both men were tired and mystified as to how they could actually come to believe what their minds told them was impossible.

Their first stop was the Cross ranch. The two men found nothing changed inside the ranch house from the sheriff's earlier visit on returning from Fairy.

The horses still wandered between the corral and the stable, and Bertram noticed a few head of Lucas' cattle had come up as well. "Adam and Donny were more than likely supposed to bring some bales of hay and spread it around. Them cattle are usually hold up for the night in Lucas' cattle barn down near the creek. They must be hungry comin' up this far. I was gonna have Howard or Gus come out here tomorrow. I'll tell them to stop by the Johnson farm—I believe that's where Lucas buys his hay —and get what hay will fit on the back of Lucas' Model T, it still being in town anyway. I'll have to see what I can do for these animals if we don't find Adam or Donny. I sure hate to see good cattle and horses neglected."

"Are we going to look around here some more?" Peterson asked.

The sheriff gazed up at the night sky. A cloud bank was moving steadily in from the north. "Looks like the weather ain't gonna cooperate much longer, not with them clouds rollin' in. Let's head out to Eli's cabin. This situation started there. That place might just be the magnet."

Driving toward the cabin, Bertram thought how three days prior it had been Lucas Cross accompanying him in the Ford to Eli Snow's place. That memory left a nagging sensation in the sheriff's stomach.

"God I'm tired," he said.

"This week has certainly kept us out of the routine

humdrum existence in Hamilton. I should be sleepy, but I'm wide awake now," Peterson said. "Exhausted, but wide awake."

"Maybe after all's said and done, Doc, and we get Eli's and whoever else's body we find to Fort Worth for a complete autopsy... Well, maybe they'll find a reason for what happened to Eli and Lucas. Maybe it's a virus like you said."

"Possibly." The doctor suddenly recalled the image of Eli Snow's body coming after them even when it was on fire. "But, if it is a virus or some other unknown microbial agent, it is one hell of an adversary." He glanced out the front windshield. In the subdued moonlight, the doctor appeared to take in the natural hollow and an outline of the cabin built inside it.

"Doc, I suppose Eli's wife could have been infected, you know a carrier or somethin', and passed it on to that unfortunate child, Jacob."

"Or perhaps, as your friend Smoke's story of the Snows would indicate, Eli's wife was indeed a monster. A real monster."

———

LUCAS CROSS PASSED through the heavy brush and trees on Eli Snow's land, eventually moving into a cleared area where the remains of the burned house stood.

The beacon that lured Lucas was strong now, and he sensed his journey was almost over. He glided to the storm cellar, its door open and lying by the side of the entrance. He floated down. A large shape loomed before him. Lucas pulled back his lips and snarled. The headless body moved aside and let the rancher pass.

Just beyond the ghastly sentry, a huddled mass undulated on the earthen floor. Sounds arose from that mass, slurping and low growling. Blood filled the dank cellar with a heady metallic scent. Lucas's mouth opened while he gnashed his new canines in expectation. He fell in with the bodies of Bonnie and Adam. He took no notice of who they were as he joined in their banquet and fought against them to pull every drop of what little blood remained from the prone, twitching form of Donny Cross.

Twenty-Two

Newell Scruggs felt empty inside. His thin frame seemed more bent and his eyesight a bit out of focus. His muscles ached deeply, especially his heart. It was as if the last few days had aged him by a decade.

Newell told himself it was only fatigue, but as he looked at the lifeless bodies of Rose and Katy Cooper, he knew the world he lived in was forever changed. He could not promise himself he would ever get a full night's sleep again.

Newell had already worked his magic on the Cooper girls. After removing their heads, he constructed a thin, flat extension consisting of sawdust and wire and placed it between the severed areas of the girl's heads and necks. He then took morticians wax and molded the spacer into what was almost indistinguishable from the girl's pale skin. The fact the girls had been bled dry made the task much easier.

He removed the pajamas from the Cooper girls' bodies. His eyes traveled sadly over the innocent flesh that was now an ashen color from massive blood loss.

Newell sighed. Remorse came to him with the certain knowledge these young girls would never know the joy of womanhood. They would never be courted, never be kissed or married, and would never hold a baby against the warmth of their breasts.

A child's death was not a novel event for the undertaker. But these two and the ghastly fate they had suffered affected him more than any other he could recall. He knew these girls, had watched them grow, and had seen them walk down the street after school to help their parents at the café. On the rare occasion Newell actually stopped by the café, Rose's and Katy's laughter had mingled with their parents' and their older sister Martha's.

Now, the two girls lay before him unaware of the cold metal under their backs or that their parents' grief filled the family waiting room down the hallway.

Newell went to his supply closet and chose two cotton gowns, one pink and one lavender. From years of experience, he had no need to measure the girls for a perfect fit.

He gently dressed Rose and Katy in the gowns and tugged the necklines flush with the space bars he had constructed between the neck and head of each girl. Although Newell was certain neither parent would notice the area where he decapitated the bodies, he had no wish to take a chance.

Before collecting Hunter and Molly for the viewing of their dead children, Newell would add color to the girls' pallid faces and hands with his array of mortician's cosmetics. And as he dusted a powder puff with makeup, Newell said to the bodies on the table, "I will make you as pretty as God's own angels, little ones, as God's own angels."

———

IF ELI SNOW's cabin had been a littered mess the previous time Sheriff Bertram Stone inspected it, what he and Dr. James

Peterson discovered now under their flashlights' beams was total wreckage.

The sheriff blew a soft whistle through his teeth. "Hell, I reckon every critter around came in rootin' for food." He glanced at Peterson. "And they were mighty disappointed, I imagine, because I don't remember there bein' too much to eat here when I gave this place the once over before."

Peterson wriggled his nose. "Now that," he said and spread the flashlight beam in an arc, "is a stench I recognize."

"Pretty bad, I know. When me and Lucas..." Bertram paused at the memory of a healthy Lucas Cross. "Anyhow, when we were out here last Monday afternoon, we discovered that odor on a knife. I told Lucas it smelled like rotten shit."

"You were pretty much spot on. I had to deal with this stink in medical school at almost every dissection. That lovely aroma is from a cut bowel."

"Bowel? It weren't from Eli then. I don't recall him havin' any gut wounds."

The doctor steadied the beam on a stain dark enough to be in contrast to the earthen floor. "That's probably part of the bowel fluid right there. That stuff is strong enough to leave a lasting memory, even in dirt."

The sheriff walked over and added his light. "There was a blood trail not far from this. That's what me and Lucas followed and how we found Eli."

Peterson changed the direction of his flashlight and spread the beam around the cabin. "Doesn't appear to be anything of interest here. Where else do we need to check?"

"There are remains of a burnt ranch house beyond the deep brush and trees on Eli's land I want to recheck, especially the storm cellar by it. I don't know how far we can get in the Ford, but if the goin' gets too tough through them thick bushes, I'll just have to wait until tomorrow and hoof it.

Course, I'll probably bring Gus or Howard with me if that happens. I imagine you need to catch up on things, sleep bein' one of 'em."

"Bertram, I don't know—"

The sound of something coming through the door stopped Peterson's voice. He and the sheriff instinctively turned the light beams in the direction of the noise.

"Holy shit!" Bertram shouted.

The naked, headless thing stood in the doorway, its decomposition now markedly advanced. Chunks of flesh and muscle oozed away from protruding bones, the stink from the slash in its belly more pungent now than the stench in the cabin.

When the thing lurched forward, the doctor screamed. He and Bertram drew their firearms and pelted the thing coming toward them, but other than a slight flinching, the headless body advanced unfazed. Bertram and Peterson didn't have time to reload before the thing was upon them. It swung wildly, struck the doctor in the ribs, and sent him painfully to the dirt floor.

Bertram charged the headless body. He slammed into its midsection and was rewarded with a heavy spray of the putrefied gut fluid. But Bertram's weight was sufficient to knock the thing down. The sheriff went to Peterson quickly and pulled him from the floor. The doctor screamed from the pain of his broken ribs.

"Come on, Doc," Bertram huffed, attempting to drag Peterson out the cabin's door. "We got to get out of here quick."

The thing on the floor scrambled around like an insect on its back. Its arms and legs flayed wildly against one another as it tried to right itself.

The sheriff pulled Peterson across the doorway. A look of agony was etched in the doctor's eyes. With the sheriff's aid, Peterson tried to walk as best he could.

"God," the doctor said through clenched teeth. Despite the

pain he picked up his pace, clearly eager to make it to the Ford as quickly as possible.

Just as Bertram opened the passenger door and slid the agonized doctor onto the seat, the headless thing stumbled through the cabin's doorway and headed forward. The sheriff backed toward the driver's side, never taking his eyes from the uncoordinated, bewildered body trying to find him and Peterson.

"*There!*"

The voice Bertram heard was cold and menacing. For a moment, he had the wild notion that the thing without a head had somehow spoken. But then he saw the floating figure of a child emerge and point a finger in the direction of the Ford.

"*There*," the horror repeated. "*Stop them!*"

Instantaneously, the headless body turned toward Bertram and began a lumbering run toward him. Bertram opened the driver side door and jumped in. He reached over and locked the passenger door and then his own. He didn't have time to check the back doors but prayed they were already locked.

Bertram turned the ignition and the Ford's engine flared to life the same moment the headless body slammed against the passenger window. Spider fractures spread across the glass. A second hit sent the window smashing into fragments on Peterson. The doctor pushed at the intruding hand reaching for him as the sheriff put the Ford in reverse and slammed the accelerator flat against the floor.

The headless thing fell forward to the ground. While Bertram kept backing up, he flicked on the Ford's lights and saw two other figures by the floating child. The headless thing stood up and sauntered back to the group behind it. The figures disappeared into the darkness, but not before the sheriff got a good enough look to notice one of them was wearing long johns.

"God, what was that thing?" Peterson asked through clenched teeth.

The sheriff fishtailed the car around in the right direction and raced it toward the road. "I seen Lucas back there...and somethin' else."

"What was it?"

"I seen Lucas and what was probably one of his boys. Christ knows what happened to the other one. And there was a child there floatin' in the air."

"So they're true? All those wild legends?"

Bertram remained silent, trying to absorb what he had witnessed. After a moment, he admitted, "Guess I should have listened to you, Doc."

"Why so?"

"Daylight's gonna be the best time to do what has to be done to them things, whatever they are."

Peterson began to chuckle, his laughs interspersed with groans.

"What's so funny, Doc?" Bertram asked.

"Well," Peterson said as his chuckles declined. "At least we know where that damned head you took out of the well came from."

———

LUCAS CROSS' face twitched and ticked with rage. His hunger had returned. Even though he had helped drain Donny, it seemed his appetite was unappeasable. He'd desperately wanted the blood of the two men who had escaped.

Adam Cross, his mouth opening and closing in a steady rhythm, stared blankly at Lucas. None of his previous humanity were left to him, the hunger and need for blood were his only motivations and his face appeared blankly feral.

Bonnie pointed in the direction of the burned house and storm cellar. *"Back,"* she said. *"Safe."*

Lucas hissed and shook his head no. "No," he snarled. "Our home. Ranch house."

Bonnie's face darkened. She drifted down and walked to her father and clutched his cold fingers.

"Danger," she hissed, her lips parting to reveal elongated canines.

Lucas released her hand and walked away. Trying to make a decision in his fevered brain, Adam glanced from Bonnie to his father and finally ambled in behind Lucas.

"No," Bonnie said, but the two moved steadily forward and away from her.

The headless body now stood by Bonnie. It quivered in confusion waiting to be told what to do. Bonnie watched the figures of her father and brother move into the darkness.

Her face creased in a frown. *"Cellar,"* she ordered the headless sentinel. *"Guard Donny."* Dripping a trail of decomposed flesh behind it, the headless thing turned and headed into the bush.

Bonnie's face went blank. Her eyes swirled red and blue and saucer-like in the cold night. She levitated and glided forward to catch up with her father and brother.

TWENTY-THREE

"Goddamnit." Bertram wrapped bandages tightly around Peterson's broken ribs. "It was all I could do to accept the notion of vampires. Now there's this thing without a head! Shit!" He pulled the wrapping too tight as he spoke, and the doctor winced and let out a yelp. "Sorry, Doc. It's just by God hard to swallow. A body without a head cain't be walkin' around, much less attack people!"

"Whatever that thing is, my ribs can attest not only is it animated but also in possession of unnatural strength no matter if it's rotting away or not."

The sheriff folded the bandage he was working with under the end of the one below it. Being in the Texas Rangers, Bertram had performed such first aid on himself and others many times, whether from assault, getting thrown from a horse, or a bullet skirting the ribcage.

After his ribs were securely wrapped, Peterson sat on the edge of the examining table in his medical office. The black bristles of his beard stood out in stark contrast to flesh made extremely pale from the pain. "Help me slide off, will you? I want to get to my desk and sit down."

"Don't you want me to get you upstairs and into bed?"

"No. I have a bottle of laudanum in one the desk drawers. After I drink some of that, it won't matter if I'm lying or sitting."

The sheriff positioned himself next to Peterson, placed a hand under the doctor's shoulders, and helped him ease off the table.

As they made their way carefully toward the desk, the doctor wrinkled his nose and said, "Bertram, you got quite a dose of that thing's bowel fluids on your clothes. It might be a good idea to take care of that before you do anything that involves being around other people."

The sheriff snorted as he maneuvered the doctor into the desk chair. "Is kinda potent, ain't it?"

In obvious pain, Peterson nodded yes and reached for the middle drawer.

"I'll get that, Doc. This it?" The sheriff pointed to a dark green medicine container lying next to a bottle of bourbon.

"Yes," Peterson said, grabbing his chest while he spoke.

"Hell, why not take both?"

"That, would certainly cure the hurt all right, but it might put me to sleep permanently. You see, there's already an ample base of alcohol mixed with the opiate. If I add the bourbon, my diaphragm could become paralyzed." He grinned against the pain. "And I wouldn't be able to breathe."

"Guess that's a bad idea then." The sheriff heard a clattering on the roof and the office window. "Figured them clouds we saw rollin' up earlier would dump some more sleet on us."

Peterson took a drink from the green bottle and then reached over and picked one of the many cigar stubs from ashtrays cluttering his desk.

"Need me to light that for you?" Bertram asked.

"No, I'm going to chew on it for a while until the laudanum kicks in."

Bertram retrieved his hat and coat from the rack by the front door. As he adjusted his Stetson, he glanced at the wall clock. It was a quarter of three in the morning. "Still a little early to pull Gus away from the Cooper girl. Damn shame about her younger sisters. Suppose I should have a word with Hunter and Molly. I imagine Newell done shown them the bodies by now." He walked over toward the doctor. "But all that can wait awhile. I reckon Hunter and Molly are still in shock."

"That type of tragedy doesn't wear off quickly," the doctor said, his eyes drooping under the laudanum's influence.

"Anything else I can do for you?"

Peterson shook his head no.

"Then I'm goin' over to the courthouse and hit the bathtub in the basement. I got some of Abraham Tanner's lye soap and a bristle brush. Don't know as that'll get all the stink off. Most of it's on my clothes though. I'll probably have to burn them."

"Check on me in a few hours if you're awake. Just make sure I'm still breathing."

"Will do."

As the sheriff was about to open the door, the doctor added, "Hold up, Bertram. What was that schoolteacher's name who said the head belonged to Jacob Snow?"

"Vivien Hagler. But why you askin' about her?"

The doctor swayed his head from side to side as if to try and unscramble gathering laudanum cobwebs. "If you can spare a few minutes sometime after sunrise, ask Miss Hagler if she or someone she knows has any reference books on the supernatural, superstitions, or unexplained and unnatural occurrences."

"You mean from around here?"

"Not necessarily. Local history would be nice, but general

information will do. I want to cross reference elements of your Indian friend Smoke's story."

Bertram suspected the narcotic was already screwing with the doctor's mind, but then the sense of Peterson's request came through. You have to know your enemy. "Sure. I'll check with her after I send Howard out to the Cross ranch first thing in the mornin' to tend to those horses and cattle."

The doctor didn't reply. His eyes were closed, his chin resting on his shirt collar while the cigar stub remained clamped tightly between his teeth.

———

The three horses in Lucas Cross' corral moved about nervously. They paid no attention to the sleet pellets stinging their flesh. The animals whinnied and snorted, their eyes wide and wild and alert. They knew something dangerous was nearby.

Like flowing ink spilt from its well, a shadowy figure slid from out of the stable. Another shadow soon followed, and in a circular approach, both separated and fanned around the horses. By now the animals were frantic. They reared up trying to knock down the corral slats.

The larger of the stalking forms jumped on one of the horses. The animal bucked wildly, the cry from its throat more like a human scream. The figure wrapped its arms around the horse's neck and buried its head there. The horse went berserk, spinning and kicking as its cries escalated to unearthly wails.

The horse then fell. The sound of it hitting the earth provoked the other horses' panic even more. The corral slats were broken under a frenzied attack of hooves. The remaining two horses bunched into a wad of arching bodies, each struggling against the other to get out. In the process, one animal stumbled and fell. The second figure in the corral leapt on it and tore into the horse's throat.

The last horse broke out of the corral and rushed into the night. The cattle that had been gathered there earlier were long gone before the melee with the horses ever started.

The two fallen horses were bled rapidly. Their cries vanished. Their trembling ceased.

The sleet increased in intensity along with the north wind. The warm blood spilling from Lucas and Adam Cross' sucking lips sent vapors of fog rising against the cold air. They paid no attention to the wandering body that approached from behind.

Bonnie drifted down by her father and nudged her head against his. Lucas growled deeply in his throat but still allowed space for her to join in the feast.

———

VIVIEN HAGLER HAD NEVER MARRIED. Whether she had been in love or even close to the wedding aisle was discussed by some of the townspeople of Hamilton, but Vivien herself offered no clues. If one of the women from church or school had enough gall to dance around the subject, Vivien silenced them abruptly with "I do not wish to talk about such personal matters."

Vivien had taught school since she was a young woman. Born in Waco, Texas she lived there with her mother and father during her first teaching appointment. After the deaths of her parents, Vivien decided to seek out a smaller town. "Waco's getting too big for its britches," she once confided to a Sunday school friend.

Vivien drifted from one place to another, eventually putting down what she considered final roots in the small town of

Hamilton, Texas where she taught school, attended the Baptist church, and was active in community affairs.

She began each day at five in the morning. She went to bed at eight each night. This routine was never broken unless an emergency had to be dealt with—such events occurring twice since her move to Hamilton. First, for a ruptured appendix, her own, requiring a short hospital stay in Fort Worth. And then the accidental drowning of one of her students, Vivien's favorite—a girl named Elizabeth Fleming, who the schoolteacher deemed a budding scientist. Vivien considered Elizabeth a young lady talented and intelligent enough to shake up the male dominated world of medicine. Elizabeth's death put Vivien in a state of grief and distraction for weeks. After she came out of her despair, Vivien swore to never lose that kind of personal control or composure again.

Every morning after she rose from her bed, Vivien put on a kettle of water for tea, heated up biscuit dough prepared the previous evening, took either apricot or strawberry jam, the only flavors she purchased, from her meager supplies in the cupboard and then sat down for breakfast. A morning bath was followed by a light powder dusting to her wrinkled skin. She then sat before a vanity mirror and arranged her graying hair into a severe bun she felt appropriate for her position as schoolteacher.

Vivien only let her hair down on Saturdays unless she left the house, which was rare as she spent most of those days planning her next week's lessons, reading whatever fiction she allowed herself for pleasure, and, after supper, studying the Bible for the next day's Sunday School gathering.

On Sunday, her hair would be reconstructed into the bun until she returned home after a pot-luck lunch at church. The rest of that day was spent gardening, if weather permitted, and, if it did not, a little more reading and a long afternoon nap.

Vivien's life was a series of routine activities. She preferred this. It offered stability and an even keel. So, when she presently heard a soft tapping on her door a little after sunrise as she was about to take off her robe and nightgown and slip into the bath, a line of irritation wrinkled her brow. Any break of her routine usually meant trouble. When she pulled back the curtain covering a small, rectangular frame of glass on her front door and saw Sheriff Bertram Stone standing on the porch, Vivien knew this morning's break from the ordinary would prove to be no exception.

She unlocked the door and cracked it slightly.

Bertram peered in. He smiled and tipped his hat. "Mornin', Miss Hagler. Sorry to disturb you." He noticed she pulled her robe's collar up higher around her neck. *Cain't be too careful of exposing flesh to us old letches*, the sheriff thought with an inner chuckle.

Vivien stared briefly at Bertram and then started bunching her hair behind her neck and wished she could somehow arrange it into that protective bun. "What can I do for you, Sheriff Stone?"

"Actually, Miss Hagler, Doc Peterson asked me to stop by and see if you might have some specific books or know someone else who might."

Snowflakes started to fall. Vivien watched them drift down and cast little shadows on the sheriff's shoulders. "Would you care to come in out of the cold, Sheriff?"

"No, thank you, Miss Hagler. I got a lot to deal with this mornin'."

Suddenly, Vivien was aware of the fatigue on Bertram's face. "My word, Sheriff, the circles under your eyes are quite a caution. Have you been sleeping well?"

"Not much, Miss Hagler. We got a situation that's been takin' up most of mine and the doc's attention. Not to mention all that Newell Scruggs has had to deal with."

"Goodness. I haven't heard of anything out of the ordinary other than the discovery of that head, which was placed on vulgar, public display. Does it involve that incident?"

The sheriff hesitated and lowered his eyes a bit. "Well, I guess I cain't keep the cat in the bag anymore. Thing's done gone too far. The whole town's bound to find out, and they really need to know for their own protection."

"It does have something to do with that Snow boy's head, doesn't it?"

"Yes, ma'am, and a whole lot more."

Vivien opened the door. "You just go sit at the kitchen table, Sheriff. I don't drink coffee, but I can make you some extra strong tea. You certainly look as though you could use a lot of caffeine."

"Really, Miss Hagler, I got so much to do."

She grabbed his arm and pulled him forward. "Nonsense. You come in and tell me what's been going on and just what books Doctor Peterson needs."

"I suppose I could spare a few minutes, and I could use that tea." Bertram walked across the threshold and removed his hat. He quickly backtracked and kicked the ice and mud from his boots as best he could on the porch and then came back in and followed Vivien after she had closed the door.

She led him to a small kitchen and offered him a chair at the table. She then put a kettle of water on the stove and sat down across from Bertram. Vivien no longer attempted to arrange her hair. It fell wild and tangled on her shoulders.

"Miss Hagler. Before I share what's been goin' on since last Sunday, I want to see how you feel about the word...vampire."

Vivien squinted and asked, "Excuse me, Sheriff. Did you say vampire?"

He nodded yes.

The kettle started whistling. Vivien pulled the collar of her robe up even higher. "Oh, my," she said, getting up to pour boiling water in the teacups. "Vampire?"

———

DR. JAMES PETERSON drifted into an opium-laced dream. In it, he sat on the edge of a riverbank and held a fishing pole. The filament of line from the pole was slack and moved lazily on the water's surface.

The sky above was a mixture of the most marvelous swirling colors. Blues and reds combined with greens and purples like melting, colored wax. Peterson felt a great serenity as he stared at this weird and wonderful display.

He felt a slight tug and saw the fishing line had gone taut. Something pulled on it with severe force, but he did not want to catch anything. He only wanted to gaze at the mysterious tints in the whirling sky.

"No," the doctor said as he tried to release the fishing pole. "No." He felt tears of frustration welling in his eyes. "No! No!"

"Doc! Doc, wake up!"

Peterson's drugged dream state evaporated. He squinted and found Sheriff Bertram Stone standing over him. The doctor was still seated behind his desk. The cigar butt he had previously been chewing lay slimy and cold on the desk's top.

Because the doctor remained a little drunk from the laudanum, he had forgotten about the injury to his chest. He tried to get up and his ribs stopped him with an alarming jolt of pain. He cried out and grasped the bandages around his chest.

"Take it easy, Doc. I just came by to check on you. Hell, I thought you'd stopped breathin'," Bertram said.

"Oooo. It might be better if I had."

The sheriff opened the desk drawer and took out the bottle of laudanum. "You want more of this?"

Peterson held up his hand and shook his head. "I just need to get my bearings. I moved too quickly and at a bad angle. I was so deep in a laudanum stupor I forgot all about my ribs." He relaxed as the pain ebbed. "There now, that's better." He glanced up at the sheriff. "Thanks for keeping an eye on me." Peterson picked up the errant cigar butt. He clenched it between his teeth and glanced at the wall clock and saw it was going on eight in the morning. "Anything new happen?"

Bertram removed his hat and coat and hung them on the coat rack. He then sat in one of the uncluttered chairs. "I sent Howard out to the Cross ranch to check on them stock animals. Gus is asleep over at the Coopers. Newell told me Molly passed out when he showed her them girl's bodies. Said Hunter just went crazy. Newell said it was a painful thing to see Molly and Hunter in the state they was in. He helped Hunter carry Molly back home. Newell said she was just comin' 'round when they put her in bed."

"What about their other daughter? Martha, is it?"

"Yep."

"Is she all right now? Should I make up some tranquilizer for her and Molly?"

"Maybe for Molly. I think Martha's come out of her shock. She asked Newell to take her down to the Baptist church and talk with Pastor Jones about arranging services."

The doctor stopped chewing on his cigar butt. His brow wrinkled. "Shouldn't those two bodies be watched for a while? Just to be sure they won't... Well, you know."

"I done had Newell take care of that," the sheriff said and drew a trembling finger across his throat.

"Oh, I see."

"I went by and asked Vivien Hagler if she had any of those books you mentioned."

The doctor arched his eyebrows. "How did that exchange go?"

"Okay, I suppose. Course, I told her most everything that's happened since Sunday and swore her to secrecy until I say otherwise. All except that headless thing. I figured she'd think I was crazy enough without that particular detail."

"Did she?"

"Not really. And that kinda surprised me. She seemed to take it all with a grain of salt. Said when she taught in Gatesville there was some evidence of witchcraft being practiced. Said even if people believe they are part of a dark art, it don't really matter if it really exists are not. People believin' a thing strong enough makes that thing real."

The doctor gingerly leaned forward. "Did she have any reference books?"

"Only one." The sheriff held up a large volume. "Has to do with Indian folk tales. She said the Catholic priest, Father Dobbins, down at St. Jude's might have more. Said he talked to her class once about how Halloween got started. About ghosts and goblins and such."

"That church is farther out of town. Dobbins doesn't have much of a parish anymore from what I hear."

"Used to be a lot of Catholics around here. Bunch of Polish and Czech settlers established farms around Hamilton, but over the years a lot of them went south down toward Temple. Soil was supposed to be richer there."

"Dobbins might be inclined to cordial conversation now, seeing how his flock has thinned. I might take a drive down there later today if my ribs feel up to it. Will you need the Ford later?"

"Howard took it. I done forgot to tell him to pick up some hay in Lucas' Model T for the livestock. I'll deal with that later. So, Lucas' automobile is still in town. Don't imagine there'd being any reason why you cain't use it. If you're feelin' up to it, that is." Bertram placed Vivien's book on the desk. "As for me..." He got up and reached for his hat and coat. "I'm going to my office and try to put together something I can tell the citizens of Hamilton about this mess without making a fool of myself, and then I'm goin' down to the stable and get Lucy and go back out to Eli Snow's place."

"You should take Lucas' Model T instead, and you shouldn't go alone, Bertram, even if it is daylight," Peterson remarked while scrutinizing the book's table of contents. "I might not be of much help, but I would certainly accompany you, if you need me."

"Naw, you work on keepin' them ribs as still as possible. Where I'm goin' it's easier to get through the brush and trees with a horse. Besides, you wouldn't catch me out there anywhere near sundown. Not after what we seen."

"Well, be careful. I don't have any wish for you to be brought to my examination table." Peterson shivered when he thought of the throat wounds he had witnessed lately.

"And I don't intend to grace that metal table, neither." Bertram opened the front door of the medical office. "See ya, Doc."

Through the medical office's window, Peterson watched the sheriff walk down the wooden porch and then out of his viewing range. The doctor then moved a finger down the table of contents of the book borrowed from Vivien Hagler and, eventually, stopped at the chapter dealing with shamans, demons, and black magic.

TWENTY-FOUR

Newell Scruggs couldn't get Molly Cooper's screams out of his head.

"Oh, my God, my babies, my babies!" Molly had shrieked over and over as she covered her daughters' corpses with kisses until she swooned and hit the floor.

"Damnit, Newell!" Hunter Cooper had said as he tried to comfort his distraught wife. "Who could have done such a thing?" His eyes had been wild and pleading. "Ain't nothin' like this ever happened here in Hamilton. I know these people. They eat my food!" He had cradled Molly's head as he spoke. "By God, I ever find the sumbitch done this, Newell, so help me, I'll cut off that spineless bastard's balls and make him swallow them!"

The undertaker was very thankful the repair work he'd done on the girls' severed heads had held them securely in place. He could not begin to imagine what would have happened had the heads detached.

All these thoughts passed through Newell's mind as he sat beside Martha Cooper, who was discussing the funeral services with the Baptist minister, Pastor Jones. Martha was still distraught and had to wipe tears from her eyes between words with a well-drenched handkerchief.

"If you would rather come back later, Miss Cooper," the pastor said, "I see no need to rush these proceedings. You and your family need more time to deal with this tragedy."

Martha wiped away a fresh set of tears. "No, I want to have everything ready, so Ma and Pa don't have to suffer through the arrangements."

Pastor Jones was nearing seventy years old and had been pastor at the Hamilton First Baptist Church for over thirty of those years. Possessing a benevolent face lined with wrinkles, his sermons were never fever pitch and concentrated on the love of Christ and how members of his congregation should learn to profess a similar love. He wore a pair of slim spectacles and smelled faintly of Bay Rhum shaving tonic.

Pastor Jones looked on Martha with an expression of compassion. "Is there any particular Bible verse you would like me to read at the service, Miss Cooper?"

Martha teared up again. "Something about little lambs... Something from 'Matthew 19:14...'" She broke down into heavy sobs, her shoulders heaving up and down in a torrent of weeping.

The pastor got up from behind his desk and came to her. Newell tried to comfort Martha as well by placing a long, bony hand gently on her back.

"I think I should take her home, Pastor," Newell suggested.

"By all means, Mr. Scruggs. These arrangements can be dealt with at another time." The pastor bent close to Martha's ear and added, "Your parents need not be involved right away, Miss Cooper. That will spare them any more initial hurt. You can come back tomorrow and decide on the funeral service then."

As Newell and the pastor were helping Martha out of her chair, the rectory door opened, and Deputy Gus Greenwood walked in. He dusted powdery snow from the shoulders of his coat. When Martha saw Gus, she ran to him.

"I'm sorry I fell asleep." Gus put his arms tightly around Martha. He then said to Newell and the pastor, "I'll take her home." Gus gently guided Martha to the coat rack where he took down her wrap and scarf. "You need to bundle up, Martha." He helped her slip on the cold weather gear. "The snow's pickin' up."

After Gus and Martha left the building, Newell sat back down and asked the pastor, "If you have a minute, there are a few items I'd like to discuss with you?"

Pastor Jones went back behind the desk and lowered himself into his chair. "Certainly, Mr. Scruggs. How may I help you?"

Newell hesitated as the memory of Eli Snow's corpse rising hungry and stalking sent chills across his flesh. "Well, Pastor, other than Jesus Christ, what do you know about people rising from the grave?"

———

As FALLING snow swirled around him in the corral at the Cross ranch, Deputy Howard Sparks stood dumbfounded.

"Gawd Almighty," Howard whispered with the dead and ravaged bodies of two horses a few feet in front of him.

There wasn't much left of the horses' throats. Loose folds of ragged flesh hung from ruined tissue, muscles, and vessels. The horses' eyes were wide open and vacant, snowflakes sticking to them in expanding, white mounds.

Howard bent down, examined the wounds closer, and let out a sigh. "Maybe there's a mountain lion loose," he considered and then recalled the Cooper girls' throat wounds. A chill surpassed the cold, snowy morning and crept up his spine.

Howard rose and glanced across the area beyond the corral

and found nothing but spinning clouds of white flakes. He decided he would take the Ford and drive further across Lucas Cross' land. He knew there was a barn Lucas built away from the ranch house near a grove of mesquite and pecan trees because of the shade the trees provided during the heat of summer and early autumn. He just didn't remember exactly where that barn was.

"Think it's north," Howard said out loud. "Maybe northeast. About a mile or so."

He decided not to do anything about the dead horses yet. He figured Sheriff Stone might want to have a look. Besides, the animals wouldn't decompose anytime soon in this freezing weather.

As he passed through the stable and into the yard toward the Ford, Howard saw something scurry under the ranch house porch. He shivered and pulled his side arm free of its holster. "Them things ain't supposed to be able to move about in the daylight," he told himself while approaching the house.

Howard was almost to the front steps when he saw a tail jutting out from under the porch. The hackles on his neck rose. *Do vampires have tails like devils?* the deputy asked himself as an old, gaunt face appeared from under the wooden slats of the porch. A shiny nose gleamed with moisture.

Howard laughed under his breath. "You sure gave me a fright, old boy," he said to Turk. "Cain't recollect your name, but I don't imagine you care about that." Howard knelt down, took off one glove, and extended the back of his hand. Turk reluctantly sniffed it and then slipped out his tongue for a brief lick. "No one around to feed you lately?" the deputy asked as he put his glove back on. "Come on, boy. Let's go inside and see if I can round you up some grub."

The dog crawled forward and then stopped.

Howard urged him on. "Come now, old boy. I know you got to be hungry."

Eventually with a tail barely wagging, Turk emerged from under the porch.

"That's better," Howard said and walked up the porch steps to the front door of the ranch house.

The door was unlocked, so Howard made to push it open, but there was something heavy on the other side stopping him from doing so. He gave a couple of strong shoves and managed to budge the door open wide enough to slip in.

Once inside, Howard said, "Damnation but it's dark in here." He waited a moment for his vision to adjust and discovered the kitchen table had been pushed against the inside of the door. He slid it away and then opened the door completely. "Oooeee," he said and blew a stream of air across his teeth. "Ain't this one hell of a mess."

The living room and kitchen had been ransacked. Furniture was overturned, eating utensils, pots, pans, and plates were strewn about chaotically. The wood slats from the couch and chairs had been pulled away and nailed across the windows, which had been covered with blankets underneath those slats.

The deputy slipped off his hat and scratched his forehead. "Hell, no wonder it's as dark as pitch in here," he said studying the windows.

Turk let loose a high, miserable howl that caused Howard to jump and draw his gun. He looked out the front door and found the old bird dog standing there. Turk then issued another eerie yowl.

"Shush, boy. Might be somebody in here."

Hackles rose on the back of Howard's neck as he remembered the mangled bodies of the horses. He kept his gun drawn and went down one hallway. Turk ran in, leapt ahead of the deputy, and headed straight for the bedroom at the end of the hall. The dog whined and scratched on the door and glanced in Howard's direction as if to say 'Hurry up! Down here!'

Keeping a constant vigil behind as well as in front, Howard advanced cautiously. It seemed an eternity before he stood by the dog still frantically scratching on the bedroom door.

The deputy turned the doorknob and felt resistance behind this door too. He shoved harder and again managed to get enough opening to squeeze through. He reached behind the door and discovered a bed had been pushed against it. The object was heavy enough to cause Howard considerable effort to move it to the side and away from the door.

Howard realized this must be Adam and Donny Cross' bedroom because of teenage boy objects in it. Those items, like the ones in the front of the house, were tossed about as if from an internal storm. Boots, hats, bed sheets, and a Winchester rifle littered the floor.

Even with the bedroom door wide open now, it was hard for Howard to see clearly in the gloom. But he did see well enough to notice a second bed had been turned over and glimpsed the tip of a boot slide under that bed as what little light intruded and brushed against it.

And then, from behind the deputy, Turk issued another ghastly howl.

Howard turned around and said, "Sshh, boy." It was at that moment he heard a rustling sound.

He cocked the hammer of his revolver and inched farther into the room. By now Howard's vision had adjusted to the dimness. He spotted a wad of blankets in one corner and noticed an outline pushing from underneath the material.

"All right now," he said. "This here is Deputy Sheriff Howard Sparks, and I want you, whoever you are, to get out from under that blanket." He then glanced briefly at the bed. "And from under that bed too. And put your hands up when you do." There was no response. Howard came closer to the clump of blankets and repeated, "Get out from under them blankets and the bed right now!"

This time the form under the blanket shifted, and a low hissing sound came from it. The hair on the nape of Howard's neck bristled. "Sounds like a cat hissing. Don't by God look like no cat, though."

Whoever or whatever it was made no move to leave its protective cover. The deputy gritted his teeth and reached for the blankets. "One, two, three," he said to himself before he grabbed a handful of fabric and quickly jerked it away.

Howard had to suppress a scream when Lucas Cross turned his face around and glared red-eyed with lips opening and closing over long, upper canines. Lucas' face was smeared with dried blood wafting an odor of metal and salt and corruption into the air. The rancher's hissing turned into a guttural growl.

"Hard gettin' around in the daytime," Howard said through a dry throat. "Ain't it, Lucas?"

Lucas' eyes narrowed and he straightened up. No longer dressed in long johns, he'd had the presence of mind to put on some old jeans and a flannel shirt. The absence of the long johns made Lucas appear even more terrible as he struggled to move toward the deputy.

Howard backed away and aimed the revolver's barrel dead center on the rancher's forehead. Lucas lunged at the deputy, and Howard fired. The back of Lucas' head exploded, and he fell backward.

Turk yelped and ran away down the hall. Howard glanced over his shoulder and saw the dog had fled. "I'd do the same, old boy, but there's still one under that bed."

Howard grabbed the bottom legs of the bed and flipped it over, leaving a heavy mattress still covering what lay beneath. He holstered his gun, grabbed the mattress ends with both hands, took a deep breath, and pulled it forward uncovering the upper half of Adam Cross' body. Adam struggled to get out from under the mattress. Like his father, he spat and growled and bared fearsome teeth.

Howard pulled his weapon and fired into the side of Adam's head. The boy tensed momentarily and then fell forward. The deputy sighed. His body shook. He went to his knees and felt tears roll down his cheeks. "Goddamn but I'm sorry about this, Lucas. Adam. I had to; don't you see?"

He regained as much composure as possible and stood up. As he holstered his gun, Howard saw the clump of blankets move again.

Sobered by this new development, the deputy approached the blankets and pulled them away. Bonnie Cross slowly turned her head and opened her eyes.

Howard drew his gun as if in slow motion. "Not a child. I cain't shoot no little girl."

Bonnie snarled and rose sluggishly. Her face contorted. With teeth snapping like an advancing trap, she stumbled toward the deputy and raised her arms. Her eyes moved quickly from side to side as if searching for something before she growled and jumped forward with surprising speed. The gun exploded as she flew at Howard. The impact of the bullet smashing into her skull threw Bonnie back hard against a wall where she slid down in an immobile heap.

The smoke from the revolver drifted around Howard's tortured expression. "Goddamnit. Goddamnit all to hell."

TWENTY-FIVE

"What did Pastor Jones say?" Bertram asked.

Newell Scruggs glanced across Stone's desk, frowned, and said, "The good pastor informed me, with as much cynicism he could muster, the only thing rising from the grave, besides Jesus Christ, was someone who wasn't dead in the first place. He then asked me to leave and told me such a ludicrous question was highly improper in lieu of the young Cooper girls' deaths."

The sheriff groaned. "Hell's bells. I imagine that's the kind of reception my news to the citizens of Hamilton is gonna get."

"What do you plan to do? Have a general meeting?"

"That thought crossed my mind, but I don't think anybody is likely to believe the truth. I suppose a little white lie may be in order."

"What would that be?"

"Well, we haven't had a good epidemic around here since the flu outbreak a few years back. I can issue an alert that Lucas and his boys, along with Eli Snow, contracted an infection of unknown type and suffered symptoms of murderous hostility."

"A disease like rabies, perhaps?"

"Yep. That will keep most of our good citizens holed up and alert until I can destroy the real monsters roamin' around."

Newell coughed to clear his throat. "I haven't had a chance to catch up with what you and Doctor Peterson found at Eli Snow's cabin, but by your haggard appearance, it was probably not pleasant."

"I tell you, Newell, if you think vampires are a mind-bogglin' development, I got somethin' we ran into at Eli's place that'll top 'em."

———

THE PAIN from his broken ribs dulled by the help of bourbon shots, Dr. James Peterson sat at his desk. He had decided to lay off laudanum and stick to alcohol, which he found he could tolerate and still keep a relatively clear mind.

On his desktop lay a writing tablet and pencil. Peterson had written at the top of the tablet's first page: **Things We Know**. At the beginning of the second page, he had penciled the heading: **Reference from Legends and Folklore**.

Peterson had just picked up the tablet when Bertram and Newell walked into the medical office. The opened door allowed a burst of cold air to enter with them. The sheriff and the undertaker dusted snow from their shoulders, both men keeping their coats and hats on. Being too occupied with his injured ribs and research to worry about the cold medical office, the doctor had yet to make a fire.

"Damn, Doc," Bertram said. "You plan on freezin' them cracked ribs numb?"

"What?" Peterson asked with distraction. He looked at the two men and saw they were shivering. "Oh, yes, a fire. Would one of you mind? I've been filled with warming liquor and haven't noticed the temperature. Of course, I don't think I would have been able to load wood into the stove without causing myself a great deal of pain."

"I'll see to it, Doctor," Newell said and walked to the far corner of the office behind the examination table. He opened the door of an iron stove and placed some cut logs stacked by the side in it. He then looked around and asked, "Is there any of your littered office paper I can use to get the fire started?"

The doctor chuckled. "Anything's game except my medical books."

Newell grabbed some wadded paper balls from the floor and arranged them under the logs. A box of matches sat on the stove's top. He struck one and soon had a fire going. Newell held his hands in front of the stove. "That's much better," he said, rubbing his hands briskly before closing the grate.

Bertram appeared to glance down at the writing tablet. "What you been workin' on, Doc?"

"I decided to approach this dilemma much like I would a medical one." Peterson pointed to the top of the first page. "I have listed the things we know. Those being what we've witnessed and also the rumors, founded or not, about Eli Snow and his family, most of those from your Native American friend, Bertram."

"You mean Smoke," Bertram said. By this time, Newell came over to join in.

"On the second page," Peterson said as he flipped the first over. "I have written what material I gathered on superstitions, legends, and folklore of Native Americans from the book Miss Hagler was kind enough to lend Bertram."

"Vivien Hagler?" Newell asked. "Did you share what has been going on with her?"

The sheriff nodded yes. "Everything except that headless thing. You're the second one to hear about that, Newell, after the doctor, here."

"I can't imagine what Miss Hagler thought," Newell said with a feeble grin.

"Well, either she was humoring me, or Miss Hagler wasn't quite as skeptical as you'd think." Bertram turned back to Peterson and asked, "What's first on your list, Doc?"

"We know these creatures are nocturnal. They have a strong aversion to sunlight, although I'm not certain what happens to them physically when exposed. And that it's very difficult to destroy them."

"That night with Eli Snow," Newell said. "It was only fire burning him that was effective, wasn't it? Not even being shot by you, Sheriff, even though Eli's brain exploded from his head."

"I couldn't believe Eli got up after I put a bullet in his skull. But he did, and, by God, he was still comin' for us after he was set on fire," Bertram said.

"That's something else we know," Peterson said. "These things are relentless when going after what they want."

All three men glanced at each other. It was Newell who finally said, "Blood, isn't it? They want blood."

"Goddamn vampires!" Bertram exclaimed. His face turned red. He took off his coat and hat and hung them on the coat rack. "Gettin' hot in here now," he said as he sat down and pulled his chair close to Peterson's desk. Newell hung up his coat and repeated the sheriff's action with a chair of his own.

"We also know that whatever makes these creatures vampires, or whatever they are, is transmitted by their bite. I still believe there is some viral agent or microbe involved," Peterson said.

"Then the Cooper girls?" Newell questioned. "Even though I severed their heads, will they still be able to...rise? Their bodies, I mean, like that headless creature Sheriff Stone told me you found at Eli Snow's cabin." He hesitated before asking, "Should they be burned then?"

"Good Lord," Bertram said with disgust. "Cain't we do something else? Hunter and Molly Cooper been through so much horror already. Ain't there some other way?"

Peterson sighed. "That's one of the things we don't know for sure. I've got a suspicion that unless the corpse has been reanimated..."

"Reanimated?" Newell asked.

"Yes. As I see it, that's what happens. The host is bled dry or the infection itself kills the host. Then the organism, by all that defies science, causes the body to rise from death." The doctor saw the stares from Bertram and Newell. "Believe me, gentlemen. Eli Snow was dead. No pulse, no breath. And Lucas Cross was almost dead when we had to leave him and deal with the newly risen Eli Snow."

Bertram visibly shivered. "I guess we'll have to burn the Cooper girls' bodies after all."

"As I was saying, I suspect unless the body had already been reanimated by the disease, it's quite possible that removing the head is sufficient. But I can't be certain. The only way to find out is to watch the Cooper girls' corpses after sundown. If they are going to turn, it will be then."

The sheriff snorted. "And what if they do come back? Are they gonna pick up their heads and leave? Are their heads gonna reanimate too?"

"There's just no way to be sure," Peterson said. "It's either burning the bodies or taking a chance."

"Damn. I guess this is where bein' sheriff sucks," Bertram said. "And to think I left the Rangers for this job so I could relax and ride off into the sunset at peace with myself. Burnin' little girls' corpses and chasing vampires wasn't what I had in mind."

Newell and Peterson laughed nervously.

After a few moments, Bertram asked, "What about the legends, Doc? Anything helpful in Miss Hagler's book?"

Peterson folded first page of the writing tablet under its back. "There's quite a bit here, actually. That word your friend Smoke used, the one you couldn't pronounce. Could it have been Tlahuelpuchi?"

"By God, that's it," Bertram said and snapped his fingers. "The very word Smoke spoke to me."

The doctor frowned. "Then, if Eli's wife was one of these powerful sorceresses and because of her alleged cannibalism took on the spirit of a wendigo as well, gentlemen we are in for a terrible fight indeed with the fruits of what she spawned."

"Why the wendigo connection?" Newell asked. "I do know a little about that Native American legend. Wasn't it a superstition of the more northern tribes? Linked to starvation in the winter and the wasting state of tuberculosis victims?"

Peterson smiled. "That's what it says in the book, Newell. I didn't realize you had knowledge of the wendigo."

"My mother read me a story about it when I was a boy," Newell said. "I was plagued with nightmares for a long time after."

"So, if Eli's wife had a bastard child made even more damnable because of incest, would that child inherit the traits of the sorceress and the wendigo?" Bertram asked. "I still don't see no vampire in that scenario."

"That's just it," Peterson said. "A child like that could have become anything. You told me Vivien Hagler said Jacob Snow was frightening in appearance. She mentioned he had feral features."

"She did," Bertram said.

"So, maybe Jacob Snow wasn't necessarily a vampire. Maybe he was an unnatural beast. With the powers he inherited, Jacob could do anything to his victims, even make them vampires if he chose to," Peterson said.

"But aren't these creatures susceptible to the same weaknesses that any vampires would be?" Newell asked. "The repelling objects we hear about as children?"

"You mean garlic, crucifixes, holy water...a stake through the heart?" Peterson asked with a strange smile on his face.

"Yeah, sure," Bertram said. "There's other ways to kill them things besides fire. Just might not be as reliable"

The doctor reached into a desk drawer and pulled out a new bottle of bourbon. He dug around until he found two more shot glasses and set them on the desktop. Without having to be asked, Bertram and Newell took the glasses and the bourbon Peterson poured into them.

The doctor took a drink and touched his bandaged ribs tenderly. "This book of Vivien Hagler's also has some reflections of scholars and men of science. The crosses and holy water have been dismissed by most as European religious influences. I mean, what would happen if you held a cross up to a Buddhist vampire?"

Newell smiled. "Oh, yes. I see their point."

"As far as a stake through the heart, there was never any conclusion other than that act probably killed more innocent people than monsters. Fire seems to be the accepted way to ensure destruction."

"What about garlic?" Bertram asked.

"The scholars and scientists think garlic may indeed repel vampires, if vampires do exist, but only in an allergenic way. Certainly, it would not kill them." Peterson pushed the writing tablet aside. "All of these legends and theories lead me to believe what we call vampirism is a disease from an organism similar to rabies." He poured himself and his two cohorts another glass of bourbon. "The idea of an evil spirit being the cause can be debunked for the same reason as crosses. It is not God or Satan at work here, gentlemen. It is some type of microscopic, infective agent."

The men were silent for a while. It was Bertram who broke that silence. "Funny you should mention rabies, Doc."

Shaking windows and rattling wooden boards, a north wind whistled around the building.

———

After shooting what had once been a little girl, Deputy Howard Sparks descended into quiet desperation in the Cross brother's bedroom. Time slipped by him in a vague blur. It took the distant and unworldly howling of Turk to bring the deputy back down to earth.

Howard glanced at the bodies of Lucas, Adam, and Bonnie Cross. When he felt sobs threaten to grip him, he stood up from his kneeling position and ambled to the door and walked out, moving down the hallway like a somnambulist. Howard stopped by the kitchen table and glanced around as if unaware of where he was and then walked down the other hall and into Lucas' bedroom.

The room was trashed like those in the rest of the house, its window covered and boarded as well. From under Lucas' bed, the deputy discovered the neck of a bottle glistening in the dim light sifting through the boarded window. He pulled the bottle out and heard another one clink against it. He bent down and found three more bottles besides the one he held. The seals on each bottle were unbroken, and they were all full of rye whiskey.

Howard carried the bottles back to the living room. He sat three of them on the kitchen table and carried the fourth outside. He sat on the top porch step and broke the bottle's seal and then took a long drink before setting the bottle on the wooden planks of the porch.

Snow was still falling, but it was not as heavy as earlier and came down in a steady tumble disturbed occasionally into a swirling, white image by the erratic north wind.

Howard stared at the drifting flakes as they fell on the snow-packed ground. He grabbed the bottle of rye and took another long drink. His mind ticked like an over-wound clock.

When images of the things the Cross' had become appeared, the deputy would tilt the bottle again until, finally, the alcohol put him into a wakeful coma. Somewhere in his brain a question surfaced Howard had not considered when shooting those three things in the bedroom: Where did the Cross girl come from? Hadn't she been missing for over ten years? Why had she not grown in all that time?

The answers were buried under inebriation, and he chose not to disturb his numbness by digging deeper for an explanation. With bleary eyes, Howard scrutinized the land around the house, the stable, and the empty corral. In the distance, he heard Turk baying that God awful and desolate sound again.

Suddenly concerned for the dog's well-being, the deputy told himself, "Best see to that old boy. No need in all the Cross' being wiped out."

Howard stood and swayed until his legs felt secure enough to walk down the porch steps. Continuing to drink from the severely depleted bottle of rye whiskey, he staggered forward through the falling snow in the direction of the howls.

TWENTY-SIX

D r. James Peterson filled out the official forms needed to alert the townspeople of Hamilton that a rabies quarantine had been issued by him at the order of Sheriff Bertram Stone.

The sheriff collected Deputy Gus Greenwood from Martha Cooper's side and instructed him and Newell Scruggs to take the notices to all of the town's businesses. He directed the two men to offer an explanation that the people living in town were not to leave their homes or stores unless it was unavoidable.

"How long?" an irritated Abraham Tanner asked. "I can't let my business be closed for too many days. There're people who come from outside Hamilton needing supplies." He eyed the falling snow and added, "Especially since the weather's turned nasty."

"Don't know for sure," Gus said, placing a quarantine notice on the General Mercantile's front window. "But I'll tell you, Mr. Tanner, I done seen what that disease can do to a human, and believe you me, you don't want no part of it."

"What do you mean? You talking about Eli and Lucas? That

what killed Eli and made Lucas sick? And what about Eli's remains being stored in my meat locker? Are they contagious?"

The deputy started to tell Abraham more about Eli and Lucas but then remembered his strict orders from Sheriff Stone. "Sheriff said to be sure everybody in town knew what's goin' on. I ain't supposed to say no more than that."

———

NEWELL ENCOUNTERED similar questions with the other residents and store owners he alerted and gave the same vague information. When he came to the Koffee Kup Kafe, the undertaker's stomach tied into a knot. He wasn't quite certain how Hunter and Molly would react to being kept from their daughters' remains for an unknown period of time.

It was Molly who answered his knocking.

"I'm sorry to disturb you at such a time, Mrs. Cooper, but I have been instructed to place a rabies quarantine on all businesses, and also homes down on the edge of Hamilton."

Molly never said a word about the quarantine. She grabbed Newell's arm and said, "Why, Mr. Scruggs, it's so good of you to drop by. Please come in. I'll fix you a nice breakfast." There was a strange, distant look in her eyes. The genial smile she wore quivered as if struggling to stay in place.

"Oh, no, Mrs. Cooper. You should be resting. I'll just put this notice on your door and be on my way."

"Mr. Scruggs, you come in out of the cold and snow. I'll get some coffee going first, and then I'll fry you some eggs and bacon and throw together a batch of biscuit batter."

As he stood in the open doorway, waves of sympathy flooded Newell. "But Mrs. Cooper."

"Now don't be silly," she said, walking behind the counter

to fill a coffee pot with water. "Hunter's a bit under the weather, but I can get you a good breakfast in no time."

"What's goin' on?" The voice behind Newell caused to him jump. Sheriff Bertram Stone put a hand on the undertaker's shoulder. "Sorry, Newell, didn't mean to spook you." The sheriff gazed at Molly, busy cracking eggs and frying bacon between sifting out flour for biscuit dough. She was humming some religious song. "Just a Closer Walk with Thee" came to mind, and he felt his cheeks begin to flush.

"Why good mornin' to you too, Sheriff." Molly beamed when she saw him standing behind Newell. "You just come on in with Mr. Scruggs and have a seat. There'll be some coffee ready directly."

Newell turned and whispered to Bertram, "Poor woman's in shock. What should we do?"

The sheriff shook his head and was about to say something when Hunter Cooper came in through the back door. He glanced at Bertram and Newell with sunken eyes welled by dark, purple circles. Hunter nodded to the men in the café's doorway and then tenderly grabbed his wife's arms to make her stop cooking.

"Come back to bed, dear. I missed you when I woke up," Hunter said.

"Why, Hunter, can't you see we've got customers? Put on an apron and help me, you old lazy bones," Molly said.

"Molly." Hunter pulled her arms away from a mound of flour she'd deposited on the wooden cooking island beside the grill. "Come on back with me now."

Molly's smile vanished. She jerked away from Hunter, tossed flour in the air, and said, "Stop it! Let me go." Making them look like quarreling ghosts, the flour settled on their faces and bodies. Hunter reached for Molly again and she made to slap him, but he caught her hand midair. She stared wide eyed for a moment before collapsing into a sobbing mass on Hunter's shoulder.

Hunter held up a hand to let Bertram and Newell know he had control of Molly. The sheriff tugged on Newell's shoulder and pulled the undertaker backward through the threshold. Bertram then closed the door to the café, and said, "You can come back and tell Hunter about the quarantine later. Let's give them some time."

"I'll see to it." Newell noticed the increasing snowfall. "You still plan on riding your horse out to Eli Snow's cabin? You might be hard pressed in this weather."

"Nope. Old Lucy wouldn't speak to me for a week if I made her brave these conditions, although there were times she's hauled me through some pretty unpleasant weather and never complained." He grinned and said, "Hell, ain't none of us gettin' any younger, I reckon."

"Doesn't your deputy, Howard, have the Ford? And don't you need to get out to Eli's long before sundown, snow or not?"

"Damned straight I do. After what I seen, you won't catch me out alone after dark, even in town here. I still got Lucas' Model T. Never did get the chance to take it back out to them boys." The sheriff frowned. "Battry's probably down, but I can charge it and pump some gas from Abraham's store and still have plenty of time to go to Eli's place. I'll just have to get through that thick brush beyond the cabin some other way to check on what I'm goin' there for."

"What would that be?"

"There's an old burned down ranch house deep into the property with a storm cellar. When I was out that way before, the day Donny Cross come lookin' for me to help with Lucas, I thought I heard somethin' rustlin' around down in the bottom of that cellar. I looked in it, but it was black as pitch, and I couldn't see nuthin' but shadows. An old tomcat came runnin' out so I thought it was him makin' the racket. Course, after what me and Doc Peterson run into out there, I expect it might be somethin' bigger than that old scrawny cat that likes to hole up in the bottom of that cellar."

"Sheriff Stone, I would be glad to go with you. I don't imagine Dr. Peterson will be able to help much with those broken ribs."

"Thanks, Newell. I'd feel a damned sight more at ease with a second, but I'd rather you and Gus stick around town. I'll probably run into Howard on the way out there. More than likely he's still at the Cross ranch. I'll stop by and get him to go with me."

The undertaker nodded, looked at Bertram, and found the shadow of the old, fierce Texas Ranger emerging from the sheriff's eyes. Newell tipped the brim of his stovepipe hat, turned, and headed toward the next store down the wooden walkway.

———

BERTRAM HAD no trouble getting Lucas Cross' Model T up and running. He headed out of town just before ten in the morning, affording him plenty of daylight. He was about halfway to Eli's cabin when the vehicle started sputtering.

"No you don't," Bertram said as he attempted to keep the engine going. The snow had increased as well as the wind. Bertram struggled to keep a vigil on the road through slow moving windshield wipers while steadily pressing the gas pedal to prevent the engine from stalling. "Probably somethin' in the gas line," he said, still pumping the pedal.

A burst of wind buffeted the side of the Model T, and he lost control. The vehicle swerved harshly and jolted the sheriff against the wheel. When he got things steadied, the engine smoothed out.

"Whew," Bertram said through a strained laugh. "That hit from the wind must have helped clear the gas line."

Bertram relaxed, dug under his coat, and pulled out a tin of rolled cigarettes from his shirt pocket. Holding the steering wheel with one hand, he opened the tin with the other, pulled a cigarette free and lit it deftly, his eyes never leaving the meager field of view in front of him.

Bertram spit bits of tobacco away and took a long drag. He was just blowing the warm smoke from his lungs when a deer suddenly appeared in his path. The heavy snowfall had veiled the animal until the sheriff was nearly on top of it.

"Damnation!" Bertram swore, steering hard away from the shocked and petrified animal.

The Model T went down into a shallow gully by the road-side and then bounced back up, breaking through a line of barbed wire that was tightly strung between fence posts bordering a field. The wire screeching down the sides of the vehicle were like fingernails on a blackboard. The Model T finally came to a halt with its front end down in a deep plowed row, causing Bertram's head to bang solidly against the steering wheel. He briefly lost consciousness, his vision filling with an infinity of swirling, black dots as he fought to regain his senses. There was an uncomfortable warmth on one of his legs that grew into a hot bolt of pain as a fallen ember from the cigarette burned though the sheriff's khakis.

"Hot damn!" Bertram yelled, the pain bringing back his senses.

He swiped the ember off his leg. The ember landed on the floor and glared a single, red eye up at Bertram as if in condemnation of being denied flesh to fry before Bertram crushed it under his boot heel.

The sheriff's hat had been knocked off during the collision with the steering wheel. He grabbed it from the dashboard and put it back on. His fingers brushed something warm and sticky. "Sure nuff," he said with exasperation as he rubbed blood between his fingers.

Bertram glanced in the rearview mirror and saw a gash across his forehead. Blood welled in the wound's groove and spilled over, sliding into his left eye. He reached in his back pants pocket, pulled out a handkerchief, and scrutinized it. "Not too snotty," he said with a chuckle while folding the handkerchief into a thick square. He then held it tightly against the cut on his head and leaned back, taking long, deep breaths. He sat that way for a while before retracing what had occurred. The wide eyes of the deer came back to him followed by the memory of the vehicle crashing through the fence and landing front down in the plowed row.

"Busted my noggin a good one," he said out loud. "Should have come out on old Lucy after all. She's been in worse weather."

The handkerchief quickly saturated with blood as the sheriff saw snow was piling on the angled engine's hood, and he knew he had to get moving. He pushed the driver's door open and slid out still pressing the wadded hanky tight against the cut.

When his feet came down on the packed snow, Bertram was immediately overcome with vertigo. He leaned against the side of the Model T. Nausea gripped him. He took more deep breaths. The icy air helped ease his dizzy, queasy feeling, and in a few moments, he felt his body stabilize.

By now the handkerchief could absorb no more. Blood ran freely down Bertram's face. "Damnit!" he said, attempting to keep blood out of his eyes. "Damned deer!"

Bertram guided himself down the side of the vehicle, which leaned at a forty-five-degree angle. He grabbed a handful of snow off the hood and shaped it into a flat mass. While replacing his handkerchief with the wad of snow, the fabric stuck to the gash briefly and tugged at the torn skin before separating. The pain was intense for a moment, but a blessed numbness soon followed. As if in reverberation from the cut on his forehead, the back of the sheriff's head began to pound dully.

Bertram looked down with eyes teary from the cold compress and focused on the plowed row where the automobile's grill rested. "What in hell was the sumbitch who owns this land plantin' anyway. Must be one goddamned giant group of seeds." Then, it came to the sheriff. "I'll be a stupid sumbitch myself," he said, his head now completely numb. "Fuckin' irrigation ditch. Probably gonna lay some pipe come springtime."

Bertram sensed the bleeding had slowed. He pulled the cold wad off his head, made a fresh one, put it back on the cut and then surveyed exactly where he was and how far off the road he'd traveled. The sheriff glanced back at the Model T and saw its rear wheels were off the ground. He realized there was little chance he could right it and get the engine started without someone's help.

He looked for any chimney smoke nearby, but the snow still fell thickly and obscured his view. "If I remember correctly, the farmhouse connected to this field is way back off the road," he said. "Just cain't clear these cobwebs enough to recall in which direction."

Bertram leaned against the driver's side of the vehicle. He dispensed with the current snow pack, shaped another, and placed it on his wound. After a while he took it off and gingerly traced the line across the abrasion. He looked at his fingers and discovered very little blood. He decided to stop placing pressure packs of snow on the cut to see if it would bleed again or not, and he was soon satisfied the bleeding had slowed down to a small seepage. Bertram then made up his mind to walk down the road toward Lucas Cross' ranch, which would be closer than going back to town. He tested his cut again and was content the bleeding had stopped and walked away from the four-wheeled heap.

He had gone no more than twenty feet when sudden dizziness sent him tumbling to the snow packed ground. His head hit first, reopening the wound.

The sheriff struggled to regain his footing and then fell down face first in the snow. Warm blood flowed freely down his head again. His skull was in a bent position allowing the blood to snake around his hat brim and pool inside of it.

He reached a shaky hand up and pulled off his hat. He clumped a small hill of snow together and laid his cut directly on it as if it were a frosty pillow. Closing his eyes, Bertram drifted off briefly only to be awakened by the sound of something walking toward him. He felt a surge of hope certain that Deputy Howard Sparks had been heading back to town and saw Lucas Cross' floundered automobile.

Squinting against the falling white flakes, Bertram raised his head. The deer that caused him to swerve off the road stood warily out of reach with its ears back, its eyes scrutinizing the fallen human.

The sheriff couldn't help but laugh. "Come to apologize?" he asked through the dull throbbing in his head.

Hearing Bertram speak, the deer backed away and stood very still. Its neck stiff and elevated, it turned and trotted away into the field. The sheriff watched as the fleeing figure was eventually swallowed in a haze of plummeting white.

Bertram rolled over. The bleeding had stopped again. He felt dried blood crackle as he wrinkled his brow under an escalating headache.

"Well," he said. "Best face the music and take it easy for a spell. No use faintin' and freezin' to death."

He raised himself slowly off the ground. Still a little weak in the knees, he stood and tried to regain his balance. When he felt he had steadied, the sheriff entertained the idea of reaching down to gather his hat. He bent slightly and felt an immediate lightheadedness again.

"Damn," he said. "Me and that Stetson been through a lot over the years." He sighed and walked tentatively back toward the Model T. "Maybe the weather won't treat it too unkindly."

It seemed an eternity to travel those few feet to the pickup, and Bertram had to stop occasionally to maintain steadiness. Finally, he found himself by the driver's door, which he opened with slow deliberation before hefting his body in the seat and closing the door behind him.

Bertram lay sideways on the seat, wooziness clinging to him. With a headache that promised to be thunderous very soon, he watched snow fall on the outside windshield's glass.

"Ain't supposed to have this kind of weather until December no how," the sheriff said, closed his eyes, and drifted away below the pain and gathering fog in his skull.

Twenty-Seven

Its fleshy rot slowed by cold weather, the headless thing lay in the storm cellar's darkness. Heavy snow packed on top of the door above, some falling through the cracks and drifting down like cold feathers onto the thing's rotten form.

But the thing did not feel the wet cold of the snow, nor did it comprehend the earth above was covered in a majestic, frozen blanket of white. It only felt a void and an absence knowing the girl was not there. That fact filled the thing with dread and confusion. There was another here in the deep recess of the underground room, but it was not the girl, and it did not call to the thing.

It could not have told you how, but the thing was aware the sun, floating fiery and distant above a mass of clouds, was still in the heavens.

Its abdominal wound opening briefly in a mimicked and morbid putrid smile, the headless thing stirred. It had no sense of time, no notion of the universal gears spinning in a wound clock that moved forward. But somehow, a memory traveled the dead nerve fibers of its body with images made for an absent brain. The thing and Eli Snow and the girl journeyed that line of recollection down dead pathways to an evening years ago when Jacob Snow and the girl had stirred from their hellish slumber. Blood and gore from their last kill clung to their lips and hands. The body of a pig lay nearby, its stink flat and subtle in the bowels of the dirt cellar.

———

Jacob felt the arms of Bonnie Cross wrap around his neck. She glanced at the pig's carcass and licked her lips. "Hungry," she said. "No blood left."

Jacob pulled her arms away from his neck and stood up. A line of fury filled his heart. "You up there, old man?" he asked. "You ever gonna let us out of this hole?"

The door at the top of the cellar stairs creaked open. With a burning torch gripped in his hand, Eli Snow stood above like an Old Testament prophet come to judge the wicked. "If I have any say over it, you and the creature you made of that innocent child will never walk on this land again."

"You'll slip up one night, old man. Now that Arlis run away, you ain't got nobody to help you. You can sleep all day, but you still got to find time to take care of your land. And most of that got to be done in the daylight." A smile spread over Jacob's feral features. "You'll get lax sooner or later. Bound to."

Bonnie grabbed Jacob's leg and stared at Eli with curiosity. Her eyes reflected red against their underlying deep cobalt. Her mouth was partially open. Sharp canines protruded over her lower lip.

Eli shuddered. "Why didn't you kill that one, boy? Whole damn county and then some was lookin' for her back then. You could've brought ruin down on me and your brother."

Jacob reached under Bonnie's rear and hefted her up. He cradled her between his arm and chest like a father carrying an exhausted child. "I needed company."

"Company? Hell, boy, me and your brother was company."

"No. You was keepers."

"That there ain't all true. I just couldn't let you run wild. I made you promise not to go off this land, but you broke your word and then did something far worse than killing livestock." Eli pointed a finger down at Bonnie. "You took a human and, by God, decided to make her like you."

"She ain't exactly like me," Jacob said and set Bonnie down. Picking up the pig's body, Jacob ripped a large chunk of its flank away with his teeth. He chewed the dry, stringy flesh and grinned up at Eli. "She don't eat no meat," he said. Jacob heard Bonnie groan. He glanced at her and saw saliva stringing from her mouth. "It's blood she wants."

Eli turned to Bonnie and found her eyes locked on him. She was grinding her teeth, her face strained in a kind of ravenous rage.

Jacob saw her too and laughed. "She sure would like to drink your blood, old man."

Eli stared at Jacob and the slick juices running down his chin in the reflected torch light. It locked him in a state of fascinated repugnance for an instant, and he didn't see Bonnie race up the cellar steps until she was almost on top of him.

Eli thrust the torch into Bonnie's face. She screamed and fell back down, landing hard on the dirt floor of the cellar. "Damned she-devil!" Eli shrieked.

Jacob put the pig meat down and wiped his sticky hands on his deteriorating overalls. He had removed his shirt, socks, and shoes years ago because they'd rotted away.

Jacob laughed a dry and dusty sound. "And she's a fast she-devil, old man," he said with a big grin. A part of the pig's hind leg bone rested between Jacob's teeth. He crunched it and let the marrow spread over his back molars like honey paste. "Hmmm. I do love bone marrow."

HEARING HIS SON CRACK BONE, Eli felt a sick shudder move over him. He noticed Bonnie was already stirring, and he put his guard back up.

Jacob glared at Eli for a while before asking, "Well, did you bring us somethin' or not? I guess you done figured out my playmate here is kinda thirsty."

Eli set the burning torch down with its end hovering in the opening of the storm cellar. Jacob and Bonnie instinctively moved further back and away from the heat coming down.

The stomps of Eli's heavy footsteps came back with another sound accompanying them. It was a funny, strangled noise, high pitched and panicked. Eli picked up the torch while simultaneously dropping a canvas bag into the cellar. The contents of the bag struggled wildly once it hit the floor.

Jacob grinned sardonically as he watched Bonnie fall on the bag and pull impatiently at the leather strip binding it. "Sure don't sound like no pig," he said with relish. "That's a pleasant surprise, as I was tiring of pork."

Bleating insanely, a lamb broke out of the bag. It didn't make it a foot away before Bonnie lunged and grabbed it. She snarled, digging her fangs into the creature's neck. She hung on to the struggling animal while Jacob pulled the lamb on its side, eviscerated it with his teeth, and gobbled intestines and blood like a ravaging beast.

Eli turned away. He closed the cellar door against the dying cries of the lamb and the ghastly sounds of the two feeding on it. He touched the torch to a circle of kerosene he'd poured around and slightly away from the storm cellar's door. The fuel lit up in a ring of fire that would burn for hours. Later, when the fire died down, Eli would come back and set a new one, and another after that one, and still another until sunrise.

TWENTY-EIGHT

Standing inside the medical office, Deputy Gus Greenwood said, "It's gettin' to be late afternoon, Doc. I'm beginnin' to get a little worried. Ain't heard from Howard or Sheriff Stone. Won't be long 'til sunset." He frowned and pulled air across his teeth. "You know what that means."

Dr. James Peterson had been sound asleep when the deputy arrived. He was still lethargic from another laudanum dose prompted by recurring pain from his broken ribs.

"Let me get my head cleared." Peterson rubbed his face. "That drug really put me under. Now, you say you haven't heard from Bertram or Howard."

"That's right, and its goin' on four o'clock. Sun starts settin' around five thirty or so."

The doctor took a shallow breath. His ribs responded with a dull ache. "Did you try phoning the Cross ranch house? Howard might be inside waiting out the snowstorm." He glanced out his office window and saw flakes still falling in a steady, thick motion. "Doesn't look like it's going to stop anytime soon. The weather's probably delayed both Bertram and Howard."

"I don't know, Doc. I did call the Cross place several times but got no answer. Howard's been gone since about eight this mornin'. Sheriff Stone headed out around ten. Hell of it is they took the only two vehicles in town. Ain't nothin' left but horses, and I don't imagine I'd make good time riding out to look for them even if I wanted to, which I don't, not in this weather and it only being a few hours 'til dark."

"Where is Newell?"

"Mr. Scruggs is next door. Said he needed a little nap. Said somethin' about staying up all night watchin' the Cooper girls' bodies. Wouldn't tell me why exactly, but it don't take much imagination."

The doctor scanned the ashtrays on his desk for any salvageable cigar butt. He finally decided on a severely short one because it had the driest chewed end. He stuck it in the side of his mouth and began gnawing on it. "Maybe we should call the Hico or Gatesville police departments."

The deputy shook his head no. "I done tried that hours ago. Must be somethin' wrong with their phone lines. Probably this weather. I didn't get nothin' but crackly static."

Peterson removed the cigar butt from his mouth, looked at it, frowned and then put it back between his lips on the opposite side of his mouth. "Well," he said. "If the weather wasn't so bad, I'd suggest you head out on horseback, but I have to agree with you, Gus; it'd be too risky. You'd better stick around the sheriff's office in case a call comes through from Howard. Nothing much else we can do but wait it out."

"Anythin' I can do for you before I head back to the courthouse?"

"No. I think I'll try to walk over to Newell's and keep him company for a while."

"Want me to help you? I mean, them busted ribs aren't gonna like you walkin' none."

"I'll take a few shots of bourbon. That should help me get over there later."

Gus tipped his hat. "Well, I'm gonna stop by and check on Martha for a bit before I go to the courthouse. But if you need somethin', call either place and I'll come and help you out."

"Thanks, Gus. You take care now."

The deputy grabbed the doorknob and opened the medical office door. The cold air drifted in as he said, "See you later, Doc." Then he strode out into the waning afternoon.

———

IN THE DISTANCE, Bertram heard a subdued tapping. He opened his eyes slowly. Blurred vision greeted him along with a rhythmic throbbing in his head.

Tap tap tap.

The sheriff gingerly pulled himself up. His vision began to clear. He then remembered the deer on the road, the crash into the field, slamming his head on the steering column, and having to stay in the vehicle because of dizziness.

He saw nothing now but solid snow obscuring the Model T's windows and windshield. "Where's that tappin' comin' from?" he asked under his breath.

Bertram coughed a wad of phlegm and held it in his mouth until he could reach into his pocket for a handkerchief. When his hand didn't find anything, he recalled using the hankie to hold against the bleeding gash on his head. The handkerchief was outside somewhere probably frozen stiff and buried in snow. With a look of disgust, he swallowed the mucous. "Damned nasty," he said with a frown.

Something caught his eye in the center of the driver's window. Little bits of snow were being flicked away. Fingertips emerged as they hurled the frozen precipitation aside.

"In here," Bertram shouted. "I'm in here. I'm hurt."

"Sheriff Stone?" The words from outside were muffled, but the sheriff recognized Deputy Howard Sparks' voice.

Bertram scooted over to the door and unlocked it. "Pull on the handle, Howard. I'll push at the same time." He felt a hint of vertigo when he strained against the frozen door, but he kept leaning his weight against the metal until the door began to budge. One last effort along with Howard's pulling on the other side opened it.

"You okay, Sheriff Stone?" Howard asked.

A wave of boozy breath made the sheriff's eyes water. "You been drinkin', Howard?"

With a stupid grin on his face, the deputy nodded. He pulled a bottle of rye whiskey from inside his coat and held it out to the sheriff. The bottle was a third full. "Care for a snort? Imagine you're pretty cold out here in this metal bucket." Howard eyed the vehicle's upended rear. "What the hell happened?"

"Deer ran in front of me, and I had to swerve. Lost control and ended up here. I hit my head pretty hard on the steering wheel."

The deputy shoved the bottle toward him again. "This might help then."

"No, thanks. I think you done had enough for both of us." The sheriff glanced outside and realized that daylight was waning. "What time is it?"

"Ouch!" Howard said when he looked over the gash on Bertram's head. "You did bang er a good one, Sheriff."

"Never mind that. What time is it?"

"Oh, yeah." Howard glanced at his wristwatch. "Quarter of five."

Bertram slapped the dash hard. "Damned if I didn't doze the day away. I'll never get out to Snow's place in time now. Shit!"

"Snow's place? Why there?"

"I needed to check something out before sunset. Just have to wait on it now, I guess."

"Hell," Howard said. Bertram noticed the deputy was swaying a little. "I'll go out there with you. I done shot three of them things dead out at the Cross ranch. Reckon there cain't be no more left anyhow unless that younger Cross boy, Donny, is out where you was headed."

"Shot who?"

The deputy lowered his head. "I couldn't help it, Sheriff. They was comin' for me in that back bedroom."

Bertram pulled himself out of the Model T. His legs felt much steadier now.

"Slow down, Howard. Tell me what you're talkin' about."

The deputy bent over. "I ain't feelin' too well all of a sudden," Howard said before vomiting.

The sheriff grabbed hold of Howard's collar and eased the deputy down on his knees. It wasn't until there was nothing left in his stomach and after the dry heaving ceased that Howard could be helped up on shaky legs.

———

BERTRAM ADJUSTED his Stetson he had rescued from partial burial under a small mound of snow as he moved the Ford his deputy had been driving back toward Hamilton. He had wanted to swing by the Cross ranch, but the dimming day and the heavy snowfall made him give up the idea.

"You sure it was Lucas you shot?" Bertram asked.

Howard was bent forward, his head lying on the dash. "Him and Adam and a child, a girl." He took a long breath to combat nausea. "Shot all them through the head."

"Where was they hiding?"

"In the back bedroom. The boys' room. They was all dug up under mattresses. It was still daytime outside."

"And you shot them in the head?"

The deputy turned his face toward the sheriff and scowled. "Hell yes, Sheriff Stone. I done told you I did." He then turned away. "I ain't too proud of it, neither."

"I doubt they're dead then."

This time Howard raised himself from the dashboard. He looked at the sheriff with irritation. "You callin' me a liar, Sheriff? You know me better than that."

Bertram could just make out a few dim lights in the distance through the snow and knew they were close to Hamilton. "No, Howard. I believe you shot them like you said you did. It's just that me and Doc Peterson and Newell have been studyin' on them things." He sighed before he said, "Vampires, I guess. And you have to destroy them with fire. You shoot them, they just keep comin' back."

"Sheriff, I saw brains and bone fly out the back of them heads. They cain't have survived."

Bertram looked at his deputy briefly before turning attention back to the road. "Howard, I shot Eli Snow just like you did them others. The impact threw him backwards. I knew a head shot like that had to have killed him, but it didn't. He got back up and came for us on those broken legs of his like he'd only tripped. We had to burn him, and even as he was burnin', he still tried to crawl to us."

"So, the ones at the ranch, the ones I shot?"

"What time is it now?"

"Huh?"

"The time."

Howard seemed confused as to why Bertram hadn't answered his question. The deputy stayed mute.

"The time, Howard. What time of day is it?"

The deputy checked his watch. "Right at five thirty."

"Then to answer your question, those three you shot are probably about to open their eyes any minute now."

———

DR. JAMES PETERSON attempted to push himself up from the desk chair. He had every intention of somehow maneuvering his aching body over to Newell Scruggs' funeral home and stand watch over the Cooper girls' bodies during the evening with the undertaker, but his ribs didn't care for the idea.

"Damn!" Peterson cursed as pain rode a hot circle around his chest. He sat back down about the time Sheriff Bertram Stone pulled the Ford in front of the medical office.

The doctor grimaced as he peeked out the window and saw Deputy Howard Sparks slide out the passenger door of the Ford slowly. The doctor heard Bertram say something from the other side of the vehicle but couldn't make it out. Whatever was said, the deputy nodded and then walked away on wobbly legs.

Bertram entered the medical office soon after. He brushed snow from his hat and coat and stomped it off his boots.

"Howard looked a little green, Bertram," Peterson said, still in obvious discomfort.

The sheriff smiled. "Seems Howard and rye whiskey don't see eye to eye."

"Howard Sparks? Deputy Howard Sparks?" Peterson asked, grinning against the ache around his chest. "I didn't take him for a hard drinker." He then noticed the large contusion on the sheriff's forehead. "Good Lord, Bertram. What happened?"

———

"Feel any of this?" Peterson asked as he pulled another suture through the skin on the sheriff's forehead.

Bertram lay flat on the examining table. "Just a dull tug."

"Good. Almost done." The doctor was forced to perform the stitching while sitting in a high back chair. His ribs couldn't endure him standing. "Probably have a nice scar. Packing this with ice saved you a lotta swelling though." The doctor tied off the last stitch. "Twelve. Nice even number, Bertram."

"Can I get up now?"

Peterson placed a hand on the sheriff's shoulder. "I'd keep still for at least a quarter hour. Give your head a little rest. You took quite a blow."

"Okay. It'll give me time to think on things."

As he collected his instruments into a metal bowl filled with disinfectant, Peterson asked, "So Howard said he shot all three?"

"Yep. Don't think that will be the last of them though."

"No, I guess not." The doctor gently eased up and went back to his desk and sat down with care. He considered pouring a shot of bourbon and then nixed the idea as his stomach rolled at the thought. "I was about to try and go over to Newell's when you drove up. I intended to share watch with him over the Cooper girls' bodies."

"I'll help Newell later. Best give them ribs a rest, Doc. After I lay here a spell, I'll go over and check on Gus. Might try to get some help from Gatesville and Hico too."

"Gus already tried phoning them. Said the lines outside town must be down due to the weather."

"Guess we'll just have to wait it out 'til sun up then. I wonder if them things will try to come into town tonight."

"Well, they are not bound by the same natural laws as we are. It's possible they can move faster than we think. I'm not certain Howard's shooting will have an effect on them, but I'll bet it alters their perception."

"What do you mean?"

"I had the impression they still sensed who they used to be. Whatever took them didn't really destroy memories. It only made those recollections ineffective," the doctor elaborated.

"So Howard blowing out some brain might change that?"

Peterson shrugged. "Maybe. And it might make them more ruthless than before. Mindless."

"Then I hope they lose their sense of direction as well."

The doctor chuckled and then grabbed his chest and chided himself for the extra movement inflicted on his rib cage.

———

"Well, I'll go check on Gus to bring him up to speed on what happened with me and Howard," Bertram said. "Then I'll make sure Howard is sleepin' it off like I told him to before goin' to Newell's." He glanced at the wall clock and saw it was a little after seven in the evening. He rose slowly, his head still numb where Peterson injected a local anesthetic.

"You might wait a few more minutes, Bertram," Peterson said and placed a cigar butt in the corner of his mouth.

"Naw. I ain't dizzy or nothin'. Best get things prepared in case we have some unwelcome company later." Bertram eased off the table and walked to the coat rack to retrieve his coat and hat. "Be back shortly." He opened the front door and then turned back around and said, "And thanks for stitching me up. You do a hell of better job than me or my old Ranger buddies ever could."

TWENTY-NINE

The headless thing sensed darkness and a slow movement in the belly of the storm cellar.

It rose and moved up the steps until it reached and pushed open the door.

Donny Cross gazed up at the snowy night consumed by an indescribable thirst. With an inner beacon moving him forward, he got up from the earthen floor, climbed the steps, and followed the headless thing out into the cold dark night.

———

Because of their head wounds, the three stirred later than usual. They could not explain the weighty sensation presiding over them. Had they still been human, they would have described a hangover type feeling to whoever wanted to know.

Eventually, Lucas, Adam, and Bonnie Cross did awaken fully. Tissue juice and blood still trickled slowly from their skulls where Howard Sparks' bullets had shattered the bone. As Adam's head had been turned slightly when he was shot, there was a more expansive hole on one side of his skull where clots of blood and brain matter stuck tenaciously. Lucas and Bonnie had received their wounds in the forehead, leaving a more consistent exit wound on the back of their heads.

But none of them were concerned with these issues. All they felt was a driving need for blood, a need that made them anxious. They growled at one another. They snapped their teeth and hissed in frustration. What inner memories they once possessed or any sense of direction they had held was now dulled by their injuries.

The three staggered about the bedroom until they managed to guide themselves out the door and down the hallway.

———

LUCAS FELT some recognition return as he moved toward the front of the house. It was like a weathervane had been spinning inside his mind and had now settled, pointing in one direction.

Lucas walked out the front door and into the snowy night. Adam and Bonnie followed as they began to regain a hold on direction themselves. And the farther the three walked, the swifter their steps, until they were virtually gliding toward Hamilton.

Two other figures were on the road further behind them. One moved spasmodically as the other patiently followed.

———

FROM UNDER THE front porch of the ranch house, Turk came out of hiding. He took a long look at the receding forms of his former master and the children who had once laughed and played with him, taken him hunting, and let him sleep in the same room as them. If a dog could feel sadness, that is what

Turk felt; that and a sinking sensation in his stoic heart telling him they would never return.

The old dog did not howl this time. He walked through the open door and headed straight to Adam and Donny's bedroom. He crawled into the old blankets he had slept on for years without even stopping to sniff the gore spread about the floor.

————

Sheriff Bertram Stone stretched out in a comfortable armchair that was situated in the family viewing room of the funeral home. Since Newell Scruggs had taken a good nap earlier that afternoon, it was decided Newell would take first watch over the Cooper girls' bodies.

"Believe me, Sheriff Stone," Newell had told Bertram. "If even one pinkie finger moves on their hands, I will alert you promptly." He had frowned and added, "After my experience with Eli Snow, there won't be a second's hesitation on my part; I assure you."

Newell sat just inside the entrance of the embalming room on a very uncomfortable metal stool. Even though he rested well during the day, he didn't dare risk his life by dozing off now.

The Cooper girls were stretched out side by side, their heads still attached by the makeshift material Newell had constructed. The thought of pulling the heads away from their bodies was too gruesome for even Newell to consider. He had convinced himself that since the heads had been removed soon after the girl's deaths, nothing would probably occur.

The undertaker glanced at the countertop and found the head from the well of Eli Snow that had started this entire chain of events still there and enclosed in its canvas bag. "Doctor Peterson seems to think you belong to that thing he and Sheriff

Stone ran into at Eli Snow's cabin," Newell whispered to the bag.

A sudden shiver gripped him at the insane idea the headless thing might come to reclaim its head. Newell realized similar, morbid thoughts were bound to come to mind if he didn't occupy himself, so he got up and perused some old books he had stacked in one corner. The undertaker finally decided on Dickens' *Bleak House* to help divert his thoughts from what gruesome trappings this long night would surely bring.

———

Bertram rested fitfully in the funeral home's family viewing room, his head experiencing sporadic bouts of pain from its wound. There was also a heaviness slipping over him, something Dr. Peterson told him to expect.

"You had a severe concussion, Bertram," the doctor had explained. "You might feel a little muddle-headed later. It's possible there could be some brain swelling. I'll check you periodically to make sure nothing critical develops."

And that was just how the sheriff felt now: muddle-headed.

When Bertram woke from his doze, he looked directly at the hallway and recalled how Eli Snow had lumbered down it menacingly toward him, Dr. Peterson, and Newell Scruggs. He now wished Newell had joined the utility company so there would be ample lighting instead of the paltry illumination from lamps and candles, whose low, yellow glow made the atmosphere unnerving.

The sheriff drifted off again and thought he heard just the slightest of sounds as his brain plummeted. It was a swishing noise, like ladies' skirts cutting the air during a waltz.

Bertram grinned. The recollection of a fancy dance held for the Texas Rangers' anniversary in Waco, Texas years ago came to mind. He'd bowed out of that one when the governor's wife asked him for a spin on the ballroom floor. "Two left feet," he'd bashfully explained to the woman.

Swish, swish.

Sheriff Stone turned his head and opened droopy eyes. The two Cooper girls stood by his chair in their burial gowns. They held their decapitated heads in front of their bodies. The eyes on both were red and fiery, mouths pulled open revealing vicious fangs. Their lips tried to speak, but no sound could come from the severed tracheas.

Bertram felt a terrible panic as the heads were pushed forward toward him with teeth clicking in anticipation of biting his neck.

"Sheriff Stone?" Newell's voice was distant. Bertram couldn't figure out why the undertaker wasn't trying to help him.

"Sheriff Stone?"

Bertram's eyes flicked open. The nightmare faded.

"You all right, Sheriff?" Newell asked, looking disturbed by the fright in the sheriff's eyes.

Bertram rubbed his face and attempted to pull away the cobwebs of frightening images clinging to his subconscious. "Whew," he said. "I'm okay, Newell. Just had a nightmare, that's all."

"You were making some odd noises. That's why I came to check on you."

Bertram leaned forward in the chair. "'Bout what time is it?"

"Just a little past ten. A long time yet until we switch our vigils on the bodies."

The sheriff's head felt clearer but still had that weighty sensation. "Doc says I had a concussion and might feel a little odd. He was damn sure right about that." He looked at Newell's concerned stare and said, "Maybe some coffee would help."

. . .

Newell poured Bertram another cup of coffee. The sheriff sat on a stool beside Newell in the embalming room. "Might sound funny," Bertram said. "But uncomfortable sitting actually makes my head feel better. That and the coffee, of course. Sure you won't join me?" he asked, holding up his cup.

"No, thank you," Newell said. "I never drink the dark brew after seven in the evening. Gives me a solid case of jittery nerves." He glanced at the Cooper girls' bodies. "I certainly don't need any more stimulation than I already have."

The two men sat silent for a while until the sheriff spoke. "Damn shame about these girls. But I imagine you've seen your share of tragedy in this business."

"Indeed. But never one this strange."

"Amen to that. I keep thinkin' I'll wake up and find myself back at last Sunday and that everything happening this week didn't occur. No head. No Eli Snow. No Lucas and his family turning into those god awful things.... And especially no headless body chasing me and Doc around Eli's cabin."

The undertaker looked at Bertram and smiled nervously. In a minute, both men laughed above the insanity of the situation.

"I know," Bertram said as tears from laughter welled his eyes. "I cain't help but find it crazy enough to be funny myself."

They continued to cackle until a loud thud on the back door sobered them.

The sheriff glanced at the clock on the embalming room wall. It was now a quarter of midnight. He slid off the stool and looked at Newell, who had gotten up as well, and motioned for the undertaker to follow him. Bertram then drew his revolver and inched toward the source of the thud.

With Newell close behind him, the sheriff slowly opened the back door. A rush of frigid air along with a good deal of swirling snow entered. There was almost no light outside other than what spilled into the street from the back door of the embalming room.

The sheriff held his revolver in front of him. He squinted into the snowy night and tried to find anything that could have made that thud.

"See anything?" Newell asked and shivered from the invading elements.

Bertram shook his head no when a wild fluttering came from the right side of the building. He held up his hand to alert Newell and then moved outside carefully checking to his right and left and front as he did.

The fluttering sound recommenced.

"Newell, bring me a lamp," Bertram said.

A few moments later, the undertaker handed Bertram one of the kerosene lamps from the embalming room. The sheriff went further outside holding the lamp in front of him in one hand and his revolver in the other.

Newell stayed in the doorway, looking nervous. The spinning snow gave off hissing sounds as it hit the hot chimney lamp and coupled with the fluttering sound in an uncanny, macabre duet.

The sheriff stopped. "I'll be damned." Bertram moved the light lower to the ground. He then looked over his shoulder at the undertaker. Bertram's face took on an exaggerated and misshapen cast in the odd shadows from the lamp, and Newell gasped. "It's an owl," Bertram said.

"An owl?"

"Yep. It must have been blinded in the snowstorm and bumped into your back door."

"I can't imagine why the animal would venture out in this harsh weather,"

"Had to be really hungry, I imagine." The sheriff walked

back and handed the lamp and his gun to Newell. "If anything creeps up on me, just aim and shoot at it."

"What are you doing?" Newell asked, handling the gun gingerly.

Bertram didn't answer. He walked back out, bent down, and picked up the dazed bird. He came back to the door holding the owl. The animal fluttered, its eyes opening wide along with its beak for a few seconds with each flap of its wings.

"Got some kind of old box?" Bertram asked while Newell shut and locked the back door. "Maybe some blankets or towels?"

Newell sat the lamp back on its table along with the revolver. "I have some old wooden crates my reagents are shipped in. They still have an ample amount of stuffing inside."

Bertram gazed at the owl. It was a typical Gray Barn Owl, fairly large and a little heavier than the sheriff would have guessed. "Listen, old man," he told the owl. "Newell's gonna let you get your senses back and warm up. So you behave yourself."

Newell returned with a large crate overflowing with straw stuffing. The sheriff gently placed the bird in the crate and arranged the stuffing around the owl as best he could. "There now," Bertram said. "Looks like there's two old birds in here tonight with bruised noggins." He winked at Newell, who had a curious smile on his long face.

"I'll set him in my bedroom upstairs," Newell said. "If he comes to after a while and is overstressed by disorientation, I'll just open the window and let him out. I'm fairly certain he'll be able to find his way home."

"Thanks, Newell. I just didn't want this bird freezing to death."

After the undertaker took the owl upstairs and then returned, voices filled the hallway. As he walked toward the embalming room, he found Dr. James Peterson standing stiffly against the wall.

"Goodness, Doctor," Newell said as he scrambled to move an armchair from out of the viewing room. "You must sit down at once. Your ribs are in no condition for so much movement. Did you actually walk over here?"

"Walked over and knocked," Peterson said with a grimace. "By the way, you forgot to lock the front door."

"Doc came up on me from behind and scared the bejeezus out of me," Bertram said. "Lucky I'd left my gun where Newell set it or I just might have plugged you."

"Really, Doctor," Newell said. "You need to sit down."

Peterson complied and eased his body down in the chair. "There isn't as much pain as before."

"Get lonely at your office, Doc?" Bertram asked.

"Not at all. I came over to look in on my patient," Peterson said, pointing at Bertram's skull. "I did say I'd check on you periodically because of the concussion, remember?"

─────

Molly and Hunter Cooper slept fitfully even under the dose of sedative Dr. Peterson had prescribed. Martha was in her room lying in bed with Deputy Gus Greenwood. She was under the covers with Gus outside them. They would doze from time to time with the deputy keeping track of the hour in-between catnaps.

Gus had come over to the café's upstairs rooms from the courthouse after the sheriff checked in on him earlier that evening, and the deputy intended to go back once he was certain Martha had fallen into a deep sleep.

The wind outside had abated considerably. Every so often a

gust would urge the snow against the window in Martha's bedroom and create a soft splattering sound on the glass.

Gus faced that window. Between drooping eyes and the moments he actually closed them, his fatigued mind invented shapes out of the gobs of snow sticking to the window pane. A dog morphed into a cat and then a goat and then a moth. He smiled when the form became that of a woman's erotic figure. He sighed and closed his eyes and drifted between sleep and hazy consciousness.

When Gus opened his eyes again and searched out the snow clusters, he found the woman's erotic shape had changed into a monstrous shadow. His eyes narrowed and he focused harder. He heard a scraping sound like something sharp being dragged across the glass.

He slid out of his spoon position next to Martha and sat up. She moaned and rolled over but did not awaken. Gus shook his head slightly to clear the drowsiness, rubbed his eyes, and stared at the window once more. This time the shadow moved. Gus watched long extensions like fingers glide across the pane in fast, erratic movements as if clawing to get in. The hair on Gus' neck rose. He gently placed a hand on Martha's shoulder and shook her as hard as he dared.

"Hmmm?" Martha asked dopily. She turned over and found Gus staring at her. He had a finger to his lips, urging her to be silent.

Gus bent down by her ear and whispered, "There's something tryin' to get in your window."

Martha's eyes widened. A slight gasp escaped her throat.

Gus put his fingers to his lips again and motioned for Martha to get out of bed. She did so, and when she stood up, he had to catch her when she almost fell from the effect of sleep and the sedative. Once she stabilized, Gus led Martha to the bedroom door.

"Go and wake your parents," he whispered.

Martha shook her head. "You come too," she said in a trembling voice.

"Go on now," he told her. He reached over and pulled a gun from the holster he had draped over a chair. "I'll be along directly."

Martha protested again.

Gus shushed her and pointed to the door. "Your parents need to be warned."

Reluctantly, Martha went out the door and down the short hall to her parents' room. Gus pulled the bedroom door open wider in case he needed a quick and unhampered escape route. He then inched toward the window where the scratching sound had escalated into something like panic.

The deputy bent down next to the window and attempted to see what was on the opposite side of the frosted pane. He caught a movement and detected what looked like the tips of fingernails trying to cut through the glass. Gus pressed his face even closer and found another face mirroring his on the other side. It was the visage of what had once been Lucas Cross. The monster had returned to the place where it had found food before.

Lucas' lips peeled back in a snarl. Seeing the deputy on the other side of the window, Lucas went crazy. His nails scratched fanatically. The frustration of having food so near overcame him. He hurled his body against the window and burst through it, sending shards of broken glass spinning outward. Gus was hit directly by Lucas' body and the glass.

The deputy tried to raise his gun, but Lucas slapped it out of the deputy's hand. Before Gus could scream, Lucas tore out the deputy's throat and gobbled the pulsing, arterial flow like a man finding a desert oasis. Gus beat weakly on Lucas' back, but it was an act of futility. The ravenous Lucas almost bled him dry in a few minutes.

As Gus' eyesight faded, he saw three other forms glide in through the window with a soft swirl of snow following behind them.

———

"Damnation," Hunter Cooper said as he dropped the sixteen-gauge shotgun shells. His hands were shaking so badly he couldn't get the double barrels loaded.

It had been hard for Martha to get her parents out of bed until the loud crashing of the window down the hall sobered them quickly.

"Here, Dad," she said as she picked up the shells from the floor. "Open the breech and I'll load them for you."

Hunter nodded. The gun shook from his trembling, but Martha got the shells in. He closed the breech. The quick snapping sound made Molly utter a gasp. Hunter looked at her and Martha. He took a long deep breath to calm himself.

"You two stay put," he said over a hard swallow. "I'm going down to Martha's bedroom."

"We are not staying here, Hunter Cooper!" Molly said.

"Molly, please," Hunter said.

"No way. Not without a weapon we're not."

"But the revolver's down in the café," Hunter said.

"And we ain't about to go wandering down there alone, either," Molly said. "You just the lead the way. Martha and I will be right behind you."

"Damnit, woman!"

Molly, standing firm in her decision and her heavy nightgown, pointed a finger at Hunter.

"All right then, but you two stay back a ways." Hunter

jerked off his nightcap and slung it down. "Damned nuisance," he said under his breath.

Hunter inched into the hallway. There was very little light there. He stopped.

"Martha," he said.

"Yes, Pa."

"Turn the light switch on by our bedroom door. I cain't see shit."

Martha did as her father asked. The wattage was low, but it gave enough illumination for better vision down the hallway. As soon as Martha had clicked on the light, a low, distant growl floated down the hall.

"Good Lord," Martha said as a chill grabbed her "What's that noise?"

Hunter, Molly, and Martha were covered with goosebumps as they slowly moved forward. Hunter stopped in the doorway of Martha's bedroom and held up a hand, urging his wife and daughter to halt where they stood. The cold air breezed through the broken window. It made Hunter's flesh even more frigid. He started to flick the light switch but stopped when he detected a black mass undulating on the floor close to the smashed window.

Hunter moved his hand away from the light switch. He cocked the shotgun hammers, never taking his eyes off the movement in front of him. Small drifts of snow had started building against the wall under the window. Occasionally, something would extend out of the mass and disturb the little, white mounds. Hunter saw a boot and then a hand and then a naked pale foot brush in and out of the snow. Once he had the shotgun's hammers cocked securely, he flicked on the light. The same low wattage filled the bedroom. This time the growl was louder.

Lucas Cross raised his head from Gus' body. Donny and

Adam and Bonnie glanced up briefly before going back to draining the corpse of any remaining blood they could suck from the multiple bite wounds on the deputy's cold flesh.

"Holy Mother of God," Hunter said in a hushed tone as he raised the shotgun and aimed into the huddled heap of monsters.

Lucas rose slowly to his feet. He moved his head quickly from side to side as he advanced toward Hunter. Adam stood up from Gus' body and snaked forward behind his father. Lucas' mouth opened and closed in quick, ticking movements. A low growl like that of an angry cat was building in his throat.

"Just you two stop right there," Hunter said. "Whatever you are don't matter to me. I'll blow you both to kingdom—"

Martha's piercing scream startled Hunter and he fired both barrels prematurely.

"Gus!" Martha screamed again while Hunter dug in his nightshirt pockets for more shells.

"Hush, girl!" he said. "Molly! Come get her away from the door."

Hunter managed to reload with no problem this time. He closed the breech, cocked the hammers, and took aim straight ahead.

The room was full of smoke from the previous explosion. He squinted through it and saw the prone, ruined body of Gus Greenwood and one other. Most of Adam Cross' face was gone along with a huge hollowed out gully where his chest had been. The other three creatures were no longer in the room.

Hunter glanced at the window and saw streaks of blood snaking over the sill.

"Goddamn," he said. "I knew I hit more than one."

Hunter rushed to the window and stuck himself out of it with the shotgun ready. He was rewarded with a cold waft of air and an empty roof. He turned back and found Martha kneeling next to Gus' body. She sobbed deeply and chanted the deputy's name over and over. Molly stood next to her daughter and, in morbid fascination, gazed on the twitching mass of blood and tissue lying next to Gus. What had once been Adam Cross tried its best to rise. Molly then glanced at Hunter with a terrified expression and pointed a shaking finger at her husband.

"What?" Hunter asked.

Molly covered her mouth and pointed again. Hunter looked down and saw his nightshirt was soaking through with blood. He hadn't felt the sharp shards of glass still stuck in the broken window frame pierce the nightshirt or his flesh.

THIRTY

The distant sound of a shotgun blast startled Sheriff Bertram Stone, Newell Scruggs, and Dr. James Peterson like a splash of icy water.

"What the hell?" Bertram asked as he jumped up off a stool.

"Sounds like it came from somewhere right across the street," Newell said as he too got up quickly.

Peterson attempted to rise from his chair, but Bertram gently eased him back down. "You stay put, Doc. You too, Newell."

Both men protested, but the sheriff shook his head. "No, sir," Bertram said as he grabbed his coat and hat from among the white lab coats hung on a rack near the embalming room's entrance. "I ain't about to have them two Cooper girls' bodies disappear like Lucas Cross done when we went out after Eli that night."

Newell nodded in agreement. He looked even paler than usual. "As you wish, Sheriff. You are right, of course."

"You still have that old Winchester of yours?" Bertram asked Newell.

"Indeed, Sheriff, I do."

"Best check to be sure it's loaded then." Bertram pulled his Stetson on. "Oh, last I checked the phone lines in town are now workin'. So one of you might give Howard a call at his home and alert Gus at the courthouse just in case either one of them didn't hear that blast."

"We'll take care of it," Peterson said. "And, Bertram?"

"Yeah, Doc."

"Unless my direction is off because of the cracked ribs and the laudanum, that shot came from the Koffee Kup."

"You ain't wrong, Doc. That's exactly where it come from."

The sheriff closed the front door of the funeral parlor behind him and moved at a quick jog toward the café with his gun drawn and cocked. He made it to the front door when Molly came rushing around the corner of the building. She pulled Hunter along with her.

Bertram saw the soaked, bloody nightshirt. "What happened?"

"Them things," Molly said, trying to catch her breath. "They come in through Martha's bedroom window. Busted through the windowpane. Hunter cut himself on the glass still stuck in the frame when he hung himself outside to see where them things took off to."

"One of them is still upstairs," Hunter said feebly. The sheriff saw the man was very pale. "I blowed most of its face away." Hunter coughed and a new line of red appeared on the nightshirt. "I'm pretty sure I hit another one, but it went out the window with them other two."

"Best get him over to Doc Peterson's," Bertram said to Molly. "You'll have to fetch the Doc from over at Newell's. That's where he is right now."

Molly nodded and started toward the medical office.

"Just a sec," Bertram said. "How many were there?"

"Four." Hunter gritted his teeth and clenched his fists in

what looked like an attempt to keep himself conscious. "It was Lucas, Adam, and Donny Cross, and a young girl. I think it was Adam's face I blew off." He slid down a bit.

Molly tightened her hold on him and started toward the medical office.

"Martha's upstairs," she said over her shoulder. Tears welled in her eyes. "With Gus Greenwood."

"Gus? He's supposed to be in my office," Bertram said, but Molly was already across the street with Hunter. "Guess Gus got here before me," Bertram said as he went around the side of the café and up the outside stairs.

The sheriff noticed a line of something dark trailing from under the crashed window. Sobs came through the broken pane. He went through the door at the top of the stairs and headed toward the weeping. The air in the hallway still smelt of spent shotgun shells.

Bertram walked into Martha's bedroom and found her kneeling next to Gus. She glanced up at the sheriff with red, puffy eyes.

"He wanted to save us," she said.

Bertram looked down at the ravaged body of his deputy. The vampires had ripped most of Gus' clothing away along with his boots in their search for more blood. The deputy's face, arms, torso, abdomen, legs, and feet were covered with hundreds of puncture and tear wounds.

"Jesus," Bertram said. Gus' eyes were wide open, his mouth agape. The deputy wore a mixed expression of surprise and terror on his frozen face.

Bertram reached down and closed Gus' eyes. He patted Martha on the shoulder. "I'm sorry, Martha. Gus was a good man," he said with a lump growing in his throat. It was then he saw the remains of Adam Cross crawling toward the window. Most of Adam's face was gone. The chest wound had opened his

315

back into a gaping hole. "How in the hell is that thing still alive?" Bertram asked.

Martha grabbed Gus' gun from the floor and rushed the thing that was trying to escape out the window. She fired all six shots into the vampire's pulverized face before Bertram could get to her.

"Damn you to hell, Adam Cross!" Martha screamed. As the sheriff tried to pry the gun from her, Martha kept firing, the firing pin dully clicking repeatedly on used cartridges. She then beat her fists on Bertram's chest. "Damn all those Crosses to Hell!" she screamed over and over until she fell weeping into the sheriff's arms.

Bertram moved Martha to the bed and laid her on it. She rolled over and pushed her face into the pillow, her shoulders heaving up and down all the while.

The sheriff started to say something but checked himself, realizing consolation could not be given right now. He turned his attention back to the body of Adam Cross and found it still trying to reach up and grab the window.

"Son of a bitch fuckin' vampire!" Bertram screamed.

Leaving a trail of gore behind, the sheriff grabbed Adam's boots and dragged the squirming thing out of the bedroom and down the hall to the back door. At the top of the outside stairs, Bertram backed down the steps and pulled the body with him. Once at the bottom of the stairs, the sheriff hauled the body to the middle of the street. Bertram huffed and puffed from the effort, but his blood was up now, and he didn't care what strain was put on his heart and lungs. He looked up and saw a figure moving quickly toward him from further down the street. Bertram pulled his gun, cocked it, and aimed.

"Wait!" the figure yelled. "It's me, Sheriff. It's Howard."

Bertram sighed and holstered his gun as Howard came forward. The sheriff then asked his deputy, "Doc call you?"

"Yes sir," Howard answered and then gasped when he saw the ruined body twitching in the street. He recognized the clothes from his encounter at the ranch that morning. "But that's—"

"Adam Cross," Bertram said.

"But I shot him and the others this morning."

The sheriff's head wound started to pound from recent physical activity. He placed his cold hand on the contusion. "Yep, like I told you earlier, you got to do more than shoot these things." His vision blurred slightly and then came back into focus. "Your hangover gone away enough that you can fetch some gasoline from Abraham's pumps?"

"Still a little sick at my stomach, Sheriff, but I'll be all right. I'll go wake Mr. Tanner and get that gas."

Bertram felt faint. He dropped to his knees.

"You okay, Sheriff?" Howard asked with concern.

The sheriff held up his hand. "I'll settle down in a minute. Just got a little worked up. Go on and get that gas."

"Yes sir."

The deputy turned to go when Bertram stopped him. "Hold on, Howard."

"Yes, sir?"

The sheriff thought of Gus with a feeling of utter dread and frustration. "Best bring an ax back with you too," Bertram said.

———

The headless thing had not been able to keep up with Donny Cross. Now that Bonnie's brain was damaged by a gunshot, she could no longer send impulses to the headless body. Donny had ignored the thing completely, hunger the only factor driving the boy to catch up with his family.

The headless thing was forced to wander without direction.

It went into the fields by the road leading to Hamilton and ambled into a wooded area where it got tangled in some low hanging tree limbs. It thrashed and swirled, eventually tumbling into a deep snowbank. There it lay immobile and began to freeze as snow steadily covered it.

———

LUCAS CROSS KNEW ONLY one hiding place—the old warehouse. Lucas had fed more than Donny and Bonnie, and they complained with growls and gnashing teeth as he guided them away from buildings lining the main street of Hamilton where they sensed fresh blood.

Lucas did not feel the injured flesh on his side from Hunter's shotgun blast, nor did he notice the progressive flow of blood from that wound. But Donny and Bonnie smelled it. Their eyes darted back and forth from their father in constrained desire.

Once Lucas had moved them into the warehouse, he tried to form a plot in his injured brain, but any thoughts other than those of feeding were so tangled and abstract he could not outline anything coherent. He hissed and snarled in frustration at his own inability. Donny saw an opening when Lucas seemed distracted. The boy had not been shot by Howard. His thought processes were keen, and he lunged and knocked his father to the ground and latched on to the bleeding wound. Bonnie's brain may have been injured, but she certainly had no trouble following her brother's lead. She jumped on Lucas as well and nudged into the bleeding tissue along with Donny.

Lucas kicked and struggled but could not shake them off. Eventually, he lost his strength and gave in like a mother hog offering up teats for her famished young.

"IT LOOKS WORSE THAN IT IS." Dr. James Peterson sat rigidly on a stool by the medical office's examining table. He traced the long cuts on Hunter Cooper's chest with a cloth soaked in alcohol.

"Damn that smarts, Doc!" Hunter said.

"You hush up and let Doc Peterson clean you up," Molly Cooper said with little conviction while squeezing her husband's hand. The thought of her dead daughters being watched by Newell Scruggs next door still plagued her. Molly shook her head and struggled to disrupt the hurtful knowledge of her two youngest being lost forever. "Will he need stitches, Doc?"

"This one might," Peterson said, pointing at the longest and widest cut. "It's still oozing quite a bit. But these other two have stopped bleeding." He took a shallow breath and winced from his rib pain.

"I can help, if need be, Doc," Molly said. "I used to sew up my dad's wounds when he was working on the ranch. He never did cotton too much to doctors."

The doctor smiled. "I think I may close that big cut with some surgical tape for a while and see if it holds. No use suturing unless we have to."

"It was one of them things—that the Crosses become, I mean—that killed our little girls, wasn't it, Doc?" Hunter asked while Peterson went about taping the wounded flesh together.

Peterson paused. He glanced at Molly and Hunter. Their faces were cragged with lines of fatigue and devastation and pain. The doctor then sighed and started to work on the laceration again. "The one that used to be Lucas. It was that one." He stopped his work again. "So he brought the others with him this time? All his family?"

"Except for that girl," Hunter said. "Don't rightly know who she was."

"My guess is that she is Lucas' daughter, Bonnie," Peterson said and started taping again.

"The one that disappeared over ten years ago?" Molly asked. "Why, she'd be a grown woman by now. Hunter said that girl-thing was only a child."

Peterson continued without taking his eyes off his work, "You knew Eli Snow, didn't you?"

"We knew very little about him," Molly said. "He didn't come into town too much. Martha knew his oldest, Arlis I think his name was, and she used to say she felt sorry for him. Something about his weird father and younger brother."

"That oldest boy was killed in France during WWI, wasn't he?" Hunter asked.

"Martha said Arlis couldn't take his family no more. That's why he joined the Army and got away from here," Molly said. "But what does that have to do with Bonnie Cross?"

"There are many things I've learned over this week," Peterson said, examining his handiwork on Hunter's cut. "If a week prior to this one someone had told me I would actually believe the strange things occurring in Hamilton, I would have told them that I'm an educated man who knows there is a logical explanation for everything." He cut off a section of unused tape and used it to fasten both ends of his repair job. "But I have discovered there are some things that defy explanation."

"You mean what the Crosses become, don't you?" Molly asked.

"Not only them, but the Snows as well," Peterson said. "I believe it started with that youngest boy, Jacob. And I also believe it was Jacob who kidnapped Bonnie Cross and made her into the thing she is." He blushed. "A child vampire who can never grow old."

"But how? Why?" Molly asked.

Peterson got off the stool and gingerly walked to his desk. He sat down, found a used cigar stub, and committed his nasty habit of chewing it while pulling the bottle of bourbon from the desk drawer. He asked if the Molly and Hunter wished to join him.

"Never touch the stuff," Hunter said, lying as still as possible on the examining table.

Molly came over and sat down across from the doctor. She nodded, and Peterson poured her a full shot glass. She took a stiff drink, scowled and then took another.

"Eli Snow had an Indian wife," Peterson began. "She was supposedly versed in witchcraft. When Eli was off fighting in the Spanish American War, she did this terrible thing with her only son, Arlis."

Molly glanced up and pushed her shot glass across the table for another. "Go on, Doc," she said with eyes tired and filled with grief. "I'm listenin'."

———

Newell Scruggs was bleary-eyed from his long vigil over the bodies of the Cooper girls. He shrugged and figured if they were going to transform with or without their heads they would have done so by now.

Newell got up from his uncomfortable stool and stretched his long, lanky limbs. From a distance, he heard an owl hoot.

"In this weather?" Newell asked himself. It took a moment for him to remember the sheriff's earlier rescue that evening. Newell glanced at the ceiling above and said out loud, "Finally got your bearings back, did you?" He smiled and made his way up the stairs to check on the visitor.

Entering the dark bedroom, Newell saw just a glint of the

owl's eyes. He lit a kerosene lamp and sat it on a nightstand. The bedroom flooded with light and the shadows cast by it. The owl sat on the windowsill as if patiently waiting its release. It turned its head in Newell's direction and gave a low hoot.

The undertaker grinned and walked carefully toward the bird. He unlatched the window and slowly raised it. The owl never moved until the window was completely opened. Then, it took a final glance at Newell before unceremoniously flying out the open window.

Newell stuck his head out the window and watched the large body glide away into the night.

"You're welcome," Newell said.

He glanced at the sky and saw clouds were breaking up. A pallid, half moon peeked through balefully. Newell shivered and started to close the window. He peered down the street to the edge of town and saw two shadowy forms moving quickly toward Abraham Tanner's general store.

Newell pulled the window down and locked it. He grabbed the lamp from the end table and rushed downstairs. He made a quick check on the Cooper girls' bodies and found nothing changed, and then the undertaker hurried next door to the medical office.

Newell entered without knocking. Peterson was at his desk and Molly sat across from him. Hunter was lying on the examination table. All three looked up in surprise when the undertaker came in.

"What's going on, Newell?" Peterson asked.

"Sorry to barge in unannounced like this," Newell said. "Do you happen to know where Sheriff Stone is at this moment?"

"He was over at the café just a while ago," Molly said, slurring her words. Newell noticed a half-filled glass of what he guessed to be the doctor's bourbon grasped in her chubby fingers.

"Thank you, Mrs. Cooper," Newell said. "I should warn all of you that from my upstairs window I saw two people coming into town. They looked very suspicious."

"In what way?" Peterson asked.

"In that they were gliding rather than walking," Newell said. "I think it would be a good idea to light several of these," he said and pointed to the lamp he held. "You just might need them, Doctor, and not necessarily for light."

The doctor nodded yes and started to get up.

"Keep your seat, Doc," Molly said. "Just tell me where the kerosene lamps are, and I'll take care of it."

"There are still four or five of them left over from before I had electricity installed. They're on the bottom shelf of a storage rack by the back door." He then told Newell, "You better go and alert Bertram." Peterson then shuddered and added, "From what I gather from Hunter and Molly, the things escaping Hunter's shotgun hadn't shared their meal all that well." He gave the undertaker a pale look. "So, I imagine some of them will be starving by now."

————

After Howard Sparks finally got an angry, heavy-eyed Abraham Tanner settled down about giving up gasoline in the middle of the night, the deputy took two five-gallon cans and began filling them.

Abraham, still in his night clothes, came out mumbling about how the city took advantage of him and rarely paid its bill. He leaned an ax that Howard had also requested against the store's outside wall.

"Mind if I at least get what sleep time I have left for this night, Deputy?" Abraham asked sarcastically.

"No, sir," Howard said with a slight of grin. "Sheriff Stone will be much obliged for your cooperation."

"I'd rather have cold, hard cash than thanks, Deputy," Abraham said as he was about to go back inside the store. "You tell him that for me, you hear?"

The deputy held up a hand. "Sure thing, Mr. Tanner. I'll—"

Howard was suddenly pushed forward as if struck by a large object. Then Abraham was hit and catapulted into the store, where he landed face down on the hard wood floor.

Abraham rolled over and tried to focus through swirling dots saturating his vision. He heard what sounded like an animal growling prior to something falling on his chest. Due to the fact Abraham's wife had passed away five years ago, there was no one in the store to help him when he cried out in pain as the teeth of Bonnie Cross ripped into his throat. He tried to pull her off, but Bonnie's arms locked around his neck, her legs around his chest. Struggling to free himself, Abraham rolled across the floor. As Bonnie pulled deeply from the arterial flow, Abraham's movements slowed until he finally lost consciousness.

———

Outside, Howard fared better. Donny Cross had slammed hard into the deputy but failed to secure an adequate hold before Howard was able to react. As if performing an acrobatic circus act, the deputy rolled backwards, pushing out with his boots, and kicked Donny away.

Howard jumped up, pulled his gun, and shot an enraged Donny Cross between the eyes. Donny fell backward with his eyes open and fixed on the clearing sky above. The deputy acted fast then. He took the gasoline hose and flooded Donny with gas and then pulled a match from his pocket, lit it, and tossed it on

Donny's body, which by that time was trying to right itself. Donny burst into flames but somehow managed to pull himself up and stumbled away as if trying to escape. Donny made it about twenty yards before he fell. The flames then consumed him.

Howard stood in shock. His body shivered. He couldn't take his eyes off the burning vampire. It was the smell of roasting flesh that finally brought the deputy around.

"Abraham!" Howard cried out and ran into the store just as a sated Bonnie Cross was rising from Abraham Tanner. She glanced with menace at the deputy.

Abraham had turned on only one overhead light when he'd answered the deputy's knocking earlier, so the store was dimly lit, but even so Howard could see a look of vile hatred on Bonnie's face. She drew her lips back in a snarl and lunged forward. Weighted down by the heavy blood meal, her actions were hampered enough to give Howard the second he needed to blow half of her head away.

The deputy went over and tried to shake Abraham awake. The gruesome condition of the merchant's throat and the cold paleness of his flesh left no doubt he was dead.

"Good Lord," Howard said in a hushed whisper. He then turned to see what was making noises behind him and discovered Bonnie attempting to get up.

Howard grabbed her by the neck and rushed outside. Amazingly, even with the damaged bone and tissue, Bonnie's jaws snapped, trying to bite Howard's hand.

"No you don't!" Howard said and threw Bonnie on Donny's flaming body.

Bonnie's clothes ignited immediately. A wretched scream made it through her damaged mouth. She swirled up from Donny's body and twisted for a moment in the air. Sparks flew free from her spinning form like a Fourth of July firework display. Then, she tumbled down into the blaze below twitching for what seemed an eternity before finally lying still.

Howard slumped to his knees. A shadow fell over him from behind. He was about to turn and fire when Sheriff Bertram Stone's large, calloused hands fell securely on the deputy's shoulders.

"Newell said something was up," Bertram said, watching the flames ebb and flow over the bodies of Donny and Bonnie Cross. "Looks like he was right."

———

By the time Bertram and Howard returned to the street in front of the café, Adam Cross had dragged himself to the bottom of the stairs on the side of the building. Even with a damaged brain and severely wounded body, the vampire knew there was more blood upstairs.

"Goddamnit!" Bertram said.

"I got it, Sheriff," Howard said as he walked to the struggling form at the foot of the stairs, grabbed its boots, and dragged it into the middle of the street. Adam waved his arms uselessly while being hauled away.

Once Adam was back in the street, the sheriff poured gas from one of the five-gallon drums over the convulsing vampire's body. Bertram then pulled a matchbook from his shirt pocket, lit the match, and flipped it onto what had once been Adam Cross. Like his brother and sister, Adam's clothes ignited instantly. He struggled to get up, but he'd sustained significant injuries from Hunter Cooper's shotgun and Martha's gunshots and was unable to stand.

Adam's resistance was short-lived, and his battered and burning form soon lay still.

A great emptiness overwhelmed Bertram. He sat down in the snow-packed street and lowered his head.

"You okay, Sheriff?" Howard asked.

Bertram glanced at his deputy. Under the clearing, night sky, the sheriff's eyes felt ancient and tired. After a moment, he asked, "Did you get that ax at Abraham's store?"

"Yes, sir. It's back sitting outside the store."

"Give me a minute to catch my breath and I'll go there with you. We can take care of Abraham first, and then we can come back and tend to Gus."

"Gus? What's happened to him?"

Bertram sighed and then said, "They got to him in Martha's bedroom. Ain't an inch of him not bit up." Bertram shuddered, "I'll let you get Martha out of the way once we're finished with Abraham."

"I don't get it, Sheriff. If Gus and Abraham are dead, what are we goin' to do to them? Ain't that Newell Scruggs' territory?"

The sheriff rose slowly. By now, the smell of burning flesh was heavy in the air. Mixed with gasoline, the odor made Bertram's stomach roll. He glanced down the street and saw the other fire was burning down, the two bodies outlined inside its glow.

"We got to cut off Abraham and Gus' heads," Bertram said as he started walking away.

"*What*? Their heads!?"

The sheriff stopped and stared directly at Howard. "Unless you want them to come by and pay you a visit one night after they turned into the things they surely will turn into. They won't be comin' by to be social neither."

Howard's face fell. "Oh," he said with sadness. "I get it."

Bertram turned and headed in the direction of the general store. "Best come on then," he said.

THIRTY-ONE

After being bled by his children, Lucas Cross was severely weakened. He tried to stand but his legs gave way each time he did. He rolled his eyes from side to side scanning the inside of the warehouse. His attention finally focused on coffins in storage for the funeral parlor. Somewhere deep in his injured brain a fragment of a memory prompted Lucas to crawl to those coffins. A portion of a torn tarp lay discarded on the warehouse floor. He wrapped the stiff material around his shoulders. With great effort, Lucas pulled himself up by grasping the top of one of the caskets. He opened the lid and, after three attempts, managed to crawl inside. He then pulled the lid shut and curled under the tarp in welcome darkness. There he slept waiting for strength to return.

———

NEWELL SCRUGGS ENTERED Tanner's General store about the time Sheriff Bertram Stone was raising an ax.

"Sheriff Stone!" Newell cried.

The sheriff stopped mid-swing. He and Deputy Howard Sparks turned their attention to the intruder.

Bertram relaxed his arms and held the ax loosely by his side. "Sorry you have to see this, Newell. But Abraham and Gus have both been drained by those things. That means their heads have to come off or they'll change." He started to raise the ax again and said, "If it bothers you, you might want to look away."

"Wait," Newell said. "There's no need to do this so barbarically."

The sheriff flushed. He'd been called many things, but barbarian wasn't one of them. Especially not by a friend. "What'd you call me?"

"Not you, Sheriff. The act. I can remove Abraham's and Gus' heads in the same manner I did the little Cooper girls. It would be more respectful."

Bertram frowned and let the ax fall from his grip. It landed on the hardwood floor with a dull thud. "God Almighty," he said in a low voice. "What's got into me? I was gonna chop two of my friends' heads off with no more concern than if they was Thanksgivin' turkeys."

For a moment it felt like Bertram would collapse. Howard grabbed one of the chairs Abraham kept around a cracker barrel and brought it to the sheriff.

"Best sit down," Howard said as he gently helped Bertram into the wooden chair.

After sitting for a while, Bertram groaned. His head abrasion throbbed unmercifully now. "Newell's right, Howard. I should have thought of taking Abraham and Gus to him. I'm just screwed up in my head right now."

"As we all are, Sheriff Stone." Newell glanced at Howard and suggested, "You stay with Sheriff Stone, Deputy Sparks. I'll go get things prepared for what I need to do to Deputy Greenwood and Mr. Tanner. I'll return here after that, and you and I can move this body and the one at the café back to my embalming room."

The deputy nodded to the undertaker.

———

BERTRAM CLOSED his eyes and leaned back. "Much obliged you came over, Newell," he said. "Kept me from makin' myself a bigger fool than I already am."

"You can't blame yourself," Newell said. "We are all under strain and doing an even stranger business."

The undertaker walked out of the store. He discovered Molly Cooper was standing by the smoldering bodies of Donny and Bonnie Cross. He noticed Molly was dressed only in her nightgown and robe, and that she was barefoot.

"Dear me, Mrs. Cooper," Newell said. "You shouldn't be out in the cold like this. My goodness, you are going to suffer from frostbite standing in the snow with bare feet."

Molly glanced at Newell as if he were a stranger. "There's another one back in the street in front of our café. That only makes three. Where's that fourth got off to?"

The undertaker placed his hands on her shoulders and gently turned her around. He then directed her toward the medical office. "Just come along now, Mrs. Cooper. Let's get you in a warm building and see that those feet are properly tended to by Dr. Peterson."

"But the fourth one," Molly repeated as she walked. "Where is it?"

"I'm certain the creature will be found soon. Sheriff Stone and Deputy Sparks will discover it in no time."

"But the fourth one," she repeated over and over, never seeming to hear a word Newell Scruggs uttered.

———

BERTRAM AND HOWARD scoured the town and its buildings until sunrise. Fatigue played a major role in their search. It was Howard who searched the warehouse. He soon tired of opening storage boxes and the coffins mixed among them. Howard actually opened the coffin in which Lucas lay sleeping under the tarp but was so tired and disgusted by that point he didn't judge the tarp in the coffin's bottom as being anything other than packing material. The deputy closed Lucas' hiding place without consideration to look under the stiff tarp.

Honestly, neither Bertram nor Howard had expected to find Lucas in town anyway. They anticipated he'd cleared out after the mêlée that had taken place.

What did occur to the sheriff was to put the three burned bodies, along with the remains of Eli Snow, which Howard removed with disgust from Abraham Tanner's storage freezer, in the middle of the street so the rising sun would make certain the monsters had been completely destroyed.

Since the skies had cleared and the wind had calmed, the imminent day promised to be a pleasant one filled with sunshine, and it was that sunshine striking the vampires' remains like a blast of flame that quickly reduced the corpses to a pile of ashes.

Sheriff Bertram Stone, Newell Scruggs, and Dr. James Peterson were the only witnesses. The rest of last night's human participants, including Howard Sparks, were fast asleep from exhaustion or misery.

As smoke swirled from the incinerating vampire corpses, the sheriff grinned malevolently. "I'll be a son of bitch" was all he could think to say.

———

"Lucas cain't have gone far, I reckon." Bertram sat in the medical office with Peterson. The sheriff glanced at the wall and shivered, knowing that on the other side Newell Scruggs was busy with his grisly task of decapitating Gus Greenwood and Abraham Tanner. "But then again, them things can do a lot you wouldn't guess. Hell, Lucas might have made it back to his ranch."

"It's possible," Peterson said. His ribs were still painful, but he could move around easier than yesterday. "You said there was no sign of that...headless thing being in town?"

"No. Just the Cross brothers and the unknown girl."

"More than likely Bonnie, don't you imagine?"

The sheriff frowned and shrugged his weary shoulders. "Anything's possible."

"Those aspirin I gave you helped your head yet?"

"Some. I still feel a little befuddled and could stand about a week's worth of sleep," Bertram said with a weak grin. "Since vampires don't keep regular hours, I suppose I'll have to wait for that shut eye though. Best to try and find Lucas in the daytime."

The doctor grabbed one of his ubiquitous cigar butts and clamped his teeth on its end. He frowned at the stale taste. "I could use a nap myself. Why don't we give Howard a couple more hours of sleep? You can wake him and send him out to Lucas' ranch. Now that the sky has cleared, the snow on the roads should be melting soon. He can take the Ford. While he's gone you can catch about four hours of sleep. I'll ring you up, and then I'll get some rest once you're awake." He glanced at the wall clock. "That should give us most of the afternoon to try and figure where Lucas is if he didn't make it back to the ranch."

"What about Newell? He's got to be draggin', too, especially after what he had to do with Gus and Abraham."

"Did I hear my name?" Newell's bass voice drifted from the

medical office's doorway. He poked his cadaverous head through. "I was just about to ask you gentlemen if I could lie down in my upstairs bedroom for a while. I'm quite exhausted."

The sheriff nodded yes. "We was just discussing dividing up some sleep time, Newell. You go on and get that rest. Me and the Doc have the remainder of the day planned out."

"You will awaken me if you need my services sooner?" Newell asked.

"Certainly," Peterson said. "By the way, did you...?"

The undertaker nodded and said before the doctor completed his question, "Deputy Greenwood and Mr. Tanner are quite at peace now."

———

Deputy Howard Sparks didn't much feel like another trip to the Cross ranch. After all that happened to him there the day before, his stomach had knotted when Sheriff Stone gave him the order to search for Lucas.

"And if he did happen to make it back there and is hidin' in the house and you stumble on him," Bertram had said after waking Howard. "Don't shoot him again by God. Drag him outside and let the sun do the work. He'll fight you all right, but he'll be too weak to harm you."

"Easy for him to say," the deputy spoke out loud as he drove the Ford through the slush on the road.

Up ahead, Howard spotted a shape cross the road and head into the neighboring field. By the time he arrived at the spot and slowed down, whatever had run across the road was nowhere in sight. Howard shrugged and sped up again.

———

THE MOUNTAIN LION that crossed the road watched the Ford move away. The animal had no idea it was a suspect at the beginning of the week, nor did anyone know that the big cat had moved out of its hunting ground from the cliffs of Glen Rose to Hamilton County, although such early speculation was presented because of Eli Snow's neck wounds.

The cat was a rogue male and ventured from Glen Rose because of dwindling food supplies. Being frightened of the strange, two legged creatures it encountered over the years, it tended to stay clear of humans it came across.

When the big cat was satisfied the vehicle it had seen was gone and would not be a threat, it moved toward a forested area paralleling the field. The animal was glad the snow had stopped falling and, once in the forest, stopped for a while to sprawl in the sun. Even though it had killed a young steer recently, hunger pains were emerging.

As it rose to continue on its way, the cat spotted a crouched form emerging from a pile of melting snow. The animal approached the figure cautiously. It sensed the form was human, but the animal also felt something was wrong. The figure never moved or gave any indication it knew the animal approached. When the cat was standing in front of the human, it made a quick swipe with its paw and the figure fell over on its side. The cat saw something was strange but had not registered this particular human had no head.

The cat sniffed the frozen flesh and felt its stomach growl. It pounced on the figure and bit into rotten skin. An immediate sense of disgust was quickly replaced by a strong urge for survival. As repellent as the meal seemed, the cat ate anyway. The animal slurped and tore at the muscle, tissue, and what organs remained in the wounded and open abdomen of the headless thing that once was Jacob Snow. When all the meat was consumed, the big cat cracked bones to gnaw the dead, dry marrow.

THIRTY-TWO

Lucas Cross was never found. Nor was the headless body of Jacob Snow. Because of these facts, Sheriff Bertram Stone expected he would probably sleep poorly for the rest of his days.

———

IT WAS a curious act of fate that took Lucas Cross away from Hamilton, and a much more natural one that removed any trace of Jacob Snow except for scant remaining tissue and tiny fragments of bone that the mountain lion left unconsumed.

Newell Scruggs possessed one small coffin, but he required two for the Cooper girls' funeral service. He called a fellow undertaker in McGregor, Texas to see if a trade might be arranged for one of Newell's larger caskets.

"I do have some smaller units," the undertaker from McGregor said. "However, I am quite overstocked with larger sizes. My brother, who runs a parlor in Lubbock has contacted me for any extra adult-sized caskets I can spare. As I stated, I am overstocked with that particular size. I was going to send my brother some by rail freight later this afternoon. If you could bring one of your larger units here before that time, I could ship it along with mine and give you the child coffin in exchange."

So, Newell planned to load the adult coffin into the Ford that Deputy Sparks had returned just after noon. The deputy relayed he'd found nothing at the Cross ranch other than "That damned cantankerous old bird dog in the back bedroom lying under a pile of blankets. Almost shot it when it came out growling. Scared the crap out of me."

When Howard and Newell loaded the coffin in which Lucas slept into its original shipping crate and transferred it to the Ford, Lucas, still weakened by the loss of blood, never stirred.

"Hell, I'll take this down to McGregor for you Mr. Scruggs," Howard said. "It ain't but thirty miles. I could damn well use a break from Hamilton anyway."

And Newell kindly accepted Howard's offer.

———

AROUND FIVE THAT AFTERNOON, the coffin Lucas slept in, along with ten other caskets, was loaded in a freight car for the long trip to Lubbock, Texas. About halfway on the trip, Lucas came out of his slumber. He had now recovered and had regained his inhuman strength, a strength allowing him to easily break the sealed box in which he'd been hiding.

Lucas felt the movement of the train and slid open the freight car's door. The cold night beckoned. His hunger now raw and raging, Lucas jumped from the moving train and landed without harm in an open space near the edge of a pine forest. He breathed in the sharp odor of the pines and moved deeper into the woods. He stopped abruptly when he noticed the dim lights and curling chimney smoke from a distant cabin.

THIRTY-THREE

The family plots belonging to Hunter and Molly Cooper were actually located in Johnsville, Texas, which was a small farming community between Hico and Glen Rose about forty miles north of Hamilton.

Johnsville had one small general store with a single gas pump and one church, The Johnsville Church of Christ, serving as a place for community meetings and events. Molly's relatives were buried in a cemetery behind that church. Hunter had never contested the fact Molly wanted her and Hunter to be buried there as well, but he never in a million years considered he'd be putting his two youngest children there long before he or his wife left this mortal coil.

The service took place on Sunday. It was seven days after the strange and deadly dealings began in the quiet town of Hamilton, Texas. Hunter, Molly, and their oldest daughter, Martha, were attended by a small group of family and friends, some making the trip from Hamilton and nearby farms.

The day was overcast. A fine, cold mist prompted umbrellas to unfold as the Church of Christ minister read from the Good Book and the Cooper girls were lowered into the earth.

Newell Scruggs was present. He stood in the distance, his lean frame, dark suit, and black stove pipe hat blending with the somber weather and occasion.

The funeral service for Abraham Tanner and Gus Greenwood was scheduled for Tuesday.

"It's Martha Cooper," Sheriff Bertram Stone had explained to the Baptist minister. "She and Gus were a couple. Just wouldn't be right to have her bury her sisters and then turn around and see Gus laid in the clay. Givin' her a day in between seems like the Christian thing to do."

And the Baptist minister agreed, saying he would conduct Abraham's and Gus' funerals as a dual service. Both men were to be buried in the Hamilton Cemetery located across from the schoolhouse. Most of the town attended the service. Even Vivien Hagler made an appearance in a faded, black dress complete with mourning veil.

As far as the proceedings for the Cross and Snow families, the sheriff and Dr. Peterson gathered up what remained of the burned bodies from the back of Newell Scruggs's funeral parlor and divided the remnants into coffins as best they could. It was difficult as there was no way to precisely separate the ashy mounds. Bertram figured some of Donny Cross got mixed in with Adam Cross and what was Bonnie Cross, and that probably Eli Snow was in the concoction too.

"One damn big mess," Bertram had grumbled to Peterson.

The only item the two men were certain of was the head of Jacob Snow, which they left in the leather bag it had been placed in the day the sheriff pulled it from the well. They placed it in the coffin designated for Eli Snow's remains.

"Seems more like a month than only a week since all this started," Peterson had said.

"More like a lifetime," a very exhausted and solemn Bertram Stone had replied.

Bertram and Peterson and Deputy Howard Sparks determined they would bury the Crosses at their ranch and Eli and Jacob's head near Eli's cabin that Tuesday after Abraham's and Gus' service. The sheriff didn't think a preacher should be involved.

As far as Lucas Cross was concerned, Bertram decided he would put a marker above an empty grave. He figured Lucas was really dead, or undead if a person wanted to put it that way, so there would be nothing wrong in doing so.

Bertram had no immediate plans to locate Lucas' relatives. As far as the sheriff knew, none had ever come to visit the rancher since Bertram had been elected sheriff. And if any of those relatives did show up, the sheriff concluded he'd have ample time to concoct a plausible explanation for what had happened.

Once the plans were made, the funeral services completed, and the remains of the Cross and Snow families buried, Bertram Stone went to the livery stable and visited with his horse, Lucy. He apologized for his recent disregard of her company and gave her an extra feed bag and apples as acts of contrition. He then went to the courthouse basement and collapsed in his office. It was the first time since he left the Texas Rangers that he'd fallen asleep in his clothes and boots.

Thirty-Four

Springtime was pleasant and peaceful in Hamilton County that year.

"Don't reckon we'll see any storms 'til early summer," Sheriff Stone said as he sat atop Lucy at the Cross ranch. He'd seen to the livestock's needs and, with the help of Deputy Sparks, Dr. Peterson, and Newell, had cleaned up the ranch house and stayed there a few nights a week when he came to take care of the one remaining horse and what cattle were still there.

"Why don't you retire and move out to the Cross ranch," Peterson had suggested one morning over breakfast at the Koffee Kup Kafé, which was now run mostly by Martha Cooper. Molly and Hunter helped occasionally, but they were never able to break from a constant state of melancholy and tended to stay in bed most of the day.

"Don't seem right to stay there all the time," Bertram had said, frowning at the bitterness of his coffee. "Martha just ain't got the knack her momma did for coffee," he'd whispered to Peterson.

The doctor had grinned and held up his teacup. "You ought to switch over, Bertram. It's hard to ruin a cup of tea."

Now as Bertram gazed over the Cross ranchland before him, Peterson's suggestion didn't seem so far-fetched at all. Besides, no relatives of Lucas Cross had ever been located, and, despite what he'd originally decided, Bertram had actually tried to find them. There was a brother supposedly still alive who'd been living in Fort Worth managing a boarding house, but he was no longer there, and the sheriff had not been able to find him elsewhere. So...

But Bertram still had trouble convincing himself to take over the ranch, even if he had paid county taxes at the beginning of the year.

"We'll just keep it goin' like it is," he told himself and Lucy. "See what comes up between now and next January."

On occasion, Bertram took a trip to Eli Snow's place. The spring growth was beginning to overgrow the cabin, and the sheriff felt no urge to stop it. "Let nature take its course," he said.

The grave dug for Eli and the head of Jacob Snow had not yet settled. A prominent hump of earth still rose there in a macabre reminder of what lay beneath.

Bertram had removed the picture of Arils Snow dressed in his Dough Boy uniform and put it in the coffin along with Eli's ashes and Jacob's head the day they were buried. He thought this act might somehow neutralize the malevolence, and besides, it seemed like the right thing to do.

Back at the Cross ranch on this calm, spring day, Bertram put thoughts of the Snow family in the distance. He breathed in clean air and let its essence remain in his aging lungs awhile before exhaling. He then urged his horse forward until he was at the small cemetery Lucas Cross made for his wife and missing daughter over ten years ago. A figure lay curled between Adam and Donny Cross' headstones.

"Hey, old boy," Bertram said. The figure by the headstones stirred and stretched its arthritic limbs and moaned. "This warm weather's better on them bones, ain't it?" Bertram asked as Turk stood on shaky legs. "I know it's helped mine."

The sheriff reached in his saddle bag and took out several strips of steak he'd brought along and tossed them down in front of Turk. The dog sniffed them for a while before its tail began to wag feebly. The animal then glanced up at the man he'd come to accept as a friend who brought food.

Bertram smiled as Turk began to work on the steak strips. "Don't know how them teeth of yours is fairin'. But you can always gum it, I reckon."

Bertram pulled Lucy's reins back and headed toward the fence line at a slow pace. He stopped when they were at the spot where the Cross boys had ventured onto Eli Snow's property the thirty-first of October the year before. Lucy shook her head, her bridle suddenly loud and metallic in its clicking. A shiver raced up Bertram's spine as he glanced beyond the fence at the remains of the well on Eli Snow's land.

"Will never get it out of my mind or out of my dreams," Bertram said with a tremor in his voice. He briefly glimpsed a vision of himself crawling down the rope ladder as Lucas Cross sat on it for support while Adam and Donny snickered when their pa wasn't looking. "It all started with that damned head," Bertram said with abhorrence. "That damned head."

A sudden breeze came up. The ghost of the previous autumn dwelt in its surprising chilliness. The sheriff shivered until the gust passed and left the warm, spring air behind.

He knew his face was lined with permanent fatigue from each glance in the mirror, his constitution briefly defeated until the sun warmed him, Bertram turned Lucy away from the fence. He bent down and patted the horse's neck. "Let's head on back and check out that cow, old girl. She should be calving any day now."

Bertram led Lucy away. The crumbling stone eyes of the old well lingered on his back all the while.

EPILOGUE

The woman no longer possessed the concept of night or day. She was animated by instinct and hunger alone.

She did not remember the night that previous November when a monster entered her cabin and killed her husband and infant daughter. She would not be able to explain why she'd been kept alive—alive but changed.

She awoke from her sleep at sunset. At this time of day, her body was empty and yearning. The monster came to her then, its long, ragged nails tugging her from the bed of moldy earth in the root cellar. Together they would glide through the night in search of blood—blood from livestock, wild animals, or the most delectable humans.

The monster had learned over time to be cunning. It guided the woman so she would not be foolish and make a mistake and expose them.

Tonight, a full, yellow moon rose above the pines. The woman's restlessness was evident in the gnashing sound from her teeth. The monster took her hand and kissed it.

"Lucas," the woman whispered as she briefly recalled a name that shook her being.

The monster pulled the woman forward through the forest. They moved without effort through the cool evening.

Discovering the soft glow of a campfire, they slowed their progress. Voices rode on the wind. Laughter bounced against trees.

"Be catching that next freight around midnight," one voice said.

"No strong boss on that one," another added.

"Be in San Antone before you know it," the first one said.

The laughter again. A smell of cooking meat, and the smell of blood that flowed fresh and hot beneath unwashed flesh.

The monster and the woman inched forward.

They licked drool from their lips.

Other Books By

WICKED HOUSE PUBLISHING

- Mr. Nightmare by Joe Scipione
- The Monster on Mulligans Hollow by Patrick Reuman
- In Grandma's Room by Justin Boote
- Salt and Bone by Alyssa Grimley

About the Author

Timothy C. Hobbs is a retired medical technologist living in Temple, Texas. His flash fiction piece Luna appeared in the Deep Water Literary Journal. His anthology Mothertrucker and Other Stories and novel Veils were published through Publish America. Novels The Pumpkin Seed and Music Box Sonata and novella The Smell of Ginger were published by Vamplit Publishing in the United Kingdom and republished by Visionary Press Collaborative. Netherworld Books published his novel Maiden Fair. A collection of flash and short fiction, In the Blink of a Wicked Eye, was published in 2015 by Sirens Call Publications. He has also published other short stories in various anthologies and magazines including The Saturday Evening Post's Great American Fiction anthology 2019.

Made in the USA
Las Vegas, NV
04 March 2023

68485737R00206